HONOR

BOUND

Book V

ATHENA RYALS

Third Printing, 2025

ISBN 978-1-7346805-8-4

Edited by Ky R. Bean

Cover design by www.ebookorprint.com

Author photo by Lucy Schultz Photography

www.athenaryals.com

Thank you to all my readers, new and old. This story would not be what it is without you.

Chapter 1

Isaac stripped off his damp t-shirt, reaching his arms over his head and groaning at the stretch. His muscles ached with a sweet, comforting sort of burn, one that didn't come from fighting. He'd been conscripted into helping Edrissa today: first by climbing up on the rickety ladder and cleaning the gutters, then by moving wheelbarrow after wheelbarrow of earth from one end of the backyard to the other – *"to level it out for when I plant the corn next year,"* she had said – then by finally kneeling in the dark soil of the garden with her to pluck the weeds that, to him, looked exactly the same as the herbs he was told to spare. The only break he'd taken all day was to have lunch and a tall glass of ice-cold lemonade to stave off the heat of the late July day. Edrissa hadn't taken any other breaks either. Isaac was happy to help, happy to be *needed* for something other than what he'd spent most of his life being needed for.

He must have groaned again, because Gavin chuckled. Isaac flushed and turned to look at Gavin lying next to him on the bed, and his stomach fluttered as it always did at the deep green of Gavin's eyes, the smile that curved at his lips, the planes of his bare chest. Isaac's throat tightened. He swallowed and tried to clear his throat.

"What?" he croaked, unable to stop the smile that tugged at his mouth. He couldn't tell if the heat in his face was from his day in the sun or from the warmth of Gavin's gaze.

"Just looking at you," Gavin said. That only made Isaac's cheeks blaze more.

"Well... stop it," Isaac said, lips aching from trying to suppress his smile. He snatched a pillow off the bed and flung it at Gavin.

Gavin caught the pillow and tossed it away against the headboard. The blankets shifted as he leaned forward, reaching for Isaac's hand. Isaac let Gavin pull him down and they fell into bed together, a tangle of limbs and laughter.

"Stop looking at you?" Gavin said with an impish grin. "Impossible. Have you *seen* you?"

Isaac didn't think he could blush any harder. *"Stop,"* he said, smiling, and covered Gavin's mouth with a kiss. Gavin sighed and tipped his head back against the mattress, pulling Isaac close. Isaac shivered and let his eyes fall closed at Gavin's touch, Gavin's fingers tracing the healed-over cane marks across his back. He kissed Gavin until they were both breathless.

"You get freckles when you tan, did you know that?" Gavin said against Isaac's lips.

Isaac huffed out a laugh and pulled back. He braced his elbows on either side of Gavin's head, their noses almost touching. There was a softness in Gavin's eyes that made the strength run right out of Isaac's body; he was grateful he wasn't standing anymore.

"I don't know if I knew that," Isaac confessed. "Haven't owned a lot of mirrors in my life."

"I've probably owned too many," Gavin said. The smile was still there, but… tight. Frozen. There was guilt there, and Isaac's heart ached as he saw it.

He cleared his throat. "Well…" The room was suddenly colder; the warmth that had enveloped them only seconds ago was gone.

Gavin's smile was bittersweet, now, but it was real. "What's the next project?" he said weakly.

Isaac rolled off of Gavin, grateful for the change of subject. "Outside?" he said, leaning on his elbow. One hand caressed Gavin's waist. His palm tingled where it touched Gavin. "Next we're going to dig some holes for fence posts." He stroked Gavin's ribs with his thumb. "Gray wants to build a fence around the yard."

"That would be nice," Gavin said gently. "A little, um… extra safety. And… and privacy."

Isaac's smile was tight. "A privacy fence," he said, leaning forward and pressing a kiss to Gavin's lips. "For the house that has no neighbors for miles and miles."

∴

Isaac opened his eyes. He looked around, dazed and blinded by the sunlit snow. The cobblestones of the square were covered in a layer of fresh, sparkling white. Flakes fell gently from the sky, settling in his hair and melting in the fog of his breath.

2

He raised his gaze to the crowd of people standing around him. Most had hatred written on their faces, twisting their features as they jeered at him. He shivered in the freezing air.

He looked down at his right hand. He held a cane. It was coated in blood. Red trickled from the cut on his forearm and dripped onto the snow beneath him. His hand shook.

"Isaac?" a voice said softly. Isaac's head snapped up and he saw Sam in front of him, on their knees, their hand clasped in Gavin's.

Gavin was on his knees, too. His hands were tied to the light pole in front of him. He was slumped against it, whimpering softly. His back was a mess of red stripes. Blood trickled down his back under his shirt.

"Oh, fuck," Isaac whispered.

"You know what you have to do, Isaac," someone said. Isaac raised his gaze to the crowd, his eyes already stinging with tears. Daniel Schiester stood in front of everyone else. His cold blue eyes burned into Isaac's. He nodded at Gavin where he knelt at Isaac's feet. "You know what we agreed."

"But I've already given him fifty," Isaac croaked. Gavin stirred against the pole, murmuring wordless pleas.

"Is that what we agreed?" Daniel said, arching an eyebrow.

Isaac wracked his brain. Yes, fifty was what they agreed upon. Gray delivered eighteen, Isaac delivered thirty-two. Sam had counted with him. Sam had held Gavin's hand through it all.

"Yes," Isaac breathed. "I did what we agreed on."

Daniel laughed mirthlessly. "No, we agreed on justice. *While he lives, there's no—"*

"This isn't how this went," Isaac whispered. His heart hammered in his chest. The cold air was like a knife in his lungs. He tried to release the cane. He strained to open his fingers. They stayed locked around the cane. He stared down at his own hand in horror.

"Isn't how what *went?" Daniel said sardonically.*

"This... I... this isn't how..." Isaac swallowed dryly. He had the strangest feeling of déjà vu. He'd been *here before, hadn't he? He'd been in the square in Crayton, with Gavin tied and beaten, and he'd paid for his crimes that way.*

He'd paid for his crimes a hundred times over, now.

Daniel laughed softly, as if he could read Isaac's mind. "You really think he's atoned for everything he's done?"

"He saved me," Isaac rasped. Gavin whimpered softly on the ground. "He... he saved us."

"And that counts for... what, exactly?" Daniel shrugged. "How many lives did he end before he ever got hands on them?" Daniel nodded at Sam. Sam jutted their chin out at him defiantly. "How many lives did he destroy as part of his family's syndicate?" Daniel's lip curled with contempt.

"What did they do to you?" Isaac said through his teeth. "The Stormbecks are dead. Why do you hate him so much?"

Daniel smirked. "Wouldn't you like to know."

Isaac clenched his jaw. His vision swam as he looked at Gavin, bleeding in the snow, then back at Daniel, and back again.

"What he does for the people he's claimed means nothing at all," Daniel hissed. "Many syndicate members are kind to their playthings. Many keep them as well-cared-for pets. I imagine he's capable of—"

"We're not his fucking playthings," Isaac snarled. "We're not his pets. He loves us. Loves... loves me."

"I'm afraid I simply don't give a shit about that. Now," Daniel smirked. He pointed at Gavin. "Administer justice, like we agreed."

"No," Isaac growled. His hand tightened around the cane. The temperature of the air dropped again. He could feel his exposed fingers freezing around the handle. "We're done here."

Daniel's eyes flashed with amusement. He tilted his head. Isaac went to take a step towards Daniel, but found himself rooted to the spot. His eyes went wide and he looked at Daniel.

"What—"

Daniel pointed at Gavin. "We discussed this, Isaac Moore. We agreed. 'Meager justice,' as Gray called it. And I only call it meager because I'll allow you to do it quickly." He folded his hands in front of him and took a step back. "Kill the Stormbeck boy, Isaac. Like we agreed."

"I never agreed to anything, you—" The words were suddenly muffled by the gag in Isaac's mouth.

"No!" Sam screamed. Isaac looked down and saw Sam was tied to the light pole now, too, throwing themself against the ropes at Daniel. "Don't!"

Daniel laughed. "I'll let you go as soon as Isaac is done, little one," he said lightly. "No need for you to be causing trouble."

"Isaac," Gavin moaned softly. "Please..."

"I don't want to," Isaac whimpered. He could hear himself through the gag, but he knew no one else could understand him. "I don't want to."

To his horror, his body took a step forward. His feet planted themselves in the snow. His fingers, numb with cold, tightened around the cane. He screamed as his body raised his arm and brought the cane down on Gavin's back with a snap.

Gavin screamed. Another line of red bloomed on his back. Tears poured down his face.

"Isaac," he moaned. "Isaac... help me..."

"I'm trying," Isaac said. All that came out was a muffled groan. His arm raised again and brought the cane down on Gavin's back.

Isaac heard one of Gavin's ribs snap. He shuddered and raised the cane again.

Daniel's pale blue eyes watched as Isaac brought the cane down on Gavin again.

"Stop!" he screamed at Daniel. "Stop... please!"

Daniel kept silent, as if he hadn't heard Isaac make a sound at all. He watched Gavin, fascinated, as he jerked and screamed under another blow.

"Isaac," Sam wailed. "Isaac, no! He's good! He didn't... Isaac, stop!"

"I want to," he mumbled through the gag. He reached up to claw at the rough fabric in his mouth with his free hand. There was nothing there. "Please." His voice was thick behind the gag.

"Isaac," Gavin whispered. "Please wake up."

"Don't make me do this," Isaac sobbed. Again, he raised his arm. Again. Again.

Gavin gasped and shuddered under the cane. His blood ran red into the snow, and it steamed where it melted beneath him. Sam jerked at the ropes around their wrists.

"No!" they shrieked. "No!"

"Please," Isaac begged. The sound reached no one. Again, he beat Gavin. Again. Again.

Gavin's shirt was torn, the mangled flesh of his back showing through. Still, Isaac laid Gavin open. The cane broke his skin open down to the bone. Gavin's eyes rolled back.

"Almost finished," Daniel said softly.

"Isaac," Gavin whispered. "Shh."

Blood cut deep rivulets through the snow as it ran over the cobblestones. Isaac's hands were sticky with it. His head spun with the smell. Tears poured down his face. His right arm was numb.

The blows rained down on Gavin's back until he lay still, his ribs exposed and shattered, his skin ghost-white and smeared with his own blood. Only when his breaths had ceased, and the light in his eyes had dulled to a cold, flat green, was Isaac allowed to stop.

He dropped the cane and fell to his knees beside Gavin.

"No," he sobbed, as he clutched Gavin's body to him. He winced as fragments of bone shifted under his hands. Tears wet his cheeks. The gag was gone. He could speak again. "No, no, no, no..."

Sam was no longer bound. They reached out and touched Gavin's face, wrists still raw from their struggling. "Gavin," they whimpered.

Isaac cradled Gavin to his chest and looked up at the sky. The snow melted on his face, stung his skin. His mouth fell open in wordless despair.

Then he was falling, falling, and finally landing roughly into the arms of the man he'd just killed.

"Gavin," Isaac whimpered, and clutched at him. The room was dimly lit by the nightlight plugged into the socket in the corner, a soft yellow light that pushed away the worst of the darkness.

Gavin's scent was all around him, his skin warm under Isaac's hands. Isaac buried his face in Gavin's neck and sobbed.

"Shh," Gavin murmured, and wound his arms tighter around Isaac. "It's okay."

"F-fuck," Isaac gasped. *"Shit."* His skin was on fire with terror. His stomach lurched. His heart beat hard in his throat.

"It was just a nightmare," Gavin soothed, and pressed a kiss to Isaac's forehead. "It's okay."

"N-no." Isaac's fingers dug into Gavin's back.

Gavin winced and pulled Isaac closer. "Shh," he whispered. He gently smoothed the sweaty hair off Isaac's forehead. "You're safe."

"But *you* aren't," Isaac whimpered. His face was flushed and tear-stained. "You... G-Gavin, you're... you're *not...*"

"I am, because I'm with you," Gavin whispered. "We're safe."

"But I... I-I... killed you, Gavin," Isaac sobbed brokenly. "During the caning. I... I *killed you*. Schiester made me *kill you.*"

"No, he didn't," Gavin murmured gently. "That'll never happen. It was just a dream."

"Fuck." Isaac pressed his mouth against Gavin's shoulder to muffle his gasping breaths.

"Breathe, Isaac," Gavin whispered. His fingers twined gently through Isaac's hair. "Just breathe. Deep breaths. There you go."

"Sh-shit," Isaac mumbled against Gavin's shoulder. "I *hate* this."

Gavin's hand moved slowly through Isaac's hair. "Hate what?" he said evenly.

"Hate *this*," Isaac ground out through his teeth. "We're safe. We've been north for... for almost three fucking *months*. It's been... *six* months since I caned you. We're safe. This is *bullshit*. I'm still..."

"Still hurting?" Gavin gently cradled the back of Isaac's neck.

"Yes," Isaac whimpered. "How long until that's over? How long until I can fucking... *sleep* without seeing you *hurt?* And... and everyone else I care about *hurt?*"

"I don't know," Gavin admitted softly.

Isaac's heart beat slower, no longer thundering in his chest. He drew in a deep breath and trembled against Gavin's side. Gavin was here, Gavin was warm, Gavin was *alive*.

"But we *are* safe," Gavin murmured against Isaac's hair. Isaac pulled back and looked at Gavin for the first time since he woke up. There were dark circles under Gavin's eyes – evidence of the sleepless nights he'd spent since the family reached the north, screaming from his nightmares of being forced to hurt the others, or holding Isaac as he screamed through his. They weren't getting better; they were getting *worse.*

At least Gavin hadn't had a migraine in a few weeks.

Gavin's mouth was drawn. His dark hair was sticking up on one side of his head. But his eyes – they shone as they stared into Isaac's, vulnerable and *trusting.*

Fuck, I hope I deserve that trust.

Unthinking, Isaac pulled Gavin forward into a kiss. Gavin groaned softly against Isaac's lips. His hand slid up the back of Isaac's neck, across his cheek, to gently cradle his face. Isaac opened his mouth to trace Gavin's lips with his tongue.

"You kept us safe," Gavin murmured against Isaac's lips. A thrill went through Isaac.

This is how I keep them safe.

Gavin pulled back to catch his breath. "You protected us. You and Vera… and all of us are safe. You don't have to fight anymore. We're safe. It's over."

Tears burned in Isaac's eyes. He tried to swallow the lump in his throat. "I always have to fight."

"Not anymore," Gavin said firmly. "It's over. Not anymore."

"There's always a fight," Isaac breathed. His eyes closed tightly. "There's *always* a fucking *fight.*"

"But not for *you,*" Gavin said, tilting Isaac's head up. "Hey. Look at me."

Isaac blinked his eyes open. He trembled as Gavin's eyes blazed in the dim light. Isaac's throat moved painfully in a dry swallow.

"Your fight is over," Gavin said, his voice like steel. "We're saving rescues, yeah, but…" He shook his head. "There's no fight anymore. You can be safe, and free, and…" His hand shook on Isaac's jaw. "…and *mine.*"

"If we keep taking people like Zachariah," Isaac said softly, "Then there will be a fight. Daniel *will* find out eventually. And then…"

"So we fight then," Gavin replied. His voice didn't waver. He held Isaac's gaze. "But right now…" Gavin's mouth pressed into a hard line. "Right now… you're safe. *We're* safe. And…" Gavin pulled Isaac close and pressed his forehead against Isaac's. "…and I swear to god, I will do *anything* to keep you safe." Isaac's eyes slowly closed. "Absolutely *anything*."

"Y-you, um…" Isaac wet his lips. "You too, Gavin."

"Yeah, I know," Gavin said with a gentle laugh. His breath was warm on Isaac's face as he nuzzled Isaac's cheek. "You've shown that. Vera would call you a dumbass."

"She's probably right," Isaac grumbled, and cuddled closer against Gavin's side. His eyes slowly closed. He breathed in deep, taking in the warm, comforting smell of him, so *close*, and let it out. Gavin pulled the covers tighter around them both. Isaac let out a breath and forced the muscles in his jaw to relax.

Chapter 2

Finn balanced the shopping bag with one hand and pushed open the door with the other. Ellis sat alone in the living room, staring blankly at the mostly unfinished puzzle in front of them. Their face was pale, their eyes dull and sunken. Finn wet their lips and closed the door behind them. Ellis slowly lifted their head.

"Hey, babe," Ellis said softly. "How was the trip?"

"Frustrating," Finn said as they hung up the car key on its hook beside the door. "The rizatriptan came in this time, but the ondansetron didn't." They walked to the kitchen and set the paper sack on the counter. They looked at Ellis over the half-wall between the kitchen and the living room, lined with barstools on the living room side that were pushed up against the counter. "I'm sorry, babe."

"It's all good," Ellis said weakly, and slumped down against the couch. "I'll be okay."

Finn chewed their lip as they pulled the multivitamins out of the sack and put them in the cabinet, next to the spices. "Yeah, I know, but I… I would have *liked*…"

"Yeah, me too," Ellis murmured. Their gaze returned to the puzzle in front of them.

Finn watched them for a moment, then tucked the can of pickled ginger into the fridge. "You doing the new puzzle?" they said softly.

"No," Ellis said. Their voice sounded thin as a string. "Just looking. You know I wouldn't keep doing it without you."

"Damn right." Finn huffed with a laugh.

Ellis laughed, too, and the sound was soft heat in Finn's chest. Finn looked over at them where they lay on the couch, staring at nothing. Their hands went still.

"Ellis?" Finn said softly. "Is… is something wrong?"

Ellis shifted, then blew out a deep sigh through their lips. "Um... no," they said, finally.

Finn abandoned the paper bag and went to Ellis's side. They sat down on the couch next to them. Ellis shifted onto their back and stretched their legs across Finn's lap. Finn gently rubbed Ellis's knee, their hand inches from the spot where if Finn grabbed Ellis's knee just right, just above the joint, Ellis would shriek and laugh and push them away, their cheeks flushing, their eyes sparkling...

They squeezed gently. "Babe," they said, and watched Ellis's eyes laze slowly over the puzzle. "What's wrong?"

"I want to move out," Ellis croaked. Their voice was tight.

"Oh." Finn drew in a slow, deep breath, and winced around the ache that formed around their lungs as they did. "Okay."

"With..." Ellis waved their hand vaguely in the direction of the back of the house. "...the new plan, the new rescue, taking in people DFS would have killed... it's..." Ellis raised their gaze and met Finn's. "It's... *dangerous,* Finn."

Finn swallowed hard. "Yeah," they rasped. They reached out and took Ellis's hand. "But that's... we... we knew that, babe."

"We did," Ellis said softly. Finn gently rubbed their thumb over the back of Ellis's hand. Ellis's free hand went to their belly. They weren't showing yet. They wouldn't, after only three months. The baby was only the size of a large strawberry now, according to the book Finn had purchased in town. They and Ellis had looked at the book together just yesterday, and laughed at how the drawings of fetuses looked more like newly-hatched chicks or baby dinosaurs or anything other than a *baby*—

"It has your eyes," Ellis had said, pointing at the two little black dots resting at the top of the little blob.

"And your tail," Finn had said, and Ellis had pushed them away, laughing, then pulled them right back in for a kiss...

Ellis took in a slow, deep breath. Finn's hand drifted to rest over Ellis's, over the baby. Ellis's hand was cool, but Finn could feel the electric current of excitement under it, the *knowledge* that the tiny little blob inside Ellis was half Ellis's, half theirs.

"I…" Ellis cleared their throat and swiped at their eyes. "I love this family. More than anything. You… you *know* that." Finn nodded. "And…" Ellis blinked tears out of their eyes. "And we support each other. We keep each other safe. But with… with *that*…" They waved again at the back of the house. "I…"

Finn took both of Ellis's hands and squeezed, their knuckles going white as they met Ellis's gaze. "I think I—"

"I've already lost two babies," Ellis said, heavily. Their eyes filled with tears that rolled down their temples and into their black hair, limp from not being washed for a few days. "I… I love this family, and I love this cause. But…" Ellis looked down at their stomach. Their shirt was pulled up just the slightest bit, revealing a thin stripe of skin. "No amount of refugees will be worth losing another baby. Or… or being killed, so she has to grow up alone."

Finn's mouth pulled into a strained and rueful smile. "I thought we decided it was a boy."

"Might be," Ellis said softly. "Sex organs form around week seven, right?"

Tears burned in Finn's eyes. "Right," they murmured. They held Ellis's hand to their mouth and pressed their lips firmly against the knuckles.

"So… I… I can't live here, if we're going to be bringing refugees through. DFS will find out eventually. He's got… who *knows* how many people working for him. And I can't… I *refuse*… I *can't*—" Ellis's voice twisted in a sob. "—lose *this* baby, too."

Finn's stomach lurched, and their heart squeezed painfully in their chest. Their hands tightened on Ellis's.

Daniel Schiester will die if he threatens my baby.

Finn bit down hard on their lip. "I… I know." They'd *always* wanted to be in the thick of it, *always* wanted to go where things were hardest.

Why the fuck did I sign up to be a medic, then?

Because I'm a coward, and deep down I'd rather be on the sidelines than be the person to take the bullet.

Ellis looked at Finn. "What is it?" they murmured.

"Um…" Finn blinked and pressed their thumb against the healing scar on their right forearm, where Vera had sliced the Stormbeck brand until it was beyond recognition back in June. It was still tender – the only scar they had from their time in Colleen's murder house. It was all they had to show for being in the fight.

They wet their lips. Their eyes focused again, and they saw Ellis staring at them, a little wrinkle between their eyebrows. Finn bent forward and kissed the worry line. When they leaned back again, Ellis's worried expression was still frozen in place.

"Um…" Finn chewed their lip again. "I… I know."

"So…" Ellis swallowed hard. Finn's heart broke as they looked at the uncertainty behind Ellis's eyes, the worry. "Will you, um… will you… come with me?"

Finn's stomach dropped, and the air rushed out of their lungs like they'd been punched. "Ellis—"

"I know there's so much work to be done," Ellis said softly. They pressed their lips together, although Finn could see them trembling. "There's so many people to save. DFS is an evil motherfucker and he needs to be stopped. But…" Ellis's face hardened. Their jaw set. Their eyes flashed. Their walls came up. "Sorry, but nothing is worth risking this baby for. Are you coming with me or not?"

Beneath the fierceness, the anger, was the terrible, wounded vulnerability Finn knew so well. Ellis looked up at Finn, their eyes still brimming with tears.

Finn leaned forward and pressed a soft kiss to their lips. "Yeah," they said gently. "I am. They're my baby, too. And… you're my fucking *family*."

Ellis whined softly. They pulled Finn down on top of them and clutched at them, holding them tight against their chest, as they pressed the kiss deeper.

"We could move into that little cottage down the road," Ellis sighed. Finn's hand went to cup Ellis's face, then slid down their neck, over their shoulder, down their side until they pressed their fingers into Ellis's hip. "It's like a ten-minute walk, but far enough that we have plausible deniability. It's kind of a shithole but the others would help fix it up. We…" Ellis gasped as Finn pulled them hard against them. "We just need to tell the others."

The back door swung open. Finn groaned and pressed their forehead against Ellis's. Then they extricated themself from Ellis's embrace and sat up.

Ellis pushed themself up to sitting and pulled their knees into their chest. A faint blush burned on their cheeks.

At least they had some color now.

Gray, Zachariah, Edrissa, and Sam all filed into the kitchen. Zachariah carried an armload of zucchini – or some kind of squash, Finn didn't actually know – and set them on the counter. Edrissa carried two fistfuls of leafy herbs. Sam and Gray followed behind, holding a bowl of fresh string beans each.

I still can't believe we're letting Zachariah outside.

Finn's stomach grumbled. "Are we having all of that for dinner?"

"No," Edrissa said with a playful glare. "Do you know of anything I can cook that combines all these things?" She tossed her head at the vegetables.

"I don't know, you're the one who knows how to cook," Finn grumbled under their breath. Gray put the bowl of string beans down on the counter and came into the living room.

"How are you feeling?" they said gently to Ellis, and sat on the couch next to them. "Still nauseated?"

Ellis shrugged weakly. "A little. I don't think I have anything left to throw up."

"Let me make you some tea!" Edrissa called from the kitchen. She darted to a cabinet and pulled down a tin with *'for Ellis'* scrawled across it in Edrissa's looping handwriting.

The corner of Finn's mouth pulled up as they looked at Edrissa. Bustled around the kitchen to prepare the tea as Zachariah followed behind her like an enormous shadow.

Gray looked at Finn. "The trip into town go alright?"

"No ondansetron," Finn said flatly. "But the rizatriptan is in. Hopefully no more migraines for Gavin."

"That would be ideal," Gray said dryly as they rubbed their forehead.

"And… we've been talking about moving out," Finn said, the words sour in their mouth. They glanced at Ellis, throat tightening, and squeezed their hand.

Gray's eyes went wide. They sat back slowly and folded their hands in their lap. Finn chewed their lip and waited for Gray to speak.

Gray wet their lips and slowly opened their mouth. "I... understand," they said, finally.

Finn blew out a slow breath and looked up to see Sam and Edrissa standing at the half-wall, looking out with identical expressions of hurt on their faces. Zachariah stood behind them, his arms crossed across his chest, eyes darting nervously between them all.

"We love you, so much," Ellis said in a rush. "We love this family. Gray, I've been with you for, for *seven years*." They gave a weak laugh. "And I'd kill for any of you. But... with DFS doing his bullshit..." Their hand drifted again over their belly. "...I *can't* risk my baby. There's a cottage just a bit down the road. We'll visit all the time. But at the end of the day, when DFS comes knocking, because he *will*..." In the kitchen, Zachariah flinched. Ellis raised their shoulders jerkily in a painful-looking shrug. "...I can't let this one get hurt. I... I..." Ellis heaved in a shaky breath, then another, then another. "I thought Finn was dead. I lost my family once already. And I can't... I c-can't—"

Gray leaned over and pulled Ellis into their arms. Ellis shivered and clutched at Gray. They breathed hard against their shoulder, their fingers digging into Gray's shirt, as Finn rubbed slow circles on their back.

"I absolutely understand," Gray said, their voice pitched low.

Finn leaned over and pressed a kiss to Ellis's shoulder. They drew in a slow, deep breath, and felt Ellis doing the same. They smiled.

"This is your baby. You protect your family, above all else." Gray leaned back and their lips curved up in a watery smile. "Besides. You're thirty-five years old. Plenty old enough to be moving out of the house."

Ellis playfully smacked Gray's shoulder, barely hard enough to even make a sound. "Fair enough."

Gray took both of Ellis's hands in theirs and squeezed. "This baby deserves all the protection in the world. I think it *would* be safer for them to be distanced from this..." They threw a glance at Zachariah where he stood in the kitchen. "...operation."

Zachariah stared at the floor. His shoulders stooped, as if that could hide his towering height from invisible, watchful eyes. Sam leaned against his side; their brow furrowed as they looked up at him.

Ellis nodded jerkily. Their eyes shone with tears. "Thank you for understanding."

Gray leaned forward and pulled Finn and Ellis both into a hug this time. "Of *course*, I do," they said softly.

"They'll be your first grandchild," Ellis said in a small voice.

Gray squeezed Finn and Ellis tighter. Finn could feel Gray trembling, and they swore they heard a sniffle. When Gray pulled back, their eyes were red.

Ellis wiped their eyes on their shirt. "You'll have to think of what you want them to call you," they said softly.

Gray let out a tight laugh and smiled wide. "I'll give it some thought," they said. Their voice broke. "Never thought that would, um… h-happen." They drew their hand over their face. "I'm certainly *old* enough to be a grandparent."

Ellis grimaced. "Don't say that."

Gray tilted their head in concession. "Fine," they said with a laugh. "I'm a fifty-three-year-old spring chicken."

"Speaking of chicken, what's for dinner?" Finn said, looking towards the kitchen.

Ellis shot upright and gagged weakly. They smacked their hand over their mouth and dashed from the room. They disappeared down the hallway, and Finn could hear the weak sound of them retching into the toilet. Edrissa's mouth puckered. She turned to the stove and stared at the kettle as it came to a boil.

Finn bit their lip. "What… what was it?" they said weakly. "They did okay with chicken yesterday—"

"I think it's just the mention of food," Gray said. "This is… a rough pregnancy for them."

"It shouldn't be Rh incompatibility," Finn said as they wrung their hands. "We're the same blood type. They checked at—"

"I think it's the stress," Gray said softly. "They…" They blew out a slow breath through their lips. "You *all* have survived… a lot."

In the kitchen, the kettle began to whistle.

Chapter 3

Sam glanced at the kettle as it came to a boil. Zachariah whistled softly, matching the tone. Edrissa snatched up a potholder and took the kettle off the stove. As Sam turned to get a mug for Ellis, Zachariah was already there, pulling one down.

How does he already know the kitchen so well? It took me a week to— I guess he's been here a month and a half. Huh.

Sam's head spun. It didn't feel like it had been a month and a half. It felt as if Zachariah had arrived ages ago – or yesterday.

Time was strange up here, even without pain meds clouding things. Sam was grateful not to need the pain medication as much anymore. Still, the days were so long, so they spent as much time outside as they could. Edrissa was constantly pushing them outside, urging them out into the fresh air – and then coming with them, lacing her fingers through theirs, walking the lake and pulling them behind trees for furtive kisses. No one was up here to see, but Sam liked it.

Sam liked everything about it up here. The air was cool and crisp, and the sun rose so early, warming their skin with its rays, seeming to melt the jagged edges of their pain. At night, they slept in a warm, soft bed, with the lights off, so unlike the cold, hard concrete and constant hum of the fluorescent lights that lit their cell in Colleen Stormbeck's house. They could even stand to go without the sling sometimes, gently moving their arm in guided motions with Finn's help, slowly bringing the strength back.

Sam glanced up as Ellis returned from the bathroom, looking green, their skin gleaming with a thin layer of sweat, the circles under their eyes darker than before. They slumped onto the couch and folded into Finn's arms.

Sam looked away. They didn't think about how they still couldn't move the fingers on their right hand, and couldn't feel a good deal of their arm. They were getting stronger. And they were safe.

17

Sam turned to the fridge to reach for the milk – and Zachariah was already there, too, pulling out the bottle that they would refill in Burmingham. Sam felt a prickle of irritation. They bit their lip and caught Zachariah's gaze.

"I can do that," they said softly, trying so, so hard to keep the hurt out of their voice. They made themself smile. "You don't have to do everything."

Zachariah's eyes went wide and he pressed his lips into a line. Edrissa took the milk out of his hand, outstretched and frozen in front of him. He stared at the floor and swallowed loudly.

"S-sorry," he mumbled. "I'm not trying to… to do everything. I know you can do it. I just…" He slowly retracted his hand and curled it into a fist. "I just want to… to *help*. To help you."

Zachariah raised his gaze to Sam, and Sam's stomach fluttered as his light brown eyes met theirs. He couldn't be much older than they were. They remembered, faintly and in flashes, him carrying them down the stairs from the Stormbeck house, how he'd screamed just before Sam was shot. And he was…

He was *pretty*.

Sam shook their head and cleared their throat. "Um. Well. Thank you. But…"

Zachariah wrapped his arms around his chest. "Yeah. I'm sorry. I don't mean to, um… to do stuff for you. I just want to help."

Sam knew what he meant: *I just want to make things right.*

Sam glanced at Edrissa where she stood behind Zachariah, the cup of tea held tight in her hand. She was staring at Zachariah with an unreadable expression on her face. She blinked and walked out of the kitchen with the tea. She held out the mug to Ellis, and they took it with a grateful glance at Edrissa. Finn rubbed distracted circles into their back as Gray stared at the floor, their face torn between expressions of joy and worry. Ellis held the cup to their lips. They didn't take a sip.

Sam chewed their lip and turned back to the kitchen. Zachariah was staring over the counter into the living room, his eyes fixed on Edrissa and Ellis.

"H-how did you do it?" he whispered.

Sam blinked. "What?"

Zachariah's throat worked and he brought tear-filled eyes to theirs. "How did you… *survive?*"

18

A twinge of fire shot through Sam's wound, lighting up their arm with pain. They hissed in a breath through their teeth and clutched at the wound with their left hand. It didn't help.

This was the only time they could feel those parts of their arm anymore: when the pain burst through them, when it felt like their arm was being held down in a pot of boiling water. Sam slowly pushed a breath out through their lips. The pain was already fading, like it always did. The shock of electricity was already ebbing away, leaving the inside of their forearm and the palm of their hand tingling, then numb once again. Sam shivered at the sudden dampness of their skin. They threw a glance into the living room, but Finn was looking at Ellis with their near-perpetual look of worry, and Gray was still staring at the floor. Sam breathed out a meager sigh of relief.

They raised their gaze to Zachariah. He was staring back at them, his gaze fixed on their arm, his hands slightly outstretched.

"Are... are you alright?" he rasped.

"Y-yeah," Sam breathed, and pulled their hand away from the wound.

"Is that...?" Zachariah wet his lips and drew in a deep breath. "I c-can't believe that bullet didn't kill you. I thought..." He squeezed his eyes shut and shook his head.

"I was very lucky," Sam said tightly. Zachariah opened his eyes to look at them. "Both with where the bullet hit me... and the fact that I had Finn." They looked back to the living room and watched as Finn laced their fingers through Ellis's and squeezed.

They jumped as Edrissa appeared at their side. The motion sent a wave of pain through their arm – but it wasn't unbearable this time. It didn't feel like a knife going through their flesh, or a flame held against their skin. It was a pinch of soreness. Nothing more. They heaved a sigh of relief.

Edrissa brushed her lips against Sam's cheek and squeezed their hand once, shooting a glance at Zachariah. She turned toward the fridge. Sam's stomach burned as they glanced at Zachariah, how he watched them both with reddened cheeks. Their gaze moved over him, lingering on his shoulders as he crossed his arms over his chest, and on the dark, bruise-like circles under his eyes that had only just begun to fade.

"Hey, Sam?" Edrissa called.

Sam blinked. They glanced at Edrissa; she stood framed by the light from the fridge, the edges of her hair lit up like they were on fire. A warm, fluttery feeling blossomed in their chest as she smiled and beckoned them over.

"Come help me with this," she said with a grin. Her lips were pressed flat, her eyes lit with a mischievous gleam. Sam was across the kitchen before they realized their legs were moving. Just as they drew to her side, their hand already outstretched to rest gently on her arm, she whirled and dabbed a bit of whipped cream onto the tip of their nose.

Edrissa leapt away with a squeak as Sam stood frozen beside the fridge, blinking slowly, letting their mind catch up. The whipped cream was cold. They stuck out their tongue and licked at it, savoring the sweetness.

Finally, they turned and fixed Edrissa with a playful glare. She giggled and held her hands to her mouth, shuffling backwards. Sam turned and glanced into the fridge, eyeing the large ceramic bowl of whipped cream. They scooped their left hand in and turned back, hand completely full of whipped cream.

Edrissa shrieked and dashed to the other side of the kitchen, throwing open cabinets, searching for a makeshift weapon. She finally emerged with a large baking sheet that she held out in front of her like a shield.

Zachariah's eyes darted between the two of them, his hands held out as if he was going to ward both of them off.

Sam grinned. They lunged forward and drew a stripe of whipped cream across Zachariah's cheek.

As they stumbled back, they caught Edrissa's eyes on them both, how her gaze moved between him and them. They flushed as Zachariah slowly, distractedly wiped the whipped cream from his face, and then licked his fingers clean.

Everyone froze.

Then, Sam turned and snatched the heavy bowl of whipped cream from the fridge. Their left hand made smears of cream on the outside of the bowl. They plunged their right hand in and shivered as one side of their fingers felt the cool, soft, sticky texture of it, and the other side felt nothing at all.

Edrissa let out a high-pitched peal of laughter and darted behind Zachariah for protection. His eyes went wide as she leapt onto his back and wound one arm around his neck.

"Get the bowl!" she cried and held the baking sheet out in front of them both with her free hand.

Sam lunged forward and swiped weakly at Edrissa with their whipped-cream-covered hand. Zachariah jumped away, just as Edrissa brought up the baking sheet to block. Sam realized with a start that they could move their injured arm without agony, without the stab of pain that had gripped them over and over since they'd arrived north. Their arm was weak, and Sam could feel the strain of muscles that hadn't been used in months, but they could *move it.*

"Hey, no fair!" they said with a laugh. "I can barely move my arm and there are *two* of you!"

"You have a whole bowl of whipped cream," Zachariah said tentatively, standing like a deer in headlights.

Sam chewed their lip as they regarded the two. Subtle heat flushed under their skin as their gaze moved over them both. Edrissa's light blonde hair was wild around her face, her cheeks pink, her eyes sparkling with that same something Sam caught glimpses of on their walks together. Zachariah's eyes caught Sam's, and his muscles flexed under his shirt. He scooped his hands under Edrissa's legs to hold her up until she wrapped them tightly around his waist. She laid her chin on his shoulder and whispered something to him, lips brushing his ear.

Sam's cheeks burned as they imagined, just for a moment, how it might feel to be between them, to feel all their hands on them at once, kissing Edrissa... and maybe going a bit further than that with Zachariah...

Sam grinned. It seemed like Edrissa was maybe getting that idea, too.

They walked to the opposite side of the kitchen and put the bowl down on the counter – but not before they dipped their left hand in again and emerged with a gigantic handful of whipped cream.

"Come and get it," Sam said with a smile.

"Oh, we will," Edrissa said, her eyebrows pulled together in a way that Sam figured was supposed to be menacing. On her, it just looked goofy.

Zachariah took a slow, plodding step forward, his lips pulled into a smile. "Better watch out, Sam," he said, grinning.

"Or what?" Sam shot back, also taking a step forward, the handful of whipped cream held out threateningly in front of them.

"Or *else*," Edrissa said. Zachariah took another step forward.

"You'll never take me alive!" Sam yelled, holding their hand aloft. They charged at Edrissa and Zachariah.

"Nooooo!" Edrissa cried, holding out the baking sheet and blocking Sam's first attempt. Zachariah jumped back and dodged the second, as Sam swiped at his nose. Sam was backing the two of them into a corner. Heat curled in their chest as they thought about what they might get to *do* when they won.

"Zachariah!" Edrissa said, brandishing the baking sheet. "Get the whipped cream!" Her grip around Zachariah's neck tightened.

Zachariah leapt past Sam, just escaping the whipped cream on their hand. He skidded to a stop on the wood floor and bumped into the counter. Edrissa leaned down and snatched up the bowl of whipped cream, triumphantly holding it aloft with both hands.

"I got it!" she shrieked. Sam lunged forward, both arms outstretched, ready to absolutely *cover* the two of them in whipped cream.

Zachariah darted to the side. Edrissa lurched sideways, not able to catch herself with her hands busy holding up the bowl. The bowl slipped from her hands.

As if in slow motion, Sam watched the bowl tumble to the floor, a little dollop of cream spilling over the side. The bowl shattered.

The pieces flew across the kitchen. Sam didn't even have time to blink before one drove into their leg, just below their knee. They gasped at the bite of pain and stumbled backwards. Their foot landed on another shard. They staggered back, blindly, and tripped over their own feet.

They toppled over and fell directly onto their injured arm.

Pain exploded through them, sharp as a knife, knocking them loose in their own mind. Their lungs were crushed in their chest. They struggled to breathe around the pain that twisted inside them, choked them.

They struggled to breathe around the phantom collar around their neck.

They fumbled blindly for their arm, feeling for the blood, for the pain that radiated across their hand, their forearm. There was no numbness now. It was all fire. It was all agony. There were no bones left, no muscles, no skin. There were only nerves, and they were nothing but pain.

Their throat was raw before they realized that the sound they heard tearing through their ears was their own scream. Their eyes rolled back and they twitched on the floor, chest heaving, skin damp with sweat, holding their arm tight to their side and shuddering at the pain crashing over them in unbearable waves.

"S-Sam?"

"Sam, are you—"

They trembled and wailed against the floor. The pain spiked and sank claws into their brain, pushing everything else out.

There was nothing but pain. Just like when they'd been shot.

Was I shot?

Sam writhed against the cool, hard floor, twisting against the pain and trying desperately to push it away, to *breathe*. They felt hands in their hair, on their shoulders, pushing them up and leaning them back against something hard. Blonde hair flashed before them, then dark skin, then hazel eyes, a kaleidoscope of faces and colors and voices. None of it made sense. They retched against the pain.

"Sam. *Shit.*"

"Oh, oh god, Sam... I'm so sorry, I didn't mean to...!"

"Get my kit. Did they hit their head?"

"U-um, um, I—"

"Edrissa. Did they hit their head when they fell?"

"I d-don't think so... Zachariah...?"

"Um... n-no. I didn't... see them hit their head."

"Okay. Edrissa, go get my kit. You know where it is."

Sam panted as fire poured into their veins. They clutched at their arm and sobbed, pressing themself back against the hard surface behind them. They blinked their eyes open – *when did they close?* – and found Finn. Their face was drawn, pinched with worry lines that hadn't been there... before. Before...

"F-Finn," they croaked. Tears wet their cheeks. "Finn..."

"I'm here, Sam. You just hurt your arm. You're alright. Can you—"

Sam sobbed and leaned their head back against the wall behind them, shivering against the cold that crept into their bones as their arm blazed with agony.

Colleen wanted their pain. And she would take it, every day.

"F-Finn, Finn, can you fix it, please, please…?" Sam's eyes streamed with tears.

"Working on it," Finn mumbled.

Sam knew that Finn only had ten minutes to fix them up, then they'd be dragged back to their own cell to be chained to the wall again.

A guard knelt beside Finn, wearing only a t-shirt and shorts, no vest, no belt, no knife, no gun. Sam blinked in confusion and turned their head away.

This one hasn't hurt me yet, but he will.

Finn looked over their shoulder at someone and pulled their kit to their side. Sam looked at Finn, only at Finn, desperate and sick and sobbing with the pain. Finn gently pulled Sam's sleeve up to reveal the wound on their arm.

They shot me. The guard shot me. Please, Finn, please please fix it before they take you away and chain me to the wall again… Their hand drifted up and they reached for the collar around their neck. Their fingers brushed bare skin. They shivered.

Sam groaned as Finn pushed gently against Sam's arm, their fingers sure and light.

"Don't feel any breaks. You may have torn something inside." Finn's voice was rough as sandpaper.

"P-please, Finn," Sam begged, arching back against the cold cement wall behind them. "Pl-please, please, please, please make it numb again, please, Finn, give me something to make it numb again…" Their tongue stuttered over the words. Their lips tingled.

Finn blanched where they crouched in front of Sam. "Wh-what?" they breathed.

"M-make my hand numb again, *please*…"

Finn's hand trembled on Sam's shoulder. "Make your… your hand…?"

The guard kneeling beside Finn looked away. He had a nice face. He was waiting for Finn to finish fixing Sam up, giving them time, instead of laughing from outside the bars of the cell door. He was giving Finn time to fix Sam before he dragged Finn away, to be chained again.

Finn still stared at Sam, horrified. Sam blinked tears out of their eyes but their vision didn't clear – it was still fuzzy at the edges, still spinning around them, colors and light pressing down into their eyes, against their skin, too bright for the cold, dim gray of their cell.

As they cast their gaze around the room – it was unfamiliar, but then, most of the rooms in this house were – their heart stuttered and sank in their chest. A bitter curl of terror twisted in their stomach, and they heaved forward with a desperate sob.

In the doorway stood Gavin Stormbeck.

Chapter 4

Isaac heard the crash. His head snapped up towards the house where he sat on the grass in the backyard with Gavin beside him.

He heard the scream that came after and leapt to his feet.

Gavin was up in an instant.

The breeze played with the hair at the back of Isaac's neck. He shivered in the warm afternoon sun as he stumbled forward, not even aware that he was moving, only aware that he had to go find Sam – because he knew it was Sam, he'd recognize the sound of their screaming anywhere – and stop whoever was hurting them. The long grass swished under his feet as he rushed to the back door, the grass that Edrissa had asked Gray not to cut, because it was so nice to lay on, so nice to see the imprints of where the family laid after they got up—

Isaac threw the back door open and rushed in, Gavin right on his heels. He dashed past the laundry room and skidded to a stop on the wood floor of the kitchen as he took in the scene.

It looked like a bomb had gone off. The floor was absolutely covered in what looked like whipped cream. Shards of a blue ceramic bowl littered the floor. Blood was smeared on the floor in a trail that led to—

Just as he saw Sam, they turned their head and looked up at him. Their eyes widened in terror when they saw him.

No, not him. *Gavin.*

"P-please," Sam whispered, not even seeming to register Finn's touch.

Isaac was across the room in an instant. "Sam," he croaked. He reached out to touch their leg, only to see that their pants were stained with a thin line of blood just below their knee. "Oh, *shit.* Sam…?"

"We were just playing," Edrissa whimpered, standing back and covering her mouth. Zachariah stood beside her, his hands held out as if he didn't know how to help – or whether he could help at all. "We were just… it was an *accident…*"

"Finn," Isaac snapped. "What's wrong? What—"

"I don't know," Finn rasped, their hands outstretched towards Sam, shaking. "They... Sam, is your hand... *numb...?*"

Isaac's heart plummeted.

"Please," Sam whimpered. "Please, *please,* G-Gavin, *no...*"

Isaac threw a glance over his shoulder and saw Gavin standing in the doorway, tears shining in his eyes and a look of horror on his face.

"Gavin, you don't... you d-don't *have* to, Gavin... I'll... I'll t-tell... please, *no...*"

"Oh, no, no, no, no, no..." Gavin whimpered softly. "Oh... *Sam...*"

Isaac stood again and held a hand up toward Gavin. "Gavin, just... maybe wait outside, I'll—"

"Isaac!" Sam cried, arching back against the cabinets. "Isaac, don't go, *please!*"

Isaac froze where he stood, his gaze fixed on Sam.

"I... c-can't find any, um, s-signs of, of new injury," Finn said flatly, crouched in front of Sam, their eyes wide. "But... Sam, has your hand b-been numb for... a wh-while?"

"It's..." Sam sniffled and clutched their arm, their gaze still fixed on Gavin. "Y-yeah, it's been, um, for a while..."

"What?" Finn said dully.

"Finn," Isaac said with a shaking voice, crouching again and reaching out with shaking hands. He was hollow on the inside. There was nothing but endless space for Sam's pain. "What's wrong with them? What happened?"

"Um..." Finn blinked and swallowed hard, looking around as if they'd forgotten what they were doing. "Um... they f-fell. I think... hurt their arm again. And—"

"S-Sam," Isaac said, and there was an edge to his voice that he couldn't smooth out. "Sam, where do you think you are right now? Do you think you're in... C-Colleen's house?"

"Isaac," Sam sobbed, and clutched at their arm. "Isaac, *please...*"

"You're safe, Sam," Isaac said. His vision was blurry. He blinked, and tears streamed down his cheeks. Sam was suffering again, and it was his—

It was his—

It was his fault.

He shoved the thought away. *This is not about me. This is so far away from being about me.*

"Finn," he rasped. His throat was dry. "Can you...? For the pain, is there something—"

"Vicodin won't do shit for a while," Finn snapped. "But it's what I have." They already had the bottle out and dumped a pill out into their palm. "I'll get water. You get them... get them back. Okay? You get them back." The words twisted as Finn spat them between their teeth. They stumbled to their feet and stepped back, avoiding the shards of broken bowl.

Isaac swallowed his despair and guilt, pushed them down until they settled into a bitter weight in his stomach. "Sam," he said softly, cradling their face and turning their head towards him. "Sam, look at me."

"I-Isaac," Sam sobbed. "Isaac... he... please, make it stop, I'll do *anything...*"

"Shh," Isaac murmured. He kept their head turned away from the doorway. He could see Gavin there, in the corner of his eye – Gray was at Gavin's side now, gently rubbing his shoulder and pulling him towards the living room. Gavin didn't move. He seemed rooted to the spot.

Isaac glanced at Finn. They were by his side again, their shoes squishing in the whipped cream. They crouched in front of Sam.

"Open up, Sam," they grumbled, and held the pill to Sam's lips.

"P-please—"

"This will help," Finn said, and Isaac's heart twisted at the pain in their voice.

"Sam," he said softly, as Finn tapped the pill against Sam's lips. Sam obediently opened their mouth, sobs pouring out with every breath, and took the pill. They held their breath as Finn tipped the glass of water against their lips and helped them take a drink. As the pill went down, Sam gasped and looked to Isaac again.

Isaac wet his lips. "You're in the north house. Look around and let's say things we see. Alright? Deep breaths."

"Isaac," Sam sobbed, tears rolling down their cheeks. They winced as Finn pulled their pant leg up to check the cut, but kept their eyes on Isaac. "Please, it hurts..."

28

"Finn's helping you," Isaac murmured. "Take a deep breath, Sam." He drew in a slow, deep breath. He pushed away the shroud of numb panic that had been cast over his mind as soon as he heard Sam's scream. Something in him shifted, and his hand tightened on Sam's leg.

"This won't need stitches," Finn mumbled. "Neither will, not the leg or the foot."

Isaac glanced down. Finn was gently wiping the cut on Sam's leg with alcohol. They made quick work of cleaning and bandaging Sam's leg, then their foot, and then slumped back, their eyes red-rimmed and unfocused.

Sam panted as they leaned their head back against the cabinets. "Isaac," they whimpered. "Why...? Isaac..." They blinked rapidly and cast their gaze around the room – Isaac watched how Sam's eyes skipped over Zachariah and lingered on Gavin.

"Deep breath, Sam," Isaac said, taking both their hands in his now, being careful of their injured arm. "Deep breath. Finn just gave you some medication that should help. And... look around, Sam, tell me what you see?"

"I... I s-see..." Sam coughed and whined softly against the pain. "K-kitchen?" Their eyebrows pulled together. "Why... in the kitchen?"

"You're north, Sam," Isaac said heavily. "Do you remember...? We made it north. We've been north for... th-three months." They drew in a slow, quavering breath. He nodded. "There you go, Sam. There you go. Good. Take another deep breath, there you go. Are you with me?"

Sam's gaze finally returned to Isaac's. Their lips trembled, but they nodded. "Isaac..." They pulled their hands out of his grasp and gently touched their right hand with their left, their fingers brushing against the skin from front to back and front again... as if feeling for sensation on one side, and numbness on the other.

"That medication is gonna take a bit longer to kick in," Finn said numbly. "But... Sam, it looks like the pain is... a little better?" The lines on their face looked deeper than they ever had been. "Sam... your hand... why didn't you... *tell* me?"

Sam swallowed hard and wrapped their uninjured hand around their right wrist. "Um... I... I w-was hoping it would... g-get better on its own."

29

Finn let out a wordless groan and leaned forward, burying their face in their hands.

Sam bit their lip and whimpered. "F-Finn..."

"We can talk about it later," Finn whispered. They raised their head. Their eyes looked haunted and faded behind their swimming tears.

Sam nodded weakly. They raised their gaze to Gavin. He still stood in the doorway with Gray's hand resting solidly on his shoulder. Isaac doubted anything could have moved him from that spot.

"Gavin," Sam murmured, their lip trembling. Their face was clouded with *guilt,* but why would Sam ever feel guilty? It wasn't their fault, it was Isaac's, it was *Isaac's* fault...

He forced down his tears, and forced down the thought. *I never helped them by thinking that.*

Except for the time it saved them.

Sam cleared their throat. "Gavin, I'm s-sorry..."

"N-no," Gavin stammered as he fell forward a step. He kicked a piece of bowl and it skittered across the floor. He didn't seem to notice. "Sam... you don't have to *apologize,* Sam, it's, it's okay..."

"I know you're not going to hurt me," Sam rasped, trembling from head to toe. They drew in another breath and whined softly, clutching their arm. "And I'm... I'm... *sorry.*" They blinked and looked at the ceiling before their gaze drifted to Edrissa and Zachariah. "I... I'm sorry. It was just a-a game—"

"And it still is," Gray said from Gavin's side. "It was a game, and it was fun, and it was an accident that you got hurt, Sam." Their mouth pressed into a thin line. "It's no one's fault." They cocked an eyebrow, and threw a pained half-smile at Sam, Edrissa, and Zachariah in turn. "Although, I'm wondering if you *knew* how much I was looking forward to having some of that whipped cream with the berries from the garden for dessert tonight."

"I'll make more," Edrissa whispered, looking away from Sam for the first time to meet Gray's gaze.

"And I'll get a mop," Gray said. They squeezed Gavin's shoulder, and then went to the supply closet in the living room. "Isaac, if you could get the large pieces of the bowl? I don't have shoes on. We'll get this place cleaned up and then… Edrissa, I hope you're as serious about making more whipped cream as I am about wanting some."

Edrissa nodded, her lips pressed into a trembling line. Isaac glanced around the mess of the kitchen. A shard of the bowl lay next to him on the floor, the painted blue edge of it razor sharp.

Chapter 5

"You good, Isaac?" Finn murmured as Isaac stared at a piece of the broken bowl on the floor.

Isaac jumped as if he'd been shocked. "Y-yeah," he mumbled, still staring at the shard. "Sure." He stood and looked around, as if he'd already forgotten what Gray had asked him to do.

Finn turned their attention back to Sam. There was a faint sheen of sweat on their face, and they still clutched at their wrist, but their breathing was slowing down, and their tears were drying on their cheeks. Finn bit their lip as they reached up and wiped Sam's tears away with their thumbs.

There was a *clink* behind Finn as Isaac began to pick up the biggest shards of the shattered bowl. Sam watched him forlornly over Finn's shoulder. "I guess I won't be able to get up until that's clean," Sam murmured.

"Yeah," Finn said distantly. "Probably a good idea to wait until the floor is clean, yeah."

"So I guess…" Sam sniffed. "I guess we should… talk about it now." They looked down at their lap.

Finn groaned as they sat down and leaned back against the cabinets beside them. "We don't have to, Sam," they said softly. "We don't… ever have to talk about it, if you, um… don't…" They trailed off and trembled as a wave of guilt washed over them. They buried their face in their hands.

Sam was silent for a long time. The drying whipped cream under Isaac's shoes made a tacky *pop, pop, pop* sound as he crisscrossed the kitchen, picking up pieces of the bowl that lay scattered in every corner.

"Finn?" Sam said softly. Finn raised their head to look at them. Fresh tears stained their cheeks. "I'm… I'm s-sorry."

"Don't be, Sam," Finn said heavily. Edrissa and Zachariah were busy wiping up the whipped cream with towels. Gavin had maneuvered past the mess and into the living room. Finn could hear a bucket being filled with water in the laundry room. "I… understand."

"But—" Sam bit their lip. "I didn't want you to find out... like this. I was hoping you'd never have to, um, f-find out at all. I thought... I thought maybe..."

Finn jerked their shoulders up around their ears in a painful shrug. "It still might get better, I guess," they croaked. "If... if it's caused by, um, by inflammation, or, or s-something like that, then once the, ah, swelling goes down, you might... might get..." Finn looked down at their hands. "I don't think..."

"It wasn't your fault," Sam whispered.

Finn's hands slowly curled into fists. "You don't, um... don't know that, Sam. I could have... while I was, um, fixing you up, I found a nerve that was in the way... I was careful, I was—" Their voice twisted. They cleared their throat, swallowed against the lump there. "I was *so fucking careful.* I thought I stayed clear of it. I thought I..." They let their head fall back against the cabinets with a *thump.* "I thought I did it *right,*" they whispered.

"You did," Sam said weakly. "I'm... I'm p-pretty sure..." They cleared their throat. "I'm pretty sure the nerve was, um... already messed up. By the bullet."

Finn's head snapped forward, and they stared at Sam. "What do you mean?"

"Um..." Sam swallowed noisily. "I... th-think I remember... even before the surgery, I..." They looked down at their right hand. "It... hurt. In my hand, and right here..." They drew their pointer finger across the inside of their forearm. "All the way up to here." They gently ran their finger over the inside of their arm, all the way up to the sleeve of their t-shirt. "I... think I remember... feeling like something was wrong."

Finn stared at Sam. Their heart squeezed painfully in their chest, hope washing through them, flushing the bitter shame out of their veins. "Sam... are you... You're not just saying that because—"

"No," Sam said, and met Finn's eyes. "I'm not."

Finn slumped back against the cabinets. "Then... then it's not..." They wet their lips. "Then it's not... my fault?"

Edrissa drew near, wiping the floor clean of whipped cream. Sam glanced at her before they returned their gaze to Finn. "No," they rasped. "It's not your fault."

Finn's breath rushed out from between their lips, leaving their chest aching. "Oh," they murmured. Tears burned in their eyes.

"You did a good job, Finn," Sam said softly.

"Maybe," Finn rasped. They jerked the collar of their shirt up and wiped their eyes. When they dropped their shirt again, Isaac stood over them both.

"Um…" Isaac bit his lip. "We're about done, Gray just needs to, um, to mop." Isaac glanced behind him just as Gray walked back into the kitchen carrying a bucket of steaming water and a mop. The lemony scent of the cleaner washed over Finn, drowning out the sweet smell of the whipped cream.

"Yeah," Finn mumbled. They pushed themself to their feet. They glanced up to see Ellis standing at the counter, looking in from the living room. Their hands were locked on the edge of the counter and their gaze was fixed on Sam. Gavin stood beside them, looking stricken. Ellis didn't even seem to notice him.

Finn blinked and reached down for Sam. Sam took their hand, and Finn pulled Sam to their feet. Sam wobbled, holding their injured foot up, and looked across the expanse of the kitchen floor towards the hallway to the bedrooms.

"I can hop, but I'll get the floor all whipped-cream-y," Sam said, glancing at the foot they were balanced on. Whipped cream clung to the sides of their foot.

"I can carry you," Isaac said at Finn's shoulder. His voice was pitched low, his gaze moving over Sam. Sam chewed their lip before nodding once.

Finn burst out laughing as they realized Sam was covered in whipped cream from head to toe. They bent forward at the waist, cackling and gasping for air. "Oh my… how did you three even… manage to *make* this mess?" they wheezed, holding their side. "How… holy *shit?*"

"We won, though," Edrissa muttered, standing by the sink, scrubbing the bottom of her foot with a wet towel. Zachariah stood next to her.

"Yeah, because there were *two of you!*" Sam cried, scandalized, their eyes wide in a look of mock hurt. "It wasn't *fair!*"

"You can discuss the legality of their win once the kitchen is all cleaned up," Gray said with a smile, dipping the mop into the bucket of steaming water and whatever it was that smelled like lemon. They wrung out the mop and let it fall to the floor with a *smack*.

"And once *I'm* cleaned up, too," Sam said. They wiped at a streak of half-dried whipped cream on their cheek. "I need a shower. Holy shit."

Gray laid a towel down on a clean patch of floor at the doorway between the kitchen and the living room. "Here, Isaac," they said. "Take off your shoes here as you take them to the bathroom. Finn, you need to wipe your feet there, too. Unless you'd like to wipe down the cabinets."

Finn blinked and realized there were spatters of whipped cream on the cabinets, too. "Damn," they breathed. "Sure, I'll help with the cabinets."

Finn turned as the front door opened and Tori and Vera stepped into the house.

Tori froze as she saw everyone standing in the kitchen, covered in various degrees with whipped cream. Vera was right behind her carrying two canvas bags. She glanced at Tori and followed her gaze into the kitchen. Her eyebrows slowly pulled together.

"Uh... what'd I miss?" Vera said.

"Edrissa and Zachariah cheated," Sam grumbled.

"*She* jumped on *my* back," Zachariah said, his gaze flicking between Sam and Edrissa. "As you'll recall, I wanted no part in this. I only wanted to save myself." He pressed his lips together, but a smile still pulled at the corners of his mouth. "I am merely a casualty of war."

"Did you use up all the whipped cream?" Tori gasped. "No!"

"I told Gray I would make more!" Edrissa protested.

"We leave for two hours, and the whole house goes to shit," Vera muttered as she set the bags on the floor and bent down to tug off her shoes.

"What'd you bring us?" Ellis said as they made their way from the counter back to the couch. Gavin remained at the counter, glancing at Sam every now and then, but mostly keeping his gaze down. Ellis shrugged. "I hope you had more luck than Finn did."

Finn's heart twinged. *Maybe Crayton could get the nausea meds sooner. I wonder if I should call their general store...?*

"Made some inquiries in Burmingham," Vera said as she bent to pick up the bags. "They didn't get any apples this week, which makes them think there was a disturbance in the southwest supply lines. No news yet about who's taking over the western sector." She walked over to the kitchen and stopped at the towel Gray had laid down in the walkway from the living room. "Do I need a password?" she said sardonically and cocked an eyebrow at Gray.

Gray snorted. "The password is, 'I don't want my socks getting sticky.' I'll take the bags." They leaned the mop against the counter and took the bags from Vera's hands. Vera wandered into the living room. "Isaac, Finn, this would be the ideal time to leave the kitchen."

Isaac nodded and looked to Sam. "Ready?" he said softly. Pain flickered in his eyes, tightened in his mouth.

They met his gaze and nodded. "Sure."

Isaac bent and let Sam wrap their arm around his neck. He gently lifted Sam in his arms and didn't even seem to notice the whipped cream smearing on his own shirt. He walked with Sam to the towel and kicked off his own sticky shoes. He disappeared with them down the hall. After a moment, Finn heard water rushing through the pipes. Isaac came back around the corner with an armload of Sam's clothes.

"These need to be washed, I guess," Isaac said as he stopped at the towel that now served to bar entry to anyone with clean feet.

"Your shirt has whipped cream all over it," Vera said from the couch, where she sat with her arm around Tori's shoulders.

Isaac glanced down. "Oh," he said, and pulled at the hem. "How... This got *everywhere*, Jesus," he huffed. He dropped Sam's clothes onto the towel and pulled off his own shirt in one fluid motion.

Everyone in the house went silent at once. Isaac stared at the shirt in his hand as if dumbfounded at what he'd just done. His scars shone white against the tan of his skin, crossing his chest, his arms, his back. He shivered and folded his arms across his chest. A flush crept up his neck.

Finn couldn't even remember the last time Isaac had had his shirt off around the others. It certainly hadn't been since he'd first been captured by Gavin – more than a year ago, now.

Gray took the shirt from Isaac's hand and let it fall onto the small pile of Sam's clothes. "Thank you, Isaac," they said casually, as if nothing had happened. "We'll get these in the wash."

Isaac blinked and took a step back. "Yeah... okay, thanks, Gray," he murmured. He turned and disappeared down the hall. When he emerged again, he had a long-sleeved shirt on. He went to Gavin's side at the counter and pulled him close. Isaac pressed his lips to Gavin's forehead, his gaze unfocused.

Edrissa all but materialized in front of Finn, holding a towel. *That girl walks so quietly. I swear to god, she'd make a perfect assassin.* Finn shivered as they realized why it might have suited Edrissa to learn to walk so quietly in the first place. They wet the towel at the sink and began to scrub the whipped cream from the cabinets. As Finn cleaned the cabinets, Gray mopped the floor. The whole room smelled of lemon, now.

Sam wandered back into the living room, limping slightly on their injured foot. Finn leapt forward to help them before Sam held out a hand.

"I'm good," they said softly. "And I, um, figured out how to take the bandages off and put them back on once I was clean." They lifted their head and grinned at Finn and Isaac in turn.

"Oh," Finn said, and a smile spread slowly across their face. "That's... geez, Sam, you trying to force me out of the job?"

"Oh, I gave you a run for your money," Sam said with a laugh.

"Hey, um, Sam?" Edrissa said softly from the kitchen. Her cheeks flushed red. "Do you and Zachariah, um... want to help me make more whipped cream?"

Sam's grin widened. "You bet," they said, and limped back into the kitchen.

Edrissa pointed to a high shelf. "Zachariah, could you...? The big bowl."

Zachariah smiled gently and reached up to get the large yellow bowl.

Chapter 6

Even though Vera had just brushed her teeth, she could still taste the sweetness of the whipped cream and berries she and the rest of the family had had for dessert tonight. She sighed as she closed the bedroom door behind her and turned to face Tori. Their room was lit only by the lamp on Tori's nightstand, which cast a golden light over Tori's brown skin that made her look... perfect. Divine. Like an angel, or a goddess, or a dream. Vera licked her lips and smiled as she met Tori's gaze.

She forced her eyes to hold Tori's gaze, instead of drifting down to the two small scars on Tori's neck where the prongs of the shock collar had pressed in. Tori's eyes were bright tonight, focused, and she gazed right back at Vera. Vera swallowed hard as her hand left the doorknob. Her lips pulled tentatively into a smile.

"What?" Tori said softly, a smile creeping across her face, too.

Vera shrugged and wrapped her arms around her chest. "Nothing."

Nothing. You're beautiful. You're amazing. And you're looking at me like I'm really here, and that's all I want right now.

Tori held out her hand to Vera. Vera took a slow step forward, then another, until her hand slid into Tori's and squeezed. Tori gazed up at her with shining eyes, near-black in the dim light, her curls catching the light around her head. Her hair was just starting to shine again, after the dull and tangled mess it had become while locked in Colleen's cell − after Gavin and Colleen had gripped her hair over and over to drag her around, hold her down as she convulsed against the shocks. The bruises around Tori's wrists had faded. The marks on her neck were completely healed.

"I'm really here, you know," Tori said softly.

Vera's mouth went dry. "I... I know." She squeezed Tori's hand again. "I know that."

Tori chewed her lip. "I... I know I... haven't been."

"It's not your fault," Vera said quickly, and sat beside her on the bed, desperate to see Tori smile again.

Tori's mouth twisted. "I, um, I know." She nodded slowly as her eyes unfocused.

"Um..." Vera's thumb moved nervously back and forth across the back of Tori's hand. "I was just, um... looking at you. You're beautiful."

Tori's eyes focused again, and her lips pulled into a shy smile. Impulsively, Vera leaned forward and kissed her.

Tori made a small, surprised noise in the back of her throat, and Vera pulled back. Tori's hands settled on either side of Vera's face. Tori gently pulled her forward and pressed her lips to Vera's again.

Vera groaned and grasped Tori's waist to pull her closer. She could feel Tori's warmth even through her shirt. She slipped her hands up under the hem and pressed her fingertips into Tori's skin.

Tori ran her tongue gently against Vera's bottom lip and sighed. Vera's heart squeezed painfully in her chest. She knew she had no right to ask, after Tori had taken all the pain the three weeks they were in Colleen's house, and for nearly a year Vera had been the one to push Tori away when all she could feel was Joseph's hands on her waist, her legs, her throat – but right now, she wanted Tori. Desperately.

Her lips trembled on Tori's. "Um..."

"I have an idea," Tori said softly against Vera's lips. Vera's stomach flipped nervously. "Can... can you..."

Vera leaned back and met Tori's gaze. "Um, yeah," she said. "What do you need?"

"Can you...?" Tori flushed. Vera leaned back farther, and her gaze danced over Tori's face. Her heart fluttered as Tori bit her lip again. "Um... can you get, um, go get the bowl of whipped cream?"

Vera couldn't help the grin that spread across her face. It fell a moment later. "Oh. I, uh... I think we used it all with dessert, babe."

"We didn't," Tori said, her blush deepening. "I set some aside. The small blue bowl, next to the milk."

Vera stumbled to her feet. "And that won't... hurt your stomach? I can't remember what Finn said about—"

"My stomach will be fine," Tori said, smiling gently. "I know you're just trying to take care of me. It'll be fine. Besides—" She shrugged. "—*eating* it wasn't really going to be the point."

Vera's cheeks burned. "You got it. One order of whipped cream, coming right up." She pulled the door open and padded down the hallway.

She ran her hands up and down her pajama pants, trying to calm the pounding of her heart. She pushed down her hope, her want, crushed it down into a sharp point inside her chest. *She might just want to have some whipped cream in bed. She might just be hungry. She might not want...*

Vera bit her lip as she crossed through the empty living room. She walked to the refrigerator and pulled the door open.

Just like Tori said, there was a small ceramic bowl of whipped cream, covered by a plate. Vera smiled as she took the bowl from the refrigerator and walked quickly back to their room. She couldn't help but smile as she passed another room, just barely caught the sound of a sighing breath behind the door. She walked further down the hall, to her and Tori's room. She pushed the door open and closed it behind her, the soft smile still on her lips.

Her smile widened to a grin as her gaze settled on Tori. Tori lay stretched out and completely naked on the bed, smiling right back at Vera. Vera's gaze moved over Tori, lingering on the silvery scars from the cane down her legs, up her arms. Vera knew many more spanned Tori's back, long healed now. The light caught Tori's skin, made her eyes sparkle. Vera nearly dropped the bowl from the dizzy rush that swept over her.

Tori was so goddamn beautiful.

Vera waggled her eyebrows and sauntered to the side of the bed. "Um. Wow. Are you...?" She held out the bowl with a smile. "Am I...? Or are you...?"

Tori leaned forward and took the bowl from Vera's hands to set it on the nightstand. She pushed herself up to her knees on the mattress, reached out again, and pulled Vera close.

Vera trembled as Tori gently pressed her lips against Vera's. Goosebumps rose under Tori's fingertips as she slid her hands beneath Vera's shirt.

"Can I take this off?" Tori whispered.

Vera fumbled at the hem and nearly fell over at her eagerness to yank her shirt off over her head. She tossed it into the corner and pulled Tori's mouth hard against hers.

"Pants, too?" Tori whispered. Vera smiled as she stepped back and slid off her pajama pants and panties. She straightened and stood naked before Tori, her skin rippling with goosebumps, her chest rising and falling with her heavy breaths. Tori gently took Vera's hands in hers and pulled her forward, guiding her down to lie beside her on the bed.

Tori smiled as she reached for the bowl of whipped cream on the nightstand. She looked at Vera as she dipped one finger into the whipped cream. "Now... where should I put *this?*" Tori murmured, and her nose wrinkled with her smile.

"Oh, I have... *so* many ideas," Vera rasped. She cleared her throat. "Babe..." She let her head fall back against the pillows.

"Hm," Tori said, drawing her eyebrows together. "Should I put this... here?" She playfully dabbed a bit of cream on Vera's nipple and giggled when Vera sucked in a breath. "Or... here?" She dabbed some cream on Vera's other nipple.

"S-symmetry is, is nice," Vera sighed. She half-wanted to tell Tori, *forget the whipped cream and just let me put my mouth on you, please.*

"Hm," Tori agreed. She dipped her finger in again and drew a line of cream from the space between Vera's collarbones, down her sternum, all the way down to her navel. Tori wet her lips as she looked at Vera, her eyes dark with a want that made Vera melt.

Tori put the bowl aside to straddle Vera's hips. Vera gasped and whined softly as she felt Tori's wetness, as her own desire rose at the heat between Tori's legs. She gently stroked the outside of Tori's thighs, gazing up and drinking in the sight of her, beautiful and mischievous and *safe.*

Tori is safe.

Tori bent over Vera until she licked gently at the whipped cream just above Vera's navel. Vera groaned and let her head tilt back further. Her eyes slid closed.

"Mmm," Tori sighed as she ran her tongue slowly, gently, up the line of cream, up Vera's abdomen and chest. Vera whimpered softly as Tori brushed

41

her lips against Vera's throat. Vera's hands trembled on Tori's thighs, and she slid her hands back, gently cupping Tori's ass, scratching her nails up Tori's back, running her fingers up Tori's flanks, up her sides, to gently caress her breasts. Tori drew in a quavering breath and sat up slightly. With a grin, she dipped her head and ran her tongue across Vera's chest, over her breast, and gently took Vera's nipple between her teeth.

"Oh, *fuck,*" Vera moaned. Her eyes flew open and she grasped Tori's hips again, grinding her down, wanting desperately to taste Tori, wanting to feel how open and ready she was.

Vera looked at Tori as Tori sucked gently on her nipple, her curly black hair trailing across Vera's chest, tickling her. Her heart swelled. Tori was naked with her, safe with her, open with her. Tori *wanted* her. Tears pricked Vera's eyes as she opened her mouth.

"You wanna get married?" Vera croaked.

Tori froze, her mouth still pressed to Vera's breast. "Hmph?" she mumbled. Her eyes were wide and fixed on Vera's.

"Um..." Vera swallowed hard, her nerve faltering. "Do you, um... wanna get married?"

Tori slowly pulled back, her mouth closing. She stared at Vera. A smile played on her lips.

"I..." Tori wet her lips, then licked at a bit of whipped cream at the corner of her mouth. "I..." She wiped her mouth with her arm. Her face broke into a grin. "*Fuck yeah* I wanna get married," she whispered.

Vera huffed out an incredulous laugh. "Y-yeah?"

"Yeah," Tori sighed. She leaned forward and caught Vera's mouth in a breathless kiss.

Vera moaned into the kiss, opening her mouth for Tori's tongue. She pulled Tori hard against her, rolling Tori's hips against hers. The whipped cream was sticky between them.

Vera laughed. She let her fingers tangle in Tori's hair and held her close, their mouths moving together, their breath mingling, fingertips brushing across brown skin. Tori pulled back and flashed Vera a smile.

"Edrissa's going to go absolutely apeshit," Vera said with a grin.

"Oh my god, she *is!*" Tori squealed. "She's going to want to make both of our dresses."

Vera laughed again, and it felt *good.* "She can have at it. I have no idea how she sews the stuff she does with what we've been able to get for her. I mean... as long as she can make a dress that isn't all poofy..."

"You know she'll make you whatever you like," Tori said, and ran her thumb across Vera's lower lip.

"Then..." Vera tilted her head, thinking. "I want... a maroon dress, a little off the shoulder... little bit of an hourglass thing going on, maybe..." She blinked, and her eyes flicked to Tori's lips. "And you... I don't know, do you think Edrissa could make something that sparkles?"

Tori snorted. "And how do you know I want *sparkles?*" Her teeth flashed white as she grinned wider.

"Because I know *you,*" Vera said, and kissed the tip of Tori's nose. After a moment she bit her lip and pulled back. "Speaking of. Do you want—"

"I want a ring," Tori said, then blushed a furious red. "I want... I want a ring. I know it's stupid, and it really doesn't matter and it's hard to get out here, but—"

"I'll get you a ring," Vera said softly, tucking Tori's hair behind her ears. It slipped right back into Tori's face, tickling Vera's neck. Vera shivered. "What do you want?"

"Um..." Tori chewed her lip. "I mean... I think I'd... really like you to—"

"Surprise you?" Vera said, her voice gentle.

Tori held Vera's gaze, then nodded. "Yeah," she said, in a small voice.

"Then I'll surprise you," Vera said. She pulled Tori close and pressed a kiss to her forehead. "I'll find you something... amazing."

"Do you want a ring?" Tori said softly against Vera's neck.

Vera blinked. She hadn't even expected to ask, let alone for Tori to say yes. She'd never even dreamed of having something like this, something like what she had with Tori, their nights together, their kisses, their dreams, their conversations. Their *love.*

Vera cleared her throat. "Yeah," she said. Her voice cracked, and she cleared her throat again. "Yeah, I... I think I would. Something... practical, that won't get caught on things when I, um, fight."

"Something practical," Tori murmured. She giggled. "A pair of brass knuckles, then. Got it."

"Oh, yeah. Get the spiked ones." Vera laughed and cradled Tori closer, smoothing her fingers through Tori's hair, rubbing her thumb back and forth against Tori's side. Vera pressed a kiss to Tori's forehead, her nose, her cheek, her mouth. She smiled at the sweet taste of cream on Tori's lips. "We're going to need a shower," she whispered. "We're all sticky."

"Hm." Tori tilted her head back and shone a smile at Vera. "That's too bad. We have so much whipped cream left."

"Oh, I didn't say we were done with it," Vera said, reaching for the bowl with a grin on her face. "Not even close." With one hand still holding the bowl aloft, she rolled with Tori until Tori was pressed into the mattress beneath her. She knelt between Tori's legs and dipped one finger into the cream again. Her gaze moved over Tori's body. "Now, where should I...?"

Vera's gaze settled on Tori's throat. Vera leaned forward and drew a line of whipped cream from the angle of Tori's jaw, down to her collar bone, and leaned forward to eagerly lick it off. Tori gasped, and her body rose to press against Vera's. Vera moaned as Tori rolled her hips. She wondered how she was supposed to focus on the whipped cream at all.

Chapter 7

"What kind of tea do you want?" Edrissa asked, her head in the tea cabinet. "I have chamomile, mint, the spice tea, basil and mint, lemon balm, green tea, Gavin's headache tea, and that new black tea I got yesterday that's really really good. It's almost like Oolong but it's a little more, I don't know, intense? Maybe it's an Oolong blend. I haven't figured it out yet. Mx. Sadey said the labels fell off when the box got wet and so it's just kind of a surprise anytime they pull teas from that box..."

Sam glanced at her from where they stood at the counter kneading dough with one hand. Their right arm was slinged again. It was feeling better with three days of rest, but Finn wasn't taking any chances. It still throbbed sometimes, still sent those agonizing stabs of pain through them when they moved wrong. Still, that was nothing *new*. And that was a good thing.

Edrissa's blue eyes met theirs. Their heart squeezed as she blushed.

"Umm..." They scrunched their nose as they thought. "Chamomile, please."

Edrissa nodded and turned her gaze to Zachariah, who stood across the kitchen at another counter chopping onions for the stew. Edrissa's lips curved into a faint smile.

"I'll, um, take chamomile too, please," Zachariah said softly.

Edrissa nodded once and pulled the tin from the cabinet. She flitted to the stove and began to heat the kettle. Then she spun and went to Sam's side, her hip just brushing against theirs. Sam wanted to pull her close and kiss her, right there.

"How's the bread going?" she murmured, and Sam flushed, hoping that she dropped her voice so she'd have an excuse to draw even closer. The faint, sweet flowery smell of her shampoo wafted over Sam.

"Um, good," they said, and their voice cracked. They cleared their throat. "Good. I think it just needs to sit... right?"

Edrissa beamed. "Right. We'll let it rise, then place it in the pans. Speaking of." She darted to the oven. "I should preheat this."

Zachariah set the knife down on the counter and crossed to the stove. He steered clear of Edrissa as he slid the onions into the stew pot. She watched him carefully, her gaze following his hands. Her eyes flicked to his face and back, and she smiled again.

It would be so good if she liked him, too, Sam thought with a flush.

"Celery next?" Zachariah said, already crossing to the refrigerator.

"Yeah," Edrissa said. She pulled three mugs down from the cupboard as Zachariah took a giant stalk of celery from the refrigerator. Edrissa scooped three spoonfuls of chamomile into the tea strainers and set them each into the mugs.

"What're you making us?" Vera said as she walked into the kitchen. Sam looked up at her and saw her smile as she wandered over to the stove. "Need any help?"

"Not yet," Edrissa said. "Actually…" She glanced at Sam and Zachariah. "I think we might have it covered."

"Fair enough," Vera said with a nod. She turned and went to the barstools that stood along the counter that looked into the kitchen. She sat down with a groan.

"Where's Tori?" Sam asked as they gently placed the dough into a bowl and covered it with a cloth.

"Reading," Vera said with a shrug. "She wanted some alone time, so I'm out here harassing you." She laughed. "Are you feeling harassed?"

"No," Edrissa said, raising her eyebrows at Vera.

"Yes," Sam said at the exact same time, throwing an impish grin Vera's way.

Vera snorted and looked to Zachariah. "What about you, kid? You break the tie. Are you feeling harassed?"

Zachariah's eyes went wide and his face went pale as he looked up at Vera. His gaze darted to Sam and Edrissa and back to Vera. He swallowed hard, his hand curling around a stalk of celery. "Um… y-yes?"

Vera burst out laughing and clapped. "Mission accomplished," she said with a smile.

Sam looked towards the back of the house as the door opened. They smiled as Isaac and Gavin wandered in, Isaac's arm slung over Gavin's shoulders. In the corner of their eye, they saw Zachariah tense and turn back towards the cutting board. Edrissa didn't seem to bat an eye, but returned to Sam's side, winding her arm around Sam's waist and pressing a kiss to their cheek. Sam flushed as they pulled her close and kissed gently into her hair. Their flush deepened as they noticed Vera was looking at them. She waggled her eyebrows at them and grinned. Sam rolled their eyes.

"How's the lake?" Vera said as she turned to Isaac and Gavin.

Isaac drew his free hand through his hair and laughed. "Completely devoid of fish, as far as I can tell," he said with a shrug. "At this point we've put lines down the whole way around the lake and caught nothing."

"It doesn't count if you're making out the whole time and not watching the lines." Vera cocked an eyebrow at Isaac.

Isaac and Gavin both flushed a painful-looking red. Isaac opened his mouth to protest. "I…"

"Oh, just ignore her, Isaac," Sam said good-naturedly, their uninjured arm still around Edrissa's waist. "She's been *harassing* us since she sat down."

Vera idly chewed a fingernail. "Which, as I said, was my mission," she said. "And I think I'm pulling it off beautifully. Who else am I supposed to bother if Tori's not around?"

"Lucky us," Isaac grumbled, but shot a winning smile in Vera's direction. "I think it might be worth it to talk to someone in Burmingham about stocking the lake. Having meat around would be good."

Edrissa wrinkled her nose. "Oh, good. More fish."

The kettle whistled. Edrissa playfully pulled away from Sam's side to go take it off and pour steaming water into the three cups on the counter. "I can make tea for you guys, too," she said, and looked up at Vera, Isaac, and Gavin.

"No, no thanks," Gavin said quietly, his cheeks still red. Isaac shook his head.

Vera smiled. "I'm okay, thanks," she said.

Edrissa nodded and put the kettle back on the stovetop. She took one mug to Sam, carefully passing it into their left hand before she kissed them gently on the cheek again. Then she went to Zachariah's side. He dwarfed her, standing taller than Isaac and broader in the shoulders and hips. Sam's heart skipped as Edrissa handed him the cup, having to crane her head back to look up at him, her pale blonde hair looking like white gold against Zachariah's warm brown skin. Sam's throat bobbed as they swallowed, their mouth going dry at the thought they'd had ever since Zachariah appeared into their life again.

Maybe...

Zachariah smiled shyly at Edrissa as he took the cup. "Thanks, Edrissa," he murmured. "You're a sweetheart."

The smile on Sam's face disappeared. Their stomach lurched. Gavin and Vera both gasped.

Edrissa spun around to look at Vera, and her gaze drifted to Gavin. "W-we don't say that word," Edrissa said tightly.

Zachariah fell a step back, his hands still clutching the mug. He shrank before Sam's eyes. "I'm... 'm sorry," he said through trembling lips. "I didn't... I... I'm sorry."

Sam glanced at Vera. She was staring at the counter, drawing in slow, deep breaths, her hands clenched into fists in front of her. She squeezed her eyes shut and rolled her neck, and Sam could hear it pop from across the kitchen. They chewed their lip.

Movement in the corner of their eye drew their gaze to Gavin. He stood huddled against Isaac's side, his eyes wide and filled with horror – and staring right at Vera.

"Oh, fuck," Gavin whispered.

Vera opened her eyes and blew out another breath through her lips. She met Gavin's gaze. "Well," she breathed. "That's a fucking horrifying realization."

Zachariah blinked and looked at Vera. "Wh-what? I'm... I'm sorry, I didn't—"

"It's okay, you didn't know," Vera said evenly, but her hands shook as she clasped them together. She looked up at Gavin, and the pain in her eyes made Sam's chest ache in sympathy. "And I didn't even... make the connection."

"N-neither did I," Gavin whimpered softly as his fingers tangled in Isaac's shirt. Isaac pressed an anxious kiss against Gavin's temple.

Sam wet their lips. "Um, Zachariah…" They walked to Zachariah's side, standing just beside Edrissa. They could feel everyone's gazes on their back. "We, um, don't say that word because, um… that's what Joseph Stormbeck used to call Vera when he… captured her." They gently rested their hand on Zachariah's arm, and felt Zachariah relax slightly under their touch.

Vera's voice was rough. "And that's what Colleen Stormbeck called Gavin while she—"

"My whole life," Gavin said with a hollow voice. "That's what she called me my whole life. That's what she called all her playthings. And I never even… *noticed*."

"I'm sorry," Zachariah said in a small voice. "I'm sorry." He raised his gaze and looked around at the others. Sam turned and saw Gavin still looking at Vera, saw Vera looking right back at him with a matching expression of horror and understanding. Sam's hand slipped from Zachariah's arm, and they flexed their fingers as their hand fell to their side. Edrissa's eyes were fixed on Sam, a strange sort of sadness crossing her face.

Slowly, Vera pushed herself up from the barstool and crossed to Gavin's side. Tears shone in Gavin's eyes. Vera's were dry, fevered. She held out a hand to Gavin.

Gavin slid from Isaac's embrace and fell against Vera as she wrapped her arms around him and crushed him to her chest. He squeezed her tight and laid his head on her shoulder.

"Now we know," Vera said heavily, her voice tight with tears.

"H-how did we… *miss* that?" Gavin said, and his voice broke.

Vera huffed out a broken laugh. "Don't make me remind you this early in the afternoon that you're a dumb—"

"I'm a dumbass," Gavin grumbled against her shoulder. "I know."

Isaac stepped forward and wrapped his arms around them both. "I'm… um… s-sorry," he croaked. "For both of you. That they… *hurt* you that way."

Vera sniffed and pulled away from the hug. She still held Gavin by his shoulders. "Yeah," she said weakly.

Zachariah shifted uncomfortably next to Sam. "So… so they… Gavin, you…"

"Yeah," Gavin said, and swiped at his eyes. "I mean, I knew she… *used* me, but I didn't realize… she…" He cleared his throat. "Um…" He blew out a slow breath and shrugged out of Vera's grip. "Isaac… I'm going to go, um, change."

Isaac met Gavin's gaze, and Sam's stomach tightened at the pain they saw there. *He always blames himself. He always feels like he has to fix it.*

Isaac nodded. "Okay. Do you want—"

"I just need a minute," Gavin rasped, and sidestepped Isaac. He disappeared down the hall.

When Isaac finally looked away from the now-empty hallway, he turned to Vera. "Do you…?" He held out his hands to her.

"Yeah, sure," Vera said brusquely, and dragged Isaac into a crushing hug.

At Sam's side, Zachariah crossed his arms over his chest and looked at the floor. "Is there, um… any, anything else I shouldn't say?"

Sam glanced at Edrissa. "Edrissa… Do you—"

"Honey," she said with a tremulous voice. She set her jaw. "H-he called me 'honey'."

Zachariah nodded.

Sam wet their lips. "And… please don't call me, um… Sammy," Sam said, looking up at him. Their heart sped up as his light brown eyes found theirs. They glanced to Edrissa, then to Vera and Isaac. They stood with their shoulders touching, Vera leaning just slightly against Isaac. "Guys, can you think of anything…?"

"I think that about covers it," Vera said, a hint of bitterness in her voice. "I mean, I'm guessing we'll be finding shit like this for a while." She fixed Zachariah with her gaze, and he withered under it. "But it's not your fault, kid. Okay?"

Zachariah swallowed loudly. "Um…"

"It's not," Sam said gently, finding their own hand reaching for his. "We all make mistakes with this stuff, and you didn't know."

Zachariah's mouth twisted. "But I do now," he said. He looked at Edrissa as she crossed to Sam's side. "And I'll… I'll remember."

Sam nodded at Zachariah, then turned to look at Edrissa. She looked back at them with a sad, wistful smile on her face.

Chapter 8

Isaac's hand hovered above the doorknob to his room. Gavin was in there – Isaac hadn't seen Gavin leave, and the bathroom was empty – but Isaac didn't know if Gavin wanted to be seen yet. *"I just need a minute,"* Gavin had said. It had been fifteen minutes, now. Zachariah, Edrissa, and Sam were still in the kitchen, browning meat and chopping herbs for the stew. Vera was still sitting at the counter, chatting with the three of them with forced calmness. Isaac could feel his heart beating in his chest, every moment keenly bringing an awareness that Gavin was behind this door, Gavin was suffering, Gavin was *alone…*

Isaac set his jaw and knocked. "Hey, Gavin?" he said softly.

A sniff, behind the door. "Y-yeah?"

Isaac squeezed his eyes shut and gently rested his forehead against the solid oak of the door. "Can I… can I come in?"

There was a long silence, and every second dragged at Isaac's chest. He bit down hard on his lip. His hands tightened into fists.

Then he heard Gavin's voice, soft and muffled, behind the door. "Um… yeah."

Isaac let out a huff of relief and opened the door.

Gavin sat on the bed, a small pile of books on the mattress beside him. He clutched at one of the books, his fingers tight on the pages as he looked up at Isaac with despair. Isaac's heart clenched as he stepped into the room and closed the door.

"Um… what're you doing?" Isaac said gently.

Gavin wiped his nose and let the book fall from his hands onto the bed – *When Home is a Nightmare: Recovering from Childhood Abuse* by Lander Coply. Isaac had seen Gavin poring over it, ever since Gray brought it home from Crayton the first week they'd been back.

Gavin read every book Gray brought home – novels, philosophy books, how-to manuals. He'd even read Finn and Ellis's baby development book, when they were off fixing up the little house just down the road. Gavin had his own collection of books, now spread out over the bedspread, that Gray had brought home just for him. Isaac's stomach lurched as he saw the desperate, frenzied pain in Gavin's face. He took a step closer, his hands held out in front of him and slightly to his sides.

"Gavin?" Isaac said softly.

"I never..." Gavin whined softly and rocked back and forth, hugging himself. "I n-never... how did I never... *see* it? She called me... called me... *that*... my whole fucking life, then turned around and called our fucking *playthings* the exact same thing. That's what she called Vera and Tori. I... *I* called them that, because I knew it would help. I knew it... *fuck, I knew* calling them that would make my mom think I was breaking. And how can I... I..." Gavin groaned and leaned forward, pressing his face into his hands.

Isaac took another step closer. "Gavin... do you... want to be touched right now?"

Gavin pressed on as if he hadn't even heard Isaac. "How could I go through my entire *fucking life* and not even realize my parents were treating me like... like... like a fucking *plaything?*"

Isaac swallowed dryly. "Um... Gavin... sometimes we... don't pick up on things until, um, way later—"

"But this was fucking *obvious,*" Gavin snarled. He snapped his head up and fixed Isaac with a glare. "This... maybe if I... realized *this* a long time ago, I wouldn't have..." Gavin's gaze moved over Isaac's arms, over the scars there. He made a sound of disgust and shoved himself to his feet. He started pacing around the room.

"What am I supposed to do?" Gavin panted, tearing his hands through his hair. "What the fuck am I supposed to *do?* If I didn't realize *this,* then... how can I even... how can I expect to... to get *better?* How can I... Gray gets me all these books so maybe they'll, they'll *help,* but..." Gavin snatched a book up off the bed and flipped through it roughly. The corners were dog-eared, lines and passages underlined, notes written in the margins.

Those books didn't look like that when Gray got them.

"See?" Gavin spat and dropped the book onto the bed. "Th-this one is, is about recovery from, um, narcissistic parents. And *this* one—" He grabbed another and rifled through it. "—is about brainwashing. It's a book about parents, but there's some cult stuff in there, too. And this one—" He tossed the book onto the bed and picked up one with a worn cover, pages crinkled with water stains. "—is about h-how, how to, to heal from abuse. And all these *fucking books*..." Gavin dropped the book, and it thumped to the bedspread. He threw his hand out, toward the pile of books. Tears shone in his eyes.

"Gavin," Isaac said softly, and stepped forward, hands outstretched. Gavin shoved his hands away.

Gavin swiped at his eyes. "All th-these *fucking books* talk about shit my parents did. They talk about the lying, and the conditioning, and the n-neglect..." Gavin sniffed furiously. "Even th-though I had everything I could ever ask for..." His eyes unfocused as Isaac watched him. Then his gaze snapped back to Isaac. His face looked torn with grief, his mouth in a terrible agonized snarl and his eyes wide and desperate. "And they... they talk about... *symptoms.*" He spat the word. "They talk about... *common manifestations of trauma.* And I have... I ha-have... *s-so many* of them." Gavin sobbed weakly and dashed the tears from his eyes. "Depression... anxiety... a feeling of impending doom... nightmares... migraines... flashbacks... blaming myself... a feeling of emptiness... And I..." He clawed at his chest, breathing hard.

Isaac stood in front of him in shock. His mouth opened, then closed.

"I f-feel empty... all the *time,*" Gavin rasped. He raised his frenzied gaze to Isaac. "But you... you're enough. This whole family, you're enough. Y-you're more than, than I c-could... ever *deserve.* But there's this emptiness inside me that doesn't go away, no matter what I feed into it..." His eyes were streaming tears now. Gavin didn't even try to wipe them away. "Every time you touch me, or Gray tells me I did something *right,* or Vera smiles at me, or Edrissa fucking... *trusts* me with the tiniest little thing..." Gavin gasped. "It feels so good, and I just want *more.* I want more of, of *everything.* And these... these... *fucking books*..."

"Gavin," Isaac said softly, his blood pounding in his ears. His hands shook. "Breathe. Breathe. Just—"

"These books tell me how this kind of, of *trauma*—" Gavin's chest heaved with a sob. "—affects you. They tell me it'll be hard to establish solid relationships. That it'll be hard to trust myself. That I'm gonna hurt, for the rest of my life, and every time I read this shit it feels like I'm reading my own fucking *eulogy*." Gavin sank to the bed and wrapped his arms around his chest. "And... I just..." He shook his head, defeated. Isaac trembled with the need to help and the terror of not knowing how.

Gavin heaved a shuddering breath. "I just don't know how this is supposed to work." He gestured weakly between himself and Isaac. "It feels like... *impossible* fucking odds that I could ever be... be happy." He wiped his nose with his sleeve.

Isaac knelt in front of him. He clutched at Gavin's hands and held them in his, warming Gavin's freezing fingers in his grip. He ducked into Gavin's eyeline, seeking his gaze. Gavin stared at the floor.

Dread burned in Isaac's gut, but he reached out with one hand and cupped Gavin's face. Gavin shuddered under the touch, but pushed slightly into Isaac's hand. Isaac's heart ached as he stroked Gavin's cheek with his thumb. He leaned in close and ducked into Gavin's eyeline.

"*Fuck* the odds," Isaac whispered.

Gavin's lips parted and he looked at Isaac, his eyes searching. Questioning. Hoping. "Wh-what?"

"Fuck. The. Odds," Isaac said softly. "Fuck what those books say. Fuck what the, what the fucking... *world* says, Gavin. You've already..." His throat tightened. He swallowed hard. "You've already done so much."

Gavin's mouth twisted in an ugly grimace. "Stop it, Isaac," he said bitterly. "Stop. Please. Don't—"

"According to everything I know," Isaac said, his lips trembling, "I should be dead."

Gavin fell silent and stared at Isaac. His eyebrows pulled together, and Isaac longed to lean forward and kiss away the worry lines there.

"According to everything I know," Isaac murmured, "You should have killed me. I should be... should be dead. In your basement, or in the Crayton house, or... or b-by my own fucking hand. That's what I know. But I'm... I'm alive. I'm alive... because of *you*."

Gavin whimpered. "Isaac…"

"You saved us," Isaac breathed. He slid his hand down Gavin's neck, over his shoulder, down his arm, to grasp Gavin's hand. "You were born syndicate and raised by those fucking… *monsters* that called themselves your parents. And you left. You *left*." Isaac raised his free hand and lightly tapped Gavin's chest. His own heart pounded, his mouth dry with the words that burned his tongue, with the words he couldn't say.

You're good. You're mine. Please don't leave me. Please don't lose yourself.

Isaac pressed his lips together to stop them from trembling. "Do you know how hard that is? Do you know… how m-much courage that took?"

"I o-only did it to save myself," Gavin whispered bitterly.

"Bullshit," Isaac snapped. "*Bullshit.* You left because you couldn't be who you were anymore. And leaving was what you needed to do to survive. To… to *escape.* You left that life even though you had nowhere else to go."

Gavin held Isaac's gaze like it was a lifeline. "You did it, too," Gavin murmured. "Y-you… you left."

Isaac chewed his lip. "Yeah," he said softly. "I did. And… and you… you found us. Gavin… You changed because of the good *inside you.*" He rested his hand lightly on Gavin's chest.

Gavin's eyes fluttered closed, and he drew in a deep breath. "B-but… where did it… did it come from?" Gavin rasped. "My parents put… evil inside me. If I'm good…" He gripped his hands together tightly and looked at Isaac. "If I'm good…"

"You're good because it comes from inside you," Isaac said, steadying the tremor in his voice, the desperation. "It's who you *are.*"

"B-but I still… I still… want to hurt people, sometimes," Gavin said, his voice dropping. His face twisted with shame, and his head fell forward.

"Everybody does sometimes," Isaac said softly. "Sam does. Gray does."

"But it's different with me," Gavin said through his teeth, as if holding back a scream. "Because I… I *remember* how it felt to feel someone's blood on my hands, feel them…" He squeezed one hand into a fist. "F-feel the life drain out of them when I… when I bled them. Or choked them." He raised his head to meet Isaac's eyes. His gaze bored into Isaac. "I know exactly how it would have felt to kill *you*." Gavin's eyes were blank, unfocused. Isaac's stomach pitched at the sight of Gavin's gaze so broken, so *shattered*. He wet his lips and squeezed Gavin's hands.

"And I know how it would have felt to kill *you,* in that safehouse basement," Isaac said softly. "There's no point in—"

"How am I supposed to stop hurting, Isaac?" Gavin rasped. His eyes suddenly blazed with rage, with pain, with *grief.* "Even when I, um, feel good, even when I'm with you and with the family, even when things are good…" He moved his hand to his chest and pressed there. "I still hurt. Here. And in my head. I still feel it in my, my hands." He whimpered and leaned forward. His head dropped onto Isaac's shoulder. "I just want to stop *hurting.*"

Isaac pushed himself up to sit beside Gavin. He pulled Gavin into his arms and held him as Gavin's hands wound into his shirt, pulling Isaac close, clutching him as if his life depended on it. Gavin unraveled and collapsed into Isaac's arms, heaving great, wracking sobs with each breath.

"H-how, do, do I, do I s-stop *hurting?*"

"I don't know," Isaac murmured into Gavin's hair. His eyes pricked with tears. "But… please… *try*. Please try. I want to try with you. And I want to be… w-with you, Gavin. Please." He pressed a kiss against Gavin's temple. *"Please."*

Gavin whimpered wordlessly. "How?" he whispered. "How do I do more?"

"I didn't mean do *more,* Gavin," Isaac said. He squeezed his eyes shut and pressed his lips into Gavin's hair. "I meant… please… just *keep* trying. You don't have to read those books if you don't want to. You don't have to be… *good,* Gavin." Isaac gasped as hot, bitter sorrow punched through his chest. Gavin whimpered and clutched him tighter. "You don't have to be *good.* You don't have to do it *right*, for me to love you."

Gavin shuddered and sobbed against Isaac's shoulder. Tears pricked Isaac's eyes as he pulled Gavin tighter to his chest, holding him as he trembled.

Isaac rocked him slowly, shivering at Gavin's breath against his neck, the warmth of his body in his arms, the sound of his sobs in the quiet room. He kissed Gavin's hair, breathing him in, holding him tight, even as his own chest ached.

"Please, Gavin," Isaac rasped. He cleared his throat. "You don't have to do it right. You don't have to… to be *good*. But please keep trying. Please… please stay with me. Please remember I love you, and it… it wasn't your fault, what your parents did." Isaac's throat was so tight he could barely get the words out.

Gavin was silent for a long moment. Isaac's eyes stung as he held Gavin tight, feeling Gavin's chest move as he breathed, feeling the shudders move over and through him with each quiet sob.

Please, please stay with me.

Isaac's heart clenched in tremulous relief when he felt Gavin wind himself closer into Isaac's arms, and nod against his chest.

"I promise," Gavin whispered. "I'm… I promise."

Chapter 9

As Sam carried their bowl into the kitchen after dinner, Edrissa met their eyes with a shy smile. They passed Isaac and Gavin on their way to the sink. Isaac piled the cooking pans by the sink as Gavin moved the compost bin closer for the food scraps, Gavin's eyes a little red-rimmed. Sam stacked their bowl by the sink as Vera rolled up her sleeves and turned on the hot water. Tori kissed Vera gently on the cheek and stood to the side of the sink, ready to dry dishes as Vera handed them to her. The kitchen seemed emptier than usual without Finn and Ellis; the two of them had decided to eat dinner in Burmingham after they'd spent all day fixing up their house.

Zachariah hovered at Sam's shoulder, an anxious, near-constant presence since he'd called Edrissa 'sweetheart' that afternoon. He wrung his hands, glancing every now and then at the sink where Vera was distractedly scrubbing the dishes.

Without thinking, Sam gently placed their hand on Zachariah's arm.

Edrissa's gaze flicked to Sam's hand, then back to their face. Her clear blue eyes darkened, just a little. Her smile was still there, as gorgeous as ever, but the corners of her mouth fell slightly as Sam watched. They wet their lips to speak.

"Want to go for a walk?" Edrissa said first. Her gaze flicked to Zachariah, then back to Sam. "Um... just... just you and me." She smiled wider, but it still seemed forced, that sadness still tightening in her eyes. "You know, might not... might not be safe, still."

Sam's mouth went dry, and they swallowed. "Yeah," they rasped. They glanced at Zachariah and squeezed his arm.

Zachariah's eyes went wide. He glanced around at the others.

"They won't bite," Sam said gently. They stepped away and followed Edrissa to the back of the house and out into the warm night.

The sun was still up and shining over the lake, not even behind the trees yet. Sam blinked and tilted their head back, breathing in the clean air, the smell of the grass and sand and trees. They felt the wind play through their hair, felt Edrissa's warm fingers clasp through their own as they walked through the overgrown yard. The grass was patchy, giving way to sand that shifted under Sam's bare feet.

The moon had just started to rise. It was barely a sliver in the sky, almost the new moon – Edrissa kept track of things like that, the moon, the seasons, the time when the herbs in the garden sprouted and bloomed. She had a little journal Gray had given her where she drew plants and charts of the stars, patterns for clothes, sketches of Nata where he sat in sunny windowsills. It occurred to Sam that the last time they saw Edrissa scribbling in her little book, she'd been close to the end of it. Sam had seen a shop in Crayton that sold pretty things like Edrissa seemed to like: notebooks, pens, tiny jars of colorful ink that they'd seen her staring at when they went into town. They were unbelievably expensive, all of it either taken off luxury syndicate shipments or purchased from black market dealers – *who knew there was a black market for fountain pens?* – but if Sam started volunteering with the refugees and saving the credits Daniel Schiester gave them...

Maybe I should get her a new notebook, they thought to themself. *Maybe she'd like the one with the pink flowers on the cover. Or... she seemed to like the leather ones, too. Maybe I could get one for her birthday. When was that again? I think it was—*

"We missed your birthday," Sam blurted out.

Edrissa blinked and looked at them. "What?" The sun shone on her hair, making it shimmer like liquid gold.

Sam reached out and tucked a lock behind her ear. "Your birthday," they said softly. "It's in May, isn't it? We... we missed it."

Edrissa shrugged and looked down. She turned and they both began to walk along the shore of the lake. "It was May fifth. You were, um... s-south," she murmured.

Sam froze. "Oh."

Edrissa stopped beside them and squeezed their hand. "It's okay," she said gently. "Gray celebrated with me. We went into town and went to that restaurant that makes the cheese they light on fire. Then we went to Ms. Clancy's nursery and Gray let me pick out any herb I wanted." Edrissa glanced back at the house. "I picked the lemon balm. It's *loving* the cooler weather up here. That's what I made the tea from."

Sam turned to face Edrissa. She had the look in her eyes she always got when she talked about her beautiful things. The breeze tousled her hair to frame her face, and her lips curved up into a smile.

Without a word, they cradled her face and brushed their lips against hers.

Edrissa sighed and pulled Sam close, her fingers winding into their shirt. She trembled as Sam carefully pulled their right arm out of its sling and wound it around her waist, holding her close. Their right shoulder was sore, but there was no flash of pain, no bolt of agony through the wound. Edrissa ghosted her tongue over Sam's lower lip and they whimpered softly. They didn't meet her tongue with theirs, though, because Edrissa didn't like that.

But Edrissa liked kissing Sam, and Sam *loved* that.

Edrissa pulled slightly away, breaking the kiss but keeping her forehead pressed against Sam's. She shivered in the warm breeze and blew out a slow breath.

After a long, sweet moment, they gently pulled their hands away and let them fall to their sides. Their right arm twinged, and they chewed the inside of their cheek as they held back a groan of pain. Their gaze moved over her face. Her fingers tightened in Sam's shirt and she bit her lip like she was holding back tears.

Sam's eyebrows drew together. Their stomach dipped. "Edrissa?" They wet their lips. "What's the matter?"

Edrissa finally released Sam and wiped her eyes. She sniffed. "Um... I was just thinking... um..." She shrugged jerkily. "I've been, um... w-watching... you. And Zachariah."

Sam's eyebrows shot up, and they pushed down the stir of warmth in their chest. "Y-yeah?"

"Yeah," Edrissa said. She cleared her throat. "And you, um... you seem to, um, do really well together. You look, um, good."

Sam ventured a smile. "So do you, Edrissa," they said gently.

Edrissa waved the comment away. "He's... he's big, and, um, and strong, and he's really nice."

"Yeah, he is." Sam reached out and squeezed Edrissa's hand.

"And... he seems to like you." Edrissa shrugged again. She wrapped her free arm around her waist and looked at the ground.

Sam's heart skipped a beat. "You think so?" they croaked, and glanced back towards the house, shining pale yellow in the sun.

"He'd be really good for you, Sam," Edrissa said, and a hint of sadness – of dismay – entered her voice. "He's good, and kind, and he'll protect you. And he'd probably be okay with... he'd... probably..." Edrissa released Sam's hand and wrapped her other arm around her waist, squeezing herself tight. Tears glittered in her eyes.

Sam's eyebrows pulled together, and they tilted their head as they looked at her. They chewed their lip. "Edrissa... I don't..."

"What I mean to say is," Edrissa said, tight-lipped, "Is that... I think you two should be together."

Sam watched her carefully. "Okay..."

"Because... I would understand if..." Edrissa blinked, and tears ran down her cheeks. She swiped them away and stared at the ground again. "You deserve... everything, Sam," she rasped. "You deserve someone who's strong, and not broken, someone who can, um... h-have *sex*. I don't know if I'll... ever want to. I don't know if I *can*."

Sam reached out to her. "Edrissa, I—"

She stepped away from their grasp. "He's good for you, Sam," she whimpered, her voice trembling. "You're good *together*. And I mean... he's... he's *gorgeous*... and so considerate, and he'd... he'd... treat you s-so well..."

Sam's heart pounded in their chest. "Edrissa, are you... breaking up with me?" Their chest ached. Their skin felt too tight, their lungs not quite able to expand.

"No!" Edrissa cried and grabbed Sam's hand. "No, I... I want to be with you, I just... I want you to be... *happy*. And Zachariah can make you happy."

"You make me happy, too," Sam whimpered. Their mind reeled. "And... you like him too, right?"

Edrissa blinked. "Well... yeah, I mean... he's... he's wonderful. I like his arms, and his voice, and his lips, and how he always wants to help me in the kitchen, and... and his, um..." She blushed a furious crimson.

Sam drew in a deep breath, trying to calm their pounding heart. "So... if you like him... and I like him..."

"He'll choose you," Edrissa whispered. "I know he'll choose you. You're..." Edrissa's gaze flicked up to Sam and back down. "You're... He'd have to be *crazy* not to choose you."

Sam looked at Edrissa for a long moment, searching her face with their gaze and swallowing against the lump in their throat. "Um... Edrissa, we could just... be with him... together?"

Edrissa blinked and raised her gaze to Sam's. "Huh?"

Sam shrugged. "I mean... you don't have to? But... if you like him, and I like him, and he seems to like both of us..."

"You think so?" Edrissa breathed. Her eyes shone with painful-looking hope.

Sam thought back to Edrissa clambering up onto Zachariah's back, holding the baking sheet aloft like a shield – and of how Zachariah's hands had gently curved around her legs, how he'd been so *careful* as he dodged Sam's handful of whipped cream, how he'd kept her safe, even from that innocent attack.

"Yeah," Sam said with a nod. "I think so."

Edrissa swallowed hard. "Is that... something people do... a lot?" she murmured. "I thought... I don't know, I've never seen that before. My parents were married only to each other, and my boyfriend and I were only with each other, and my o-owner only ever had—" She cut herself off with a gasp and looked back down at her feet sinking into the soft sand.

"I just know it's something people do," Sam said gently. "And we don't have to if you don't want to. But... Edrissa..." They stepped forward and cupped Edrissa's face, tilting her head back so they could see her eyes. "I would, um... really, really like that. If we could all... be together. And... please know that..." They leaned forward and gently kissed Edrissa's cheek. She drew in a short, quick breath. "I like you. A lot. And just because you've been through... what you've been through..." They kissed her other cheek.

"…doesn't mean I don't want to be with you. I told you." They gently pressed their lips to hers. "I don't need to have sex, if you don't want to have it. You're my… my girlfriend." They smiled at the shiver of her breath against their lips as they said it. "And you told me what you wanted when we started this, and I told you that's what I wanted, too."

"Oh," Edrissa murmured. She pulled Sam close and laid her head on their shoulder. "So… did you want to talk to him… tonight?"

Sam's stomach flipped at the idea of pulling Zachariah close, kissing him as Edrissa touched him, too, as he touched them both. Their mouth went dry. "Um, yeah," they croaked, then laughed softly. "Yeah. Tonight. Sounds good."

They turned back towards the house. Sam slung their left arm over Edrissa's shoulders. She wound her arm around their waist. They laughed as they bumped hips and stumbled over the sand.

Chapter 10

The first thing Gavin became aware of was a throbbing pain behind his left eye. His eyelids fluttered open, and he winced as the hot, dull ache stabbed through his head. He squeezed his eyes shut against the light that filtered in through the curtains. He groaned, his hands pulling into fists, and curled into a ball under the blanket.

"Gavin?" came Isaac's soft, concerned murmur.

"Nnngh," Gavin moaned, swallowing the saliva that pooled in his mouth as his stomach heaved. "H-head, *agh…*" He whimpered softly and winced as even the sound of his own voice seemed to crush his brain against the inside of his skull.

Cool, gentle fingers carded through Gavin's hair. He cracked his eyes open to see Isaac lying next to him, his eyebrows pulled together in worry. "Another migraine?" Isaac whispered.

Gavin's head moved a fraction of an inch in a weak nod. He blew out a slow breath between his lips. "Y-yeah," he rasped. His eyes slid shut.

The mattress jostled as Isaac smoothly pushed himself out of bed. Gavin longed to reach out and pull Isaac back down to the bed and beg to be *held,* just to beg for Isaac to stay with him through what Gavin knew would be an agonizing day. He lay perfectly still, trying even to stop his own heartbeat, to relieve the pounding ache in his head. He wet his chapped lips and curled further into himself.

"I can go get your medicine," Isaac whispered over the sound of clothes rustling. "The riz— the migraine meds Finn brought a few days ago. We can see if that works."

Gavin groaned his assent and tugged helplessly on his hair. He tried, desperately, to think of what helped last time – but each beat of his heart shoved away his thoughts until all he could focus on, all he could comprehend, was the pain of each second that crept by.

The door creaked open, the sound thundering through his brain, and Gavin was alone. He trembled beneath the blanket, his skin breaking out in a sweat as waves of nausea rocked through him. He rolled onto his other side and let his head hang against the edge of the mattress, above the waiting trashcan. After a long moment, the door creaked again, and Gavin could hear Isaac's bare feet on the rug as he walked to Gavin's side. The mattress dipped under Isaac's weight. Gavin's stomach lurched with the feeling, and he opened his eyes.

"Here," Isaac whispered. He held out a light orange, oval-shaped pill in his fingers. Gavin moved to take it from him and sucked in a breath as pain exploded through his head.

Isaac pressed his mouth into a hard line and gently held the pill to Gavin's lips. Gavin let Isaac drop the pill into his mouth, and shivered as Isaac cupped his chin and held a glass of water to his lips. He took a long sip and slumped against the mattress again. Helplessly, he prayed he wouldn't throw up the water, and the pill, before it had time to kick in. If it would help at all.

"Finn said it should kick in within an hour," Isaac whispered.

Pain spiked through Gavin's head with the thought of relief. "Hmmn," he groaned. He closed his eyes and tipped his head back as Isaac drew his fingers through Gavin's hair again. That brought a hint of relief. "Wh-what…" He swallowed hard. "Do you need to go into town today?"

"No," Isaac said softly. "No, I can stay home today. Although, when I went to get your meds, the others were talking about heading down to the lake and maybe bringing a picnic lunch. Finn and Ellis are pretty much moved into their new house. It sounds like Gray and Edrissa wanted to have a going-away party for them, even though they'll be right down the road." Isaac huffed out a laugh. "I think Edrissa's going to bake a cake."

"You should go," Gavin groaned. "I'm… 'm good." He squeezed his eyes tighter, and sparks shot through his head.

Isaac's fingers paused in their path from Gavin's temple to the back of his neck. "But I can stay here with you," he murmured.

Gavin whimpered and reached up, lacing his fingers through Isaac's. "But… if it's their last d-day… *fuck me,* if, if it's their last day at this house, then you sh-should… ahh…"

"But—"

"They're your... *family,* Isaac." Gavin wondered if he would be able to fall back asleep if Isaac left. Maybe, if he could lie in the dark and not move, maybe his head wouldn't explode...

"You're my family, too," Isaac breathed. He squeezed Gavin's fingers. "And you're... you're sick."

"I'll have plenty of migraines you can help me with," Gavin said bitterly. "Isaac... *please,* go, I want you to have a, um, a g-good... Fuck, this is worse than before..." He gagged weakly. The mattress lurched as Isaac lunged for the wastebasket and thrust it under Gavin's chin. Gavin shuddered and swallowed bile, pressing his face against the sheets. He *wanted* Isaac to stay, but the pain ratcheted higher, like a railroad spike being driven into his left eye socket, at the thought of Isaac missing Finn and Ellis on their last day at home. His throat clicked dryly as he swallowed. "Isaac..."

"I can get you a cold compress," Isaac said weakly. "Would that help?"

"Um... I don't know," Gavin groaned, wanting to scream from the pain and knowing the sound would shatter him if he did.

"Okay. I'll go... I'll go get one." Isaac's fingers slid out of Gavin's grip, and the mattress dipped as he stood.

Gavin drifted in the pain, his heartbeat marking the time as each moment crawled by. He jumped when something cool pressed against the back of his neck. He hadn't even heard Isaac come in over the pounding in his head.

Gavin sighed as the compress pushed away the pain, just a little. "Thank you," he whispered.

"Yeah," Isaac said softly. "Do you... Gavin, if you really want me to go—"

"Once the meds start working, I'll come out and join you," Gavin ground out through his teeth. "Right now I just... need to focus on not... *ahh...*"

"Okay," Isaac said quickly, and Gavin's heart wrenched at the concern in his voice. "Okay. If you, um..." The compress shifted as Isaac pulled his hand away, and Gavin reached up to hold it in place. "I'll come check on you in a few hours if you're not out by then."

"S-sounds like a plan," Gavin breathed. He twisted against the sheets, desperate to find a position that would ease the pressure building in his head.

"I love you," Isaac whispered, and Gavin felt the soft press of a kiss into his hair. His heart thudded in his chest.

"Love you, too," Gavin whispered back. After a long moment, the soft sound of Isaac padding to the door and the creak of it shutting behind him stabbed Gavin like hot knives.

He whimpered softly and pressed the cold compress against the back of his own neck. It cooled his damp hair. Each heartbeat rocked through his head, each breath echoed loudly in his ears, each roil of his stomach threatened to bring up the pill and water. He drifted in the pain.

∴

Gavin blinked his eyes open. He stirred beneath the sheets and squinted in the dim light filtering through the curtains. The cool compress on the back of his neck made him shiver. He swallowed, and his throat felt dry.

The pain in his head was gone.

Tears of pure relief stung Gavin's eyes. His chest swelled with gratitude for Finn, and he made a mental note to thank them later. He experimentally pushed himself up off the bed. The room swam oddly around him.

He put a hand to his head and groaned. It was as if a thick fog had settled inside his brain, blunting the edges, dulling each thought. Still, his stomach felt settled, and the light no longer stabbed his eyes. He dropped the cold compress onto the nightstand and sat up.

There was a pair of dark blue swim trunks lying at the foot of the bed.

Tears blurred Gavin's vision all over again. He swung his legs over the side of the bed and clumsily got to his feet, wobbling before he got his balance.

I don't remember feeling this weird after.

Gavin shuffled forward and pulled the swim trunks on. After a moment, he crossed to the dresser and took out a t-shirt. He pulled it on over his head and shivered as it settled on the scars on his back. His fingers drifted over his chest, just below his right collarbone, over the scar there – the one that matched the scar on Gray's left side.

He shook his head and pushed the door open. The house was silent as he wandered down the hall. As his head swam, he made his way to the bathroom and brushed his teeth. He caught himself staring in the mirror, his gaze flicking from the scar on the bridge of his nose, to the one on his cheek, to the one stretching from the outer corner of his left eye and up into his hairline. Isaac always kissed those scars in exactly that order. Gavin blinked and bent over his rinse out his mouth.

He wandered towards the back of the house with a strange, detached feeling. It was almost as if, as he moved through the air, it was thicker than normal. He seemed to only notice everything a second after it happened. He walked through the laundry room and pushed open the back door, blinking in the sudden sunlight.

It wasn't quite overhead, but then, it never got that high this far north. Even in late August, the sun still cast shadows at noon. Gavin stumbled out into the long grass of the backyard and wandered down towards the lake.

Gavin blinked again; everything was stunning. The sun was warm on his face, and a gentle breeze ruffled his hair, still slightly damp with his own sweat. He felt comfortable in his t-shirt and trunks. The sun glittered on the surface of the lake, and his feet brushed through the grass as it gave way to rough, granite-gray sand. Gavin drew in a deep breath and felt a smile pull at his lips.

Down near the lake, Finn and Ellis sat on an electric blue towel, Ellis's legs draped over Finn's, both of them turned towards the water. Zachariah stood waist-deep in the water – Gavin fought back the prickle of unease at seeing the young rescue outside and found himself glancing around, half-expecting to see figures watching him from the trees.

Zachariah laughed, joyously fending off Edrissa and Sam as they both climbed him like a tree, Edrissa's squeals and Sam's laughter carrying over the water. As Gavin watched, Zachariah's large hands closed around Edrissa's waist and he heaved her farther into the lake. She disappeared with a splash and broke the surface again, shrieking with laughter, her pale skin flushed red from the cold water. Sam giggled as they wound their legs around Zachariah's middle, locking their ankles together and hanging onto his back with one arm. Edrissa flipped her soaking wet hair over her shoulder before she clumsily swam to

Zachariah and threw her arms around his neck. She planted a kiss on his cheek before he hoisted her and hurled her back into the water, laughing the whole time.

Tori and Vera stood at the edge of the water in their own bathing suits, their arms around each other's waists. Even twenty yards away, Vera's scars stood out pale against the dark brown of her skin; Tori's scars shone pink against her black skin. Vera's had faded with time. Tori's would, too, someday.

They both laughed as Sam splashed Edrissa from their protected spot on Zachariah's back. Zachariah ducked his head as Sam pressed a kiss to the side of his neck. Gavin smiled at the sight of the three of them together.

Gray sat in a lawn chair turned towards the lake, wearing a t-shirt and shorts and a straw hat to keep off the sun. Gavin couldn't stop the laugh that bubbled in his throat.

They look retired.

Isaac was pawing through a basket set on top of another towel, this one a blaring yellow. He looked up at the sound of Gavin's laugh. Gavin felt Isaac's gaze like a thump in his chest. His smile stretched wider as he made his way to Isaac's side.

Gray glanced up, and Gavin realized that they held a glass of lemonade in their hand.

All they need is a book, and the look is complete.

"Hey!" Gray said with a grin. "He lives!"

"Yeah," Gavin mumbled, and blushed as Isaac wound an arm around his waist and pressed a kiss to his temple. "That medicine did the trick."

Finn glanced over and perked up when they saw Gavin. "Oh, hey!" they said, gently guiding Ellis's legs off of theirs and climbing to their feet. "You feeling better?"

"Um, yeah," Gavin said as he looked down at his own sandy feet. "I'm a little dizzy, but…"

"Yeah, that can be a side effect," Finn said, and chewed their lip. "You feeling anything else? Pins and needles? You drowsy?"

"Yeah, a little drowsy," Gavin murmured. He glanced up and flushed an even more painful red when he realized Finn, Ellis, Gray, and Isaac all had their eyes on him. "Sorry I, um—"

"You should be," Ellis sniped, and they climbed to their feet and picked up the towel. Gavin found his gaze flicking to their abdomen, hidden behind a black one-piece bathing suit. They still weren't showing, and probably wouldn't be for another month or two. That's what their baby book said. He blinked and returned his gaze to their face.

"We were waiting on you to have lunch," Ellis said with a roll of their eyes, although their cutting voice was softened by a slight smile.

"No, we weren't," Isaac said with a playful grimace in Ellis's direction. He looked back at Gavin. "I was just going to come get you. You hungry?"

Gavin's stomach grumbled. "Yeah," he croaked. "I am, actually. Really hungry."

"Good," Isaac said. Gavin melted at the smile shining on Isaac's face.

Ellis turned to the others still in the water. "Hey, young people!" they shouted. "Get your asses over here, it's time to eat!"

Zachariah stopped mid-toss, holding Edrissa up over the water, as his head snapped towards the shore. Edrissa shrieked as he dropped her unceremoniously into the lake, laughing, and began to trudge toward the beach. Sam stayed latched onto him like a barnacle. Edrissa giggled as she grabbed Zachariah's arm and let him pull her to shore.

As Zachariah reached the edge of the water, Sam slipped off his back and landed lightly in the sand. Edrissa scrambled out of the water and tucked herself under Zachariah's arm, shivering. Her lips were blue as she turned her head and kissed his shoulder. Gavin smiled.

"Glad you're feeling better," Sam said through chattering teeth. They made their way over to a pile of towels beside Gray's chair and toweled off their hair, wrapping another towel around their shoulders. "The rizatriptan worked?"

"How come everyone can say it but me?" Isaac mumbled at Gavin's side.

"Yeah," Gavin said, and took another towel for him and Isaac to sit on. "Doing a *lot* better." He spread out the towel next to the basket and pulled Isaac down to sit next to him. Isaac's scars shone pearly white in the sun. Gavin laced his fingers through Isaac's.

"I spent all morning getting this ready," Edrissa said as she knelt by the picnic and began pulling out containers of food and sandwiches wrapped in napkins. "Potato salad for everyone… Egg salad for Ellis…" She passed the sandwich to Ellis. "Turkey for Finn, PB&J for Sam, turkey for Gray, tomato mozzarella pesto for Vera, ham for Tori, double turkey for Zachariah, mozzarella pesto for me…" she murmured as she passed out each sandwich. "Chicken salad for Isaac, Gavin I made one of those for you, too…"

Gavin gratefully took the sandwich from Edrissa and pulled the cloth napkin away. His stomach growled louder. Edrissa kept pulling food out of the basket. "Pickles, olives – gross, chips… these chips are really good, they're made by this married couple in Burmingham, they fry them in peanut oil, you have to try them… cookies…" A small pile of food was spread out on the towel next to the basket. "And if anyone wants more lemonade, I can just bring the pitcher…"

"Yes please," came the chorus of replies.

Edrissa scrambled to her feet. "I'll go grab it," she said.

"I'll help," Zachariah said with a grin.

"I'll come, too," Sam said as they tripped after them.

Gavin smiled and wondered how much time the three of them were going to spend actually bringing the lemonade.

As Gavin looked around at his family, he smiled even wider. Vera was laughing as she kissed Tori, and Tori's eyes were bright, focused, clear. Gray looked more relaxed than Gavin had ever seen them. Ellis and Finn had spread out their towel again next to the food, and Ellis was swatting away Finn's attempts to tickle them through peals of laughter.

And Isaac… Gavin allowed himself a moment to look at Isaac, and was instantly, desperately lost. Isaac stared right back at him, the look in his brown eyes making Gavin's stomach lurch like he was falling. Isaac reached over and laced his fingers through Gavin's. Gavin's heart ached with happiness as he squeezed Isaac's hand.

Isaac leaned forward and brushed his lips against Gavin's scars: nose, cheek, eye. Gavin turned his head and sought Isaac's lips with his. He smiled when Isaac lingered on the kiss. Isaac's beard tickled his cheeks.

"Oh, get a room," Ellis said good-naturedly. Gavin broke the kiss, and his cheeks blazed.

"May as well start eating," Gray said with a laugh. "Who knows when those three will be back. Apparently getting drinks is a strenuous three-person job."

Gavin took a bite of his sandwich as he looked out across the lake. The wind stirred the trees on the opposite shore.

Chapter 11

Gavin shivered and yawned on the couch. The sun was low in the sky now, not yet behind the trees on the opposite side of the lake. His head felt clearer now, the effects of the rizatriptan worn off. His headache hadn't returned. He covered his mouth with his hand and yawned, blinking away the water it brought to his eyes.

"Tired?" Isaac said where he sat on the couch next to Gavin.

A smile pulled at Gavin's lips as he brought his gaze to Isaac. They were alone in the living room; Finn and Ellis had driven to their new house only just down the road in one of the cars, after a long goodbye. Still, Gavin understood. The family had never been willingly separated before. Sam, Edrissa, and Zachariah had elected to walk around the lake after dinner, giggling and holding hands as they left. Gray was already asleep. Vera and Tori were in the backyard, ready to watch the coming sunset that was just barely turning the clouds a golden hue.

Isaac's eyes were warm and bright, his cheeks and forehead tanned from his day in the sun. His sandy-blond hair was tousled by the wind, and Gavin reached out and ran his fingers through it. The smile pulling at Isaac's lips widened. His gaze flicked down to Gavin's lips.

Gavin cleared his throat. "Um, yeah," he said, a little awkwardly. "Tired."

Isaac nodded. "Did you want to go to bed?" he said gently, still keeping his voice low.

"Um…" Gavin flushed and looked down, pulling his hand back and resting it awkwardly in his lap. "Bed, yeah, but… sleep…" He glanced up at Isaac again and wondered if his heart would ever stop beating harder when he met Isaac's eyes. "I want… I'd like…"

Isaac leaned forward and pressed a kiss to Gavin's lips.

Gavin sighed and cradled Isaac's face. "Y-yeah," he mumbled against Isaac's lips. "This."

Isaac broke the kiss and got to his feet. He held out a hand to Gavin with a conspiratory smile. "Let's go, then," he said softly. Gavin slid his hand into Isaac's and let Isaac pull him up from the couch.

As they made their way down the hall to their room, Gavin's fingers laced through Isaac's and squeezed. Isaac squeezed back. Isaac pulled Gavin into their room and before Gavin could say anything, Isaac had Gavin pushed up against the closed door, Isaac's mouth moving with his, hot and urgent and breathless.

Gavin sighed as Isaac's hands moved to the hem of Gavin's shirt and pulled it up over his chest. "Isaac..."

"Hmm?" Isaac gripped Gavin's waist, and Gavin gasped as Isaac's fingertips pressed into his skin.

Gavin pulled Isaac against him, his heart fluttering in his chest as he savored the feeling of Isaac's body pressing him back against the door. Goosebumps raced over Gavin's skin as he raised his hands to let Isaac pull his shirt off over his head, and then fumbled to remove Isaac's. Both shirts dropped to the floor and Gavin stepped forward, breathing hard already, and pushed Isaac towards the bed.

"I w-want..." Isaac rasped against Gavin's lips. "I... Gavin, I want—"

"Anything," Gavin breathed, his cock already hardening as Isaac sat on the bed and pulled Gavin down to straddle him. Gavin rolled his hips against Isaac's and shivered at the friction. He brushed his lips against Isaac's shoulder, then pressed his lips to Isaac's again, panting against his mouth. "I... Isaac, what do you want?" He pulled back and studied Isaac's face, his heart pounding even faster with the *want* in Isaac's eyes, the flush on his cheeks. "Tell me what you want," Gavin whispered.

Isaac's throat bobbed as he swallowed, and his gaze flicked to Gavin's lips and back to his eyes. "I, um..." He cleared his throat. "I want to try... I want you to, um... t-to fuck me," he murmured. His lips trembled.

Gavin's eyes went wide. *"Oh,"* he breathed. He couldn't push away the old flash of panic, the familiar thunderclap of shame as the memory gripped him: Isaac under him, screaming, pleading through the gag as Gavin raped

Isaac, Leo holding him down. His hands shook as they settled on Isaac's shoulders, the muscle moving under scarred skin as Isaac reached up to cup Gavin's face.

Isaac's brow furrowed. "We don't have to," he said softly, his gaze darting across Gavin's face. "We... w-we don't. I just thought—"

"Are you..." Gavin gulped loudly in the sudden silence of the room. "I mean... are you... ready?"

Isaac chewed his lip and nodded slowly. "I think so," he whispered, and his eyes flicked down to Gavin's lips again. "I've been, um... th-thinking about it. A lot. And I... want to."

Nausea curled in Gavin's stomach and he shuddered as Isaac's broken screams echoed through his mind. Tears stung his eyes. "Um..."

I'm sorry, I'm sorry, I'm sorry, I'm so sorry...

Isaac's mouth hardened into a line. "I can see those gears turning," he said gently, with only a hint of a tremor in his voice. "Gavin... It wasn't your—"

"Please," Gavin croaked. "Please, can we... n-not..."

"We don't have to," Isaac said, his eyes darting between Gavin's. "It's alright." He looked away.

"It's not that I don't... don't *want* you like that," Gavin said, guiding Isaac's head up until he looked Gavin in the eye again. "I do, I... *fuck,* I really, really do." His throat worked in another dry swallow. "I just... Isaac, when we... It was..."

"It was different," Isaac said. He kept his eyes riveted on Gavin's. "It's not the same. And I... I'm ready. If you don't want to, then we won't, but please... don't... *not* do it, just because of me."

"It's not *just* because of you, Isaac, I—"

"Sorry," Isaac murmured. "I didn't mean it like that. I meant—"

"I know what you meant," Gavin said, gently cupping Isaac's face. Isaac looked back at him, and Gavin's heart squeezed painfully in his chest at the trust, the *love* in Isaac's eyes.

I could never deserve—

Stop it. This isn't about that.

Gavin blew out a slow breath through his lips. "Um... okay," he rasped. "But... I want you on top."

Isaac nodded. "Yeah, I... kinda wanted that, too," he said, and his cheeks darkened.

"Alright, then," Gavin breathed, and pushed himself to his feet. He kept his gaze on Isaac as he undid the button on his jeans and pulled down the zipper, guiding his jeans and underwear off. He carefully stepped out of them and stood in front of Isaac, completely naked. "We stop, if you want to stop," Gavin murmured. "At any point. We... we stop."

"You, too," Isaac said, and took Gavin's hand. "It... happened to you, too." Isaac's eyes shone in the dim light of the room.

Gavin's throat worked around a hot lump of tears. "Yeah," he croaked. "Can we... can we start with you... on your back? As I get you ready?"

Isaac stiffened. "We can... yeah, I just... as long as you're not... on me."

Gavin chewed his lip. "No," he croaked. "Not on you." He nodded weakly. "I promise."

I'm sorry, I'm so sorry...

He swallowed hard, pushing away the memory of Isaac writhing under him, panting, head canted back, begging— He sucked in a deep breath and shoved the thought away. Gently, he placed his hands on Isaac's shoulders and guided him to lie on his back on the bed, his head supported by Gavin's pillow. Gavin crawled between Isaac's legs and slowly, carefully, brought his hands to Isaac's waistband.

"Is this okay?" Gavin said softly, and brushed his fingers against the button of Isaac's pants.

"Yeah," Isaac whispered. "Gavin... I *want* this. Please." He looked at Gavin with something that bordered on *need*, his chest moving with his breaths, his lips parted. Gavin's hands settled over the button of Isaac's pants and snapped it open. He flushed crimson when he realized Isaac was already hard.

"Oh," he breathed.

Isaac spread his legs wider. "Gavin, I... *please...*"

Nothing quite like having a handsome plaything under me panting for me to touch him.

Gavin shook himself and bit down hard on his lip as he drew down Isaac's zipper, then pulled his pants and underwear off in one smooth motion. Gavin dropped Isaac's clothes off the side of the bed.

"Hey," Isaac said, and Gavin looked up at him, startled. Isaac lay naked on the bed, leaning up on his elbows, looking at Gavin with those soft brown eyes that stirred something in Gavin's chest every damn time. The concern on Isaac's face took Gavin's breath away.

"S-sorry," Gavin mumbled. "I didn't think this would be, um… hard for me, too."

"It happened to you, too," Isaac repeated, this time his voice barely a breath.

"Yeah," Gavin said with a nod. "Yeah, I… yeah."

Isaac's eyebrows pulled together. "We don't have to—"

"I want to," Gavin said as he let out a breath. "I… want to."

Isaac kept his gaze on Gavin as he relaxed back against the pillows. "Okay," he murmured.

Gavin was breathless and dizzy as he leaned over to grab the lube from the nightstand drawer. He slicked his fingers and looked up to see Isaac staring at him, his gaze hazy with want. Isaac's cock twitched as he spread his legs wider, looking up at Gavin.

Gavin settled himself between Isaac's legs, sliding one leg under Isaac's and tucking the other beneath him. He reached out and gently took Isaac's cock in one hand. Isaac gasped out a breath, his eyes fluttering shut as Gavin stroked him once.

"Ready?" Gavin whispered.

Isaac nodded vigorously. "Y-yes," he breathed. "Yes, yes, *please…*"

As gently as he could, Gavin eased a finger inside him.

Isaac sucked in a breath through his teeth. Gavin stroked his cock again to ease the sensation. Isaac's toes curled as Gavin pressed his finger in deeper, deeper, until he was as deep as he could go. And still, he continued the firm strokes on Isaac's cock. Slowly, carefully, he eased Isaac open.

Gavin's cock throbbed as he prepared Isaac, heat coiling inside him at the sound of Isaac's pleasure: moans, whimpers, panting breaths that Isaac drew through parted lips. He quivered at Isaac's tightness, his heat, as he added another finger.

"Oh, *fuck*," Isaac moaned, and Gavin froze. "Gavin…"

Gavin shivered and let out a breath. "Is it… Do you like this?" he murmured. Heat warmed his chest.

Isaac nodded jerkily, his body moving with Gavin's hands, his hips rolling rhythmically, his hands fisting in the sheets. He tipped his head back against the pillow. "M-more…"

Gavin's heart lurched as he nodded and added a third finger.

"Oh," Isaac sighed. His eyes rolled back, and his mouth fell open with a moan.

I'm glad nobody is in the house right now…

Gavin's own cock throbbed, painfully hard as he eased his fingers in and out of Isaac. Gavin's gaze moved over Isaac, over his scars, over the tan of his skin and the play of muscles beneath, and he trembled. Isaac was in bed with him, Isaac was moving and moaning and wanting *him*… And Gavin wanted him too, so badly he could barely keep his hands from shaking. His cock was painfully hard and leaking precum as he tried, desperately, to focus on Isaac. Isaac slowly relaxed under Gavin's touch, so different from before.

In bed with Isaac, naked with him, Gavin felt *safe.*

Gavin swallowed hard. "Isaac, um… are you… ready?"

"Yes," Isaac rasped. "Gavin…" He blinked his eyes open and turned them to Gavin. "Please…"

Gavin's hands shook as he gently pulled his fingers out of Isaac. He reached for a condom in the nightstand and pulled out the foil packet. When he glanced up at Isaac, Isaac was looking back at him with a radiant smile on his face.

"Wh-what?" Gavin said, shivering under Isaac's gaze. His fingers trembled as he tore open the packet.

"Nothing," Isaac said with a hazy smile. "You're beautiful."

Gavin looked away as he rolled the condom on. "You are, too," he said softly. "You're…" His voice trailed off into a whimper as he met Isaac's eyes again.

"Come here," Isaac whispered. He leaned forward and pulled Gavin into a kiss. Gavin's eyes slid shut and he shivered at the feeling of Isaac's lips on his, the press of his tongue, the heat of his breath. His mouth moved with Isaac's and he crawled forward. His hips jerked forward as his cock slid against Isaac's.

"Here," Isaac said softly. He placed his hands on Gavin's shoulders and guided him to lay down on the bed as Isaac straddled his hips. Gavin's breath caught in his chest as he looked up at Isaac, his scars shining in the lamplight, at the man he'd hurt and broken, at the man who saved him.

And I saved him, too.

Heat poured through Gavin's chest. Tears welled in his eyes.

Isaac's eyes went wide. "What is it?" he murmured, reaching down to touch Gavin's cheek before pulling back. "Is this—"

"It's good," Gavin rasped. His voice cracked. "Just happy." He blinked the tears away. "Just… really happy."

A smile broke across Isaac's face and he leaned forward to kiss Gavin. "Me, too," he whispered against Gavin's lips. After a moment, he pulled away and reached for the lube.

Gavin gasped as Isaac slicked Gavin's cock, gently stroking as he gazed down at him. Gavin's hips jerked up into Isaac's hand, and his mouth fell open in a moan.

"Isaac…"

Isaac smiled and raised himself up over Gavin, positioning Gavin's cock with one hand and bracing himself on Gavin's chest with the other. Gavin held Isaac's gaze, his skin tingling with anticipation. Isaac slowly slid down onto Gavin's cock.

Gavin bit back a moan. Isaac sighed with him as he rose up, then slid down again, letting Gavin fill him inch by inch. Gavin clutched at Isaac's thighs, his eyes rolling back, as Isaac adjusted to Gavin's cock, slowly took him in until Isaac's hips sat flush with Gavin's. They sat still for a moment, chests heaving together, as Gavin gazed up at Isaac.

Isaac's eyes were bright, his cheeks flushed. He braced his hands on Gavin's chest. "You okay?" Isaac said with a laugh.

"Uh…" Gavin licked his lips as he met Isaac's eyes, stunned. "Um…" Isaac rolled his hips once, and Gavin's vision went white with pleasure. *"Ahh…"*

"Yeah," Isaac whispered as he leaned down for a kiss. "Me, too." He ran his tongue along Gavin's bottom lip. Gavin closed his eyes and opened his mouth to Isaac, helpless. His head tilted back against the pillow. As Isaac pulled away, Gavin opened his eyes. His lips trembled. He jerked his hips up to meet Isaac's, and Isaac fell forward with a cry. Gavin licked his lips. The air felt electric on his skin.

Isaac braced himself and took his own cock in hand. He whimpered and moaned as he stroked himself, rolling his hips against Gavin's. Gavin let out a breathy moan and trembled with each new wave of pleasure.

Gavin drew his hands up Isaac's thighs, over his hips, up Isaac's sides and back down again, tracing Isaac's body, feeling the warmth of Isaac's skin. His fingers brushed Isaac's scars, traced the lines of them, curved over the unbroken skin along Isaac's hips and legs. Then back up, across Isaac's chest, up the back of his neck to tangle in his hair. Isaac sighed as Gavin gently grasped Isaac's hair and pulled.

"I-I… Gavin, *fuck*…"

"You're beautiful," Gavin whispered. Pleasure warmed him with every move of Isaac's hips. "I love you. I love you. I love you…"

Isaac moaned and rode Gavin harder, reaching up with one hand and bracing it against the headboard. "I l-love you, too," he breathed. "Gavin… I…"

"I love you," Gavin whispered again. His lips tingled with the words. His hands moved over Isaac's body. Heat rose inside him, pleasure building in his cock as Isaac rocked against him. The bedframe squeaked with each roll of Isaac's hips. Gavin's lungs felt too large for his chest. His mouth fell open and he gasped for breath, caught in the rising tide of his orgasm.

"*Fuck,* you feel good," Isaac groaned. "Gavin…"

"What do you need?" Gavin panted. He planted his heels against the bed and thrust his hips up against Isaac's. Isaac gasped and cried out, grinding down harder onto Gavin's cock, stroking himself faster.

"You," Isaac whispered. "I need…" Isaac rolled his hips once, twice—

Isaac's eyes squeezed shut and he came hard over Gavin's stomach, his head tilted back in a helpless moan. He clenched around Gavin's cock, and tingling heat swept through Gavin. His fingers tightened on Isaac's hips as his orgasm rocked through him. He spilled into the condom with a cry. Pleasure crashed over him like a wave, lighting every nerve, filling every inch of his body.

He slumped back against the mattress, dizzy with his orgasm as Isaac stroked himself through his. They both settled, breathing hard. Gavin brushed his fingers gently up and down Isaac's sides until his hands rested, again, on Isaac's hips.

"Mmn," Isaac moaned. Sweat shimmered on his brow. Gavin swallowed as he looked up at Isaac, his mussed hair and his sweet, sleepy smile. Isaac rose up over Gavin again and slowly slid off of Gavin's cock with a groan. Gavin clumsily pulled the condom off and dropped it into the wastebasket.

Isaac grabbed a shirt off the floor and gently wiped his cum off of Gavin's stomach. He laid down by Gavin's side on shaking arms and curled against his chest. Gavin tucked Isaac's head under his chin and drew the blanket up over them both with a sigh.

"I love fucking you," Isaac mumbled, and laughed. "That was... *mmm*." He pressed a kiss to Gavin's throat.

Gavin shivered at the touch and held Isaac tight to his chest. "Hmm," he agreed wordlessly. He could feel Isaac's heart beat fast, in time with his own.

"We could, um... try this again sometime," Isaac said as he relaxed in Gavin's embrace. "I... I want..."

"Yeah?" Gavin said, and gently kissed Isaac's forehead. "Yeah, I... I would want this again."

"Good," Isaac sighed, his breaths turning deep and slow. "Good."

"Love you, Isaac," Gavin whispered, as Isaac drifted off to sleep in his arms.

"Love you," Isaac mumbled.

A moment later, he was limp in Gavin's arms, snoring lightly. Gavin reached over and snapped off the lamp on the nightstand. The room was only lit by the soft yellow glow of the nightlight.

Chapter 12

Gavin flinched awake to a hand clamped over his mouth. He blinked, casting his gaze around the dark room, fuzzy and groggy and confused. Slowly, his eyes focused. His stomach lurched. A tall figure loomed over him, silhouetted by the nightlight. Gavin looked to Isaac and froze as terror struck him like a blow to the chest.

A man stood over Isaac, pointing a gun at Isaac's head.

Gavin's heart thundered in his chest as he realized Isaac was still asleep next to him, his eyes closed and his mouth open, breathing slowly. Gavin looked back towards the man bending over him. He couldn't quite make out the man's face as he held a finger to his lips and tilted his head at Isaac.

Gavin swallowed hard and nodded desperately against the man's hand. The man pulled his hand away from Gavin's mouth. The other man kept the gun trained on Isaac.

The man standing at the side of Gavin's bed held out what Gavin suddenly realized were his clothes. Gavin took them with shaking hands and slowly, carefully pulled on his pants under the blanket. He kept his eyes fixed on Isaac as he slid his arms into the sleeves of his t-shirt, praying that Isaac would stay asleep. He pulled the shirt on over his head and looked towards the man standing over him. The man gestured towards the door with a jerk of his head.

Tears sprang to Gavin's eyes, and he bit his lip as he looked back to Isaac. Freezing water flowed through his veins; his hands shook so badly he could scarcely feel them. Still, as Gavin looked over at Isaac, he longed to kiss him, to say goodbye. Just to feel something good before he disappeared into a car, or into a body bag.

Just to convince himself that, for a little while, Isaac had been his.

Gavin shoved down a sob as the man pointed at the door. He pushed himself out of bed, silently screaming for Isaac to wake up and save him – and begging, just as loudly and just as silently, for Isaac to stay asleep. The first man roughly grabbed Gavin's arm and pulled him towards the door, even as Gavin looked back at Isaac. Tears ran down his cheeks. The other man kept the gun pointed at Isaac as he backed out of the room behind Gavin. Gavin caught one last glimpse of Isaac before the men shut the door behind them and pulled him towards the front door. Gavin could still smell Isaac, and he realized with a start that the man had given him Isaac's shirt.

The men herded Gavin through the dark house. From the closet near the kitchen, Gavin could hear the soft hum of the refrigerator. He jumped as something brushed against his leg, cursing himself as he realized it was the cat, Nata. Nata meowed urgently as he trotted beside Gavin, his reflective yellow eyes staring up at him in the dark. Panicked, Gavin glanced around at the men, terrified that they would stop at the cat's noise and turn back. They both kept walking, one in front of Gavin, one behind.

When they reached the front door, the men paused to pull on the boots they had left at the threshold. Gavin blinked as they opened the door and pushed him out into the night, barely lit by a sliver of moon.

Gavin shivered as one man pulled his hands behind his back and the other tightened a zip tie around his wrists. The cold, hard plastic of the restraint broke through Gavin's panic as he cast about for why they waited to restrain him until he was outside.

The thought occurred to him a moment later: *after everything that's been done to him, Isaac would have woken up at the sound of a zip tie tightening.* One of the men pulled a cellphone out of his pocket and sent a quick text. The men began walking again, not pausing to let Gavin put on shoes of his own.

Gavin's teeth chattered. The cold, stony ground ached against his bare feet as the men turned west and began to walk him along the lane. Gavin thought he remembered the house being east of Burmingham, but he couldn't be sure; they had arrived at the house three months earlier in the dead of night, delirious with exhaustion, and Gavin hadn't gone past the lake since then. Underneath the gripping chill and the sting of gravel beneath his feet, Gavin's heart pounded in a frenzied, sickening thrum.

He glanced back at the men, their faces dimly lit by the sliver of the moon above them. Gavin didn't recognize them. Neither of them spoke, just prodded Gavin forward. Gavin's tears cooled on his cheeks.

They could have been walking for ten minutes or for an hour when Gavin thought he heard a car idling ahead. He turned his ear towards the sound and felt a deeper chill – definitely a car.

Everyone in the house would have woken up at the sound of a car coming in the middle of the night.

Gavin whimpered quietly and kept walking. His fingers felt numb.

The sound of the idling car grew louder until Gavin could see it, in a shallow embankment by the side of the road. One of the men tightened his hand on Gavin's arm and shoved him towards the side of the car. For a moment, Gavin wondered if his cousin Mark was in the car, here to drag Gavin back to the home he'd escaped.

The guard opened the door to the back seat. The overhead light switched on, revealing another guard in the driver's seat. When Gavin looked at the passenger seat, his heart sank in his chest.

Daniel Schiester stared placidly back at him.

I am not surviving this.

Gavin shivered as the mayor of Crayton's cold blue eyes and colder smile settled on him. Gavin flinched at the memory of the only other time he'd seen Schiester, where he'd had Gavin caned half to death. Schiester was the reason Gavin had had to remain under house arrest during the family's time in Crayton; if Gavin was caught outside that house, and outside the family's protection, their lives would be forfeit as well as Gavin's.

That was before their trip south, before they told Schiester that Gavin was dead.

Gavin's throat worked, and more tears formed in his eyes.

Please, please don't kill them, too. It's not their fault.

"Hello, Gavin Stormbeck," Schiester said almost pleasantly.

Gavin licked his trembling lips. "My name is—" He doubled over with a cry as a fist smashed into his gut. One of the men holding him dragged him upright again. He gagged weakly in their grasp.

Schiester tilted his head. "Yes, Mx. Uriah mentioned you went by something else now."

Gavin's eyes widened and he gasped like he'd been dealt a second blow. "G-Gray—"

Schiester waved his hand dismissively. "No, they didn't turn you in. They'd rather die, clearly, since that was the penalty I spelled out for harboring you."

Gavin's eyes streamed and he swallowed down the nausea roiling in his stomach. "P-please, don't—"

Schiester held up his hand. "Quiet, Stormbeck," he said lightly. "I won't take their life tonight, nor the lives of anyone else in that *family*," Schiester said with an edge to his voice. "They serve their purpose, and are worth more to me alive than dead. They will, however, almost certainly come after you once they discover you're gone. At which point they will die."

"N-no," Gavin breathed. "Schiester, *please...*" His voice sounded broken to his own ears. Gavin shivered violently against the guards' hands.

Schiester shrugged. "I'll allow you to do your part in stopping them." He nodded at the guards still standing outside the car with Gavin. "Get him inside, please."

The two guards shoved Gavin forward and he fell roughly into the back seat, sobbing weakly. *"P-please,"* he rasped, staring pleadingly at Schiester. "Schiester, please, *please,* don't kill them, don't k-kill..." He shuddered and pressed his lips together. "It's not their fault, please, *please, please, please, no...*"

Schiester watched Gavin evenly. "You care about them?" His voice was devoid of emotion.

Gavin nodded desperately. "Y-yes," he gasped. "Please... Th-they shouldn't d-die because, because of *me, please...*"

Schiester's cold gaze moved over Gavin as he cried. "You understand that I am allowing you the chance to prevent them from coming after you. And that once you do this, I will take you to Crayton to be punished for your crimes. You've already been tried and convicted by private tribunal, of course."

Gavin shivered but met Schiester's eyes. "Please don't kill them," he whispered.

Schiester continued as if Gavin hadn't said anything. "And you realize that, once you have suffered what *I* deem appropriate for your crimes, you will be put to death."

Gavin swallowed hard. "But you won't hurt my... the family?"

Schiester's gaze pierced through Gavin. He held Gavin's eyes for a long moment. "No," he said finally. "If you do your job and those people don't come after you, they'll have nothing more to fear from me."

Gavin tasted his own tears on his lips. "Wh-what do you want me to do?" he breathed.

Schiester gestured at Gavin with his chin. "Liefeste," he said flatly.

Gavin blinked, mind reeling. "Wh-what—"

One of the guards still standing outside the car leaned in and pulled Gavin towards him. He drew a knife from his belt and cut the zip tie tying Gavin's hands behind his back. Gavin rubbed at the chafed skin, staring at Schiester with hopeful terror.

Gavin flinched as Schiester reached into his coat pocket. Schiester withdrew his hand – but he was holding a piece of paper, not a gun. He set the paper on the center console and reached back into his pocket for a fountain pen that he laid across the paper.

Gavin's throat ached as he swallowed. "What do you want me to—"

"You are going to write a letter to Isaac Moore, whom I can only assume is your lover based upon where you were found," Schiester said evenly. He glanced at the guard who sent the text. "I refuse to speculate on the nature of *that* relationship. And I cannot pretend to know what makes the others tolerate your presence." Schiester shrugged. "You will write anything you need to write in order to convince Isaac Moore not to come for you. Assuming he can read, of course."

Gavin blinked away his tears. "He can—"

"Then write it," Schiester said with a wave of his hand. "If not, Isaac dies. I'll have Liefeste bring you back something to remember him by. A lock of his hair, perhaps. Or a finger. You have three minutes." Schiester glanced at his watch.

All the air rushed out of Gavin's chest. His fingers shook as he picked up the fountain pen and clumsily unscrewed the lid. He leaned forward over the center console and rested his hand on the paper. His mind was a ragged mess of fear. *I can't tell him not to come. I can't tell him it's too dangerous. There's nothing I can say that will make him understand that he can't save me from this. Anything I say will just make him fight harder.*

Cold bitterness gripped his chest. There was only one thing he could think to write that would shatter Isaac so badly he'd never go after Gavin. He gripped the pen tighter and prayed his hand wouldn't shake too badly.

Isaac,

I'm sorry I'm telling you this way, but I just couldn't say it to your face. I'm leaving. I need to be honest with myself: I love you, but you can't keep anyone safe, least of all me.

Sorry things had to go this way, but I got what I wanted. Hope you understand and there are no hard feelings.

Take care,

Gavin

Gavin let the pen fall from numb fingers. His chest ached as he forced down a broken sob. Schiester snatched up the letter and read it once, his eyes scanning it before he smiled slightly and folded it. He glanced at Gavin before handing it to one of the guards – Liefeste.

"Put that somewhere conspicuous," Schiester said flatly. Liefeste took the letter with a grunt and jogged back towards the house.

Gavin dissolved into a mess of tears. He pressed his face into his hands and wailed. His lungs felt like they were being torn from his body.

The other guard climbed into the back seat with him and closed the door. The overhead light turned off, plunging Gavin into darkness. He sobbed as the guard pulled his hands behind his back and zip tied them again. Gavin barely felt the bite of thin plastic over the tearing in his chest.

"I-Isaac, *no*, Isaac, Isaac, Isaac…"

"Want me to shut him up, sir?" the guard asked.

"No, let the child cry it out," came Schiester's cold reply.

"Isaac," Gavin moaned. Isaac's scent was all around him, wafting off the shirt Gavin wore as he rocked back and forth. His voice rose halfway to a scream in his anguish. "He, he'll think… *No!*"

"It was expertly written, I'll admit," Schiester said. "Clearly your penchant for cruelty hasn't left you."

"Isaac, Isaac, Isaac…" Gavin sobbed. "Isaac, Isaac, Isaac, I didn't… Isaac, please, no…"

"Take comfort in the fact that you're saving his life, if that means anything to you," Schiester said in the dark.

Gavin's head swam as he gasped for air. "Isaac," he whispered brokenly. "Isaac…" Tears burned his cheeks.

He jumped as the car door opened and the overhead flooded the car. Liefeste stood in the door and looked at Gavin with disdain before climbing in beside him. Gavin sobbed as Liefeste closed the door and extinguished the overhead light again. The car lurched onto the road, and the guard drove in darkness for a while before he finally switched on the headlights. The car reached Burmingham and turned south.

Gavin's sobs faded away to whimpers, which faded away to silence in turn. Anguish and dull dread gave way to numbness as Schiester and his men drove Gavin through the dark towards Crayton. The stars silhouetted the black hills around them.

Chapter 13

Gavin could hardly see the shops of Crayton's main square, his eyes were so raw from crying. There was a thin line of pink along the horizon to the east, the only hint of the coming sun. Gavin swallowed hard. His throat was dry and gritty.

I'm never going to see the sun again.

Gavin shivered. He squeezed his eyes shut as he caught a hint of Isaac's scent again. His hands clenched into fists, and he winced as the zip tie rubbed against his already chafed skin.

He opened his eyes and stared blankly out the window. The square looked different, without all the snow. The light posts that lined it shone in the fading dark. The scars on Gavin's back flared as he saw the post he'd been tied to and caned, months and months ago. He chewed his lip and shifted in the seat. He knew, with detached blankness, that the caning would be nothing compared to what Schiester was going to do to him now.

"Once you have suffered what I deem appropriate for your crimes, you will be put to death."

Gavin's throat bobbed and tears sprang to his eyes. *I begged them to kill me. I begged Vera to kill me.*

The car pulled up to the town hall and turned down an alley. Gavin couldn't find it in him to be afraid as the driver pulled into a garage behind the town hall and turned the car off. He was empty. The garage door began to slowly close behind them. A light flicked on overhead, casting the garage in a dim, sickly yellow.

The garage door closed, and the guards opened their doors. Schiester stepped out and straightened his coat – thick gray wool, stretching all the way down to his knees. Gavin thought it might be the one he'd been wearing when the family first arrived in the north. He couldn't be sure. It didn't matter. He shivered in the early-morning chill, protected by nothing but Isaac's t-shirt. The guards reached in and roughly dragged Gavin out of the car. He sucked in a breath. His toes curled away from the freezing cement floor.

Schiester looked down at Gavin's bare feet, and his brow wrinkled. "Where are his shoes?" he said casually. His breath fogged.

"Didn't bring them," one of the guards grunted. His hand tightened around Gavin's upper arm, so hard Gavin could feel it bruise.

Schiester blinked once, and then slowly brought his gaze to the guard. Gavin shivered at the coldness in Schiester's eyes, and the tightly coiled violence that he kept perfectly in check.

"You what?" Schiester said, his voice carefully even.

The guard hesitated. "We... didn't bring them. Sir." His hands tightened even more on Gavin's arm, and Gavin couldn't hold back a whimper.

Schiester drew in a slow, deep breath and let it out. It fogged around his mouth like he was breathing fire. "And what," he said softly, "Do you think his people will do when they find him missing, with his shoes still there? A coat I can understand, at the height of summer, even if it does get cold at night. But *shoes?* They'll know he couldn't get far, and when they fail to find him..."

The guard blanched. In the cold yellow light of the garage, he looked like a wax statue – or a corpse. "Um," he mumbled. "Sir... I apologize."

Schiester pierced the guard with his gaze. The guard squirmed under it and stared at the floor. After a moment, Schiester blinked slowly and wet his lips. "Well," he said softly, with a glance at Gavin. "At least this one's suffering will be *brief,* if they come for him." He turned on his heel and headed for a door at the back of the garage. One of the guards tripped forward to open the door for him.

The guard holding Gavin jerked him forward and dragged him towards the door, as if he was expecting Gavin to resist. Gavin stumbled forward on legs that felt disconnected from his body. His hands and feet were numb from the cold, from the tight zip tie, from his fear. He shivered so violently his muscles ached.

Schiester disappeared into the doorway, and Gavin was pulled behind. He blinked as he was led down a short hallway with cement walls, cement floor, and no windows, lit by the same pale lights from the garage. He panted in short, whimpering exhales that clouded in the air. Icy dread trickled down the back of his neck as he was led deep into the building – then down some stairs to the floor below.

This is what I did to Isaac, he thought with a crashing wave of despair. *I paraded him through my fucking warehouse and took him down to the basement and chained him up and beat him and hurt him and—* He did his best to hold down a whimper as shame pulsed dully through him.

Schiester glanced back at the sound, his footsteps echoing in the stairwell. He turned back with a slight smile on his face, but said nothing.

Gavin heaved a sob and ducked his head, trying to catch another hint of Isaac from his shirt. He clutched at any shred of comfort, a moment of relief from the throbbing terror that pressed against the inside of his skull. *He'll think I hated him. He'll think I lied. He'll think I never loved him. I'm going to die, and he'll blame himself... I didn't mean...* Shame lashed him as he breathed in the faint scent of Isaac's sweat and soap and skin.

His neck and shoulders ached as he shuddered, hating himself for his selfish need to keep that scrap of Isaac with him. He knew that when Isaac woke up, that letter would break him – that he would break Isaac again when he woke with the rising sun, the letter confirming Isaac's worst fears – but he was desperate. He was desperate to feel something. He could almost feel the shadow of Isaac's arms around him as he breathed Isaac's faint and fading scent from the shirt. The light was blue, here in the basement. The chill crawled deeper into Gavin's chest. It was colder in here than it had been outside, under the starry black sky.

As they reached the bottom of the stairs, Gavin looked around with blank despair. Just like the hallway upstairs, the room was cement walls and a cement floor. The ceiling disappeared in the glare of bluish lights that made his head ache behind his eyes. Along the walls were five barred cells. They were all empty.

Gavin's stomach dropped as his gaze went to a set of gallows built against the wall.

A wooden platform stood about six feet in the air, with two nooses hanging from the ceiling above. There was a lever at the side of the platform that could be pulled to let the platform drop.

Gavin's throat ached. He swallowed and choked on the memory of the rope around his neck – the burn in his chest – the bitter cold against his skin – the sound of Isaac screaming – the smell of Isaac's blood. Blood Isaac gave to save him.

Even then. He tried to protect me even then.

He realized then why Schiester's people tried to hang him in the square, instead of just putting him on his knees and shooting him dead with one of the pistols they carried on their hips. As his gaze moved numbly over the gallows, he knew. Schiester had been killing people like this since long before Gavin had ever arrived. Gavin's vision blurred with tears.

That's how I'm going to die. He shuddered as he stared at the nooses, imagining how it was going to feel when one of them tightened around his neck, the rope rough against his skin, cutting off his air while he kicked and strangled and died. He wondered what they would do to his body afterwards. Would they bury him? Did they have a graveyard of innocent people, killed because of the choices they made to survive? Was Gavin going to be buried with them, a killer and a sadist and a torturer alongside the people he would have tortured and killed?

Gavin looked around, his heart beating faster, pounding in his chest to the thrum of his own terror. His gaze returned to the cells.

He wondered how long they ever stayed full. When Gray found out Schiester was killing people, they said one of his victims was killed the same day he'd been found. But Gavin wasn't like the kid Schiester killed – Caleb, that was his name. Gavin glanced at the gallows and shivered as the temperature in the already cold room dropped. Gavin wondered, dimly, if they turned on the heat for the guards when they had someone to watch.

He hissed in a breath as the guard's hand tightened on his arm again and dragged him to the center of the room. The guard threw Gavin roughly to his knees. Gavin grunted with the ache and pulled weakly at the zip tie around his wrists. He watched Schiester's boots come closer until they stopped, inches away.

Gavin sobbed weakly as a hand gripped his hair and dragged his head up. He was forced to look at Schiester, who looked down at Gavin with a hint of vicious satisfaction. Gavin pressed his trembling lips together. Words burned in his throat, filled his mouth until he felt like he would be sick if he didn't say them.

Please. Please, don't kill me.

A tear rolled down his cheek as he bit back the desperate plea.

Daniel Schiester tilted his head as he looked down at Gavin. Gavin squirmed under his gaze. He couldn't help but feel, not for the first time, that Schiester was looking for someone else in the lines of his face, the set of his jaw, the frame of his shoulders. Gavin shivered and wet his lips. He could taste his own tears.

"Y-you knew my father," he said softly.

Schiester snorted. "Yes." He nodded, almost casual. "I did."

Gavin opened his mouth to speak again, then closed it. His knees stung. His stomach roiled as he wondered what his father must have done to Schiester to make him hate Gavin so goddamned much.

I've done enough things myself for him to hate me for. I've done so many terrible things.

Schiester tilted his head again and glanced up at the guard holding Gavin on his knees. "Alvarado," he said softly. "Show me his scars."

Alvarado grunted, and there was a pinch at Gavin's wrists as the zip tie was cut away. Gavin gasped as Alvarado dragged his shirt up over his head and yanked it off his arms.

"NO!" Gavin screamed as he clawed at the shirt. He heard seams pop as Alvarado snatched it out of his grasp and kicked him, sprawling, onto the floor. Gavin cried out as his bare chest hit the icy floor, and scrambled to his hands and knees before a boot on his back shoved him to the ground again. His breath froze in his chest.

"Interesting," Schiester drawled above him. "It seems someone felt the need to redo Uriah and Moore's handiwork. Did they make those cuts themselves?"

"I-it was my *bodyguard*," Gavin heaved as he shivered on the floor. "My mom, my mom told him to, to hurt me so I'd... tell her how I..." Tears burned in his eyes and dripped onto the floor beneath him. His voice cracked with a sob. "Sh-she tortured me so I'd tell her how to... h-hurt Isaac."

Schiester scoffed. "Fabricating a story like that will not spare your life, Gavin Stormbeck. I'm afraid you assume I feel enough affection for those people to be moved by the notion of you protecting them."

Gavin sobbed weakly and pressed his forehead into the floor. The scars stung in the cold air. Pain pounded inside Gavin's head as the sickness and agony of the moment when he'd broken and told his mother everything washed over him again. He'd given her everything she needed to torture Isaac. Everything she could use to torment Gavin's family, while he just stood there and *watched*.

The boot let up from his back, and he dragged in a breath. He lay on the floor, shivering, staring at Schiester's boots where they stood inches from his face. After a long moment, he dared to look up at Schiester with terrified eyes.

Schiester's lip curled as he stared back at Gavin. "Get him up," he snapped. "And tie him. Fifty lashes, to begin his sentence. And this time, *I'll* administer them."

Chapter 14

"N-no," Gavin rasped as the guards dragged him to his feet. "No, no, *no no no…*" He yanked against their hands, out of his mind with panic, as they dragged him to one of the cells. They threw him to his knees in front of it and forced his arms out in front of him. Tears blurred his vision and he thrashed against the guards.

His heart pounded in his chest as he remembered the agony of the cane – the fiery sting of the blows, the dull, crushing ache of his bruised ribs weeks after. Sweat prickled on his skin as he strained against the guards, whimpering as they held his wrists against the icy bars and zip tied them there.

"N-no," he sobbed, his chest heaving with panicked breaths. "Schiester, no, *f-fuck,* if you're g-going to kill me please just kill me, *please…*"

"There is no if, Gavin Stormbeck," Schiester said evenly. "Your death in not in question. As I've told you, you have already been sentenced. Your remaining time on this earth serves as penance for your crimes since I cannot kill you twenty— Well. How many playthings *have* you killed?"

He wrenched Gavin's head back with a vicious grip on his hair. Gavin whimpered wordlessly through his teeth as Schiester craned his neck back. The plastic zip tie cut into his wrists. The three guards stood back, watching impassively.

Schiester jerked Gavin's head back further and Gavin cried out. "How *many?*" Schiester growled.

"Please, please, *twenty-three!*" Gavin sobbed. "I've, I've k-killed twenty-three playthings, *please…*" He felt every single one of those deaths with every sickened heartbeat.

Schiester let go of his hair and stepped back. Gavin sobbed against the bars. "I'm assuming that means you've killed more than just *playthings,* Gavin Stormbeck," Schiester spat. "God knows how many—"

"My name is *GAVIN URIAH!*" Gavin roared. The basement echoed with his broken voice until it faded away to a stunned silence. Gavin could barely breathe as he quivered on his knees, waiting for the pain. Waiting for the bullet in his head.

Gavin shivered as he felt, more than heard, Schiester take a step closer. He flinched as Schiester placed his hand gently on the back of his neck. Gavin swallowed as Schiester slid his hand across his throat and tilted his head back, pressing his thumb and forefinger in on each side of his windpipe – a warning, and a threat.

Schiester clicked his tongue and leaned over Gavin. "No, it's not," he murmured, his voice smooth as silk and deadly quiet at Gavin's ear. "Your name is Gavin Stormbeck. You were born a Stormbeck. You killed as a Stormbeck." Gavin's stomach lurched with terror as Schiester's hand closed, just slightly, around his throat. "And you're going to die a Stormbeck. Right over there, on my gallows."

"P-please," Gavin whimpered. Tears ran the corners of his eyes and back into his hair. He shuddered at the cold on his bare skin.

In one smooth movement, Schiester released Gavin's throat and stepped away. "What was it I called this back in January? Meager justice?" He laughed once, a cold, cruel sound. "I should have dragged you from that fucking *family* kicking and screaming and put you to death that day in the sight of the entire north. People should *know* how Gavin Stormbeck meets his end. Still. This is the cost of my work. It goes unnoticed, unthanked, and uncelebrated."

Gavin glanced back behind him. He sobbed desperately as he watched Schiester strip off his coat and hand it to one of the guards. Another guard passed a long rattan cane into Schiester's hands. Schiester took his stance behind Gavin, adjusting his grip on the cane.

Gavin let his head drop and ground his forehead against the bars in front of him. His breaths were coming so fast his fingers were starting to go numb. "Please," he whispered. "Please, please, please, please, please, I'm sorry, I'm *sorry…*"

"Ah," Schiester scoffed. "There it is. The Stormbeck son is *sorry.*" He wound his arm back and brought the cane down on Gavin's bare back with a *snap.*

Gavin *screamed*. Fire shot across his back, piercing his lungs. He slumped against the bars, gasping for breath as his head spun. Before he could draw in a full inhale, the cane struck him again.

Gavin wailed against his arm and yanked against the zip ties. He sobbed and clenched his hands into fists as he strained, desperate to break free. He rocked forward with the next blow. His scream rent the air.

Another strike. There was nothing to hold on to. At least if he could clutch at the bars he could hang on until it was over, but he couldn't twist his hands enough to grab them. His hands remained clenched and empty. Sam wasn't there to take his hand and guide him through the pain, this time.

Another blow. Gavin scrambled against the floor, frantically trying to push away the pain. He froze mid-scream when Schiester struck him again.

Schiester hits harder than Isaac and Gray did.

Of course, he would. Even through the agony of the lashes in January, Gavin had known Isaac was pulling his punches. Gray struck harder than Isaac – determined, perhaps, to spare Gavin further punishment. Or maybe Gray really did hate him, then.

The thought shattered under another lash. Then another, and another, and another.

Gavin panted, and his throat burned with thirst, a dull pain compared to the fire of his back. "H-how…" he croaked. His voice twisted in a scream as Schiester struck him again.

How many is that?

Gavin's mind was a cacophony of pain. His entire body went rigid as the cane came down on him again. Sweat poured down his back, dripping down his temples and stinging in his eyes. His mouth gaped open as he gasped for breath. He went blind with a flash of white as the cane came down again.

"Sch-Schiester, please, I— *ahh!*" he cried with the next blow.

How many? His head spun.

Brilliant pain split his mind with the next blow. He shivered as his sweat and blood dripped down his back, wetting the waistband of his pants. His stomach churned with the sickly metallic smell of it.

He sobbed with the next lash. His voice was a twisted, broken thing to his own ears. It echoed off the walls and pierced back into his brain. He screamed himself hoarse with the next.

Through the roaring in his ears, he could hear Schiester breathing hard behind him. Schiester grunted as he swung the cane again. Gavin felt his flesh split under the blow.

"Isaac, please," Gavin breathed. His throat was too tight to make a sound. "Isaac, please, please, Isaac, please…"

The blows stopped. Gavin sobbed with relief. It couldn't be over, surely it wasn't *over?* He thought that was maybe twenty. Maybe. He turned his head to look behind him. Every part of him trembled.

Schiester stood with the cane at his side, staring at Gavin with a bemused smile. There was an ugly flush on his cheeks; his eyes shone in the cold, sickly light overhead.

"What did you say?" Schiester arched an eyebrow.

Why couldn't Isaac have just killed me after we escaped? Gavin thought with despair. *I begged Vera to kill me. I begged her.*

Gavin wet his lips and heaved a sob. "N-nothing," he croaked. His throat was scraped raw from screaming. Distantly, He could hear his blood dripping on the floor. The smell was thick in his nose, chasing away the memory of Isaac's scent.

Schiester wound up and struck Gavin again. Gavin screamed against the bars of the cage.

"*What* did you *say?*" Schiester ground out, punctuating each word with a blow. Gavin gasped and sobbed.

"I w-was…" Gavin's lips trembled, and he sagged against the bars, dizzy. "I… please, I was—"

The cane struck him with a *crack* that reverberated around the room, only to be swallowed by Gavin's scream. "N-no, *no,* please, I-I—" He threw his head back and screamed with the next blow.

"These all count, by the way," Schiester said softly. "I'm not an unfair man. Now. *What did you say?*"

Gavin's skin was slick with sweat. "I... w-was begging... Isaac." He whined and squeezed his eyes shut, trying to conjure up Isaac's face. The pain shoved all other thoughts away.

Schiester barked out a cruel-sounding laugh. "Begging his *plaything,*" he muttered. "Unbelievable."

"H-he's *not* my plaything," Gavin whispered. He braced for another crash of pain. It didn't come. He heaved a sob.

"In my experience, playthings that are released never return to the world fully *human,*" Schiester sighed. "But take comfort however you like. You can pretend the man who fucks you loves you of his own accord."

Shame flooded through Gavin. *He loves me. Or... he did. He doesn't love me anymore. I've broken that. I've ruined it.* A tear streaked down his face, and he whimpered.

I love you, but you can't keep anyone safe, least of all me.

Sorry things had to go this way, but I got what I wanted.

That would break Isaac. Right now, a hundred and thirty miles away, Gavin knew that Isaac was awake, burning with hatred. He knew it.

Gavin's shame blasted apart with the agony of the next strike. His torn and broken skin seared with pain as Schiester brought the cane down hard again. And again, harder. Harder.

Gavin writhed and twisted against his restraints. *"Please!"* he shrieked. Blood smeared on his wrists, looking almost black in the cold blue light. Again, Schiester struck him, and again, and again.

Gavin's chest heaved with sobs. "P-please, *please, no, please...*"

A guard cleared his throat. Gavin had forgotten anyone else was here. "Sir, should I gag him, or—"

"No, let him beg," Schiester replied. "We always let them beg, Ziegler."

Another blow. Gavin's head spun dizzily. His hands were numb.

Another blow. Gavin slumped against the bars, his head lolling. His wrists strained against the zip ties. Gavin gasped and screamed and blinked sweat out of his eyes. His back was on fire. Every breath was agony.

The world was ripped apart by another blow. He tasted salt. He wasn't sure if it was blood, or tears.

His body shuddered with the next strike. He flinched, blind with pain, his pulse roaring in his ears. Schiester lashed him again, and his throat made a broken, animal whine. He couldn't feel his lips. The room tilted around him.

He wondered, faintly, if Schiester would keep beating him if he lost consciousness. If he would break Gavin's body with the cane, even if he wasn't awake to feel it. Somehow, he doubted he could escape that way. His eyes rolled back, and he prayed for oblivion.

He jerked with another strike. He shivered, hot, cold – shattered. His muscles quivered with strain as he struggled against the restraints. Sweat stung the broken skin of his back.

"Pl— *Ahh,* pl-please…" he mumbled through numb lips.

"We're almost finished, Gavin Stormbeck," Schiester said gently. "Card, please fetch his other restraints."

"You mean… Yes, sir."

Boots clicked on the cement floor. Gavin couldn't tell where the sound was coming from. His voice broke his scream with the next strike.

Gavin's stomach heaved at the next spike of pain, and he gagged. The smell of his blood clouded his mind. He tasted bile.

As Schiester struck him again, a black spot appeared in the center of Gavin's vision. He blinked, his eyes wide and unfocused and swimming with tears. His blood was fire in his veins. His heart hammered wildly in his chest.

"Fainting again are we, Stormbeck?" Schiester mocked. The sound seemed to reach Gavin from far away. "Ah, well. I'm not surprised to discover you cannot withstand what you dish out."

I don't hurt people anymore, Gavin thought dizzily. His shoulders ached as they twisted. He hung to the side, the zip ties cutting into his wrists. His sweat-soaked hair stuck to his temples. His vision blurred with tears, growing darker with every passing moment.

A slap rocked his head to the side, and he cried out weakly. He closed his eyes.

"That didn't wake him up at—"

"Doesn't matter. I'm almost finished. I said fifty lashes. I didn't require him to be awake." Schiester seemed to be breathing hard. Gavin felt a flash of pain, heard a scream. Tears streamed down his face.

101

His throat felt torn, with his next broken scream. The lights above him were fading. *Is someone dimming them?* He jerked as the cane came down on him again. He couldn't breathe through the pain.

He felt darkness encroaching on the corners of his vision. He'd felt it before, when Isaac had beaten him in the square all those months before. He clawed away from the pain, writhed when Schiester struck him again. He choked on a scream as fire flashed across his back, but then it was fading, fading. It was as if he was sinking under the surface of the lake at home. His head spun; his mouth gaped open as he desperately gasped in another breath.

A red slash of pain cut across his vision. Then Gavin's eyes rolled back, and he felt nothing.

Chapter 15

Gavin drifted. Sensations reached him slowly – cement leaching his body heat through his jeans, sweat drying in his hair, blood thick and cloying in his nostrils. He blinked sightless eyes, shuddering with pain that seemed to come from *everywhere*. There wasn't enough room in his body for the pain. It was pressing against the inside of his skull, pushing out thoughts of everything else.

There was a pinch at his wrists, and he crumpled to the floor. Agony lanced through his back. His mouth let out a mindless, twisted cry. Hands grasped his arms and dragged him upright.

"Sir? Preference on a cell?"

"Oh, I think this one will do just fine."

Gavin swallowed with a throat that felt scraped raw. The room spun dizzily around him as he was dragged into the open door of the cell he'd just been cut loose from. The bars of the cell slid into focus, then out again. He wet his dry lips and tried to lift his head to look at the guards carrying him.

"Please…" he rasped. "*Ahh,* please…"

"Ah, awake at last, Stormbeck. You only missed the last five or so lashes."

Gavin's head swam as he looked around for the source of the cold, steady voice. His vision was blurred still, shapes and shades of white and gray kaleidoscoping around him. "Mmmy…" His mouth felt like it was full of putty. "My n-name is…"

"Yes, your name is. You've mentioned it. And yet your name continues to be and always will be Stormbeck."

Gavin grunted as he was dropped onto what felt like a cot. He looked up and saw bars crossing above him, cutting through the dim glare of the lights. He shivered in the cold starting to creep into his bones on the heels of the fire chewing through his back. His eyes squeezed shut, then opened again as he cast his gaze around the cell – gray cement floor, shining steel bars, and a tiny metal toilet in the corner against the wall that Gavin hadn't noticed when he was first brought in. His throat worked in a swallow. He raised his gaze to Daniel Schiester as he stepped into the cell, having to duck under the doorframe as he came in.

Schiester's gaze moved around the cell as the shadow of a smile crossed his face. "Hm," he murmured. "I didn't expect how good it would feel to see Gavin Stormbeck in a cage."

Gavin blinked tears out of his eyes. *My name is Gavin Uriah.* He pressed his lips together and said nothing. His stomach pitched uneasily as Schiester took another step closer.

Schiester's lips pulled into a wider smile as his gaze settled on Gavin. He tilted his head. "You truly have no idea who I am, do you?"

Gavin blanched. He pushed himself up on the bed and whimpered as pain shot across his back. He felt as if his flesh had been split down to the bone. His throat ached as he swallowed again – fuck, he was so *thirsty*.

Schiester chuckled. "No, I suppose your father wouldn't have mentioned me."

Gavin searched Schiester's face, desperate for a hint, a clue, a memory of who the man standing over him could have been. He shivered as Schiester's cold gaze pierced into him.

Schiester rolled his shoulders and drew in a deep breath. "You will be fed twice a day," he said, his voice as flat and cold as his eyes. "You will be permitted to bathe every three days. No sense forcing my men to deal with your filth for as long as I have you."

Gavin's chest heaved as his breaths punched in and out of him rapid-fire. His back was in agony. "Every th-three... Schiester, how long will—"

"As long as it takes," Schiester said lightly. "As long as it takes until I feel justice has been done. Whether it be a few weeks, a few months... a few years..."

Gavin whimpered and sank further down onto the cot. There was the same cold emptiness in Schiester's eyes as he'd seen in his mother's – as she promised, over and over, to kill him when she was satisfied he had become a Stormbeck again. Gavin cast his eyes around the basement, finding the three guards standing outside the cell with hardened gazes and steadfast expressions. In them, he saw absolute devotion to the man who stood over him now. He saw men who would follow any order. He wondered if it would be one of their hands pulling the lever on the gallows when Schiester finally decided to kill him, or if Schiester would be the one to do it himself.

Gavin looked back at Schiester, and he knew the answer.

Schiester's lips quirked as he looked at Gavin. "You will be permitted," he murmured, "To earn your blankets, and your sleep, and my mercy."

Gavin shivered violently. Tears stung his eyes at the thought of huddling under a blanket, hiding away from Schiester's eyes and bitter accusations. "H-how?" he croaked.

"By confessing your crimes to me," Schiester said evenly. "I don't worry about you running out of things to confess. I know you started young. I can't imagine the depravity you've committed, even during your short time on this earth. Although... how old are you?"

Gavin's mouth was dry. "T-twenty-five."

Schiester snorted. "Good lord. If only someone had put you down, oh, ten years ago, how many lives could have been saved?"

Tears ran down Gavin's cheeks. *Nineteen,* he thought. *If someone killed me then, nineteen lives would've been saved.*

I begged Vera to kill me.

Schiester took a step closer to the doorway of the cell. It dimly occurred to Gavin that if it were Isaac trapped in this cell, he would fight. He would tear his way through these guards, fight for his life. Like someone brave.

Gavin had always been a coward. It was much easier to be brave when the other person was tied down, bleeding, terrified.

Gavin had never been brave in his life.

"Card," Schiester said as he held out his hand to one of the guards. The guard stepped forward and passed a coil of rope into Schiester's hand – and something else.

Schiester stepped towards Gavin again, a deadly hint of a smile on his face. "I endeavor to be a better man than the ones I protect the north from," he said, excitement tightening in his voice. "Though in this particular case... I see this only as further retribution for the life you've led."

105

Gavin's stomach dropped as he realized what Schiester held in his hand.

A collar.

"No," Gavin whispered, his eyes sliding shut. "No... no, *no*..." He blinked his eyes open and pushed himself up on the cot. He cried out as his back pressed against the cold metal bars of the cell. "Schiester... *p-please*..."

Schiester set the length of rope down on the end of the cot and took another step forward. "You deserve this," he murmured. Faster than Gavin could fathom, Schiester's hand shot out and fisted in his hair. Gavin sobbed weakly as Schiester dragged him onto his back and pinned him on the cot with a knee on his chest.

"No," Gavin heaved, writhing under Schiester's weight. Pain shot through him. He gasped and shoved against Schiester, out of his mind with agony as his back pressed against the rough canvas of the cot. *"No!"*

"Ziegler, Card, get in here," Schiester growled, and yanked Gavin's head back with a hand in his hair.

Gavin's voice broke as he screamed. "Please, *please!*" Hands encircled his wrists in an iron grip and forced them down on the bed. "Please, no, *no*..."

Schiester leaned harder on Gavin's chest. Gavin went rigid with the bolt of pain. His mouth gaped open, and he sobbed raggedly. Schiester released Gavin's hair to wind the collar around his neck. It was rough nylon, black, and it chafed against Gavin's throat. He tossed his head back, breathless, desperate, his face streaked with tears.

Schiester pulled the collar tight, just tight enough to constrict his throat, and buckled it. His smile grew wider. Gavin turned his face away in horror. The collar was closing around his throat, choking him. His heart pounded against his ribs.

"You deserve this," Schiester murmured again, his voice slithering through Gavin's mind. It froze Gavin's breath in his chest. He stared sightlessly past Schiester, at the ceiling. His eyes streamed tears.

I collared Tori.

I deserve this.

He shuddered and lay still. His head swam with the smell of blood. His wrists were released. Schiester got to his feet. Gavin realized dimly how much

106

his wrists burned from the zip ties; the blood smeared on his skin was starting to dry. He rocked forward with a sob and curled onto his side. The collar pressed against his throat with every shaking breath, every desperate movement. He swallowed and felt it tighten.

Schiester leaned forward again and hooked his fingers through a ring attached to the front of the collar, pulling Gavin's head up. Gavin coughed weakly and lifted his head.

"If you even try to remove this," Schiester murmured, "I will break your fingers one by one."

Gavin shook his head, meeting Schiester's gaze. He trembled and wet his cracked lips.

Schiester reached for the rope at the foot of Gavin's cot and looped one end through the ring on his collar. "I have no doubt your playthings have suffered worse fates," he said softly, tying the rope to the collar like a leash. Gavin didn't dare argue. "So, you will always be tied like this. If you are compliant and accept your punishment, you will not be restrained further. If not..." Schiester jerked the rope once. Panic spiked in Gavin's chest, and his hands flew up to his throat. "...I will find other, more creative ways to restrain you. Do you understand?"

Tears coursed down Gavin's face. "I-I understand," he rasped. He shivered and whimpered softly as the movement pulled at the cane marks.

"Good." Schiester straightened and tied the rope to one of the bars of the cell, leaving enough slack that Gavin could move to every corner. "Now. Would you like to earn a blanket? Or would you prefer to wait?"

Gavin couldn't help it as his hands drifted up again to tug at the collar. Schiester watched him with a coldness that chilled Gavin to his core. He forced his hands back down and wrapped his arms around himself as he shivered. He nodded weakly.

Schiester tilted his head. "Alright. Confess to me—"

"My coming back was my fault. Not theirs." Gavin bit down hard on his lip, trying to keep more tears from falling. "I... I sh-should have died," he whispered. "It wasn't their fault. Please don't... h-hurt them for it."

Schiester scoffed. "Your surviving their trip south and returning to the north isn't a cri—"

"It is to me," Gavin breathed. His hands curled into fists until his nails cut into his palms. "I wasn't supposed to live. It is to me."

Schiester watched him steadily, and Gavin trembled under his gaze. Then Schiester lifted his chin and stepped back. "I'll accept it. That earns you a blanket." He stalked out of the cell.

Gavin didn't bother following Schiester with his gaze, just curled tighter into himself and heaved a shuddering sob. He flinched as something was dropped onto the foot of his bed. He lifted his head to look. A worn, rough-looking blanket made of brown wool lay at his feet. He jerked forward to grab it – and cried out as his back screamed in protest. For a moment, he was lying in bed at the Crayton house, counting his heartbeats, breathing slow and shallow, and praying the pain would pass after Isaac had caned him. He blinked, and he was back in the cell, his hand held out towards the blanket. Schiester stood over him expectantly.

"Th-thank you," Gavin mumbled.

Schiester laughed. "If you feel the need to thank me, I accept," he said, almost cheerfully. "Although if you believe your very life is a crime worth punishing, it will be added to your punishment."

Gavin gingerly pulled the blanket over himself and curled under it without another word. He flinched again when something soft hit him in the face – Isaac's shirt. He didn't put it on, but instead clutched it tight, burying his face in the soft cotton. He didn't want the smell of his blood to ruin the traces of Isaac he still caught with every sobbing breath.

Chapter 16

Isaac breathed in deeply, feeling the slow rise of his chest before anything else. Other things came to him slowly – the softness of the sheets, the warmth of the thin blanket, the sunlight shining behind the thick curtains. He felt that sweet, familiar ache inside him, and smiled as he drifted in the memory of the night before.

"What do you need?"

"You."

Isaac's lips pulled into a smile. Longing curled in his chest as he stirred beneath the sheets – maybe Gavin would want Isaac again this morning, before Sunday breakfast. Isaac could lay down between Gavin's legs, stroke him to hardness and then take him into his mouth, taste Gavin on his tongue, hear Gavin's heavy breath and feel his body arch as Isaac brought him to the edge and over...

Isaac reached out across the sheets for Gavin. Maybe Gavin wouldn't want that just yet, might want Isaac to hold him instead, to stroke his hair and kiss his scars and tell him how beautiful he was. Isaac pursed his lips as he reached further, his brow furrowing in foggy, sleepy confusion.

Paper crinkled under his hand as he pawed at Gavin's pillow. He blinked his eyes open, fumbling at the paper in the dim light. He reached over to the lamp on the nightstand and snapped it on, his eyes still unfocused as he tried to make sense of the words scrawled across the paper in black ink.

A cold finger of dread brushed down his spine. His stomach clenched. His heart jumped to his throat and seemed to choke him as it pounded there.

Isaac,

I'm sorry I'm telling you this way, but I just couldn't say it to your face. I'm leaving. I need to be honest with myself: I love you, but you can't keep anyone safe, least of all me.

Sorry things had to go this way, but I got what I wanted. Hope you understand and there are no hard feelings.

Take care,

Gavin

Every nerve in Isaac's body lit on fire. He read the letter again. Then again, his mind struggling to comprehend the words.

I'm leaving.

You can't keep anyone safe.

I got what I wanted.

Isaac's chest heaved with panicked, hitching gasps. After everything they'd shared – after everything they'd said last night— The memory of last night suddenly seemed like a bitter lie. Isaac cast his mind back, desperate for a moment, an instant, that would have caught Gavin in a lie. His head spun as tears blurred his vision. Humiliation curdled in his gut.

You can't keep anyone safe.

I can't keep anyone safe.

He was an absolute *idiot*. He was an idiot for believing he could have this with Gavin – for believing he could have this with *anyone*. He was a fool for constructing this romance in his mind with someone who clearly didn't want him – and probably never had. It made *sense* for Gavin to attach himself to Isaac. If he was worried the family would kill him, it made *sense* to make himself Isaac's. All the way back before the team made their way south to fight Colleen Stormbeck, Gavin was attaching himself to Isaac so that he would be safe from the family. He probably never had any plan to act on it at all.

He *told* Isaac he never had a plan to act on it.

"Okay, just know that I'm not trying to make anything happen, alright? I'm just telling you this in case I fucking die tomorrow."

Isaac swallowed a broken sob. *He never loved me at all. But once I told him I loved him, he didn't have that excuse anymore. He let me do those things to him because he didn't think he had a choice.*

Isaac's hands shook as he staggered out of bed, suddenly ashamed of his nakedness. He pulled clothes on over numb skin and heard a distant crackle as he crumpled the paper in his hand. His eyes were wide and unfocused as he stumbled out of the bedroom, towards the kitchen.

When he reached the kitchen he realized, faintly, that Gray was the only person there. They were seated at the counter, a cup of coffee held in their hands. They lowered the cup and smiled as they turned around to face Isaac. They froze at the look on Isaac's face.

"Isaac," they said urgently, setting the cup down and getting painfully to their feet. "What happened? Was it a nightmare?"

Isaac numbly shook his head and held out the crumpled note.

"What's this?" They took the note from Isaac's hand and smoothed it out, their lips moving as they read it. They looked up at Isaac, horror written on their face.

"Gavin's gone." Isaac's voice was hollow. He licked his numb lips. "Gavin left."

Gray didn't breathe as they stared at the note. "I... I don't understand."

"He's gone," Isaac said. The words tore from his chest. "He had enough, and he's gone."

"No," Gray said, shaking their head. Tears tumbled down their cheeks and dripped onto the note. "No. This doesn't make any sense. Why would he—"

"It says so right there," Isaac said flatly. His throat constricted as he swallowed. "He got what he wanted, and now he's gone."

"*No,*" Gray snapped. They crumpled the now creased note in their hand and tossed it onto the counter. "This makes no sense, Isaac. This doesn't... *why...*"

"I w-wasn't enough," Isaac murmured. "He realized the liability that comes with being around me and decided to leave. I can't blame him for that. He was honest with me. He gave me a reason. He didn't have to do that."

"N-no..." Gray swiped the tears from their cheeks and sniffed loudly. "No, I mean... I don't..."

Isaac shrugged, and it felt like shattering. "He had to do what was best for him," he whispered, his throat too tight to speak any louder. His vision blurred as his gaze moved numbly across the kitchen and into the living room. The room felt darker, flatter, and emptier than it ever had before. "And I hope he finds someplace safe. God knows he deserves…" His gaze fell on the front door, where their shoes were piled. "He… d-deserves…"

Isaac's eyes focused. The hair on the back of his neck prickled. His heart thundered in his chest. He wet his lips and blinked tears out of his eyes. "Are… are those Gavin's shoes?" he rasped.

Gray looked up, their shoulders heaving with silent sobs. They lowered the hand that was pressed over their mouth. "Wh-what?"

Isaac swallowed the lump in his throat. His hand shook as he pointed at the front door. "Th-those… are Gavin's shoes," he said, his voice sliding into a low, deadly murmur. His heart rate quickened until it felt like a steady, never-ending thrum in his chest. "He… l-left without his shoes."

Gray's throat clicked loudly as they swallowed. "And… he didn't have any other shoes?"

"No," Isaac said, lurching towards the back door. His breaths were coming so fast it made his head spin. He counted the pairs of shoes at the back door. "Sam's, Edrissa's, Zachariah's…" He dashed back to the living room and counted the shoes there. "Yours, mine, Vera's, Tori's… Gavin's…" His hands curled into shaking fists. His fingers ached. "He didn't take anyone else's, either." His head jerked up and he looked at Gray. "Where's the phone?" he said, his voice barely a breath. "I'm calling Finn and Ellis. Where the *fuck* is the phone?"

Gray reached into their pocket and shakily held it out to Isaac. Isaac hit redial. His heart slammed into his throat as the phone rang once.

Twice.

Three times.

He choked on a gasp when the fourth ring cut off.

"Hello?" a sleepy-sounding Finn said.

"Finn," Isaac rasped. His voice cracked. His free hand spasmed at his side. He needed to be holding something, *anything*.

He needed to be holding his gun.

"Finn," Isaac said again, his voice a little stronger. "Is Gavin with you?"

"Hmmm? What do you…? Why would Gavin be—"

"Is Gavin with you?" Isaac snarled into the phone. "Right now. At your house. Is Gavin there?"

"Wh-what? No, I don't… babe, wake up. Do you know where Gavin is?"

A muffled *"Why the fuck would I know where Gavin is? Tell Isaac to keep track of his own boyfriend. It's seven in the fucking morning,"* reached Isaac over the line.

"Um," Finn grumbled. *"I don't… Hang on, let me put clothes on before I check the rest of the… Isaac, what's going on?"*

"He's not here," Isaac said through his teeth.

"And maybe he's just… oh, fuck, those are Ellis's… babe, where are my pants? Oh, here they…" There was rustling over the phone. *"Maybe he's just out walking, you know? He probably likes the—"*

"He left a note," Isaac said, and he couldn't help how his voice twisted with a sob.

There was a pause over the line. *"…what kind of note?"*

Isaac couldn't bring himself to go to the counter and unfold the note to read it again. If Gavin really did mean it, and somehow left in the middle of the night because he was so sick of Isaac's love and wouldn't go back even for his shoes, not even to save his own life… "Um… I d-don't… he s-said he… wanted to, um… l-leave me," he whimpered.

A sharp intake of breath. *"Oh, fuck,"* Finn whispered.

"B-but his shoes are still here," Isaac sobbed, crumbling. He sank to his knees on the wood floor and covered his face with his free hand. "And I'm worried that… I'm worried that… something happened to, to, to h-him…"

"Yeah, now I am, too. Shit. No, checked everywhere inside, he's not here. Let me go check… Isaac, are you absolutely *sure—"*

"I'm looking at his fucking shoes right *fucking* now," Isaac said brokenly. The anger coiled inside him and was just as quickly extinguished by panic. "He didn't take anyone else's. He wasn't in bed this morning and left this… this *fucking* note…"

Gray reached out for the phone and took it from Isaac. Isaac let them. They eyed him as they put it on speaker and set it on the counter. Isaac stumbled to his feet and staggered to the counter, leaning heavily on it.

Gray blinked tears away. "Finn, you're with Gray, too, on speakerphone."

"Gray. Shit. What did—"

Gray picked up the note from the counter and unfolded it. They cracked their neck and sniffed back their tears. Robotically, they read, "Isaac, I'm sorry I'm telling you this way, but I just couldn't say it to your face. I'm leaving. I need to be honest with myself: I love you, but you can't keep anyone safe, least of all me. Sorry things had to go this way, but I got what I wanted. Hope you understand and there are no hard feelings. Take care, Gavin."

Isaac shuddered at the words. He whimpered softly and covered his face with his hands.

There was a long pause over the line. Then, slowly and carefully, Finn said, *"That... doesn't sound like Gavin at* all.*"*

Isaac sobbed. "But I—"

"No," Finn interrupted. *"That... seriously, not at* all. *He's... never said... or hinted... or implied... any of that bullshit. Not... not ever, Isaac. I'm sorry, that... that letter fucking* sucks, *but... seriously. That doesn't sound like him. That sounds like... that sounds like him trying to sound like someone else."*

"That sounds like him trying to sound like Gavin Stormbeck," Gray said quietly.

Isaac's eyes blazed. "Stop trying to make me fucking *feel better,*" he growled, glaring straight at Gray. "This isn't... I need—"

"Isaac," Gray said softly, holding their hand out to him. "I'm saying I agree with Finn. I'm saying this sounds like... Gavin being *coerced.*"

Isaac whimpered and squeezed his arms tight around his chest, wincing at the ache. "I... Gray, what are you—"

"Think about it, Isaac," Finn said. *"He left that note. He left without his shoes. That doesn't... Isaac... that doesn't sound like him leaving voluntarily."*

Isaac trembled, looking desperately from Gray to the phone and back. "You... you mean...?"

"We mean," Gray said softly, "That you need to consider that this note was *designed* to break your heart and keep you from going after him."

Isaac's hand twitched toward his waistband. Frigid, placid rage slid into place inside him, fitting as if he was made for it. When he spoke, his voice was a calm, even murmur.

"Then who do you think took him?" he said softly.

"Maybe it was—" Finn began.

"Gavin has a lot of enemies," Gray said at the same time. Finn fell silent. "And as far as I know, none of those enemies knew he was *alive,* let alone *here.* So. I'll wake the others. Finn, please get Ellis and meet us at the house. We need to go over every possible angle, try to find out when and where Gavin may have been discovered.

Isaac's voice was deathly quiet as he said, "And when we figure it out – find him, save him, and kill every mother*fucker* who put their hands on him."

Chapter 17

Isaac felt like he might be sick. Finn stared at the note, their brow furrowed, their mouth twisted in a grimace as they leaned on the counter. Ellis stood just behind them, reading over their shoulder. They had circles under their eyes and looked exhausted, wrapped in the blanket they'd stolen from the couch.

Vera stood behind them both, her face like a storm cloud. She absentmindedly rubbed Tori's shoulder as she clutched her tight. Tori's eyes glittered with unfallen tears as she watched Isaac closely. Across the room on one of the couches, Zachariah, Sam, and Edrissa sat huddled in a pile of tangled limbs and clasped hands, worry stamped on each of their faces. Gray stood near Isaac, but was careful to leave him room to breathe.

As for Isaac, he stood back from everyone, watching them all through red-rimmed eyes.

Finn set the note down on the counter and turned to fully face Isaac, crossing their arms over their chest. "Isaac... listen, I don't think—"

"I know you don't think he left on his own," Isaac snapped. "But then what do you think *happened* to him?"

"Has he given you any sign he was planning on leaving?" Vera croaked, squeezing Tori's shoulder. "Has he... I don't know, done *anything* out of the ordinary?"

"Besides the obvious?" Ellis grumbled.

"Maybe not the *fucking time,* Ellis," Vera snarled at them. They pursed their lips and looked down.

Isaac tore his hands through his hair. "I... no, I... I haven't noticed... *anything,*" he said weakly. "Not a s-single... I mean..." He looked at Vera helplessly. "I don't... th-think...?" He turned to look at Gray. "Gray... I kn-know Gavin has a, a lot of people up here that want to kill him, but..." He

116

whined low in his throat. "Come on, Gray, we know someone who wants Gavin dead for *sure*."

Gray pressed their lips into a hard line as they looked at Isaac. When they spoke, their voice trembled. "Yes, we do."

Isaac's chest heaved and he struggled to force down the spike of panic inside him. "And... *fuck,* Gray, if it's him, and we call him..."

"Schiester will kill him," Gray murmured.

Tears brimmed in Isaac's eyes. "And if it's... if it's... *n-not,* and we ask Schiester where Gavin is..."

"...then Schiester will start hunting him. He'll know we lied. And..." Gray's gaze moved to settle on Zachariah. "And our lives will be forfeit."

Zachariah withered under Gray's gaze. Sam and Edrissa both clutched him tighter on either side. "Does that mean..." Zachariah hunched his shoulders up around his ears. "Is this... my fault? Did he—"

"No," Gray said firmly. "If Schiester knew about you, I have no doubt you would be dead right now."

"I need to fucking *do* something about this," Isaac growled, turning to pace the living room. "I... I need to... Gray, I need to fucking *do* something."

Finn set the letter on the counter. "We can start searching near the house," they murmured. "If... I mean, it's possible someone was blackmailing him and—"

"I would have *known!*" Isaac cried, whirling to face them. "I would have... he would have *told* me! He knows we could help him, whatever it was. He knows I... we would have done *anything!*" He whimpered and pressed his face into his hands. He knew that he was falling apart, that he was breaking; he raised his head and shuddered, wrapping his arms around himself.

On the couch, Edrissa whimpered and shrank back.

"Isaac," Gray said carefully. "Go search your room. Look for anything that could indicate someone was communicating with Gavin without us knowing. Finn, doing a search around the property is a good idea. We'll split up around the lake and around your cottage, too. I'll go to Burmingham later this morning, ask around, see if anyone's seen anything. I've got a shift in Crayton tomorrow and I can..."

"What are you going to *do*, Gray?" Isaac rasped. "You can't ask Schiester. You can't ask for a fucking… *tour* of his goddamned town hall. He told you he kept Caleb in the basement before he murdered him. He knows we know about that. That's probably the *last* place he'd keep Gavin, if he knows what we do—"

"I think Schiester is only too aware of the nature of our missions," Gray said tightly. "I think that if he believed we were coming after Gavin for a *moment*…" They pinched the bridge of their nose. "He probably has people on the roads who will tell him the moment we even *look* like we're driving to Crayton. If we assume he's the one who's done this at all."

"Who else could it be, Gray?" Isaac whimpered. "I know nothing's for sure, but… who else…?"

"I don't know," Gray confessed, their voice fading.

"Let's just… start by checking your room," Vera said evenly. She kissed Tori's hair and went to Isaac's side "I'll help."

Isaac stood frozen, not quite sure how to get his legs to work. He trembled as Vera's hand landed gently on his shoulder. He raised his gaze to her. His vision blurred with tears. He opened his mouth to speak, but no sound came out.

"Come on, Isaac," Vera murmured. "Let's go. I'll help you." She steered him from the room. Tears ran from his eyes and streamed down his cheeks.

∴

Vera folded her arms awkwardly across her chest. It felt bizarre standing there in Isaac and Gavin's room, the bed unmade, the blankets rumpled. The curtains were pulled back, letting light stream in as dust motes floated in the golden beams. It all looked so normal. There was a book on the nightstand, next to a cup of water. A shirt lay on the floor in a heap. Isaac stood stock-still, staring at it. His hands shook at his sides.

Vera took a step closer to Isaac, then another. Gently, carefully, she placed her hand on his shoulder and winced when he jumped at her touch. She chewed her lip and stepped in front of him. His eyes remained fixed on the shirt

118

on the floor behind her, his face a rictus of agony. He blinked, and tears ran down his cheeks.

"Isaac," Vera murmured.

Isaac shuddered and finally raised his gaze to hers. His throat bobbed as he swallowed loudly. Vera's chest ached with sympathetic pain.

Vera wet her lips. "I…"

"He t-took my shirt," Isaac rasped, his gaze sliding back to the shirt on the floor. Vera turned to look at it. Isaac trembled at her side. "He… I don't know if it was on purpose, or… but he took my shirt." He took an unsteady step forward. He snatched the shirt up, pressing the wrinkled gray cotton to his face, and sobbed.

Vera went to him and wrapped her arms around him, holding him as he shuddered and came apart. He sagged against her and wailed against the shirt. His tears wet her hair as he dropped his head onto her shoulder, gasping with sobs, convulsing with each tortured whimper. Vera's eyes pricked with tears. She swayed slowly with him as she drew in a deep breath and let it out between her lips. She caught the faintest scent of Gavin from the shirt with her next breath in. Her stomach lurched as she squeezed Isaac tighter.

"Wh-what if he's dead?" Isaac sobbed. His voice was tight, breaking with each word. "Wh-what if, if Finn and the others go out and, and they f-find… they… they find…" Isaac sobbed wordlessly. "What if, if Schiester came and… and Gavin went out – *why would he leave?* – and Schiester killed, k-killed him, and I… I didn't… Why didn't he wake me up? I… no matter what it was, I could have, have *helped,* I could have *helped* him, didn't… didn't he know? D-didn't he know that we… we… I *love* him, didn't he know that? I… wh-what, Vera, wh-what if he's, *d-dead,* oh *no,* Vera, no *no no…*"

"Shhh," Vera soothed, and blinked her own tears away. "Isaac…"

"If it's Schiester, then he's dead," Isaac whimpered, clutching at the shirt. "If it's Schiester… he's killed him, Vera, I *know* he has, he s-said he would when he… *no,* I c-could have saved him, no, no, *please, no, please don't let him be dead…*"

"Hey," Vera snapped as she shook Isaac. He sagged forward in her arms, tears pouring down his face and onto her shoulder. She pushed him back and ducked into view to meet his gaze. "Isaac. *Stop.* Listen to me—"

"I should have protected him," Isaac moaned. "I sh-should have, he, he *left* while I w-was sleeping and I, he *left* and, and I didn't do *anything,* I h-had *no idea,* and I... no, please, *Gavin...*"

"That's *enough,*" Vera said fiercely. She jerked his chin up in a firm grip. "Isaac... *stop.* This *isn't your fault.*"

"It is," he whispered, holding the shirt tight to his chest. "He *knows* I can p-protect him. But he wrote that... that *letter*—"

"I think we all know that wasn't really him," Vera said through her teeth. "Whatever reason he wrote that letter, it was to stop you from coming after him. Isaac..." She lifted his chin higher. He blinked tear-filled eyes and met her gaze. "Take it from someone who's had to *deal* with you lovesick dumbasses for the past few months..." She cleared her throat, trying to gentle her tone. "...he loves you. Okay? He loves you *so fucking much.* So much that..." She shivered, pushed down the wave of dread that broke over her. "So much that he wrote that letter. To save you from... whatever he thought was going to happen to him." She released his chin and put her hands on his shoulders instead, steadying him. Steadying herself.

Isaac's eyes darted across Vera's face. He shuddered and his face crumpled with another sob. "Three... th-three months," he whimpered. "I... h-had *three months* with him. And they were the best... I... I've never... Vera, we were... *safe.* And happy. The whole family. I had... I've never..." He convulsed forward and pressed his face against the shirt again. "I th-thought I'd have... longer. I thought... I..."

Yeah. I thought you'd have longer, too.

Vera shook herself. *We just have to find him. We just... have to find out where he went and go get him.* She swallowed hard and drew herself up. Her back twinged, and she winced.

Isaac's tears ran into Gavin's shirt, soaking the fabric. Vera fought the urge to pull the shirt away from Isaac's face – *if it takes us long to find him... you don't want to ruin the shirt with your tears.* She shook her head once.

I didn't even have Ryan's shirt to hold onto when—

She drew in a slow breath as she rubbed Isaac's arms with shaking hands. "Isaac," she said gently. His unfocused gaze flicked up to hers, then down again. She pushed him back towards the bed and sat him down. "If you sit here, do you mind if I look around? Try and find anything that... means something?"

Isaac nodded absentmindedly, staring sightlessly at the wall.

Vera sniffed back her own tears and turned slowly in a circle, her gaze moving methodically over the room. It was mostly bare – just a bed, a dresser, and a nightstand on each side of the bed. She pressed her lips into a line and went to the dresser.

Her throat was tight as she pulled open the top drawer. Her skin crawled with the invasion. She pushed Gavin's socks and underwear around the drawer. A short length of rope caught her eye. She left it alone and closed the drawer.

In the next drawer were shirts and pants, a few pairs of shorts. Vera checked under every single one, unsure what she was searching for. Another note, maybe. A cell phone. Something. There was nothing but clothes there. She pushed the drawer closed with shaking hands.

She knelt and pulled the last drawer open. She blinked as she looked down at Isaac's things – his clothes, a knife, and little else. She blinked away tears. Her drawer in her room with Tori had a letter written by Tori, a small white rock in the shape of a heart Tori had found on the lakeshore, a tiny sack of Edrissa's potpourri, a tiny book of poems Gray had thought she might like on one of their trips into Crayton...

Her throat worked around a swallow as she stared down at the utilitarian objects, the *functionality* of everything in Isaac's drawer. Her eyes welled with tears all over again. She swiped them away as she slid the drawer closed and leaned forward to look behind the dresser. Finding nothing, she pushed herself to her feet, groaning as her knees complained. She turned and walked to Gavin's side of the bed. She rolled her neck and pulled open the drawer on Gavin's nightstand.

Inside was a small orange pill bottle with *rizatriptan* scrawled in handwritten letters on the side. There was a pile of books that Vera carefully took out and set on the bed. One by one, she opened each book and shook it out over the covers, her heart in her throat, waiting for a piece of paper to slip out – a note from Gavin, explaining what was really happening. A letter from someone else, blackmailing Gavin, demanding he hand himself over, or threatening him—

Or something. It had to be something terrible, for Gavin to give himself up without a fight. Like threatening to kill Isaac. Or the whole family.

If Gavin gave himself up at all.

Vera set her jaw. She knew nothing else would have convinced Gavin to go. Someone, somehow, had threatened the family. For what felt like the hundredth time that morning, she lifted her chin against her tears and tried not to look at the titles of the books she was shaking out.

Unreality: The Role of Neuroplasticity in Brainwashing and Deception

Parents Who Hurt: How to Recover from Narcissistic Parenting

The Body Remembers: A Study in the Manifestations of Early Trauma and Recovery

When Home is a Nightmare: Recovering from Childhood Abuse

The books were empty. Vera's vision was blurred as she put the books back. *Gray got him these.* Her throat tightened. She closed the drawer.

"Isaac, can you get up?"

She looked over at him where he sat on the other side of the bed. Numbly, mechanically, he got to his feet. She lifted the mattress and checked underneath. As the mattress shifted, something clattered to the ground on Isaac's side.

She leapt to her feet and dashed to the other side of the bed, her eyes wide, her heart pounding in her chest. She pushed Isaac out of the way and crouched by the bed. Her gaze raked the floor and landed on a knife. The black metal glinted dully in the light. She reached out and picked it up. She looked at Isaac, who glanced at the knife and then back at the floor.

"This is yours?" Vera rasped. Her hand tightened on the handle.

Isaac nodded wordlessly. He shivered.

Vera pressed her lips together and nodded once. She turned and put the knife back, between the mattress and the bedframe. She stood and silently pulled Isaac into her arms. Slowly, his arms wound around her waist. He squeezed her tight as he began to sob.

Chapter 18

Gavin shuddered as time crept slowly past him. He thought maybe he'd been in his *cage* for a few hours, shivering under the threadbare blanket. His tears soaked into Isaac's shirt. His pulse beat against the collar pulled tight around his throat. His every breath stretched the cane marks on his back. He wondered, vaguely, if someone would be sent down to see to him if the marks got infected. Schiester had to have access to the best health care the north had to offer – but how many of those people could be trusted to know that *Gavin Stormbeck* was in Schiester's basement?

My name is Gavin Uriah.

Isaac *had* to be up by now. Everyone had to be. It was Sunday; they'd all be up, ready to cook breakfast, ready to sit together at the table, talking, laughing. Gavin's eyes stung with tears as he imagined it, as he pictured Isaac's bright smile as he was surrounded by the people he loved and who kept each other *safe*.

Not this morning, though. This morning, Isaac would be heartbroken, and his family would gather around him, trying to comfort him and tell him that the words Gavin wrote about Isaac were lies, and that they never should have believed him in the first place. They would tell him they were all fools to have ever trusted him, to have let him into their lives, and they'd spit his name like poison through their teeth: *Gavin Stormbeck.*

But it was worth it if they didn't come after him. It was worth dying hated by the only family he'd ever had, if it meant that family survived.

My name is Gavin Uriah.

Gavin licked his lips, his throat burning with thirst. He hadn't been given water, hadn't been given *anything* after Schiester tossed him the blanket and slammed the door shut with a *clang* that made Gavin's head ache. Schiester had left the basement the way he came, leaving his guard – Ziegler, that was his name – behind. The man now sat in a metal chair in the corner, as far from

Gavin's cage as he could get, his feet propped up on another chair and with a space heater blowing warmth at him in the cold basement. He hadn't looked up from his book since Schiester went upstairs. Gavin stirred and pressed his face harder into the shirt, desperate to find Isaac in the soft cotton.

My name is Gavin Uriah.

He had to keep his name. Even if Schiester took everything else away, he *had* to keep his name. The name he *chose.* The name he'd *earned,* the name that belonged to Gray. Schiester could have everything else. His sins, his shame, his guilt... he'd hand it over to Schiester eventually, he knew it. If Leo could drag out Isaac's secrets, Gavin knew without a doubt that Schiester would pry his every crime loose. Schiester could have them, if he wanted them. He could have anything but Gavin's name.

My name is—

Gavin jerked as the door up the stairs swung open. He whimpered and ducked beneath the blanket, shivering – but the cold still crawled deeper under his skin. It pounded in his chest, and he gasped for air.

"Meeting ended early," Schiester's voice rang from the stairwell. His boots clicked on each step as he came down. The noise drove into Gavin's head, making him dizzy and weak. Each breath made the cane marks on his back flare with pain.

No, he thought desperately. *No, no, not again, not already...*

His throat moved with his swallow. The collar seemed to tighten around his neck. *I visited Isaac several times a day for five days...* He blinked tears out of his eyes. *And I was going to kill him when I got bored. This is what I've done to so many people. This is what I deserve. This is my fault.*

"Approved a few bills, talked to the council about building another school on the other side of town for the older children..." Schiester said nonchalantly. "Most people who arrive here, you see, have small children if they have any at all. The older ones tend to get separated on the road. And now that we have some children old enough to need a high school..." Schiester's laughter echoed across the basement. Gavin flinched. "Listen to me, going on about the minutiae of running a town. My apologies." Schiester's voice dropped. "How was he for you, Ziegler?"

"Fine, sir. Just laid there."

A chuckle. "Well, if that's how he wishes to spend his time…"

Gavin's muscles coiled tighter and tighter as the footsteps reached the bottom of the staircase and slowly crossed the room to approach the cell. He pressed his hand to his mouth to muffle a sob.

The sound of footsteps ceased. There was the scrape of a key in a lock, and the door to the cell swung open. Gavin curled in on himself under the blanket and shuddered, his heartbeat thundering in his ears. An invisible band tightened around his chest, squeezing the life out of him. There was an electric current under his skin.

I would deserve that, too. I did that to Isaac, and I laughed when I told him to beg me to let it end.

Gavin couldn't breathe as he heard Schiester step into the cell. He cowered under the blanket, covering his head with his hands.

Hiding under the blanket so the monsters wouldn't find him, the dead men that looked back at him with empty eyes, reaching for him with their hands slick with blood, cutting him with their knives until he screamed for his parents…

Gavin sobbed weakly and blinked away the memory of his childhood nightmare. Something old and bitter dragged up his chest with every frantic beat of his heart.

"Look at me, Gavin Stormbeck." Schiester's voice was pitched low, almost gentle.

Fear wound through Gavin's body, freezing him, binding him in place.

My name is Gavin Uriah.

A huff of breath. "Look at me, boy. If I have to tear that blanket off of you—"

Gavin whimpered and pulled the blanket back away from his face. He raised terror-filled eyes to Schiester where he loomed over Gavin. His hands, clad in black leather gloves, were folded in front of him; his gaze was sharp and cutting as—

As the knife on his belt.

Tears slid down Gavin's cheeks and his lips trembled. He pulled the blanket around him as he pushed himself upright. He couldn't help his weak cry of pain as his back was shot through with fire at the movement. He cringed at the smile that slid across Schiester's face and glanced past him at the guard behind him, who now stood placidly just outside the cell door.

"I won't be visiting you every day," Schiester said softly. "So don't worry about that. No, I have a town to run, and a life outside of you. But today..." Schiester tilted his head and stared down at Gavin like he was an insect pinned to a piece of paper. "Today, I feel the need to set *firmly* in your mind who you are, since you seem so prone to forgetting."

Gavin's jaw tightened as he stared up at Schiester. Dull rage pooled in his gut. *My name is Gavin fucking Uriah and you can go to hell if you think you're taking that from me.*

He was Gray's son. Schiester couldn't take that from him. No one could.

Schiester shrugged and took a step forward. Gavin's stomach dropped. His breath froze in his chest. Schiester's eyes pierced into him.

"I opened the scars on your back well enough. I doubt you'll soon forget that. But you came to us..." Schiester took one step forward after another, until he stood beside Gavin's cot. Gavin's throat felt rubbed raw by the collar as he tipped his head back to stare up at Schiester. "...already marked, all those months ago." Schiester reached out with one hand, and his gloved fingers trailed almost gently across Gavin's left cheek.

Gavin jerked back with a gasp and cried out as his back flared with pain.

"Please forgive the gloves," Schiester said with an easy smile. "I just didn't want to have to *touch* you with my bare hands. Please allow me this one hypocrisy – I don't want your blood on my hands, although I'm content to take responsibility for your pain. I simply don't care to wash it off later."

Gavin's stomach dropped, and he bit back a sob of terror. "Sch-Schiester, no—"

"Begging will do you no good," Schiester said as the guard stepped into the cell behind him. "You need to know that. Scream if you need to, beg, plead, cry, but understand: your death is certain. All this is just..." His lip curled, and Gavin shuddered under his gaze. "...borrowed time."

Schiester glanced behind him and nodded to his guard. "Ziegler, put him on the floor please. Hold him down."

The guard grunted and stepped forward without a word. Gavin clumsily scrambled back, half-paralyzed with fear and pain and half-blind with tears. He screamed as Ziegler grabbed the rope tied to his collar and dragged him tumbling onto the cold stone floor.

Gavin jerked and went rigid at the cold cement on his bare skin, the sudden burn as his back pressed against the floor. He sobbed helplessly and clawed at Ziegler's hands as the guard pinned him to the floor and straddled his hips.

"No, *no, no, please, no!*" Gavin screamed. *"No!"* Ziegler grabbed his wrists and forced his hands away from the collar, pinning them down against the floor. *"NO!"*

Schiester knelt at Gavin's head and gripped his hair tight in his fist. He drew his knife with his other hand and held it in Gavin's face, twisting it to catch the light. Gavin sobbed and tried to turn away.

"This is your instrument of choice, isn't it?" Schiester said softly, his gaze moving along the length of the knife. "I've seen some of Isaac Moore's scars, both from your first time with him and your second. He keeps them very well-covered, you know. But there is one that travels up the back of his neck that the collar of his shirt doesn't conceal, and a few at his wrists – does he keep them covered with you? Or do you admire your handiwork when you're together?"

"Fuck off!" Gavin roared, twisting against Ziegler's hands. "It's not, it's not *like* that, you *leave him out of this!*"

Schiester snorted. "Why? You clearly couldn't. As you said, you weren't even supposed to *return,* remember? How long did you wait to twist yourself into his affections? How long until he let you fuck him?"

Tears streamed from Gavin's eyes as he tried to turn his head. "N-no, no, *fuck* you..."

Schiester laughed, the sound utterly mirthless. "There I go again, speculating. Forgive me. I just can't *fathom* what would drive someone to let you have them again after they'd escaped you. But then again, in my experience playthings never return to the world fully *human.*"

Gavin's gaze snapped to Schiester's. He heaved a sob through his teeth and spat in Schiester's face.

Schiester jerked back. Gavin's chest heaved with furious, shaking breaths.

"*Don't* you fucking talk about Isaac," Gavin snarled. "Don't, I, I will fucking *kill* you, you *don't* talk about Isaac, you mother*fucker*—"

Schiester drew his sleeve across his face with a look of utter disdain. Gavin swallowed, but stared daggers up at Schiester. He trembled as cold leached into his bones.

"How protective he is of his toy," Schiester said flatly, with a glance to the guard. Without another word, Schiester leaned forward, gripping Gavin's hair again, and brought the knife to the scar across the bridge of Gavin's nose.

"*NO!*" Gavin sobbed. The sob drew out into a wordless scream as Schiester cut through Gavin's scar. Gavin blinked as blood rushed into his eyes, hot and burning. Schiester moved again, and Gavin's scream rent the air of the basement as the knife sliced a line through the scar on his cheek.

Schiester pulled the knife away, tilting his head to admire his handiwork. Gavin heaved a desperate gasp and twisted hard against the hand in his hair, mindless with panic. Schiester yanked his head to the side and pinned it down against the cold floor. Gavin went rigid. The knife pressed, ever so gently, against the skin at the corner of his left eye.

"If I take your eye, that'll be your doing, Stormbeck," Schiester murmured. "Hold still."

Gavin convulsed as the knife cut through the scar stretching from the corner of his eye into his hairline. His eyes streamed with blood and tears as Schiester finally released him, choking on the air trapped in his throat.

All at once the weight across his hips and the grip on his wrists disappeared. He rolled onto his side, sobbing, and brought his hands to his face. When he pulled them away, his fingers were wet with blood.

Gavin raised his red-tinged gaze to Schiester as he strode out of the cell, his guard right behind him. Gavin's stomach heaved with the cloying, inescapable smell of blood. His stomach lurched and he vomited onto the floor.

"Oh, Christ," Schiester said, rolling his eyes. "If I have to cope with *that*…" He shook his head and turned his back on Gavin. "I'll fetch cleaning supplies from upstairs," he grumbled. "And if the boy is sick each time he smells blood, then so be it. He'll be sick, and I'll just keep spilling his blood."

The guard nodded and returned to his chair. Gavin's head swam with the smell of blood and sweat and vomit that clung to his skin. He crawled to the cot and dragged himself up onto it, weeping and shaking, as blood dripped from his face and back. He curled up on his side and pulled the blanket up. He held Isaac's shirt away from his face, not wanting to ruin it with his blood.

Chapter 19

If there was a breeze outside today, Isaac couldn't feel it through his long sleeves and his numbness. He squinted against the sun reflecting off the lake and the granite-gray sand of the beach. Sweat prickled under his shirt and ran down his back in rivulets, but he couldn't fathom wearing a short-sleeved shirt today. He couldn't even bear to roll his sleeves up. Not with the shame burning his every scar. He had so fucking many.

So many failures.

He shuddered in the sweltering sun and buried his face in his hands. He could go inside – he *should* go inside, to help find Gavin – but he couldn't bear to look anyone in the eye.

The one thing he had asked of Gray this morning was to let him come with them into town to make some preliminary inquiries into how missing people get found up north. And they had said no. They had said it would be better for him to stay home in case the house was attacked, but… he knew better than to believe that.

You're a liability, is what they had meant. *You're useless.*

You can't keep anyone safe, least of all me.

Isaac crouched at the edge of the water and tugged at his hair, heaving a sob. The echoing words rubbed salt into his thousand wounds. He couldn't escape from the pain any more than he could escape the truth of Gavin's words.

I can't keep anyone safe.

Gavin is gone because of me.

Because of me.

This is all because of me.

If I had kept him safe, this would never have happened.

If I had woken up when he left, this would never have happened.

If I had known *this was coming, this would never have happened.*

My fault. My fault. My fault.

Isaac's tears mixed with the sweat already dampening his cheeks as he lowered himself to his knees and yanked his hair back. The burst of pain across his scalp crowded out the onslaught in his mind. He caught his breath and tugged again. For a second, the only thing he could think about was that pain. His lips trembled as he lowered his hands. He turned them over, staring at the scarred knuckles, the sunburst of white lines around his right thumb from when he had escaped Gavin the first time. He tightened his hands into fists. He couldn't remember a time his knuckles hadn't been scarred.

No, he could remember. His eyes squeezed shut and his hands began to shake. He could remember the last time his hands were unscarred, before his knuckles had been broken open over and over by fighting with Rosa, and then by everyone else. He could remember that.

He could remember what he'd been doing to himself with those hands, too.

He could remember when it started, when he was just thirteen years old, scared and alone and confused and not even sure why he was doing it. He didn't remember where he had first come across the idea, or when, but he remembered when he started: five months after his father was killed in that accident, five months after his mother started drinking, five months after his mother stopped loving him. He remembered that he used the pocketknife his father gave him for his ninth birthday, on his inner thighs. He never wanted anyone to ever know.

He remembered using a different knife, the one Rosa gave him; she had thrown away his dad's pocketknife after he fell asleep on watch. He was sixteen. He hadn't been allowed sleep for two days before that watch. *"Excuses are like assholes, Isaac, everyone has one and yours is not my fucking problem,"* she had said.

What he remembered most of all, though, was how bringing the knife to his skin had made him feel better. Even with the blunt force of his mother's drunk hatred hammering against his skull, even with his grief for his father gnawing at his insides like carrion vultures, the blade had always made him feel better. For a little while, at least. Until he had to do it again, and it was better again, for a little while.

His throat was raw. He swallowed hard past the collar tightening around his neck. Tears pooled in his eyes, and he let him fall. The sand shifted under his knees as he reached for his belt and drew his knife from its sheath there.

He had kept it between the mattress and the bedframe before, so he could use it to protect Gavin when the time came. He failed. The knife may as well serve a purpose now.

Fingers trembling, he pushed up his left sleeve. New scars from his captivity at Fort Meyers shone palely in the sun. He didn't need to go back inside to the stifling gazes of his family to try and find some privacy in a bathroom or closet; he wouldn't be going back to the bedroom he shared with Gavin. No, with the scars on his arms, he didn't need to cut up his legs anymore. As long as he stayed in line with the scars he already had, and as long as no one saw the cuts until they were healed, no one would ever know. His heart leapt in his chest as he held the tip of the knife against the line of an old scar. His breath quickened in anticipation of the cut, and the agony in his chest faded.

But not enough. He pressed the knife in and dragged the knife across his arm.

He clenched his teeth against the groan of sharp relief. The cold, metallic sting of the blade cut through him and for a bright, brilliant moment, the only thing that existed was the white line of pain across his arm. Blood welled in the cut. Isaac pressed on the thin line he had made and sucked in a breath. It was starting to burn now, and the relief it had granted from the pain in his chest was already fading. His throat bobbed. Sometimes it took more than one for the relief to last – he remembered that, too.

He brought the knife to his arm again, to a scar just above the first. He didn't hesitate this time; he pressed the blade in and opened the scar back up again. This flash of pain was hotter, deeper. Isaac groaned and nearly dropped the knife. Tears of relief pricked his eyes as the crushing weight in his chest lifted.

Isaac steadied his hands so he could wipe the blade clean on the hem of his shirt. He gently pressed the pad of his thumb against the point, watched the ridges of his fingerprint bow in under the pressure. Isaac pulled his thumb away from the point of the knife. A single bead of blood glimmered under the afternoon sun. The knife was wickedly sharp, but then, of course it was. Isaac had kept it that way.

You can't keep anyone safe.

The air was so still that Isaac could hear a car coming down the lane, even from here.

His heart leapt in his chest and whirled towards the house. He sheathed his blade and reached for his gun in one smooth, practiced motion. His hand closed on empty air. His stomach roiled as he staggered towards the house, hurriedly wiping his hand on his pants.

He left his family alone and unguarded while he was busy hurting himself, all because he was *weak*.

He skidded to a stop when the car passed a stand of trees and continued towards the house – the family's car, the one Gray had taken into town. Isaac jerked his sleeve down over his wrist, covering the evidence of what he had done. He was grateful to be wearing a dark shirt. He would have to volunteer to do the laundry this round, just to be doubly sure. Shame curled inside him, already snuffing out any relief cutting had brought. He was pinned to the spot; he needed to go inside and hear what Gray had learned, and he needed to hide from their sight forever. Surely, they would *know* what he had done. And they would be so, so disappointed in him.

Another option struck Isaac like a bullet. An option that didn't have to include Gray – or anyone else in the family. No one else had to suffer, none of them had to put themselves on the line. It could be as it was always supposed to be: Isaac, alone, keeping the others safe. He took a lurching step towards the house.

Maybe this is how I keep them all safe.

He froze. Someone was watching him from the window. He could tell from the figure's tense shoulders and loose curls that it was Vera.

Once she looked away, then. That's when he would make his move.

And if he failed this time, he wouldn't have to worry about what came after. There was comfort, at least, in that.

Chapter 20

The room spun. Gavin blearily blinked his eyes open and squinted at the halos that ringed each light above him. The air in the room had a strange, almost familiar quality to it – he could feel it on his skin like a blanket that threatened to smother him. He had a strange feeling like he'd *been* here before, felt this strangeness in his blood, tasted it in his pores. He groaned. Gavin shook his head, and the room slid past him as if behind glass.

Pain shot through his back, and he hissed out a breath. He looked behind him, half-expecting to see someone standing there, wielding a cane, a whip, a knife. There was no one there. The cell was empty. The bars pressed in on him, leaching his warmth even from several feet away. He shivered and pulled the blanket tighter around him.

The newly-opened scars on his face still wept blood, which ran down his cheeks like tears. He whimpered and raised his hand to his face, touching the bridge of his nose, his cheek, the corner of his eye. Blood clung to his fingers, congealing and sticky and smelling like terror. Gavin turned his face away and pushed himself up on the cot. He gasped at the sudden burn of pain in the crook of his elbow.

He whimpered and looked at his arm, his entire body shaking from the effort of holding himself upright. His lips trembled as he stared at the tiny prick of blood on the inside of his elbow, fresh and starkly red above the darker, mostly-dried smears of blood on his wrists. He blinked and shook his head, trying to clear it. He could see Schiester pinning him down by his throat, having the guard hold Gavin's arm in place—

He swallowed hard, then shuddered at the rough collar rubbing along his throat. He reached up to tug at the collar, then froze.

"If you even try to remove this, I will break your fingers one by one."

His throat constricted with fear, even as his nails scrabbled along his throat, fumbling to dig his fingers under the collar and pull at it, just so he could *breathe.* Terror stabbed through his gut, and he sobbed helplessly, eyes streaming tears. They blurred the dark figure that stood in the corner, that watched him with cold blue eyes and a cruel, mirthless smile.

"I-Isaac," he whimpered, tugging harder at the collar and bruising his throat with his own fingers in the process. "Isaac, *p-please…*" Gavin, writhed against the pain, his chest heaving with sobs. "Isaac—" He squeezed his eyes shut. Sweat broke out all over his body, even as his teeth chattered from the cold. He reached out to steady himself. His hand closed on the cold steel bar of his cell. With his other, he clutched at Isaac's shirt, desperate for that comfort, for that small relief. He pressed it to his face and breathed in deep.

"Gavin."

The voice went through him like a bolt of lightning. He went rigid; his muscles strained and his heart pounded so loudly that he could barely hear the ringing in his ears. Hope crushed his chest, but terror swept in just after it. Slowly, he lowered the shirt and looked up into the eyes of a man standing in the open door of the cell – a man Gavin thought he'd never see again.

"Isaac," he breathed, and reached out to him.

Isaac lurched forward and fell to his knees by Gavin's cot. Gavin's heart was close to bursting in his chest as Isaac reached out, his hands shaking but so warm, to cradle Gavin's face. The touch seemed to come from miles away and too close, pressing under Gavin's skin. Gavin shoved the thought away and stared at Isaac, nausea swimming in his stomach.

"I-Isaac," Gavin whimpered as his fingers wound in Isaac's shirt. "Isaac, y-you… you *came…*"

Isaac pulled Gavin forward into a bruising kiss. Gavin whimpered against Isaac's mouth as tears spilled down his cheeks, mixing with the blood there and staining the cot beneath him. Isaac's breath came hot against Gavin's lips, and Gavin could feel him shaking, too. Isaac pulled back and kissed the bridge of Gavin's nose, his cheek, his eye. He pressed his forehead against Gavin's.

"Of course, I came for you," Isaac murmured. His voice was low, husky, tight with tears. It echoed oddly in the basement.

"B-but…" Gavin pulled back and searched Isaac's face. "How did you find me?"

"Just made sense," Isaac said, his gaze warm and soft. He gently stroked his fingers through Gavin's hair. "It made sense for him to bring you here."

Gavin pushed weakly into the touch. "But... the... the letter, you..." Gavin clutched Isaac's shirt even tighter, but it seemed to slip through his fingers like air. "But... h-he'll kill you, Schiester will... w-will *kill you.* Isaac... I... I didn't want you to come for me—"

"But I did," Isaac said fiercely. "I knew it was a lie. You thought I wouldn't come for you?" He thumbed away the blood and tears on Gavin's cheeks. "I always will, Gavin. I *love* you."

Gavin sobbed and sagged forward against Isaac. "Please," he whispered. "Please... Isaac... I want to go home."

Isaac fumbled at the rope tied to the collar around Gavin's neck. Gavin swallowed uneasily as the knot came loose and the rope fell away. Isaac gently guided Gavin to stand and caught him when he stumbled. Gavin's head spun. He swallowed hard. His throat was so dry. Isaac wavered in the cold air of the basement, almost as if...

"Shh," Isaac murmured, and pressed a kiss to Gavin's hair. "Shh. I've got you. I'll get you out – I promise."

Gavin clutched at Isaac and shivered against his side. His bare skin prickled with goosebumps. "Please," he whispered. *"Please."*

Isaac guided Gavin towards the door of the cell – and Gavin jolted as the door swung closed.

"No," he breathed, and looked up at Isaac. Isaac was staring back at him with terror in his eyes. "No, *no,* Isaac, no—"

The air froze in Gavin's lungs at the sound of laughter echoing through the basement, and of gloved hands clapping slowly. "So close, Isaac Moore," came Schiester's smooth, even voice. "So close."

"No," Gavin whimpered, shrinking against Isaac's side as he raised his head to look at Schiester, standing just outside the bars, looming more like an apparition than a man. "No... Schiester, *no,* don't—"

Schiester laughed as he looked at Isaac. Isaac tensed by Gavin's side, reached for his waistband – but his gun wasn't there. Gavin's throat tightened

136

as he glanced at Isaac, then looked back to Schiester. Schiester wasn't looking anywhere but Isaac.

"I was willing to forgive your little transgression," Schiester said softly, tilting his head as he looked Isaac up and down. "After all, you *did* sneak a syndicate son back into my region without my allowance, putting every person in the north in danger – but I was willing to overlook that. I was willing to let your family live. You do, after all, represent a sort of triumph over the syndicates, having survived what you have."

Isaac glared at Schiester, his jaw tightening, and said nothing.

"But *this?*" Schiester said with a glance and a sneer at Gavin. "Isaac, I gave you a chance at *life* again. I removed the syndicate threat, and you didn't even have to feel guilty about it. I did this for the safety of our people. If you like to think of it this way, I did this for *you.*"

Isaac's lip curled as he stared at Schiester and pushed Gavin behind him. "You won't *touch* him," he growled, his hands tightening into fists.

Schiester laughed. "No, no, I will. His life is *mine,* Isaac Moore, for the crimes he's committed. But I'll get to that later. Right now, however..." Schiester rolled his neck, and Gavin could hear the crack from across the room. "...I handle *you.*"

"No," Gavin sobbed, trying desperately to put himself between Schiester and Isaac. "Schiester, please, let him live, he didn't— please, kill *me*..."

"I will," Schiester said with a wave of his hand. "We've been over this, Gavin Stormbeck." He jerked his head toward Isaac. "Take him."

"NO!" Gavin screamed. He was thrown to the ground as the guards descended on Isaac. Gavin sobbed desperately and scrambled to his hands and knees, only to be shoved back down to the floor – and the floor gave under him, just a little. He felt the ghost of a blanket on his skin, or perhaps it was the air.

The guards dragged Isaac away, out of the cage. Isaac snarled as he fought, throwing his weight against the guards' grip. They threw him to his knees and forced his arms behind his back. Gavin blinked away his tears and shook his head against the fog as he sobbed. Tears streamed down his face as he watched the guards bind Isaac's wrists behind him. They kept Isaac on his knees, forcing him down with hands pressing on his shoulders, fisted in his hair, locked onto the collar of his shirt.

"I-Isaac, *no*," Gavin sobbed. "Schiester, please *no*, don't k-kill him…"

Schiester looked up from Isaac and tilted his head. A ghastly smile spread across his face, and he chuckled. "He means a lot to you, doesn't he?" His voice was almost gentle.

"*Please,* Schiester." Gavin's head spun. He struggled to focus on Isaac. "D-don't… please, don't, *no*…"

"I'm not going to kill him," Schiester said.

Gavin gasped out an agonized, hopeful sob. His eyes focused on Schiester. "Y-you…?"

"No," Schiester said with a widening grin. "Today I'm just going to give dear Isaac a little concussion."

An unbearable, bone-deep chill gripped Gavin. His eyes went wide. His mouth fell open to beg Schiester to let Isaac go, to let Gavin pay for his sins alone, to die for them, to die screaming. No words came out. He was nailed to his cot, freezing and on fire.

Schiester took a step towards Isaac, his shape wavering in the glare of the lights. "You've already lived through losing your family once. Stands to reason that you can do it again."

Gavin threw himself against the rope tied to his collar. The collar pulled tight around his throat, and he gagged. He tore at it with his fingers, fumbling for the buckle. His voice broke as he screamed his desperation.

Schiester reached out with one hand and gripped Isaac by the hair. He jerked his head back, forcing Isaac to look at him. Isaac's chest heaved with fury, his gaze flicking between Schiester and Gavin. Schiester craned Isaac's head back further. "But I can kill the Isaac you know, kill his mind, and leave his body walking around like a damned ghost."

"N-no, *no!*" Gavin screamed and writhed on the cot. His eyes unfocused.

Schiester shrugged. "His body would still be with you. I wonder, would that be enough for you? Would you still hold him, love him, kiss him after he didn't know who you are? Even after I've reduced him to some simple, trembling mess, would you be able to resist taking him?"

Each sob tore from Gavin like a knife being dragged from a wound. *"NO!"*

Schiester's lips quirked into a vicious smile. "It would never be the same. You'd have his body, not his mind. How long would it take before you went crazy from that?" Schiester released Isaac's hair, pulled his hand into a fist. Leather creaked against his knuckles.

"Kill me!" Gavin roared, sweat beading in his forehead as he clawed at the collar. "Sch-Schiester, kill, *k-kill me, please!* Not him, please, *no,* please not him…" The air was trapped in his lungs. He couldn't breathe.

Schiester pulled back his fist and smashed it against the side of Isaac's head.

Gavin's scream pierced his own skull. Isaac crumpled with a cry, held upright only by the guards on either side. His eyes were unfocused, dazed, as he slumped in their grip. Schiester wound up and punched Isaac again. His head snapped to the side. A spray of blood covered the floor.

The air boiled around Gavin and he scrabbled against the bars, trying to tear them from the floor. Sweat soaked into the cot, into the blanket. His mind was a ragged slash of agony as he watched blood drip from Isaac's mouth. Again, Schiester drove his fist against Isaac's head. Isaac slumped, senseless, against the guards' hands. His flesh split under Schiester's fist, and blood streamed down his temple, his face, his neck.

Gavin sobbed as he watched, his throat tearing with each scream that shattered him. Again, Schiester hit Isaac. Again, and again. Gavin couldn't draw breath. Every beat of his heart poured poison into his veins. Isaac groaned mindlessly like a plaything close to death.

Finally, Schiester straightened and shook out his hand, sending droplets of blood flying and spattering across the bars of the cage. He chuckled and nodded to the cell. "We're done, for now," he said coolly.

Gavin's body was tearing apart as the guards dragged Isaac into the cell. He hung between them limp, bloodied, and barely breathing. They dropped him to the floor and stepped out, closing the cell door with a clang that stunned Gavin out of his stupor.

"Isaac," Gavin sobbed as he crawled onto the floor, reaching out to touch Isaac. His hands shook as he cradled Isaac's head. Isaac's blood stained his hands. The crook of Gavin's elbow itched as he held Isaac to his chest, shivered as his blood dried on his skin.

Isaac stirred, moaning softly. He blinked his eyes open and turned his gaze toward Gavin with blank, sightless eyes.

Chapter 21

Vera stared impassively out the window at Isaac as he stood motionless in the backyard. Her jaw ached from clenching it. Her shoulders hovered around her ears, her muscles shaking and her hands worrying at each other. While she rocked nervously from foot to foot, he could have been made of stone he was so still, a statue at the edge of the yard. The only thing that betrayed him as flesh and blood was the quick, jerky glances he threw at the house every now and then.

Still, it was better than the pacing he'd been doing before – and whatever secretive motions he had been doing with his hands further down the beach, where he probably thought he had been out of sight of the house.

The front door swung open, and Vera turned to see Gray walk in. Their shoulders were stooped. Their eyes were red, just like Isaac's. Vera swallowed hard and wet her lips.

"Anything?" she murmured.

Gray passed a hand over their face and drew in a deep breath. "No," they croaked. "Nothing. I'm still not sure how I'm supposed to find someone who isn't supposed to exist, someone who's *dead,* when they go missing up here."

"Yeah," Vera whispered. She looked back at Isaac, who was still standing motionless save for the glance he shot at her. Still, she could see the tension in every line of his body.

"How's...?" Gray went to Vera's side and looked out, their face darkening as they looked for themself. "So about the same."

"He's in rough shape, Gray," Vera said. "We... w-we all are, but..."

"Yeah." Gray cleared their throat and blinked away tears. "How about the others?"

"Finn and Ellis are still hunkered down in their house," Vera said. "They haven't seen or heard anything suspicious. Tori's in our room on the phone with Mathias. Zachariah, Sam, and Edrissa are all in Sam's room. I told

Zachariah to stay inside until…" Vera looked down at her hands. "I mean… Jesus Christ, if he has to stay inside until we… I mean… we don't even know if—"

"Gavin's alive," Gray said through their teeth. Their eyes flashed as they looked at Vera. "Gavin… he's alive. He… *h-has* to be alive." Gray's voice faltered, and their eyes filled with tears.

Vera watched them for a long moment, then pulled them into a crushing hug. She could feel Gray tremble against her as they wound their arms around her.

After a long moment, Vera said, "We know who did this."

"I th-think we do," Gray rasped. They cleared their throat and released Vera, placing a shaking hand on her shoulder instead. "But that doesn't narrow down… anything. Schiester has the entire north at his disposal. Gavin could be… could be *anywhere*."

"Yeah," Vera said weakly. She shoved down the ache in her stomach, the trickle of fear down her spine. Her family needed her. Gray needed her. Isaac needed her. "We just have to…"

"Any sign that we're searching for him, any at all, and Schiester will kill him," Gray breathed. "We can't… how on *earth* do we ask the people of the north if they've seen him? 'Oh, yes, I'm looking for my son. He's five-foot-eleven, green eyes, dark brown hair, scars on his face, looks a lot like Joseph Stormbeck…'" Gray scoffed. "Anyone we ask…"

"…can immediately bring it back to DFS," Vera said weakly. "I know."

Gray looked out the window for a long moment. Vera's tears blurred her vision as she watched Isaac, still standing motionless, looking out across the lake. "What are we going to do about him?" Vera whispered.

Gray blew out a slow breath. "I don't know," they murmured. "But… he can't wait much longer like this. Vera… he… if he goes south looking for Gavin, and he confronts Schiester…"

"Schiester is fucking terrified of him," Vera said, only half-aware of what she was saying. "There's a reason… look, I'm… pretty much fully convinced DFS *made* Gavin write that letter, just so Isaac wouldn't—"

"He's seen what Isaac does when his family is threatened," Gray croaked. "Or at least… he's heard of it. He knows Isaac went to Gavin in Sam's place a year ago. He knows what Isaac did to escape. He knows you all escaped from Colleen's captivity; he knows you laid the entire place to waste. He knows that's what's waiting for him, too, if Isaac ever finds out."

"I'm going to pull Schiester's lungs out of his fucking throat," Vera growled. Her heart pounded painfully in her chest. "If— When we find Gavin, once he's safe…" She licked her lips and bared her teeth in a silent snarl. "I'm going to… to…" She heaved a dry sob and wound her arms around Gray's waist. Gray laid their cheek on the top of her head, and she felt tears dripping onto her hair.

"He's…" Gray whimpered. "H-he's my *son*."

"I know," Vera whispered. "I… I know." She glanced out the window. The backyard was empty. "Hm." She stepped forward, peering out the back window, her gaze scanning along the lake for Isaac. He was nowhere to be found.

"Did he wander off?" Gray said weakly.

"Think so," Vera murmured. She froze at the sound of a car starting. She whipped around and saw the keys were missing from the hook by the door.

Gray turned at the exact same time. "I l-left the keys under the seat," they breathed. "Shit, *no*—"

Vera lunged towards the door, with Gray stumbling right after her. She dashed across the living room and threw open the front door. The car was running, and Isaac was fumbling at the gearshift. His head snapped up. His hands jerked as he saw them, frantically scrabbling on the wheel. He jammed the car into reverse and turned his head to back down the driveway.

Vera bolted past him and skidded to a stop behind the car, her hands held out in front of her. The car's tires crunched on the gravel as Isaac slammed on the brakes. Gray moved with speed Vera had never seen and darted to the side of the car. They yanked the door open and reached inside to grab Isaac.

"Put the car in park," they snapped, their eyes wide and blazing, their chest heaving. "*Now,* Isaac."

Vera stalked to the side of the car. Tears streamed down Isaac's face, and he looked desperately from Vera to Gray and back. His lips trembled. "B-but—"

"Put the *fucking* car in *park,* Isaac," Vera hissed. Her heart pounded so fast she felt dizzy.

Isaac rocked forward and buried his face in his hands. He heaved a sob, reached down, and put the car in park.

Vera leaned in and dragged Isaac halfway out of the car. He whimpered softly and grabbed at her wrists as she yanked him upright. Vera slammed him against the side of the car.

"What the *fuck* were you thinking?" she snarled in his face.

"V-Vera," he sobbed. His face was swollen from crying day and night, and dark shadows cut deep under his eyes. "I… Vera, I ha-have to, to do *something…*"

"What, so you thought you'd steal the car and go to Schiester yourself, like you did for Sam?" Vera shoved him harder against the side of the car. "Offer yourself to *him,* too, and hope for some motherfucking reason that Schiester somehow wants *you* more than Gavin fucking— Uriah? Was *that* the fucking plan?"

Isaac sniffled. "I don't *kn-know,* I w-was—"

"What?" Vera snarled. *"What* were you thinking?"

Isaac's eyes fluttered closed, and tears slid down his cheeks. "V-Vera…"

"You thought you'd just come up with a plan as you drove down there?" Vera hissed through her teeth. "Wander through the front door of his fucking town hall, guns blazing, and just take those people out until they tell you where Gavin is? Is that it?"

Isaac slumped back against the car, silently shaking his head. He opened his eyes and looked up at the sky. "It… when I… it w-worked with Sam…"

"No, it fucking *didn't,* you fucking *idiot,* you came so fucking close to dying and Sam was *still* almost fucking killed…" Vera jammed Isaac back against the car and stepped away, holding a shaking hand over her mouth. "Jesus *fuck,* Isaac, you can't just… we… we need a *plan,*" she breathed. "This isn't *like* going to Gavin. Schiester's fucking *organized,* he has the entire goddamn *north* at his disposal. We need to know exactly where Gavin is before we move. Isaac… Schiester holds *all* the fucking cards right now. We need to be smart about this. We need to know what the fuck we're *doing* before we move like that."

Isaac hung his head and wrapped his arms around his chest, cowering against the side of the car. "B-but... I..."

"You want DFS to kill Gavin?" Vera seethed. Isaac's head snapped up. He fixed his desperate eyes on her. "Because this is how you make that happen. Isaac... How much more fucking clear did Gavin have to make it that he *didn't* want you coming after him?"

"I j-just need to... *do* something." Isaac swallowed hard.

"You can't do *this*," Vera spat. She leaned in, pressing Isaac against the side of the car. She was barely aware of Gray's presence at her side. "We can't afford to look for Gavin *and* babysit you. You want us to tie you to the fucking *bed?* Is *that* what you want?"

Isaac's gaze went cold. His expression hardened. "No," he growled.

Vera stepped back and dragged her hands through her hair. "Then... for fuck's *sake,* Isaac, you need to think about this. Going after Gavin like this gets you nothing. It probably just gets you both killed."

Isaac shrank back into himself with a whimper. Tears welled in his eyes and spilled over. "I-I... I'm sorry..."

Vera stepped forward and pulled Isaac into a fierce hug. He sobbed and wound his arms around her waist, pressing his face into her shoulder. After a moment, Gray wrapped them both in an embrace.

"I'm sorry," Isaac whimpered. "I... I j-just... we..." He swallowed hard, and Vera felt his whole body shaking. "I... I *l-love* him," he breathed. "I can't... I... we s-spent so much time being, being k-kept apart, and... C-Colleen made him hurt me, Vera, I just want to be with him and d-don't want him to h-hurt anymore..." He squeezed Vera tighter and shuddered, dissolving into bitter sobs.

"I know," Vera croaked, then cleared her throat. Her own tears ran into his shirt. "But... Isaac... you *can't*—"

"I know," he whimpered. "I... I kn-know. I just... can't *think,* right now. Schiester is... h-he's hurting him, Vera, I *know* he's hurting him..."

Vera closed her eyes against a flash of memory: the snow falling in the square, the blood on the snow, the seething hatred in Schiester's voice, the loathing in his eyes as he stared down at Gavin.

"Look at me, syndicate boy. If you betray us, lead any of your family to us, in any way jeopardize a single life during your time in my territory, I will break you in ways even your twisted mind can't imagine. Do I make myself perfectly clear?"

Vera shivered and held Isaac tighter. "Y-yeah," she rasped.

Isaac sobbed, trembling. "He's... V-Vera, he... he doesn't deserve that. He..."

"I know," Vera said. She whimpered softly.

"We'll find him." Gray's voice was tight with tears. "Isaac, we'll find him."

"How?" Isaac moaned, falling against them both. *"How?"*

"I don't know," Vera admitted. "But we will. We'll start by finding people who are sympathetic to us. I'm sure the north has more people with syndicate ties than Schiester would care to admit. We're already talking to Mathias about being sent more refugees. He told Gray there's an entire settlement of them that he's been sending people to. And... Finn had an idea."

Isaac's head shot up. He clutched at Vera, his hands rough on her arms, his eyes raw. "Idea...?"

"Yeah, um... It might not work, but... Fire safety inspections." Vera shrugged tightly. "You know, get into buildings, see every corner..."

Isaac's face crumpled, and his head fell onto Vera's shoulder again.

Vera ignored the pit in her stomach. "There are people who will help us, Isaac. I *know* there are."

"N-not when they find out who we're looking for," Isaac whimpered.

"Hey." Vera pulled back and held Isaac tightly by the shoulders. She ducked into his eyeline. He brought tear-filled eyes to hers. "We'll figure this out, Isaac."

"He sh-shouldn't suffer because of... of what his parents made him," Isaac murmured. His voice broke. "V-Vera, he's, he's *ours,* he's *good...*"

"I know." Vera blinked back tears. "We just have to find people who agree with us."

"We're not going to stop," Gray rasped. "We're going to keep looking until we find him."

Isaac heaved a sob and collapsed in their embrace. The car idled beside them. The sun burned in the sky, but the breeze sent cool tendrils over Vera's skin, drying her tears.

Chapter 22

Gavin groaned and rolled onto his side, hissing through his teeth as the cane marks flared with pain. His head swam in the dim light. He shivered as the cold air chilled the sweat drying on his neck. The faint scent of blood made his stomach roil.

Where am I?

His eyes flew open. He sat up with a gasp, only to cry out as pain tore through his back. The collar jerked him to a stop; the rope tying him down shortened until he could barely sit upright. His heart pounded in his chest as his gaze swept the cell. Isaac was gone. There wasn't even a smear of blood on the floor.

Cold flooded his chest as he raised his gaze to Schiester's face, the smug, twisted grin. Gavin licked his lips and trembled as he met Schiester's eyes through the bars.

"Wh-where is Isaac?" he croaked, terrified to hear the answer.

Schiester smiled wider. "Interesting."

"Where…" Gavin whined softly, his hand curling into a fist around Isaac's shirt. "What did you…" Gavin pulled the blanket tighter around himself, wincing as it pressed into the dried blood and broken skin of his back. His voice dropped to a whisper. "What did you do with him?"

Schiester tilted his head. "I did nothing with him."

Gavin leaned forward, clutching his head in his hands. "P-please," he whimpered. "Please let me see him, he… h-he needs *help,* please get him help…"

Schiester's lips quirked. "And what," he said amusedly, "Does he need help *with?*"

Gavin's breaths started to come faster. "N-no, no… p-please, he's not… please don't kill him, you… you d-didn't kill him…" He rocked forward and back, tears streaming from all but sightless eyes. "Isaac…"

Gavin froze as Schiester's laughter filled the basement. "It worked better than I could have hoped."

Gavin slowly raised his head to look at Schiester again. He scarcely dared to breathe. "What worked... better?"

Schiester snorted and reached into his pocket with his ungloved hand. He pulled out a small vial and held it up to the light.

Dread pooled in Gavin's stomach. "What... wh-what...?"

"I had a friend craft it for me," Schiester said conversationally. "She went through several iterations, mixes of ketamine, lysergic acid diethylamide, rohypnol, sodium pentothal, epinephrine... I'm honestly not sure what particular formula she settled on. But I would say it decidedly works."

Bile crawled up Gavin's throat and burned the back of his tongue. "Wh-what... Schiester, what—"

"What, *exactly,* did you see?"

Gavin felt dissected under Schiester's gaze. He swallowed. "What did I... see?"

"You mentioned Isaac," Schiester said. His gaze burned Gavin's skin. "Did you see Isaac? What was happening to him?"

Gavin felt dizzy. His lips were numb. "Wh-what... Isaac was *here,* you—"

"And what was I doing to him?" Schiester's eyes flashed with excitement.

The blood drained from Gavin's face. "Y-you're insane," he whispered.

Schiester stepped forward, and Gavin flinched back. The rope snapped tight again. The collar constricted around his throat.

"Tell me, Gavin Stormbeck," Schiester breathed. "What did you see?"

Gavin wet his lips and tried to think, but each thought flew through his mind with paralyzing speed. He blinked tears away as he remembered, vividly – as if in a dream – Isaac being caught, beaten, thrown into the cell with him. Panic tightened in his throat as he heard Schiester's voice, cool and deadly – an echo of his own, only last year, as he leered down at Ellis and taunted them with Finn's life.

"They mean a lot to you, don't they?"

"Today I'm just gonna give dear Finn a little concussion."

"But I can kill Finn, kill their mind, and leave their body walking around like a damned ghost."

The room spun around Gavin as he raised his gaze to Schiester again. "That... w-wasn't real?"

Schiester tucked the vial back into his pocket. "And the syndicate son figures it out."

Desperate terror seized Gavin and he reached forward to clutch at the bars. "L-let me see your hands," he managed through chattering teeth.

Schiester quirked an eyebrow. "Why?"

"J-just, let, l-let me see your fucking *hands!*" Gavin shouted. Sweat beaded on his forehead. He thought he might be sick.

Schiester hesitated, then stepped forward, holding his bare hands out, palms up. "Content, Stormbeck?"

"The backs," Gavin rasped. "Let me s-see your knuckles."

Schiester huffed out an amused laugh. He turned his hands over and held them out for Gavin to inspect. The skin across his knuckles was unbroken, unbruised.

Gavin whimpered and sank to the cot, his eyes wide. Unbearable relief flooded his body, tainted by acrid fear. He pressed a hand over his mouth. His heart thudded in his chest; blood rushed through his ears.

"Tell me what you saw, Stormbeck," Schiester said quietly, just outside the bars. Gavin jumped and whimpered with the fire that shot through his back.

"He w-wasn't here," Gavin whispered. Tears streamed down his face, smarting where they touched the opened scar on his cheek. "He... d-didn't come."

"No. Why would he?" Schiester said with a chuckle.

"He didn't... he w-won't be... hurt. Because of me." Gavin sobbed weakly and curled into a ball, pressing Isaac's shirt to his face. He sobbed harder as Isaac's scent washed over him.

Schiester was silent for a long moment. Then, with a tone that bordered on pity, he said, "Ah. You hallucinated Moore coming to your rescue."

"H-hallucination," Gavin mumbled through numb lips. "It was... w-was a, a hallucination. He won't be... hurt." Gavin felt like the floor had been

150

ripped out from under him. Isaac wasn't coming, had never come. He wouldn't be rescued.

But Isaac wouldn't be hurt.

"And what," Schiester said softly, "Did I do to him for trying?"

Gavin cowered against the cot, shrinking in on himself. "You…"

He couldn't tell Schiester. If he told Schiester the truth… and if Schiester took that information back to his family, took Isaac's mind away, turned Isaac into the walking corpse Gavin had once promised to make Finn…

Gavin tasted blood at the back of his throat as he swallowed. "Y-you tortured him," he rasped.

"How?" Schiester said through his teeth.

Gavin jerked his head from side to side. "Won't…" His voice broke. "N-not…"

Not telling.

Schiester would have to beat it out of him. He'd have to cut it out of him.

Schiester blew out a slow breath, his eyes sliding out of focus. He rolled his neck and raised his gaze to Gavin again. "Was it in a way you fear?"

Gavin blinked. His head rang with the echo of Schiester's laughter as he beat Isaac nearly to death— *But that didn't happen.* "Wh-what?"

"The way I tortured him." Schiester pinned him with his steady gaze. "Was it in a way you fear for him?"

"Y-yes," Gavin whispered through trembling lips.

Schiester's gaze was colder than the room around Gavin as he stared him down. "Alright," he said softly. "I'll accept that, for now." He relaxed his shoulders, took a step back from the cell. He walked a slow line across the basement, turned, walked back. Gavin kept his eyes fixed on him. "Interesting," Schiester murmured. "You… hallucinated *Moore* rescuing you."

Gavin slumped against the cot and pulled the blanket up over his head, hiding from Schiester's gaze. "F-fuck off," he growled.

Schiester laughed once. "It's *very* interesting to me. He… must have fully convinced you he felt something for you, didn't he?"

Cold crept under Gavin's skin, slipped down his throat, and chilled his heart. He shook his head and squeezed his eyes shut against the waves of nausea and dizziness that still clung to him from the drug. He rubbed at the pinprick of burning pain along the inside of his elbow. His fingers moved over it and he realized, for the first time, that it was a needle mark, directly over his vein.

Schiester huffed out a laugh. "I mean, it makes sense. Can't say I wouldn't do the same. When you're saddled with a syndicate threat, you do what you must."

"I said *fuck off*," Gavin whispered, hiding his head in his arms. His breath warmed the air under the blanket. He curled tighter into himself.

"I wonder at your... acumen, in this situation, then," Schiester continued, as if Gavin hadn't said anything. "Truly, Stormbeck, did you *believe* him? He would have said *anything* to keep you in line."

Schiester's words prickled under Gavin's skin. He pressed his hands against his forehead. They came away sticky with drying blood.

"I admire Moore's tenacity to protect his family even more now. I imagine it was hell to— but then again, he's made far greater sacrifices for his family than being your bed toy, no?"

Gavin groaned and uncurled slightly to relieve the burn of the cane marks. "No, th-that's not... it wasn't... *like* that..."

"But with you heir to the throne, so to speak... no wonder. It makes sense. Let you believe he feels something for you, and you're less likely to betray him. Do you not see the power dynamic there, boy? If he refuses your advances, he risks you turning on him, sending him and his entire family back south in chains. And with him being too broken to find the strength to kill you, well. What choice did he have, other than to let you have him? What other choice is there, when the alternative is death?"

"N-no," Gavin whimpered. "He... h-he *knows* I'd never..." He gagged weakly at the smell of blood and tipped his head back until his face was out from underneath the blanket. He breathed in deep the cold air of the basement. The smell of blood wasn't as strong.

"*How* would he know that, Gavin Stormbeck?" Schiester purred. "All he's ever known at your hands is torture. Pain. Obligation. Risk. This is what you bring to his doorstep, and this is why he chose to make the sacrifice of being with you. And played his part splendidly, if you saw him rescuing you, and watched him be tortured for it."

"No," Gavin moaned, clawing at his collar.

"If anything, this has increased my respect for Moore tenfold," Schiester said, chuckling. "He's already proven he'll sacrifice his body and soul for his family but... *damn.*"

"S-stop," Gavin whimpered.

"Makes me wonder how different you are from your father, though. Do you like Isaac Moore to like it? Or do you prefer him screaming under you?"

"NO!" Gavin screamed as he shot upright. Tears burned his eyes and he sobbed raggedly. "N-no, *no,* don't, don't say that, *stop*—"

Schiester paused. His lips slid slowly into a smile. "Stormbeck... don't pretend to be *shocked.*"

Gavin rocked forward, clutched at his hair, yanked it out by its roots. "N-no, no... I *didn't*—"

"I shouldn't be surprised that you can't understand that, the way you were raised. Still, there goes the last of my hope that time with that family could make a human out of you." Schiester stepped forward, eyes like a predator about to strike, perfectly focused. "But even after you all made it north, even after both your parents were dead and you couldn't even blame their influence over you anymore..." Schiester wet his lips; his eyes flashed even in the dim light. "...you raped him, didn't you? You raped Isaac Moore."

"No," Gavin sobbed. The sound drew out into a terrible broken wail. "No, *no, no,* he... he l-loved me, I didn't—"

Schiester scoffed. "Pathetic. Oh, I believe he told you that, of course, I'm not saying you're lying. Not about *that,* anyway. But... Stormbeck, I know he was lying to you, because... well, just think about it. How could a man like *that*..." He took one more step forward and leaned close to the bars. "...love a man like *you?*"

Gavin shattered. He collapsed onto the cot, his mouth pulled open in a silent scream. He'd known, deep down, that Isaac couldn't truly love him – and he had slept with Isaac anyway, even *knowing* it didn't make sense.

He had raped Isaac. Even without the chains, the restraints, the guard watching in the corner – he had raped Isaac. And Isaac had withstood it, to save his family.

Gavin sobbed wretchedly against the cot and dug his fingers into the cuts on his face. He gritted his teeth against the flash of pain. Over his sobs, he could still hear Daniel Schiester's cold laughter.

Chapter 23

Gavin knew *something* had happened. He lay sprawled in a heap on the freezing floor beside the cot. He blinked blearily in the dim light of the cell, sore down to his bones; his head swirled with a feeling that was almost familiar. He wet his cracked lips and glanced out into the basement. His heart leapt as his gaze landed on a bottle of water on the floor outside the cell, just within reach. He groaned as he rolled onto his stomach and pushed himself upright.

He froze as he saw Schiester standing back, watching him. A guard watched impassively from the corner.

Panic spiked through Gavin's body – panic, and shame. There was something in the back of his mind, something bitter that moved through his blood. Flashes of Isaac came to him – Isaac smiling in bed with him, Isaac crying out against Gavin's skin as they made love...

Then, here and gone so suddenly Gavin couldn't quite grasp the image – Isaac, in this basement, being beaten half to death by the man standing outside the bars.

An echo of Schiester's voice came to him as if from a nightmare, as if from a years-old memory.

"You raped him, didn't you?"

Then that echo, too, was gone. Gavin was left grasping after it like the last tendrils of a dream fading away upon waking.

His blood crawled in his veins, sluggish and sharp like ice. He wet his lips and tried to push himself to standing; the rope tied to his collar was now long enough that he could.

Was it shorter before?

The floor bucked beneath him, and he crumpled. A scream pressed against his teeth as pain ripped through his back. The floor felt like ice against his bare chest, and he reached up, fumbling for Isaac's shirt where it lay in a heap on the cot. He pulled it on with shaking hands and whimpered as Isaac's

155

scent washed over him. He hoped that the blood on his back was dried enough that it wouldn't ruin the shirt; he was too cold to stand being without it any longer. He pushed himself up onto his hands and knees and began to crawl towards the bars, towards the water.

"He lives," Schiester said with a sneer.

Gavin hung his head. "F-fuck off," he groaned.

He reached the bars and collapsed in front of them, his chest heaving, his stomach roiling with the dizziness that pushed him out of his own head. He stretched out one hand towards the bottle of water, his fingers dragging across the cold cement. Just as he reached the bottle, Schiester took two steps forward and pinned Gavin's hand under his boot.

Gavin grunted and tried to jerk his hand away. He squirmed and whimpered softly as Schiester leaned more weight, grinding the knuckles beneath his boot.

Gavin hissed a breath in through his teeth. "Ahh, fuck, *get off,*" he growled.

Schiester laughed. "Where are your manners, Stormbeck?"

"Truly, Stormbeck, did you believe *him? He would have said* anything *to keep you in line."*

Gavin shuddered and blinked away the tears that sprang to his eyes. His mouth was bone dry. "Wh-what did you do to me?" he croaked.

Keeping weight on his foot, still crushing down onto Gavin's hand, Schiester dropped into a crouch. He stared at Gavin through the bars. "Interesting. Anterograde amnesia. She said that could be a side effect."

"Side effect of *what?*" Gavin snapped and tried again to yank his hand out from under Schiester's boot. He glared up at Schiester but trembled at his cold, piercing look.

Schiester tilted his head. "Hm. What *do* you remember?"

Gavin blinked. The time was... *missing.*

Missing, like so much of his time in the hospital after Isaac escaped him. Missing, like the helicopter ride from his summer home to the hospital after Vera shot him. Missing, like... so many moments, after Isaac beat him so badly he nearly died from it. He swallowed hard and winced. It felt like shards of glass scraping down his throat.

He saw flashes, but he couldn't even be sure they were real. Struggling under the guard's hands as Schiester held a needle to his arm. Screaming as he watched Schiester beat Isaac and dump him in Gavin's cell. Schiester taunting him with Isaac's love, Isaac's pain...

"You raped him, didn't you? You raped Isaac Moore."

Gavin shivered and went rigid as terror and rage swept through him. He raised his gaze to Schiester again, his lip curling.

"What the fuck did you *do?*" he spat through his teeth.

Schiester chuckled and shook his head. "Alright. Not ideal, but... I can work with that." He lifted his boot. Gavin groaned and pulled back his hand, cradling it against his chest as he lay slumped on the floor.

Schiester raised an eyebrow and nodded at the water. "Didn't you want that?"

Gavin glared up at Schiester, then glanced at the water. He felt like he'd swallowed a knife. A headache pounded faintly behind his left eye. "You're gonna let me have it?" he ground out.

Schiester took a step back and raised his hands. "Wouldn't want you dying of thirst. It's an agonizing process, but... far too *short.* A few days, at the longest."

Gavin chewed his lip, his gaze fixed on Schiester. His eyes flicked to the water again once, twice, then his hand shot out to grab the bottle. He twisted off the cap and held it to his lips with a shaking hand. His eyes slid shut as the water rushed over his tongue and down his throat, quenching his blazing thirst. When he paused to take a breath, Schiester was still watching him with feverish intensity. Gavin clenched his jaw and shuffled back on his knees until he reached the cot and crawled back onto it, shivering from the cold. He pulled the blanket up and wrapped it around himself as he sat up and glared right back at Schiester.

He pushed down the panic rising in his chest, the feeling that everything – including this – might be a dream, a trick. If Schiester could do something to him to make him miss time...

Still, there was something... *different,* about that one part of it, about Schiester smiling mirthlessly, the expression not touching the coldness of his eyes, his mouth curling into a sneer as Gavin sobbed and begged.

"You raped him, didn't you? You raped Isaac Moore."

"And with him being too broken to find the strength to kill you..."

Gavin didn't know if it was real, but he had to say it, anyway. "I d-didn't rape Isaac."

Schiester blinked. "Excuse me?"

Gavin hesitated. Fear clutched at him, terror that if Schiester believed Gavin was denying something Schiester didn't even know about, he would find a way to punish him for it. Gavin didn't need any imagination at all to know exactly *how* Schiester would repay that.

But I did rape Isaac. I raped him almost every day when I was with my mother.

Tears blurred Gavin's eyes, but he forced himself to hold Schiester's gaze. "I... when we g-got back. I didn't... rape him. He—"

Schiester held up a hand. "Please don't try to convince me he was with you voluntarily, and please don't try to convince me you weren't sleeping together. My men found you naked in bed with him."

Shame crushed Gavin's chest. But even as his heart struggled to beat – even as he folded into himself, even as tears ran from his eyes – a bitter core of rage shifted inside him, cutting him open from the inside out. There was something so *familiar* about how Schiester seemed to find Gavin's shame with ease, slide the knife in, and twist. Gavin swallowed. His mouth was dry again.

Still, he could feel something rising in him, too. Something true that he couldn't logic his way past, something he'd known from the very first time he heard Isaac's voice.

Isaac is not broken.

Gavin leaned back, looking Schiester up and down, taking him in – from the shine of his boots, to the long coat keeping off the chill of the basement, to the cold blue of his eyes, to the short-cropped silvering hair. He drew in a deep breath and blew it out slowly. He could *see* Schiester in a way he hadn't even tried to see anyone for a long time.

He could see the cracks.

"I didn't rape him," Gavin said again, his voice a little stronger.

Schiester sighed. "Stormbeck—"

Gavin leaned forward. "I didn't. Fucking. Rape him. If you know a fucking *thing* about Isaac—"

"I think I know a bit more about Isaac Moore than—"

"No, *shut up*," Gavin spat. He relished the flash of surprise that crossed Schiester's face. "You shut the *fuck up.* If you think Isaac could see me as a threat to his family and not put me down in a *heartbeat*—"

Schiester took a step forward, a shadow passing over his face. "Stormbeck—"

"I said *shut up*," Gavin snarled. His fingers locked on the edge of his cot. "You've seen what Isaac can do. He... for fuck's *sake,* he escaped *me,* even after I—"

"So perhaps he's always had a soft spot for the people who see the truth of him," Schiester said darkly.

Gavin continued as if Schiester hadn't said anything. "Isaac's not broken. He's *not* fucking broken. M-maybe he... he maybe didn't... feel for me what I did for him, but... he..." Gavin dashed the tears from his eyes and grimaced. "If he thought for a *second* that I was a threat to his family, he would have put a bullet in my head before we even left my—"

"He brought you north with him," Schiester said through his teeth. "He brought you north in January when you were a threat, through and through. He let you stay in his *home,* with his *family.*" Schiester spat the word like a curse. "He—"

"I don't think you're related to me," Gavin said softly.

Schiester stopped in his tracks. "...excuse me?"

Gavin narrowed his eyes, sweeping Schiester once more with his gaze. "I don't think you're related to me," he said again. "You talk like you're from my dad's social circle, but—"

Schiester shoved his hand into his pocket and drew out the keys to Gavin's cell. Terror clutched at Gavin as Schiester took a furious step forward and jammed the key into the lock.

Gavin shoved down the panic. "Finn said you were Defense Corps. What, you and my dad liked to hang out torturing prisoners of war? You know we were in peacetime before my fucking *family* took over, right?" Gavin pressed himself back away from Schiester against the wall, hissing through his teeth as it pressed against the cane marks through the blanket and Isaac's shirt. "Is that why you started this bullshit? Not enough people around to hurt, so you had to *manufacture* an entire caste of people you could fuck with?"

Schiester's eyes blazed as he met Gavin's. His lip curled as he unlocked the door and yanked it open. Gavin flinched back against the wall, heart thundering in his chest. Heat curled in his stomach as he watched Schiester step into the cell, rage twisting his features. It spread through his chest, warming his throat, as he watched his words dig under Schiester's skin.

I used to be good at this.

Gavin's lips pulled back over his teeth in a vicious grin. "Or did my dad pick the wrong plaything, hm? Did he pick someone in the DC you *liked*? I know the bases were destroyed, but what, did my dad scoop up some poor idiot who thought they could *trust* you?"

Schiester's face contorted in a snarl of rage.

There it is.

Knuckles smashed against the side of Gavin's head, and he toppled off of the cot. He sprawled onto the floor, stunned. His mouth gaped open. His eyes rolled back. The rope tied to his collar tangled around his legs.

He whined softly as Schiester jerked him upright by the collar of Isaac's shirt. He tasted the coppery burst of heat in his mouth as blood trickled down his chin. His stomach heaved, faintly. His head lolled as Schiester pulled Gavin close, his face mere inches away.

Still, despite the burn and ache of his split lip, despite the fire of the lash marks on his back, Gavin smiled. Pleasure stabbed through him, sharp as a knife, as he saw the twist of Schiester's mouth, the tightness in his eyes as he snarled at him.

"Did I hit the mark, soldier?" Gavin said, and spat his blood into Schiester's face.

Schiester let out a cry and flinched back. He dragged his sleeve across his face, leaving a smear of Gavin's blood on his cheek. Then he pulled his fist back and drove it into Gavin's stomach. Gavin screamed and slumped to the floor, only to be jerked upright again. He let out a peal of fevered laughter as Schiester's hand fisted in his hair and dragged his head back.

"You don't know who the *fuck* you're dealing with," Gavin sneered, reveling in a feeling he hadn't allowed himself in months. "You think you know a *goddamn thing* about torturing people, but you're nothing but a fucking *Joseph Stormbeck knockoff, fucker.*"

Chapter 24

Schiester slammed Gavin onto his back against the floor. A choked cry punched out of Gavin's chest. He squirmed under Schiester as a hand crushed his throat. Tears streamed from his eyes.

"Levine, get your *fucking ass* over here."

"Yes sir."

Gavin writhed as Schiester rolled him onto his stomach and the guard forced his hands behind his back. He hissed through his teeth as a zip tie tightened around his wrists, cutting into the already broken skin. Tears streamed from his eyes as he was forced onto his back again, and he whimpered as his hands were crushed beneath his own weight.

He convulsed with terror as Schiester's hand closed around his throat again, just above the collar, pinning him down against the floor. He shuddered as Schiester leaned forward, his breath hot on Gavin's ear.

"I was a colonel in the DC, yes," Schiester hissed, his voice low and deadly and perfectly even – a horrifying contrast to the hand pressing down on Gavin's throat. "I was a friend of your father's, yes. I made mistakes. I *trusted* him. I told him things I shouldn't have. Things that helped him take the DC down. But when he told me to order the executions of the cadets in the JDC, I refused." Schiester leaned back. Gavin ground out a scream as Schiester's hand tightened, just a little more, on his throat.

Schiester huffed out a mirthless laugh. "And he destroyed me. Destroyed the social standing I had, denied me the privileges he *promised* for delivering the DC to him. And to make sure I couldn't return to my people…" Schiester's trembling hand loosened on Gavin's throat, and beneath the terror, he felt familiar warmth at the pain in Schiester's eyes. "…he brought in my best friend, a fellow colonel. He pulled a gun on me and told me to h-hurt him."

Gavin's lips pulled into a wide smile. "And I bet you did, didn't you? I bet you tortured your friend to *death* like a fucking—"

Schiester pressed his full weight down against Gavin's throat, cutting off his air.

Gavin kicked frantically against the floor, his vision going black almost immediately. His eyes rolled back and his throat spasmed under Schiester's hand. Just before he slipped into unconsciousness, Schiester released him, and he dragged in a desperate breath. He curled into himself, and a rattling cough wracked him.

Pain crushed his throat again as he was dragged backwards by his collar. His head spun as Schiester untied the long length of rope from the bars and wrestled Gavin back until he was across the cell from his cot. Goosebumps erupted over his skin as Schiester shoved him back against the wall of the cell and tied his collar tightly to the bars, keeping him sitting up but preventing him from standing.

Gavin yanked against the zip tie still binding his hands behind him. His head ached from the lack of air as he drew in breath after wheezing breath. Schiester stood over him, staring down at him with fathomless fury in his eyes. He straightened his coat and rolled his neck.

"Maybe everything that I was is still there inside me," Gavin spat through bloodstained teeth. "But you were a *normal person* and you fucking *volunteered* to help my father bring down your own fucking *military?*"

"I would stop talking *now* if I were you, Gavin Stormbeck," Schiester said softly, his voice a deadly threat.

"Or what, you'll torture me to death?" Gavin sneered, desperately ignoring the terrified pounding of his heart. "I'd give you some pointers but apparently you learned from the fucking *best.*"

Schiester aimed a kick at Gavin's ribs that left him gasping. His head fell back against the bars and his collar choked him as he tried to swallow. Without a word, Schiester plunged his hand into his pocket and drew out a syringe and a vial of clear liquid.

"The *fuck* is that?" Gavin said, forcing down the tremor in his voice.

"I'm curious," Schiester said impassively, "About what will come up with *this* dose."

"What will…" The blood drained from Gavin's face. He kicked against the floor, crushing himself back against the bars of the cell. "Schiester, what… what *is* that?"

"Retribution," Schiester growled. "Levine, hold him, please."

Cold terror flooded Gavin's body. "What… what, *no*…" He flinched away from the guard's hands as he stepped forward and shoved Gavin back against the bars, dragging his wrists out to the side until one arm was twisted behind him. He straightened Gavin's arm as best he could as Schiester stepped forward with the syringe, flicking it to get the last few bubbles out.

"Hold still, Stormbeck," Schiester said almost gently as he knelt at the guard's side. He slid the needle into Gavin's skin.

Gavin screamed as the cold liquid entered his vein, not with pain but with horror. He sobbed weakly as Schiester withdrew the needle and stepped back to smile down at him where he sat tied to the bars of the cell. The other guard faded, disappearing into the hazy walls.

Gavin turned blurry eyes up to Schiester's. The blue of Schiester's eyes seemed to deepen, to drag him in, to freeze him further in the already cold basement. His head felt detached from his body. He whined softly and drew his legs up against his chest, as if that could provide him with any sort of protection from the thing that Gavin somehow knew was about to happen. He had no idea what was coming, just knew that something was coming, something that was going to hurt him.

He cast his gaze around the room and turned his face away from the thing standing in front of him – a creature, a specter, a monster with cold blue eyes and a tongue like a knife. He whimpered softly but couldn't feel the tears that streamed down his face.

He blinked, and the specter was gone – outside the bars somewhere, where the room swirled in dark grays and blacks and blues. Inside the bars, Gavin was alone. Inside the bars, pain raced through him with every beat of his heart. He shook his head, desperately trying to get his eyes to focus. When he finally could, his heart stopped in his chest.

Sam lay on their back on the cot. Their wrists were cuffed to the bars, their arms pulled painfully over their head. Their lips trembled, and their cheeks were stained with tears.

"G-Gavin," Sam whimpered.

But this was... wrong. Sam's arm was hurt, they couldn't tolerate having their arms over their head like that. Gavin squinted, and felt, more than saw that Sam's right arm was still intact, uninjured. Their hair was shorter than he remembered it being – *when did I see them last?* – and their face was... rounder, as if they'd aged backwards. They looked so much younger.

They looked *exactly* the way they had when Gavin first took them from Isaac.

Gavin's stomach heaved and he jerked forward, only to gag as the collar choked him. "S-Sam, no, no, Sam... they didn't... t-take *you*...?" He looked around and shivered at the empty abyss that loomed just beyond the bars. When he looked at Sam again, he cried out in horror.

Leo Tierney stood at the foot of the cot, looking down at them with a hunger Gavin had seen in his face before. Bile rose in Gavin's throat as he wet his lips.

"L-Leo... no, no, I... I told you that you *couldn't*..."

Leo shrugged. "And what the *fuck* are you gonna do if I do fuck them, boss?" He gestured to his own neck and nodded at the collar around Gavin's. "Funny little predicament you found yourself in, huh?"

Gavin snarled and he jerked forward again, convulsing as the collar closed around his throat. "N-no. Leo... no, I... I will *kill you* if you touch them..."

Sam turned their head toward Gavin with wide, terrified eyes. "Gavin... p-please, I'll, I'll take the knife, I'll... *Please* don't let him... I'll... Y-you can drown me again, I—"

Gavin squeezed his eyes shut as sounds overtook him – the wet, choked screams as he gleefully poured water over the towel covering Sam's face, relishing the strain of their muscles, the thin wails when he finally let them up. He tried to clap his hands over his ears to block out the sound, but it crawled into his bones and settled there to rot.

Leo snorted and braced one knee on the cot. "All I wanted was a little fun. One little fuck. You're such a prissy little fuck, Stormbeck, you couldn't even let me have *that*. Fucking bitch." He shuffled forward on his knees onto the cot and pushed Sam's legs apart.

"N-no!" Sam sobbed, pulling helplessly against the cuffs. "N-no, *no, please, no…"*

Leo tipped his head back and drew in a slow, deep inhale. "Fuck, I love when they beg like that."

Sam looked to Gavin in terror. "G-Gavin, *please!* I… I'll t-tell you about the others, I… I'm sorry… I'll t-tell you *a-anything!"* They twisted away from Leo as he crawled over them on his hands and knees. They shuddered as he bent forward and dragged his tongue up their neck. *"PLEASE!"*

"No," Gavin croaked. "Leo, I… fuck, Leo, d-don't…"

"You made me wait so goddamned long," Leo sighed as he pushed Sam's shirt up, baring their stomach and chest, and bit down hard just below their collarbone. Their shriek split Gavin's head.

"Leo, *no!"* Gavin roared. He threw himself against the rope as Leo jerked Sam's pants down around their hips. "Leo, f-fuck, I, you can have *me,* for fuck's sake! You can… fuck, *LEO!"*

"I'll tell you everything!" Sam screamed as they heaved great, open-mouthed sobs. "I'll tell you! Please! Please don't!"

"You fucking leave them *alone!"* Gavin's scream was hoarse.

"I don't want you." Leo didn't even glance in Gavin's direction. "You're so fucking broken, you don't even fuck your own playthings. Why in the *fuck* would I want that? This one…" He drew his finger down the side of Sam's face, and they flinched away from his touch, begging wordlessly. "…is so sweet, and…" He snorted. "What the fuck is the point of fucking someone who's already broken?"

"No!" Sam wailed as they kicked out against Leo. They landed a kick to his stomach, and he grunted.

"Not like that," he growled, pinning them down to the cot. "Don't like it when you kick." He grasped their hips and jerked them towards him so the chain of the handcuffs snapped taut against the bars of the cell, the cuffs digging into Sam's wrists. They whimpered and tried to hide their face against their arm. Gavin squeezed his eyes shut and tried to catch his breath as he sobbed.

"Open your eyes, Stormbeck," Leo said with poison dripping from every word. "Open your *fucking eyes."*

166

Fresh tears streamed down Gavin's cheeks as he forced his eyes open. Leo had the fly of his pants open, his body pressing Sam down onto the cot. He met Gavin's eyes and grinned as he forced himself into Sam.

Gavin sobbed helplessly as Sam went rigid, sweat beading over their skin, their mouth pulled wide in a silent, desperate plea. Gavin begged through numb lips as Leo began to slowly roll his hips against Sam's. As Gavin watched, Leo sped up, fucking into them harder, pinning them down against the cot. They writhed under his touch, not even able to draw breath between their sobs. When Sam's voice rose with a scream, Gavin screamed with them, until the very air in the basement shook.

Chapter 25

Gavin woke to a faint pounding ache behind his left eye. The air felt so *cold,* and he felt so sick. He groaned, pushing himself upright, and froze at the horrifying familiarity of where he was – the bars surrounding him, the rope tied to the collar pulled tight against his neck, the burn of pain through the cane marks, the guard sitting at the desk in the corner, the dim lights above him that stabbed into his eyes... And he knew that somewhere outside the basement Schiester was waiting. And soon he was going to come down and hurt Gavin again.

He whimpered and let himself slump back down onto the cot, pulling the blanket up over his head. Perhaps if he laid perfectly still, the headache would go away.

Perhaps if he just ceased to exist, he'd be safe.

He pressed his hands against his forehead, tugged gently at his hair, rolled his neck in a weak, desperate attempt to push the headache out. He drew in slow, deep breaths, trying to push down the nausea that curled in his stomach. The room slowly spun around him as the pounding behind his eye became a stabbing pain bursting through his skull with every heartbeat.

The door to the basement opened. Gavin gasped and shot upright, then had to hold back a groan as the pain flashed through him. It lit his blood on fire; the lash marks flared to life just as hot, blunt agony pressed against the inside of his skull. He squinted up the stairs. Relief punched through his chest as he realized it was just another guard, a tray of food in hand.

The guard seated at the desk yawned and pushed himself to his feet, stretching his arms over his head. "Thank fuckin' Christ. Night shifts are—"

The guard holding the tray chuckled. "They suck, right?"

The other guard threw a look at Gavin that was somewhere between resentment and apathy. "We never keep them for this long. But... I mean, at least I get a differential..."

"Yeah, which you don't need, Davis," the new guard said, laughing. "The fuck are you gonna spend it on?"

Davis shrugged. "I don't know. Kids are getting bigger, they might need—"

"You know Schiester will cover what you need," the other guard said as he placed the tray of food on the desk where he would sit for the rest of his shift.

"Yeah," Davis croaked. "He's a good guy."

Gavin groaned and buried his face in his hands.

"Hey," the new guard snapped, and Gavin jerked his head up – only to clutch at the bars as the room wobbled around him. The guard turned to Davis. "Has he been moaning like that all night?"

Davis shrugged. "Nope. Mostly just slept."

The guard sighed. "Good. You on your four day now?"

"Yup." Davis gathered his things – lunch box, phone, charger. "I'll be back Saturday."

"Fun." The guard snorted. "Have a good weekend."

Davis nodded and crossed the basement to climb the stairs. "Later, Ginaro."

"Later."

Gavin leaned his forehead against the bars, for once grateful for the cold press of steel. The collar around his neck seemed only to increase the pressure in his head. His hand crept up to the buckle, fingers sliding over the metal and leather, and he fumbled mindlessly at the constriction at his throat.

"Did you not fucking hear Schiester?" Ginaro snapped.

Gavin froze. He swallowed painfully against the collar as his stomach heaved.

Ginaro snorted. "What part of 'leave it alone or I break your fingers' did you not fucking get?"

Gavin kept his eyes down. "S-sorry," he mumbled, his mouth dry.

He shivered and cringed back from the bars as Ginaro picked up the tray and stalked over to the cage. He set it on the floor outside the cage with the clatter of plastic on cement. Gavin flinched as the sound exploded through his head.

169

"Breakfast," Ginaro grunted. He turned his back and walked over to the desk, setting his lunch in the small refrigerator next to it.

Gavin looked at the tray sitting just out of his reach where he lay on the cot. There was a glass of water and a plate of dry toast with a scoop of scrambled eggs that looked somewhat fresh. Gavin thought he could see a tendril of steam rising from the eggs, although that might have just been because his left eye was blurry. His stomach lurched at the thought of eating. He groaned and curled up on his side, pulling the blanket up over his head.

"What?" Ginaro scoffed. "That food not good enough for you?"

"No," Gavin groaned. "Just—"

"Yeah, I imagine everything tastes like shit after the rich fuckin' food you're used to," Ginaro grumbled.

Gavin lifted his head and winced as he tried to focus on the guard sitting across the room, glaring at him. "I'm s-sorry," Gavin rasped, every heartbeat thundering through his head. "I… j-just…"

Ginaro rolled his eyes. "Spoiled shit," he said roughly, and pulled out his phone.

Gavin pressed his lips into a line, shivering under the blanket. He was hot and cold, goosebumps breaking out over his skin even as sweat prickled at his hairline. He wanted water. He wanted ice. He wanted his rizatriptan.

He wanted *Isaac*.

Tears brimmed in his eyes as he carefully lowered his head again. He wanted Isaac with him, to hold him through the waves of pain and nausea as the pressure grew in his head. He wanted Isaac's gentle hands in his hair, holding ice to the back of his neck, giving him sips of water and Edrissa's tea and the pills when he could keep them down. His skin ached with a longing, bitter desire so strong it burned him.

Slowly, painfully, he worked Isaac's t-shirt up over his back and shoulders, pulling it off over his head. It hung from the rope tying his collar to the bars of the cell, but he clutched it tight, burying his face in the cloth, shuddering from the faint smell of blood that permeated it now.

But underneath the metallic tang of blood, it still smelled like Isaac. Gavin had to hold onto it while it still smelled like Isaac.

Tears streamed from his eyes as he pressed his nose into the shirt. Sobs tightened in his throat, shook his shoulders, burned in his chest. He pressed a hand over his mouth, desperately trying to keep silent as his heart shattered.

He could barely breathe. He felt like he was being torn apart, slowly bludgeoned to death by the pain pounding behind his eye. His stomach heaved even as his muscles locked, trying not to make a sound. Every second dragged along his skin as he fought against himself; his throat burned with thirst, but if he moved to get the water, he thought he might be sick.

A deafening sound shot through the basement: Ginaro, scraping the chair against the floor to push it further away from the desk. The sound burst into agony in Gavin's head. He rolled in an agonized panic and vomited off the side of the cot.

"The fuck?" More noise as Ginaro got to his feet, his footsteps knocking against Gavin's brain. Sweat beaded on his face and he moaned as his stomach heaved again. The smell of his own vomit was heavy in the air around him.

"The fuck are you doing?" Ginaro snapped. "Jesus…" His voice came from just outside the bars. "Did you… Are you fucking sick or something?"

"N-no," Gavin groaned, knotting his own hands in his hair and pulling hard. "Please…"

Ginaro sighed. "Jesus Christ. You're gonna have to clean that up, I'm not fucking doing it."

Every word was like a blow to Gavin's head. "P-please," he breathed. He shoved his hands against his ears, trying to blot out the sound. "Please."

"Jesus Christ. They *said* you were fucking dramatic."

The words reached him slowly, muffled through his hands. An even fainter sound stabbed into his brain: the sound of Ginaro dialing a cell phone.

Gavin's head snapped up, and the room dipped dizzily around him. *"N-no,"* he gasped. "No, don't, don't t-tell him…" He stretched out his hand through the bars, grasping for the phone in Ginaro's hand. "Please, I-I'll clean it up…"

"I'm supposed to call him whenever you do something stupid," Ginaro snapped, and held the phone to his ear. "I'd say throwing up over nothing is pretty fucking stupid." Gavin sobbed weakly as Ginaro stepped away from the cell. He could hear the faintest murmur of Schiester's voice on the other end of the phone as he picked up, but couldn't decipher the words.

"Yeah, hey, boss. It's the Stormbeck kid."

"No, no, he didn't say anything new or…"

"No, not that, he's just… he's sick, I think."

"Puked all over the floor."

"I don't think so?"

"No, sir, just came down with his breakfast. He hasn't touched it."

"Davis said he just slept."

"Yes, sir. Did you want me to—"

"Okay. Yes, sir. I'll be here."

Ginaro hung up the phone and slipped it into his pocket.

"Please," Gavin whimpered, huddling under the blanket. "Please d-don't, *please,* he'll… h-hurt me, please, *no…"*

Ginaro scoffed. "Yeah, that's kinda the whole point of this bullshit." Gavin looked up at him pleadingly, and he rolled his eyes. "Never had to work in shifts before you showed up. You think I *like* this bullshit?" He turned and went to a door across the room. When he swung it open, Gavin could just barely make out the shapes of mops and cleaning supplies. Ginaro switched on the overhead light in the closet. Gavin flinched as the light stabbed into his eyes from all the way across the basement.

Ginaro grabbed a stack of threadbare towels, a trash bag, and a bottle of disinfectant before he turned and stopped just outside Gavin's cell. "Here," he said roughly as he passed them through the bars, one by one. "Clean that up. Towels go into the trash bag. Someone else will do your laundry for you – isn't *that* fucking nice?" He ground his teeth as he glared down at Gavin. "Get your ass up and clean. *Now.*"

Gavin groaned as he looked down at the puddle of vomit beside the cot. He pushed himself up on shaking arms and maneuvered around it, his feet landing on the cold cement floor. The cold air felt good on his head, but he shivered without Isaac's shirt. His head felt like it was about to split open as he slowly pulled the shirt back on. He crouched on the floor and pulled the cleaning supplies closer to him. The room didn't spin so badly when he was lower to the ground.

He took one towel and laid it over the puddle, mopping it up. He placed the towel into the trash bag and reached for another. He scrubbed the wet spot on the floor, shuddering, his stomach heaving weakly. That towel went into the bag too, and he reached for the disinfectant.

A deathly chill struck him when the door to the basement opened. Gavin froze, his hand still outstretched for the bottle. He trembled as he tilted his head up and squinted at the figure coming towards him, the picture of ease.

It was only when Schiester reached the bottom of the stairs that Gavin could really force his eyes to focus on him. He shuddered at the look of irritation that darkened Schiester's features.

"Is our Stormbeck guest not feeling well today?" Schiester said, his voice flat and cold. The words fell against Gavin's head like stones.

Gavin hung his head and slumped against the frame of the cot. He passed his hand over his face, wincing at the sweat on his fingertips.

"No comebacks today?" Schiester said mockingly. "No 'My name is Gavin Uriah'?"

Gavin pressed his lips together and stared at the floor. *That* is *my name. I don't need to say it to you for it to be true.*

Schiester tilted his head as he regarded Gavin. "It is interesting, though. We've had the boy for two days. Nothing in the food has made anyone else sick. Could it be…" Schiester lowered himself into a crouch, so he was eye-to-eye with Gavin. "…are you withdrawing from something? Did our Stormbeck boy get himself dependent on something we as his hosts haven't provided?" The mocking tone dug hooks into Gavin's flesh.

Gavin slowly shook his head, then leaned harder against the cot as the room dipped with the motion. His stomach heaved again and he pressed his hand to his mouth.

Schiester's eyes narrowed. "Speak to me, Stormbeck," he said, his voice a gentle threat. "Tell me what's wrong with you."

Tears rolled down Gavin's cheeks as he shivered, hot, cold, sweating, freezing. He wet his lips to speak. Even the sound of his breaths whispering through his lungs pressed against the inside of his skull.

"NOW, STORMBECK!" Schiester barked.

Gavin flinched back as if he'd been struck as pain exploded through his head. He slammed his hands over his ears and heaved a broken sob. His stomach roiled. He bent over, waiting for more bile to claw its way up his throat.

Through the roaring in his ears, Gavin could just make out Schiester's muffled voice saying, "Take your hands away from your ears, Stormbeck, or there will be consequences."

Gavin whimpered and slowly, slowly pulled his shaking hands away. A red-hot ice pick was being driven into his left eye.

"Good," Schiester said, and this time his voice was mercifully quiet. It still drilled into Gavin's head, but not nearly so much as his shout had. A smile pulled at Schiester's mouth. "Cover your ears again and I will tie your hands behind your back and blast loud music in here for as long as it takes for you to learn your lesson. Do I make myself clear?"

Gavin raised his gaze to Schiester. "Y-yes," he whispered.

Schiester nodded once. "Finish cleaning up."

Gavin blinked. He shivered as sweat soaked into Isaac's shirt. He reached out with one hand and grabbed the bottle of disinfectant. Under Schiester's watchful eye, and with Ginaro watching impassively behind him, Gavin sprayed disinfectant over the already-drying cement.

The smell was strong and bitter, and it burned inside Gavin's skull. He sobbed weakly as he reached for the last towel and scrubbed the cement until the smell of vomit was gone. Disinfectant was all Gavin could smell. It had crawled under his skin, the acrid fumes spiking the pain in his head. He dropped the towel into the trash bag and pushed everything towards the bars of the cage. He crawled to the cot and climbed onto it, barely holding down bile.

No one moved. Gavin was grateful for the silence, but he shivered with dread as he lifted his head again and looked at Schiester. Schiester's gaze burned into him.

"Tell me your name, boy," Schiester murmured.

Gavin groaned. "P-please, no."

A huff of laughter. "As I said before, Stormbeck, beg if you need to, but know that it will earn you no mercy. Tell me. What is your name?"

My name is Gavin Uriah.

Gavin wet his cracked lips. "Y-you… already know it." His insides twisted with terror, with dread, with self-loathing. *If I wasn't such a coward, I'd tell him my real name and tell him to go fuck himself.*

"Tell me your name, boy," Schiester said, voice raised. *"Now."*

"U-Uriah," Gavin whimpered, his hands creeping up towards his ears. He froze as he remembered Schiester's threat.

"Tell me your *fucking name!*" Schiester roared.

Gavin sobbed and writhed in agony. "G-Gavin Stormbeck!" he wailed. "M-my name is, is Gavin S-Stormbeck, *please…*"

The air in the basement still vibrated with the echo of Schiester's shout. Gavin trembled as he stared up at Schiester, his hands clutching the hem of Isaac's shirt.

"Now, was that so hard?" Schiester said softly.

Gavin lay stock-still under Schiester's gaze. He looked Gavin up and down, a faint smile on his face. "Ginaro," he said over his shoulder, "As long as someone is washing those towels, let's give that shirt a wash, too."

The words reached Gavin slowly, wading through the thick fog in his mind. Cold settled in his gut when he realized what Schiester meant. His fingers locked on the shirt as he looked back at Schiester, horrified.

"N-no," he breathed. "Sch-Schiester, no, *please…*"

"The thing is stained with your blood," Schiester said, his eyes fixed on Gavin like a snake as he walked to the door of the cell. "Doesn't that make you sick? Don't you *want* it clean?" He slid his hand into his pocket and drew out a set of keys.

"Please, no," Gavin whimpered, pushing himself back against the bars of the cell even as his head threatened to burst. "Schiester, *please…*"

Schiester unlocked the door and swung it open. Tears streamed from Gavin's eyes as Schiester took one step into the cage, then another. He stared down at Gavin as he pressed himself back against the bars.

Schiester reached out and gently traced Gavin's throat with one finger, just above the collar. "Move," he said gently, "And I will punish you. Do you understand?"

Gavin nodded weakly, his tear-filled eyes looking at Schiester in terror. His hands twisted in Isaac's shirt. His lip trembled. "P-please."

Slowly, Schiester untied the rope from Gavin's collar. Gavin shuddered and held still as Schiester let the rope fall to the cot. He swallowed and felt the collar press against his throat.

"Give me the shirt, Stormbeck," Schiester said, holding out one hand.

Gavin folded forward with a sob. "Please... *please,* let me keep it, *please*..."

Schiester snorted. "You are going to keep it, after it's washed. Give it to me. *Now.*"

Gavin brought a fistful of the shirt to his face and breathed, sobbing as he caught the last trace of Isaac he knew he'd ever have. His heart shattered in his chest. He shivered and clutched at the shirt, imagining Isaac's arms around him, lying down on sheets that smelled like Isaac—

Schiester grabbed a fistful of his hair and cracked his head back against the bars. Agony broke him open, and he could barely hear his own sobs as Schiester grabbed the shirt and dragged it off over Gavin's head. He was limp under Schiester's hands as they pulled the bloodstained shirt off his arms and shoved him back down against the cot. The rope was tied to his collar again. Agony stabbed his head with every heartbeat. His stomach heaved and roiled as the room spun around him, pain building and sharpening until he felt like he'd die if it lasted another moment.

And yet it lasted. He didn't die.

Every noise shattered through his skull as Schiester picked up the trash bag and the bottle of disinfectant, handed them to Ginaro, and left – his boots echoing on the cement stairs like gunshots. Gavin flinched at the slam of the door that crushed his skull. Tears streamed down his cheeks and soaked into the cot as goosebumps erupted over his skin. The guard returned to his desk. Gavin buried his face in his hands and wept Isaac's name over and over.

Chapter 26

Isaac could feel Sam's gaze on his back as he bent over his drawer. They stood in his bedroom doorway with their arms across their chest. One arm held tighter, always. Sam didn't even seem to notice anymore.

Isaac didn't think he could ever forget.

"So there's nothing I can say that could change your mind?" Sam said, their voice low.

Isaac's hand curled into a fist around the pair of socks he'd been about to stuff into his rucksack. He was already practically finished packing after only ten minutes at the task. With the drawer of his clothes almost cleared out, a few cans of food from the kitchen, and a spare set of sheets taken from the linen closet, he was ready to go. This place never quite felt like home – never quite felt *safe* – anyway. He had always been looking over his shoulder, always looking across the lake for figures moving among the trees.

Now he knew that there always was someone to fear out there, after all.

"No," he croaked. "There's nothing you can say. I'm going."

Sam made a soft, choked sound behind him. "I could—"

"And you're not coming with me," Isaac said. He couldn't force himself to look at them – not yet. He'd look at them before he left. He shoved the last pair of socks into his rucksack and fumbled to zip it up. His hands shook as he stood and swung the rucksack onto his shoulders, keeping his back to them. If he stayed in this room for a little while longer, with Gavin's things still untouched and with Sam still there behind him, he could protect the fragile thing in his chest that was about to shatter. He knew if he took that first step towards the doorway in his booted feet, then the next, then the next, the distance between him and Sam might stretch on and on and snap this time.

But if I don't go, I might not get Gavin back.

He squeezed his eyes shut, pressed his fingers into his eyelids until stars burst in his vision. This was always his choice, always had been: abandon the family he had to save the family he stood to lose. He hated himself for walking away.

If he let Gavin go, he would hate himself more.

He pulled his hand away from his face and waited for the stars to clear from his vision. He finally turned and forced himself to look at Sam.

"I need to be able to keep absolute focus," he said weakly.

"I would stay out of your way," Sam offered.

"That's not..." Isaac blew out a breath through his teeth. "I'm going to be in and out, Sam. I'm going to be following leads. Making connections with other groups. Searching with my own two fucking eyes half the time. I won't..." Another breath, and he swallowed hard, pushing down his grief and shame as he watched Sam's eyes fill with tears that they were obviously trying to fight. "I probably won't be in most of the time anyway."

"But when you are," they said, voice wavering, "I could be there. To help. If you need... anything."

"And if Schiester finds out that I'm searching?" Isaac's voice trembled. "If he sends men to the place Gray found for me and... like he did to Gavin back in Crayton? What if he does that and I'm not there?"

Sam shook their head. "Isaac... please just... let me come with you. Let me help you, *please*. I just want to... be with you, while you're hurting." They took a step forward into the room, then another. Isaac's throat ached and spasmed shut. He swallowed the lump there and blinked away his tears. "Please," Sam said as they reached out and took his hand. Isaac held very, very still, careful not to let his sleeve ride up as they squeezed his hand. "Please don't leave us right when we need you most."

A hardness flashed through Isaac's eyes. His jaw worked and he pulled his hand away from Sam's. "Gavin needs me the most right now," he said flatly. "He's the one who's dying." He leaned forward and pressed a rough kiss to the top of their head. "I'll visit when I can," he muttered as he brushed past them and left the room.

∴

Sam stared out of the empty doorway for a long time after Isaac left. Tears burned in their eyes, but they didn't let them fall. The hurt washing through Sam's veins felt almost as old as their relationship with Isaac itself. They drew in a deep breath through their nose and let it out again. Their arms fell to their sides, and they walked down the hallway into the living room.

Most of the others were there. Zachariah and Edrissa sat huddled on a couch together, hands clasped, shoulders hunched against each other. Tori stood in the kitchen and peered out at the living room as if in a daze. Vera sat in a recliner, her face drawn. Gray stood at the front window. Finn and Ellis weren't there; they had barely left their home down the lane since their initial sweep of their property. And Gavin... Gavin's absence seemed to be carved out of the room itself, as if all the air was disappearing into the chasm where he once sat.

Sam couldn't stand the room being so quiet. "He's already left?" they said dully.

Gray quickly looked at Sam when they broke the silence, as if they would have been startled if they could muster the energy. "Yes," they said. "He just pulled away."

Sam nodded and swallowed hard. "And he'll be... right down the road in Burmingham?"

"About twenty minutes away, yes," Gray said distractedly. "I found him a place – little more than a shack, really, if I'm honest – that's right by the highway that connects Burmingham with Crayton. So, it's not as close to here as it could be. But. Being close to the highway is, ah..." They trailed off into silence.

The silence grated on Sam's nerves. Hurt rankled into bitter resentment. They experimentally flexed their right hand open. The fingers twitched, but still only moved slightly. The steady throb of pain fueled the rancor growing inside them.

They opened their mouth and let the words they were thinking come out before they cared to hold them back. "Why did you help him find a place?" they demanded. The tears in their voice warped the demand into a plea.

Gray blinked, seeming to notice Sam for the first time. Realization dawned on their features. Their mouth creased into a sad, weary frown.

"Because he needed the help," they said. "He wasn't in any state to focus on the task himself, so I—"

"But is leaving really what he should be doing right now?" Sam whimpered.

Gray wordlessly stepped forward and pulled Sam into a tight hug. Sam accepted it, but didn't wrap their arms around Gray, like they used to. They pressed their face against Gray's chest and let their shirt soak up their tears.

"Isaac is allowed to leave," Gray murmured against their hair, even as Sam shook their head against the words.

"But—" Sam cut themself off. No more words came.

"Isaac is allowed to leave, if that's what he feels is best," Gray said, even fainter. "Even if it hurts. Even if it's temporary." Sam gritted their teeth as Gray whispered, just for them, "Even if I think it's bad for him in the long run, Sam, Isaac is allowed to leave *you*."

Sam pulled away from Gray's arms, and Gray let them go. They dashed the tears from their eyes and refused to look at anyone else as they stalked out into the backyard, trying not to think about who might be watching them from the distant shore.

Chapter 27

Sam chewed their lip as they stared into Isaac and Gavin's room again. It looked eerily empty, with Isaac gone now, too. Gavin's books were stacked on the nightstand and the sheets were still rumpled from the last time it had been slept in. That was days ago. The curtains were pulled back, letting in the warm afternoon sun as if nothing had changed.

Sam only felt a cold and stinging loss.

They blinked the tears from their eyes and gently touched the scar on their shoulder. The skin twinged under their fingers. Their throat was tight.

They jumped at the brush of bare feet down the hall, and the louder *thump* of heavier footsteps. Sam glanced over to see Edrissa approaching them with Zachariah just behind her, his head hanging low and his gaze on the floor.

"Hey, Sam," Edrissa murmured as she went to their side and distractedly kissed their cheek. Sam's eyes slid shut as the light, flowery smell of her perfume wafted over them, soothing the nervous stutter of their heart. They swallowed hard and met Zachariah's gaze as he shuffled to their side. They didn't think they'd seen Zachariah look this tired since...

Since he'd come to them two months ago, after almost two months on the road.

"Hey," Sam said, their gaze shifting between the two of them. "Any... any news?"

"What? Oh." Edrissa shook her head. "No. No one's back yet. But Sam, I... I w-wanted to talk to you both about... something." She glanced at Zachariah.

Sam followed her gaze. "Okay..." They let her take their hand and lead them into the living room. They shot a glance back at Gavin's room and shivered. Numbly, they let Edrissa lead them to a couch, a blanket still folded up on one arm from where Isaac had slept. Sam looked back at Zachariah. He was watching Edrissa, his eyebrows pulled together in concern. Dark circles were etched under his eyes. Sam felt the urge to glance at the window to make sure no one was watching from outside.

Edrissa stood before them both, wringing her hands, rocking forward and back. She tucked a strand of hair behind her ear and drew in a deep breath.

"Um…" She cleared her throat. "I want to… to go." She laced her fingers together. "I mean… leave. With you both."

Sam drew in a quick breath. "Go… Edrissa, it's not safe to—"

"It's not safe *here*," she murmured, meeting Sam's gaze, and they shivered with the intensity of it. "I mean… Gavin…"

Sam flinched.

Edrissa swallowed hard. "Gavin l-left—"

"He didn't leave," Sam said quickly, an ache shooting through their chest. Their eyes smarted. "He didn't. You read the note. He would *never* have—"

"I didn't mean left," Edrissa whispered. She stared down at her hands as she twisted her fingers together. "I'm… I'm sorry."

Zachariah shifted forward in his seat. His arms squeezed tight around his chest; his shoulders crept up around his ears. His voice was hoarse when he spoke. "Edrissa…"

"I didn't mean left," she said softly, rocking back on her heels. "Sorry, I meant… Gavin…" She tilted her face up towards the ceiling, her eyes shining with tears. "Someone came into this house and… and *took* Gavin," she murmured. "From… from *Isaac's bed*. Isaac was… was sleeping, and…" She shrugged jerkily. "If someone can take Gavin like that…" She fixed her gaze on Zachariah. "I d-don't want to wait around for—"

"B-but no one knows I'm here," Zachariah said, hunching forward. "I haven't been outside since… I mean… no one…" His voice faded away into silence.

"No one knew Gavin was here, either," Edrissa said softly. "At least I… I didn't… *think*…"

"But… leaving?" Sam ran their fingers over their palm, wincing at the dull pressure, the numbness. "Edrissa… where we are right now is probably the safest in the…" They wet their lips, sagged with exhaustion at the ever-present ache in their chest that had been there ever since Isaac left. "While we're still here, Isaac can…"

Edrissa shifted her eyes down. Sam sat up straighter. Anger burned in them, crowding out the ache.

"Edrissa," they said, their jaw tightening. "Isaac can… can *protect* us…"

"No, he can't," she breathed. "He isn't even *here*." She shrank back, as if expecting Sam to start shouting. As if expecting Sam to wind back and hit her.

Sam pressed their trembling lips together. Tears blurred their eyes. "We c-can't just… *leave,*" they whispered. "Everyone needs us, Edrissa. With everyone out looking for Gavin… with Gray being so upset and, and *Isaac…*" Tears ran down their cheeks, and with them, their vision cleared. "I can't leave *Isaac.*"

Edrissa fixed Sam with a long, heavy stare before shifting her gaze to the floor. "But Zachariah…" She hugged herself tight and rocked forward again. She bit her lip. "I don't know, Sam, I was just thinking that… maybe if we go further north, I mean, if we find out where Mathias was going to send him in the first place…"

"But I'm needed here," Sam said, their heartbeat quickening. The scar on their shoulder burned. "I mean, I… I d-don't do… as much as the others, but—"

"That's not true," Zachariah said, his mouth twisting.

Sam swallowed bitterness. They pushed out a slow breath and looked up at Edrissa. "I need to stay here."

"But if we go further north—" Edrissa's voice rose. "—we can stay safe. Zachariah will be… will be safe."

"We're safer with the family," Sam said, bristling. "Edrissa… with the family's work with the refugees, and with Vera and Isaac to protect us… this is where we belong. This is where we're safe."

"But—"

"I want to stay with Isaac," Sam said. Edrissa's mouth closed slowly. Sam's left hand squeezed into a fist as they looked from Edrissa to Zachariah and back.

"But…" Edrissa blinked tears away. "Sam…"

"Isaac's my brother," Sam said, their voice breaking. "And he just lost his boyfriend. And Gavin is… I love him, too."

Edrissa's eyes went wide, the blue only sharpening with the shock on her face. "Sam… Gavin is—"

"I love him, too," Sam said again. Their head fell forward as Edrissa stared at them with a look bordering on disbelief – shot through with pity.

"Sam," Edrissa murmured. "Gavin isn't—"

"If you say he's never coming back…" Sam said, their head snapping up. Their lips trembled as they looked up at Edrissa, more tears burning in their eyes.

Edrissa pressed her lips together and said nothing.

Sam pushed through their numbness as they turned to Zachariah. "Do you… d-do you want to leave?" they rasped.

Zachariah's eyes darted between Edrissa and Sam, and he shrank back even more. "I…"

"We *need* to leave," Edrissa said meekly. "Zachariah… you could be… we c-could be…"

"Who else would take me in?" he said, desperately meeting her gaze. "Mathias said he could send me somewhere else, but… who else knows about Gavin?" Zachariah plaintively held out his hands to her. "We don't know if nobody knows, or if it's this giant unspoken secret across the entire north. *Someone* clearly knew about him. Once people know where I came from, and who I've been staying with…" He glanced at Sam. "Sam? You know more about… about…"

"I'm the one who was north for the month when they were gone," Edrissa said roughly. "I know more about being up here than—" She gasped softly and took another step back. "I'm sorry," she whispered. "That… that was mean."

Sam stared at her, dumbfounded. "Edrissa… if you don't feel safe with us, then okay, we'll do our best to find you a safer place. But… it's different, for Zachariah." They looked at him. "With the tattoo, and with him being tied to the Stormbeck house…"

Zachariah bowed his head and looked at his hands, folded in his lap.

Edrissa looked at Zachariah. "Well, I'm…" She sniffed and tossed her hair over her shoulder. "I'm going. If you want to stay, Sam, fine. But… I want to find a safer place with Zachariah."

Sam froze. Disbelief jangled their nerves as they looked at Edrissa, the blue of her eyes getting colder as they watched. They glanced at Zachariah and he was looking between the two of them, stricken. His knuckles were white, hands still locked together in his lap.

"Z-Zachariah," Sam said numbly. "If… if you want to go, that's… I can talk to Gray, I can see if they can… I mean…" They fought back tears, shoved down the stinging in their chest as Edrissa's words echoed: *If you want to stay, Sam, fine.*

"I…" Zachariah looked to Edrissa. "Edrissa… I really don't…" He drew in a deep breath and blew it out slowly. "I… I don't know if I'll find anywhere… safer. I tried. I—"

"Gavin was taken out of his bed in the middle of the fucking night with *Isaac fucking Moore* in bed next to him," Edrissa snapped, eyes blazing. "This family isn't *safe* if that can happen to the person Isaac loves most—" Her mouth snapped shut as she looked again to Sam. "I mean…"

Sam slumped back against the couch, their eyebrows pulling together. Their mouth opened, then closed again. The tears spilled over their cheeks. They didn't try to stop them.

"Isaac loves me, too," Sam said softly.

Edrissa nodded jerkily, and her own tears fell. "I know that," she murmured. "I wasn't trying to say—"

"But you did," Sam said. Their voice cracked. "And now you think… what, now that Gavin's gone, Isaac doesn't care enough to protect the rest of us? Is that it?" Their right hand spasmed, and they sucked in a breath through their teeth. "Because he… he would still… die for *any* of us," they said, glaring up at her. "Including *you*, you know."

"Um…" Edrissa nervously fiddled with a strand of hair.

"And you," Sam said, looking at Zachariah. Zachariah looked at the floor.

Sam swiped at the tears still rolling down their cheeks. "I know Gavin was taken under all our noses," they said, their voice tight with bitterness. "And

I know that… it could have been… worse." Zachariah flinched. "And… maybe it isn't… *safe* to stay with us. But I don't think anywhere else would be *safer*."

Edrissa chewed her lip until it bled. "Isaac is… is *angry* that Gavin is gone," she whispered.

Sam dragged a weary hand through their hair. "He's not angry at *you*," they said heavily.

"But…" Edrissa whimpered and fell silent.

Sam opened their mouth to argue, to insist Isaac would never hurt her, would never be angry at her for this… and stopped short as a memory flashed across their mind. Isaac, shivering in the cold on their way north, telling Sam how close he'd been to killing Gavin in the woods.

"I almost killed him, Sam. And Edrissa."

"No, you didn't. You wouldn't have done it."

Sam trembled as they looked up at Edrissa, at how she pulled away from them, as if she was afraid of their touch. Their breath froze in their chest. Slowly, just like they'd seen Isaac do so many times, they put their hands at their sides, open, empty. Harmless.

"Edrissa," they said softly. "I'm not leaving. I want… I want to help the others. And…" They drew in a sharp breath. "I want to stay with them. They're my *family*."

Edrissa sniffed and looked at Zachariah. "Then… w-we'll go together," she said, and Sam wilted at the sharp bitterness in her voice. "I can ask Gray where Mathias was going to send you, and we'll go… together." She held her head high, even as tears coursed down her cheeks.

Zachariah rubbed his hands against his knees, looking from Sam to Edrissa and back. Finally, he fixed his dark brown eyes on Edrissa. He bit his lip and shook his head.

"I can't," he croaked.

Edrissa went rigid. "…what?" she breathed.

Zachariah wrapped his arms tight around himself again, muscles shaking. Sam wondered if he was leaving bruises on himself. "It's not safer anywhere else," Zachariah said, exhaustion weighing heavy on his face. "And… Edrissa… I'm *tired* of running."

"We wouldn't be running." She sounded so much younger than she had a minute ago. "We'd just be—"

"And I'd be looking over my shoulder every day," he said. Sam's throat tightened as they looked at him, and they tried not to feel the swell of relief in their chest at Zachariah's words. His gaze flicked to theirs for the briefest moment. "And... yeah, it's not exactly safe *here* but... I'd rather be here than running again."

"You can't even go outside right now," she said breathlessly.

"I wouldn't be able to go outside anywhere else we find, either," he murmured.

"Yes, you could," she said, her voice rising, desperation filling her widening eyes. "You just can't go outside *here* because someone could be watching the house."

"I wouldn't feel *safe* to go outside, no matter where we went," Zachariah said, and for the first time, his voice trembled. "This is the safest place I know."

Edrissa folded in on herself, and she fixed on Zachariah with a look of hurt that crushed Sam's heart. Their eyes smarted. Tears blurred the corners of their vision. All they wanted was to stand and pull Edrissa into their embrace, kiss the tears from her cheeks, tell her it would all be alright—

But nothing would ever be alright again, if the others didn't find Gavin. Nothing would ever be alright again if Gavin's shoes stayed untouched by the door, if his bed remained unmade forever, if Isaac never came back, if he walked around like a ghost for the rest of his life because Gavin was gone or dead or *worse...*

They pressed their hand over their mouth. They squeezed their eyes shut when they saw the others' gazes both turn to them at the same time. They wiped the tears from their cheeks and forced themself to open their eyes to meet Edrissa's gaze.

"I-if you want Gray to contact Mathias," they said, fighting to keep their voice even, "They'll see if he can find you somewhere safe for you." They swallowed the lump in their throat.

"I... I'm not going *alone...*" Edrissa whispered, looking at Sam in horror.

Sam's lips quivered. "I know Isaac scares you," they murmured, trembling. "But... this is my *family*. This is the only family I've ever had. And I'm staying here."

Edrissa blinked and looked at Zachariah, her face blank. "You?" she snapped.

"I..." Zachariah shivered but held her gaze. "This is where I'm safest. And I... w-want to stay here."

Edrissa's throat bobbed as she stared back at Zachariah. She took a step back. "Fine," she hissed.

This time, Sam did get to their feet. "Edrissa..."

"I'll take all your stuff out of my room," she said brokenly, her lips thin. She didn't look at Sam. "Then I'm going to take a walk. Alone." She turned on her heel, then stopped. "Isaac left you," she whispered, then stalked down the hall towards the bedrooms.

Sam's lungs froze in their chest. They stood, paralyzed, until Zachariah heaved a sob. His hand slid into theirs and he gently pulled them down to sit on the couch next to him. They numbly wrapped their arms around him.

Zachariah clutched at them and pressed his face against their shoulder. "I c-can't go," he whimpered.

"I know," Sam said, trying to ignore their own tears, the way their stomach tied itself in knots.

It's not true. Isaac will come back. He's already been back once, because he forgot something. He'll come back when he needs something.

"I would... would go with you, if it was safe," Zachariah rasped. "But it's not. I... s-spent almost *two months* finding you. I... didn't think I would... I'm so *tired* of running..."

"You don't have to run," Sam said, doing their best to be soothing. Their voice just sounded dead and flat.

He didn't leave me. I can... go to his house right now, and he's probably there. I could probably see him. He still cares.

He would still protect us.

"I understand why she wants to go." Zachariah looked towards the hall. "I get it. But... I... c-can't..."

Sam gently stroked his hair and said nothing. Edrissa appeared again, studiously keeping her gaze away from Sam and Zachariah. She stalked past them through the living room and headed towards the back of the house. Sam could hear the sliding door open, then thud closed. They buried their face in Zachariah's neck as Zachariah heaved another sob. This time, Sam sobbed with him.

Chapter 28

Gavin woke with a kick to the gut. He gasped and moaned weakly, covering his head with his hands as he looked up at the guard standing over him. His left eye felt too big for his skull, like it would burst out of his head if he moved too fast. His ears rang and his stomach heaved.

The guard held out a gray cotton shirt. Gavin's heart ached as he looked at it, faint brown lines still staining the back. His hand shook as he reached out to take it. Despair crept into his heart as he pressed the shirt to his face and breathed.

The shirt smelled like homemade soap and the faint tang of disinfectant. Tears burned in his eyes as he muffled a sob.

"Hold still," the guard said briefly, and reached out for Gavin's collar. Gavin gasped and jerked back, then groaned as pain crescendoed in his head.

The guard rolled his eyes. "What fucking part of 'hold still' do you not... Jesus Christ." He loosened the knot tying the collar to the bars of the cage. Gavin blinked as he looked up at the guard, who gestured impatiently with his hand. "Put the fucking shirt on," he snapped.

Gavin fumbled to obey. He pulled the shirt over his head, wincing as the motion tugged at the scabs that had formed where the cane had broken his skin. He gingerly eased the shirt down over his back and forced himself not to move again as the guard retied the rope to the collar. He pulled the blanket around his shoulders and shivered as he looked up at the guard, who still stood over him, digging in his pocket. The guard pulled out a phone.

Gavin's eyes fell shut. "P-please..." he rasped. "I was... was *good*, I did what you... w-wanted..." He opened his eyes again and stared up at the guard, tears spilling down his cheeks. "Please don't call him."

"Not calling him," the guard grunted. He tapped the phone's screen a few times.

"Th-then... what...?"

"Shut up," the guard ordered. "Boss wanted you to see something."

Dread clutched at Gavin's heart. His throat seemed to close as he tried to peek at what the guard was doing. After a moment, the guard turned the phone around and held it in Gavin's face. Ice poured through Gavin's stomach and his breath froze in his chest.

On the screen, there was the blurry image – no, *video* – of two people sitting at a table, huddled together. The woman's brown hair was a mess around her pale face, her eyes wide, her face haggard with exhaustion. The man had his arm around her shoulders, his own gaze fixed on someone standing behind the camera. Terror struck Gavin like a fist.

Lucy and Topher.

"N-no," Gavin whispered. "No, *no*…" The words died in his throat as a familiar voice came from the phone.

"Thank you for being willing to speak with me," the smooth, even voice said. Gavin's stomach heaved at Schiester's tone.

"Y-yeah," Topher said. *"Of, of course. Wh-whatever we can… can do."*

"Once we talk with you," Lucy said softly, visibly shivering despite the blurry picture, *"We can… can…?"*

"You'll be provided with temporary lodgings until we can find a more permanent solution," Schiester said. Gavin's lips felt numb as tears formed in his eyes. *"With our gratitude. I know I speak for Tori Nasser and her family when I say, I'm very grateful for the role you played in getting them north."*

"No," Gavin sobbed weakly, and pressed a hand to his mouth.

"We just, um… h-helped with what they needed," Topher said weakly. *"I'm glad we could be there."*

"Of course." There was a shuffling sound, and Lucy and Topher both looked past the camera, presumably at Schiester. *"Just a few questions. I won't take much of your time."*

Gavin clutched at the hem of Isaac's shirt as he stared at the phone, horrified.

Schiester cleared his throat. *"What was the nature of your employment in the Stormbeck region?"*

Lucy and Topher glanced at each other. *"V-vet tech,"* Topher said weakly.

"Accountant," Lucy said, leaning against Topher.

"Self-employed?" Schiester asked, and Topher wet his lips.

"N-no," Topher said. *"I worked for Fort Meyers Emergency Veterinary. But I did some stuff on the side, yeah. For people who couldn't afford the vet."*

Lucy blinked. *"And I worked for Franklin's Grocery,"* she said. *"Th-they're a, a family-owned—"*

"Thank you," Schiester said softly, and Lucy fell silent.

"No, no, no... *please*..." Gavin whispered against his hand. His skin felt like it was on fire. The guard said nothing, just held the phone out for Gavin to see.

"Now, when Tori Nasser and her people made it to your home," Schiester continued, *"You rendered medical aid to one of them?"*

"Sam." Topher's voice broke. *"Th-their name is Sam. Please, did they... d-did they make it?"* His face twisted, and he looked like he was on the verge of tears.

Schiester was silent for a long moment. Then, *"Yes. They survived. They are alive and well, living a few hours north of here."*

Topher let out a breath of relief. *"Thank god,"* he murmured. *"Oh... thank god."*

"This was on the day of the Stormbeck overthrow, yes?" Schiester said, and there was an undercurrent of a threat beneath his gentle tone. The hair on the back of Gavin's neck stood up.

"Um..." Topher glanced at Lucy. *"Yeah. When they, um, escaped."*

"Tori and her family?"

"Yes." Again, Topher and Lucy shared a look. Gavin could see the fear in their eyes.

There was the sound of rifling papers again. *"And... what of the Stormbecks?"*

Gavin thought he might be sick.

Topher swallowed hard. *"Wh-what about them?"*

The seconds dragged on, each one stabbing into Gavin's mind. He scarcely dared to breathe as he watched Lucy glance at Topher.

"Th-they're all dead... right?" she said softly.

"Fuck," Gavin whimpered, and folded forward, clutching the side of the cot. "F-fuck, *no...*"

"That is what we've been told," Schiester said, every word perfectly formed, carefully pronounced. *"That is our understanding from reports we've heard, yes."*

Topher visibly relaxed. *"Good,"* he huffed.

"However," Schiester continued, *"Reports can be... incomplete."*

The blood drained out of Lucy and Topher's faces.

"Did you," Schiester said softly, *"Provide aid to any syndicate members on that day?"*

Gavin's heart thundered in his chest. His eyes were wide, streaming with tears.

"Um..." Lucy said softly, her shoulders hunched as she leaned over the table. *"N-no. Just... just the family."*

Gavin heaved a sob and bent forward until his forehead pressed against the cot. "No!" he wailed.

Schiester pushed out a slow breath. Gavin's head snapped up again as a seat creaked behind the camera. Schiester's figure appeared on the screen, towering over Lucy and Topher where they sat huddled in their seats. They both looked up at him with wide eyes as he brushed past them and opened a door behind them.

"Ziegler, Alvarado, come in here please."

Gavin whined softly as the two guards stepped into the room, just in the camera's view. Lucy met Topher's eyes, and they both turned to look at Schiester.

"Downstairs, please," Schiester said smoothly.

"NO!" Gavin screamed. He lurched forward, clawing at his collar.

The guard holding the phone took a stumbling step back. The two guards dragged Lucy and Topher out of their chairs.

"NO!" Topher screamed, and threw a clumsy punch at Alvarado. Alvarado ducked it effortlessly and slammed his fist against Topher's stomach.

Topher doubled over with a choked gasp. Lucy sobbed as Ziegler pulled her hands behind her and tied them there.

"Topher!" Lucy sobbed. Alvarado jerked Topher upright and tied his hands behind him, too. Over the phone speakers, Lucy let out a warped, piercing scream. Gavin shivered and he lifted his head as he heard the faint echo of the scream coming from upstairs.

The guard turned off the phone screen and tucked it into his pocket. He took a step closer and grabbed Gavin's hands as he fumbled for the rope on his collar.

"N-NO!" Gavin screamed, shoving at the guard's hands. "No, *no!"*

The guard shoved Gavin back against the bars, knocking the breath out of him. As he gasped for air, the cane marks on his back burning like they were fresh, the guard dragged him forward by his shirt and pinned him on his stomach on the cot. Gavin sobbed as the guard pulled his hands behind his back. A zip tie tightened around his wrists. He looked up as the door to the basement opened. Lucy's screams pierced his skull.

"N-no, no, *please!"* Lucy shrieked as Ziegler dragged her down the stairs. "N-no I, please, please don't…"

"Lucy!" Topher bellowed as Alvarado pulled him along behind her. *"Lucy!"*

Behind them all, Schiester slowly descended, with a sick, venomous smile on his face.

Lucy's screams stopped when she saw Gavin. Her eyes went wide, and she looked back at Schiester.

"N-no," she whimpered, her face glazed with tears. "No, they s-said he was, was *good*, I, I thought… I—"

"We didn't help him!" Topher gasped as the guards reached the lowest stair and began to drag them both across the floor to the gallows. "We didn't do anything for him! He was just there!"

"Please, no!" Lucy sobbed. She twisted in Ziegler's grip as he dragged her up the steps of the gallows. *"PLEASE!"*

"Schiester," Gavin sobbed. "Schiester, please, *please,* it's not their fault, they d-didn't help me…" He shuffled forward on his knees, crawling to the edge of the cot. "Please! They, they sh-shouldn't die because of me, *please!*" He yanked against the zip tie, hissing through his teeth as hot blood dripped down his hands. The third guard stepped out of the cell and pulled the barred door closed behind him.

Topher dug in his heels and threw his weight against Alvarado. Alvarado aimed another punch at his gut and he fell to his knees, gasping.

"TOPHER!" Lucy shrieked, dropping to her knees like a stone. Ziegler wrestled her to her feet and dragged her across the platform. *"TOPHER!"*

"L-Lucy, no, *Lucy!*" Topher kicked out at Alvarado. He desperately sought Schiester's gaze. "M-mercy, *please,* we... we d-didn't do anything *wrong!*"

Schiester watched them placidly. Ziegler forced Lucy to stand as he slipped a noose around her neck and pulled it tight. She sobbed wordlessly as Topher was dragged to her side.

"Please," Topher sobbed as the other noose was pulled tight around his neck. His eyes were wild with terror. "Please."

"Sch-Schiester..." Gavin wailed as Schiester stood in front of the platform and looked up at Topher and Lucy. "Schiester, don't kill *them!* They didn't do *anything!*"

"You are being charged with collusion and fraternization with Gavin Stormbeck," Schiester said softly.

"NO!" Gavin screamed as he threw himself against the rope restraining him.

"And for that the penalty is death."

Gavin choked on the taut collar as he thrashed; the plastic zip tie cut even deeper into his skin. His wrists were a mess of blood.

"P-please, we, we didn't... we just h-helped *Sam,*" Topher sobbed. He shook violently from head to toe as he gasped against the noose. *"Please,* we... we d-did the, the right thing..."

"And I'm sure Sam Vasterling is grateful," Schiester said softly.

"Y-you, you, you *did* this!" Lucy shrieked, fixing panicked eyes on Gavin. "You sh-showed up and, and, no no no *no no please!*"

"You may give your last words now," Schiester said calmly. He folded his hands behind his back and tipped his head up to meet Lucy and Topher's eyes.

"No," Lucy sobbed, stumbling. "No, *please.*"

"I d-don't want to die," Topher pleaded. He whimpered and looked desperately at Schiester. "I don't want to die."

Schiester nodded solemnly. "I hear your last words. I now put you to death."

"NO!" Lucy screamed, sobbing so hard she could barely breathe. Topher stood frozen, his eyes wide and streaming tears, his gaze unfocused as Schiester walked to the side of the platform and placed his hand on the lever.

"Topher," Lucy whimpered, staring desperately at him. He turned blank, horrified eyes to hers.

Schiester pushed the lever on the gallows, and the platform dropped.

A wordless scream tore from Gavin's throat. Topher and Lucy fell for what seemed like an eternity before they both jerked to a stop. A *snap* echoed across the basement.

Topher hung still, his eyes blank, his body limp and lifeless. Lucy's legs kicked out, her body twitching and convulsing as the rope constricted around her throat. Her face went red, then purple; her eyes were wide and bulging as she fought for air. Slowly, her struggles weakened, then stopped. Her still face was a rictus of agony.

Gavin knelt on the cot, his eyes transfixed on them both, his heart hammering in his chest. He couldn't move. Couldn't *breathe.*

Finally, Schiester stepped forward and pulled the lever back. There was a screech of gears and the platform raised to return to its position, lifting up Lucy and Topher's corpses with it in a macabre display as they dangled from the nooses.

Schiester slowly climbed the steps of the platform as Gavin watched. Gavin's blood burned in his veins, and his throat closed as the collar seemed to tighten. Schiester went first to Topher's side, feeling for a pulse in his neck. After a long moment, he went to Lucy and did the same. Then he nodded and descended the steps again. He motioned at the three guards. Two guards stepped forward without a word, and the third went to the closet to get something – two body bags.

Schiester walked slowly to stand in front of the cell, seeming to savor the tears streaming down Gavin's face, the tortured, whimpering breaths he heaved past the collar. Gavin raised his gaze to Schiester, suddenly numb.

"You killed those people," Schiester said gently.

Gavin lurched forward with a sob. *"No,"* he croaked. "No, no, *no*..."

"Yes," Schiester said. "You showed up on their doorstep, and they made the choice to help you. Their deaths are on you."

Gavin looked pleadingly up at Schiester. His wrists stung; around the broken skin, he could feel the blood oozing into his shirt and the back of his pants. His eyes were wide and unfocused, his heart pounding weakly in his chest. Tears streamed down his cheeks. Schiester glanced behind him, and Gavin saw the guards had finished taking Lucy and Topher down. Two full body bags lay next to the platform. Gavin's head spun. His stomach heaved and he slumped forward.

There was a rattle of keys in the lock, and Gavin looked up to see Schiester unlock the cell door and push it open. Gavin fell back, his body and mind scraped hollow. He looked blankly up at Schiester.

"Your turn," Schiester said with a grin.

Gavin's eyes went even wider. "N-no," he rasped. He pulled weakly against his restraints. *"No,"* he whispered.

"Oh, I think it's time," Schiester said, and stepped into the cell. He shoved a knee against Gavin's chest and reached for the rope tied to his collar.

"N-no," Gavin heaved, writhing under the crushing weight on his chest. He dragged in a breath as the rope came away and Schiester got to his feet.

"Come on, Stormbeck," Schiester said through his teeth, his voice no longer cool and even. He gripped Gavin's collar and dragged him from the cot onto the cold floor of the cell.

"No," Gavin choked out, kicking out jerkily as Schiester dragged him across the floor, toward the gallows. Ziegler stepped forward and grabbed his legs just as Alvarado wrapped his arms around Gavin's chest. They lifted him bodily and carried him up the stairs to the gallows as Gavin twisted and sobbed.

"P-please," Gavin panted as they dropped him roughly to the platform. He cried out as pain shot through his back.

"Get one arm free," Schiester snapped.

Alvarado knelt and shoved Gavin onto his side. He reached for the knife on his belt and cut through the zip tie with one quick jerk of his hand. Gavin wrenched away from Alvarado's grip and screamed as he was forced onto his back, his right arm held out and pinned to the platform.

Schiester drew his own knife and lowered himself to his knees beside Gavin as the guards pinned him down. Sweat beaded on Gavin's forehead as he sobbed and gasped for breath.

"You'll die marked for what you are," Schiester growled, and pressed the tip of his knife to the inside of Gavin's forearm, at the wrist.

As Gavin's voice broke, an echo of memory gripped him: his mother's voice, soft and sweet: *"I'd never let you die without you remembering who you are."*

Gavin sobbed through gritted teeth before his throat went raw from screaming. Schiester carved the tip of the knife into Gavin's arm again and again, cutting a design – or a word. Gavin turned his head to look, his stomach churning with the smell of blood in the air. Schiester bent over Gavin's arm, obscuring what he was doing. Gavin thrashed against the guards holding him down.

Again and again, Schiester cut him, and dread poured down Gavin's spine with the pattern: a curving line, a cross, a circle. He turned his head and wretched with the pain. Nothing came up but bile. Tears streamed back into Gavin's hair as his screams echoed off the walls. Schiester cut deep, further and further up his arm until he reached the crook of his elbow. He wiped the blade on Gavin's shirt and tucked it back into his belt.

"Up," Schiester ordered as he got to his feet and stepped back.

Gavin sobbed and looked at what Schiester had carved into his skin, convulsing with horror at the red letters cut into his flesh, the rivulets of blood streaming from each wound:

STORMBECK.

His arms were pulled behind him and his wrists tied again. Alvarado dragged him to his feet by his collar and looped the noose around his neck. The rope pulled tight around his throat, sitting just above the collar. Alvarado stepped away, leaving Gavin trembling, heaving forward with each sob. His blood dripped onto the platform beneath his feet.

The guards followed Schiester as he stalked off the platform. Gavin tipped back his head and sobbed as Schiester's hand settled on the lever.

"I-Isaac," he whimpered, stumbling over the name. "Isaac, Isaac, Isaac, Isaac, Isaac, I'm *sorry*..." He squeezed his eyes shut, every nerve blazing, and prayed he would die fast, like Topher.

He prayed he'd see his family again, someday.

If there's something after this, I'm not going where they are.

"P-please," he choked. He kept his eyes shut. He held his breath, waiting for the drop, the *snap,* the tightening of the rope that he'd felt in January at the hands of Schiester's men. He waited to die. He waited for it to be over.

A moment passed.

Then another.

He opened his eyes, dizzy, and looked over at Schiester. Schiester was watching him with a smile. Schiester lifted his hand from the lever. Gavin dragged in a terrified breath.

"Oh, Stormbeck," Schiester murmured. "You don't think you've suffered enough yet... do you?"

Gavin stared at him, his skin burning. Every heartbeat was a knife in his chest.

Schiester chuckled. "Get him down."

Gavin dragged in a breath like he was on the verge of drowning. "Wh-what..."

Two guards climbed the stairs to the platform. They loosened the rope and tugged the noose off over Gavin's head. They shoved him towards the stairs. He fell to his knees, his legs too numb to hold himself up. He choked as Ziegler grabbed his collar and dragged him down the stairs. He stumbled as he tried to stand, to breathe.

Numbly, Gavin looked at Schiester as he was dragged back into his cell, as the rope was tied to his collar again. His forearm tingled, the pain not even reaching him as Ziegler cut the zip tie binding his wrists. He tried to find words, and failed.

Schiester stepped forward and peered through the bars of the cage at Gavin. Gavin was sure he would shatter under the ice of Schiester's gaze.

"You have not *begun* to suffer, Stormbeck," Schiester hissed. "When you have suffered enough to pay for your sins... then, and *only* then..." He glanced behind him, at the gallows. "...will you be put to death. Until then..." He turned on his heel and crossed to the stairway out of the basement. "Let me know if those wounds require stitches," he snapped at the guards. "In a few hours, wash it with salt water. I want it to scar."

Chapter 29

Weeks later

Vera chewed her lip as she put the car in park. She stared up at the house in front of her – barely more than a shack really. The weeds were overgrown in the yard, choking out the grass. The paint on the walls was peeling, flakes of it littered on the pebbles along the sides of the house. She turned the car off and opened the door. A breeze ruffled her hair, a cooler day at the tail end of summer. She drew in a deep breath as she picked her way over the cracked sidewalk up to the front door. The drapes were pulled shut over the windows, giving the already dilapidated house the look of abandonment. She raised her fist and knocked three times.

Through the thin door, Vera could hear rustling and took a step back. Her heart leapt in her chest as the lock slid back and the door opened. Isaac looked out, his eyes wide, his face haggard. His hair was pulled back from his face with an elastic, with some lank, sandy-blond strands escaping to brush his face. His beard was ragged, uneven, as if he had simply grabbed clumps of it and cut it with scissors when it got too long – and Vera had no doubt that's exactly what he'd done. Dark circles were carved under his eyes. His shirt looked worn, wrinkled, as if he'd been sleeping in it for days. When she glanced behind him, she saw a room lit only by what light had made it past the curtains, furnished with only a mattress and a sleeping bag on top.

Vera wet her lips. "Hey, Isaac," she murmured.

Isaac's eyes flicked down to the floor and back up. "Hey," he croaked. When he raised his gaze again to her, she noticed his eyes were red.

"Heard you were back." Vera shrugged. "Can I, um… can I come in?"

Isaac's eyes widened. "Is there news? Did you—"

"No," Vera said heavily. "No. I'm sorry."

Darkness settled over Isaac's face once again. He stepped back and opened the door wider. Vera passed by him, her heart aching as her gaze moved around the mostly empty room. Her boots made a hollow sound against the worn wooden floor.

"You just get back?" Vera said softly as Isaac walked past her and into the back room, a tiny kitchen with a bathroom just off to the side.

"Yeah," Isaac said gruffly. Vera's eyes settled on the gun tucked into his waistband.

Vera's heart sank as she walked into the kitchen and looked down at the kitchen table, a map spread over it and marked with scribbles of pencil at nearly every town. She stared at it for a long while. There were quite a few towns crossed out that she hadn't realized Isaac had already searched – or perhaps those had just been crossed out.

I'll have to tell Gray.

Behind her, Isaac shifted, and she finally turned to look back at him.

"Can I get you some, um, coffee or something?" he said distractedly, looking at the floor.

"No," Vera said, her mouth dry. "I'm... I'm good."

Isaac nodded and slowly raised his gaze to look at her. Even though it was still warm out, he was wearing long sleeves, pulled all the way down to his wrists. Vera swallowed hard and leaned against the wall.

"Missed you at breakfast today," she said softly.

Isaac blinked. "What day is it?"

"Sunday," Vera said, her gaze flicking to the map. "And, um... we were, uh... talking about having a belated birthday party for you this week, if you wanted."

Isaac's forehead wrinkled as he looked at her. "Wh-when...?"

"It's September twenty-second, Isaac," Vera said carefully, keeping her voice even. "Your birthday was five days ago."

Isaac pushed out a slow breath and pinched the bridge of his nose. "Oh. I'm, um... I'm sorry. I was—"

"With Saoirse and her crew, yeah," Vera murmured. "It's okay. It was a good lead."

"It was a *shit* lead," Isaac muttered, scrubbing his face with one hand. "It turned up *nothing*."

"But it was worth pursuing." Vera looked at the map again. "Looks like you've been getting a lot of Orson's region covered," she said. "And Laura in Trisland Springs said she's got a lot of—"

"Still turning up nothing, though," Isaac murmured. His eyes shone with tears. "We've gotten most of the western sector thoroughly searched, and Joshua's gone as far north as there are people living. Nothing. Whole shitload of *nothing*."

Vera chewed her lip, holding back her own tears. She traced her finger over the highway between Burmingham and Crayton. Most of the towns north, west, and east of Burmingham had been turned over, searched by friends of Gray or Mathias. Very few knew exactly *who* they were searching for, but they could probably guess. The further south they went, the less the family had been able to search.

The further south they went, the more likely it was that Gavin was there.

"It gets cold at night, now," Isaac said softly, his gaze moving over the map, too. "If he's being kept outside, then—" His words cut off with a choke. "I... we need to move faster. If he's... if he's..." His voice broke, and he trailed off into silence.

Vera glanced up at Isaac. A muscle stood out in his jaw as he stared at the map. Vera didn't have to follow his gaze to know what town he was looking at.

"Gray still doing their shifts with Schiester?" he croaked.

"Yeah," Vera said, her own gaze lingering on the map. "They do three a week. The refugees are coming in faster than ever before, especially now that summer's almost over. Crayton's got its hands full finding homes for everyone who comes through. Mathias has sent us two people... we just sent the last one to his new home a few days ago. Kiernan. Sweet kid. Younger than Sam, scared out of his mind."

Isaac's lips trembled. His hands closed into fists. "H-how is Sam?"

Vera took a deep breath. "They miss you," she said finally. "We... we all do." She chewed the inside of her cheek.

Isaac hung his head and said nothing.

Vera pressed on. "We miss having you at home. I know it's been chaotic between planning the searches and coordinating our people in Crayton, but... I mean, I know living in Burmingham gives you more access to..." She trailed off. Her finger traced along the scars around her wrist.

"I'll come home when I find him," Isaac said.

Tears stung Vera's eyes. She blinked them back. The words burned her tongue, but she forced them down.

What if you never find him?

What if he's dead?

"Isaac..."

Isaac's gaze snapped to hers. "I would do the same if it was any of you," he hissed. Helpless rage darkened his eyes. "If... If it was like with Sam and I could... could *go* to Schiester and... and..." Vera swallowed as his rage intensified, and she suddenly felt the heat of it on her face. "I could have gone to him," Isaac whispered. "I could have... have t-traded myself, and maybe Schiester would have—"

"Stop it, Isaac," she spat, crossing her arms in front of her. "Just... just *stop*. I don't want to talk about this again."

Isaac pressed his lips together and dropped his gaze. All the rage seemed to slither out of him, leaving him cold and empty. He stared at the map again.

Vera's head fell forward into her hands. She drew in a deep breath, pushed it back out again. When she lifted her head to look at Isaac, her breath punched out of her.

Isaac looked like he was being burned alive from the inside. His face was a mask of agony, his eyes brimming with tears, his hands shaking at his sides. Isaac slowly raised his gaze to hers.

"H-he was mine," he rasped.

Vera squeezed her eyes shut against the burn of tears. "Yeah," she whispered. "Y-yeah, Isaac, I know. I m-miss him too."

"I just want him back." Isaac's voice broke, and he cleared his throat. It sounded more like a sob. "I would do... *anything* to get him back."

Vera opened her eyes, and her gaze landed again on the map. On Crayton.

They both jumped as a cell phone rang.

Isaac's hand flew to his pocket and he flipped the phone open with shaking fingers. He held it to his ear. Vera's heart pounded and she leaned forward to listen.

"Neysa?" Isaac gasped, his eyes wide, his chest heaving. "Anything?"

Vera scarcely dared to breathe as she stared at Isaac and strained to hear the muffled voice on the other end of the phone.

Slowly, the tension slid out of Isaac's body, and he leaned forward, bracing one hand on the table. "Okay," he said weakly. "I... thank you. Thanks. Stay safe."

He flipped the phone closed and tossed it onto the table. Vera flinched at the clatter. Isaac leaned his other hand on the table, his head bowed, trembling.

Vera swallowed dryly. "N-no news?" she croaked.

"No," Isaac murmured. He grabbed the pencil off of the table and shakily crossed off another town in the eastern region.

"Fuck," Vera whispered.

Eyes unfocused, Isaac slowly leaned back and ran his hands through his hair. He didn't seem to notice as more strands pulled free of the elastic to frame his face.

Finally, he said, "I need more people in Crayton."

Vera nodded slowly. "Mathias is working to recruit more people. He's found a retired firefighter named Vanya to help Finn with the home inspections for fire safety." Vera shook her head and couldn't help the snort of half-hysterical laughter that seemed loud to her own ears. "Never would have believed a *firefighter* would be of any..." She trailed off and pressed her lips together when she saw the tortured expression on Isaac's face.

"If he's moving him," he croaked, "Then it doesn't matter. He could be... Jesus Christ, he could be *anywhere*. And I'd never know. He could be next-fucking-door and I'd never know if Schiester moved him before I searched it. I... How do I...?" Isaac stumbled a step back and pressed himself back against the kitchen sink. "I just..." Tears filled his eyes and spilled over his cheeks.

Vera stepped forward. "Isaac, hey..."

205

"Every time I get a call," Isaac whispered, "*Every* time, I... I think I... I'll either be told that they found him alive, or... or f-found him... dead. And it's... he's never found. It's always dead ends. It's a-always no news."

Vera reached out for him. "Isaac..."

"You saw how much snow they get up here in the winter," he croaked. "There were *feet* of snow when we got here in January. And that'll just... m-make it *harder* to find him. Some roads are impassable in the winter, for... for weeks. For *months*. I *have* to find him. I *have* to do it before the snows come. And if it takes another month or two..."

Vera stepped forward and pulled him roughly into her arms. "Hey." She squeezed him tight. She shivered as she felt his muscles tighten under the skin, as his arms came around her and crushed her to his chest. He was stronger than last time she'd seen him. Bigger. Leaner. "W-we'll find him." She hoped Isaac couldn't hear the uncertainty in her voice.

Isaac whimpered and squeezed her tighter, forcing the air from her lungs.

She shifted her feet and buried her face in his shoulder. "It would be good if you came home," she whispered. "We can help you. Seeing you would be—"

"I need to stay here," Isaac murmured. "The farm is too far away from Burmingham. Besides. If you're getting new rescues, having the extra room is good. And I'm guessing Edrissa's doing better without me there."

Vera gave him one more squeeze, then stepped back. He kept his eyes down and away. "She's... doing okay, yeah."

Isaac's throat worked. "She still fighting with Sam and Zachariah?" he rasped.

Vera blew out a breath. "Um... no," she murmured. "She's... well, she's... no. They're not fighting anymore. Sam and Zachariah are still, um, close, but..." She shrugged. "Edrissa's been pouring all her focus into the rescues, and the garden. She's still um... mad at Sam, I think. For not running with her."

"If they want to go," Isaac breathed, "Then they can go. They don't need to stick around for—"

"They stuck around because they *love* you," Vera said, a little sharply. "They love this family. Edrissa's a big girl, she can make her own decisions. And she decided not to go, once Sam refused. We... Isaac, we want to see you. We want to help you. I mean, we're doing everything we can on our searches. Please just—"

"I understand that I scare her," Isaac said softly. "And I'm sorry. But right now, I can't... I can't just... *turn off*..." He wearily passed a hand over his face. "I d-don't have the fucking *energy* to not be scary. I'm sorry. It's better that I'm here. I'm away from the rescues who scare easy. I'm closer to the people who bring me news. I'm not... I mean, I..." He took a step back. "I..."

"Isaac..." Vera's mouth fell closed. Inhale, exhale. She wet her lips. "What do you need from us?"

Isaac blinked and looked up at her. Tears shone in his eyes. "Have Gray get more people searching Crayton. I... I know I need to be searching everywhere else, too, but the longer we *don't* find him elsewhere, the more likely it is that he's *there*. And I just..." His hands tightened into fists and he shook his head. "I... I *know* he's there. I *know* it. I think... I think I've known it this whole time, and I haven't... I didn't..."

"Crayton is the place we have to be the most careful about searching," Vera said gently. "Crayton is the place we have to play it safest. It's been slow going. But Gray has a lot of good connections there, and we're starting to really branch out with the fire safety inspections. Finn practically lives down there now. And even if we knew exactly where Gavin was, we'd need a plan."

"But if I'd focused only on Crayton from the beginning," Isaac whimpered, tears spilling down his cheeks, "Then maybe he... I..."

"We're focused on Crayton," Vera said. "We've been focused on it the whole time. The whole town is... a fucking *fortress*, as far as finding allies goes. It's almost impossible to find people there that DFS trusts who aren't also in his fucking *entourage*. But it's happening. We're doing it."

"Twenty-eight days," Isaac said brokenly, staring again at the map. "Twenty-eight fucking days that bastard has been torturing him. Do you... d-do you think he'd keep him alive that long? Do you think... do you think Gavin is... is...?" He forced down a sob and shook himself.

Vera drew in a long, deep breath through her nose. "Isaac..." she said softly. "If... I think if Schiester killed Gavin, we would know. There's no way that fucking creep wouldn't tell *everyone* that he killed the Stormbeck heir—"

Isaac flinched.

Vera clenched her teeth together. "Isaac... DFS is a fucking sadist, if I ever saw one. Somehow, some way, if Gavin was dead, he would make *sure* we knew. Would make sure *you* knew."

Because there's no goddamn way he's had him for this long and not *gotten it out of him how important you are to him.*

Tears darkened Isaac's shirt. "He's... h-he's going to be... s-so... *broken.*"

Vera sucked in a breath. *I was almost broken by this point, I think.* She shook her head to rid herself of the image of Gavin, strapped down to a table like she had been, strung up from the ceiling, gagged, collared—

Be good for me, sweetheart, or I will make *you good.*

She swallowed her disgust. *If that's what we find, we'll handle it. We'll help him. He'll... he'll heal. I did.*

It took years, but I did.

A chill rolled over Vera's shoulders. "Finn is running out of places in Crayton they really think Gavin could be. And they're petitioning to, um, set up an inspection of the town hall."

Isaac's lip curled, and when he raised his gaze to Vera's, she took an involuntary step back. "If Gavin has been there the whole time," he growled, his hands shaking, "Then..." Just as quickly as the rage had gripped him, he sagged again. "If he's been under Gray's feet this... this whole time... then..."

"Then we'll make a plan to get him out," Vera said evenly. "We couldn't have gone any faster than this. This has been about finding *allies,* Isaac. Even if we knew exactly where he was from day one, we still would have... would have had to find a way inside." Vera shrugged. "We need a way to make this happen without Schiester—"

"—killing him first," Isaac finished bitterly. "Yeah."

Vera took a step forward. "Isaac..." She reached out and took his hand, smoothed her thumb over the scarred knuckles. "No matter where we find him, promise me…" She looked up and met his eyes, her heart breaking at the lines of pain on his face. "…promise me you won't… punish yourself."

Bitterness settled over Isaac's expression. Vera's stomach lurched. "Sure," Isaac snapped.

Vera shook her head. "Punishing yourself does nothing for him," she murmured. "And nothing for you."

Isaac lifted his chin and said nothing.

Vera's mouth twisted as she looked at him. He held her gaze for a beat, then dropped his eyes. She released him and wiped her hands distractedly on her pants. "Well," she said softly, "I can take off. I just wanted to drop by and, um, check on you. Do you need anything? Food? Meds?"

Isaac blinked. "Oh. I… I ran out. I forgot to, um—"

"That's okay," Vera murmured. "Which one? The prazosin?"

"Yeah," Isaac said softly. "I, um… Th-the nightmares are worse. I didn't realize I didn't have enough until I was already on the road…"

"That's okay," Vera said. "You want a hug?"

Isaac stepped forward and dragged Vera into a crushing embrace. She felt his body tremble as she squeezed him tight.

"We'll find him," she whispered, her voice muffled against his shirt. "Finn's plan is good. We'll find him."

Isaac made no sound except a twisted whimper. Vera felt tears wetting her shoulder. She stood there in Isaac's kitchen, clutching him tight, doing her best not to fall apart herself. After a long moment, Isaac pulled away and wiped his face on his shirt.

Vera's hand lingered on his shoulder. "I can collect the meds when they come in," she croaked. "Do you want to pick them up from the house? We could make a night of it. Even if you don't feel like celebrating your birthday… which I get, believe me, I do… Sam would love to see you. Would that work? We—"

"I'll come home when I find Gavin," Isaac rasped. Slowly, he rolled his neck, his gaze fixed on the floor. "Okay? It was good to see you, though. Tell everyone else I said hi."

Vera fought back tears. She gave Isaac's arm a squeeze. "I will. I'll be back soon with meds, okay?"

"I'll call if I have any news," Isaac said softly. Vera nodded and walked back through the house, not looking back as she closed the front door. As she walked back through the unkempt front yard, she heard the bolt of the lock sliding back into place behind her.

Chapter 30

Gavin jerked awake to the sound of the basement door opening. Dread gripped him; he knew, without even having to look up, who was coming down the stairs. He'd know the sound of those boots anywhere. He'd know that sound asleep, drugged, half-dead. A whimper escaped his throat as he huddled under the blanket.

His fingers traced the ridged lines on his forearm, the scar that marked him for what he was, carved into his flesh like a syndicate brand. "M-my name is Gavin Stormbeck," he whispered to himself, and felt the frantic beating of his heart calm just a little.

It's fuckin' not, though.

My name is Gavin Uriah and I had a family.

His hands twisted the hem of the gray t-shirt he wore, the shirt that used to smell like Isaac. He could barely remember how Isaac smelled, now, but he could dredge up a memory of how Isaac's eyes looked as they gazed into his. He set his jaw and raised his gaze to the man walking unhurriedly down the stairs, an easy smile on his face.

"Bath time for the Stormbeck boy," Schiester said cheerfully as he reached the bottom step, his blue eyes shining as he pinned Gavin down with his gaze.

Gavin swallowed as he looked up at Schiester. *You're never here when they wash me.* He shivered at the memory: every three or so days being led to a room just to the side of the gallows, stripped naked, tied to a pole, and sprayed with a hose. His breath froze in his chest as he remembered the icy water on his skin, the hours of shivering afterwards. He pulled his blankets tighter around him and ducked his head under them. Where no one could see, he looped his fingers under his collar and pulled, buying him a moment of relief from the constant pressure on his throat. He whimpered softly as he desperately tried to imagine what pain would come from this, if Schiester was here to watch.

The pain came either way. Even if he was left alone for hours, or days, the pain always came. There was nothing else left. Nothing but pain, and the rope that would finally end Gavin's life, hanging from the ceiling within his constant view.

No. There was something left. The only thing that was left, while he was still breathing.

Isaac Moore loved me, once. Gray Uriah called me their son. I had a family, once.

Gavin lifted his head from the warm sanctuary of his blankets as Schiester's keys rattled in the lock of his cell. He glared at his captor, his body starting to push away from the door on instinct. His hands shook as he huddled on the cot. Schiester grinned as he stepped into the cell, and Gavin would have given anything to carve the smug fucking grin right off Schiester's face.

Then carve out his heart, for forcing him to break Isaac's.

Schiester snorted. "You know the drill, Stormbeck," he said, and his hand shot out in a *get up* gesture. Gavin flinched back from the quick motion and bit down hard on his tongue when Schiester laughed. Clumsily, he pushed himself to his feet, his limbs weak from his time in the cell – *how many days? Weeks?* – able to do nothing but lie on the cot and sometimes pace, when his fucking *leash* was long enough. The rope tugged gently on his collar. He clenched his teeth so hard his jaw ached and crossed his wrists behind his back.

Schiester chuckled as he pulled a short length of rope from his pocket. They had started using the rope a lot more, lately. *Maybe they were running out of zip ties,* Gavin thought bitterly to himself. He winced as the rope tightened around his wrists, chafing skin that had only just healed after being torn open again during a particularly bad hallucination a few weeks ago.

Hallucination. He'd finally managed to get Schiester to admit that's what the drug did, why Gavin lost time. Knowing that never helped after Schiester actually dosed him with the drug, apparent now by the lines along his veins left by the needle, but it helped to remember once the nightmare passed, leaving him sobbing and soaked in sweat. *It wasn't real. It was just a hallucination.*

The pain, though... the pain was real.

When Gavin raised his head again, Ziegler stood outside the bars, staring at Schiester quizzically.

"Sir?"

Schiester quickly untied the leash from Gavin's collar and shoved him out the door of the cage. "Is there a bucket in the washroom?" he said conversationally, as if he was talking about whether there was milk in the refrigerator, not like he was talking about how Gavin was about to be stripped, humiliated, and tortured.

"No, sir," Ziegler said, his gaze settling on Gavin for a fraction of a second. "Would you like me to get one?"

"Yes, I would," Schiester said. Ziegler turned and went to the small closet full of cleaning supplies.

Gavin shivered as Schiester guided him the few steps across the basement to the washroom. It was mostly bare, with a linoleum floor with a drain in the center, a pole that extended from floor to ceiling in one corner, a hose coiled in another corner, and nothing else. Schiester snapped on the light. Gavin blinked in the yellow glare, brighter than the cold blue lights in the rest of the basement. The yellow tinge gave the room a sickly atmosphere. It made Gavin's head throb uneasily. He felt a tug at his wrists as Schiester untied the rope.

Tied my hands for a walk across the fucking room, Gavin thought, his lip curling. He kept his eyes down, even as he felt Schiester's gaze on his face. He rubbed gently at the raw skin of his wrists and wrapped his arms around his chest. Goosebumps broke out all over his body.

Schiester chuckled. "Are you somehow confused as to the purpose of this room?" he said, and Gavin rankled at the smugness in Schiester's voice. He shivered as Schiester shifted his feet. "Take off your clothes."

The blood that warmed Gavin's cheeks made no sense. Schiester had seen him laid bare – every sin, every mistake, every ounce of guilt torn out of Gavin at the point of a knife, at the point of a needle. Schiester had heard him scream, cry, beg, confess to everything he was accused of and more, just to make the pain stop. Schiester had pored over every inch of Gavin's body, pressing his gloved fingers into every scar, forcing Gavin to recount how he had received each one until he was sure even Schiester's men knew each story by heart. There was nothing of Gavin that Schiester had not seen. Still, Gavin's mind rebelled against the thought of Schiester seeing him naked again.

Schiester rolled his eyes. "You'll confess to your own plaything's rape but you won't—"

Rage punched through Gavin. He stripped his pants off with trembling fingers, flushing with humiliation as Schiester pursed his lips. He tossed the pants in a heap on the floor. His hands shook as he tugged the shirt up over his chest, and he sucked in a breath as the scars on his back stretched with the motion. Carefully, he folded the shirt and placed it on top of his pants. He stood naked in front of Schiester. Even though he knew it would draw Schiester's ire, he covered himself, wrapping his other arm tight around his chest as he shivered in the cold.

Schiester jerked his head towards the pole in the corner. "Kneel," he said, the command reverberating faintly in the small room.

Gavin's throat bobbed as he crossed to the pole. His skin already ached in anticipation of the icy water. He slid to his knees and held out his wrists against the pole to be tied. Schiester bound his wrists tightly to the pole, then turned as Ziegler walked back into the room.

Gavin kept his head down, but looked up from under his lashes at Ziegler, who was carrying a small plastic bucket.

"Thank you," Schiester said softly, and took the bucket from Ziegler's hands. He set it on the floor and began to fill it with the hose.

Gavin shivered. So, it would be this – having icy water dumped over him, instead of being sprayed. He tugged weakly against the rope, his skin rippling again with goosebumps, his teeth already beginning to chatter as he knelt on the cold linoleum.

Schiester looked up from his task and glanced at Ziegler. "And a towel," he said softly.

The hair on the back of Gavin's neck stood up as Ziegler left the room.

Schiester finished filling the bucket – a few gallons at most, not really enough to do anything more than get Gavin wet – and raised his gaze to Gavin's. Gavin felt Schiester's gaze on his skin as his eyes moved over Gavin's body, lingering on the scars from the cane, the knife, the needle. Gavin knew without a doubt that Schiester was imagining those scars on a different body, one that had Gavin's build, Gavin's eyes, Gavin's dark hair – hair that Schiester had painstakingly ordered cut just so, in a style Gavin knew without even having to look: the style his father had worn when Gavin was a child. His face was even kept shaved, to keep the lines of his jaw clean.

Can't have some fucking scruff *ruining the look,* Gavin thought, and he felt like his hatred would burn him alive.

When Ziegler walked back into the room, Schiester glanced at him. Ziegler gave Gavin a long look.

"Thank you, Ziegler," Schiester said warmly. "Now, if you would please hold that over the Stormbeck boy's face…"

Gavin's eyes went wide and he dragged in a desperate breath. "N-no," he whimpered. "No, *fuck*, no…"

In a distant corner of his mind, a bored-sounding voice drawled, *Once he's done this, that's one step closer to killing you. One step closer to this being over.*

Gavin's knees ached against the floor as he jerked against the rope. "No, *please*," he gasped.

Ziegler glanced at Gavin, then back at Schiester. "Yes, sir," he said with finality, and stepped forward.

Gavin's lungs already ached as he pulled in gasp after terrified gasp. "N-no," he pleaded, and his wrists chafed against the rope. "Please."

I did this to Isaac… how many times? To Sam? To the four other playthings I tried it on before them? A sob tore its way out of Gavin's chest.

Ziegler stepped up behind him and dragged Gavin's head back with a hand in his hair. Gavin was forced to look up at him, eyes wide with terror. Ziegler pulled the towel across Gavin's nose and mouth and used it to torque his head back further, pulling tighter as Gavin fought desperately to pull away. His breaths came heavy and thick through the towel.

He let out another sob as Schiester stood over him, holding the bucket. "Consider this justice on Isaac Moore's behalf," he purred, and let the first few splashes soak the towel through.

Icy water struck Gavin's face and chest and he dragged in a breath – an instinct. A reflex. He thrashed against the rope, and against Ziegler's iron grip on the towel, as the gasp drew water straight into his lungs. His throat spasmed as he tried to cough. In an instant, more water coursed over the towel, and Gavin was drowning.

The icy water in his lungs became fire. He jerked mindlessly against the rope, against the towel. He tried to turn his head, to let the water trickle out of his mouth so he could breathe. Ziegler tightened his grip on the towel, his fists pressing against Gavin's temples. Gavin's knees scraped to bleeding as he fought desperately against the water.

"Enough," came the cool order.

Gavin lurched forward as the towel came away from his face and heaved cough after wracking cough. Water streamed from his nose and mouth, his chest aching like it was being crushed. He sobbed raggedly and cowered against the pole.

"No, no, *please,* no more…" Warm tears mixed with the cold water on his face.

"Only twice more, Stormbeck," Schiester said gently.

"N—" His scream was cut off as Ziegler pulled the wet towel over his face, and the water came pouring in.

The stream was endless. Gavin writhed in his bonds, his mouth gaping open, his eyes open and sightless as he stared up at Ziegler. He could feel the water running down his spasming throat, streaming into his nose, burning him. His heart thundered in his chest.

"Enough."

He was let up. He heaved water out of his lungs, out of his mind with panic. He tried to speak, but the water drowned his words. As the towel pulled over his face again, he ducked, sobbing.

"N-no, no you're not doing it right, you're *not doing it right,*" he babbled, desperate. Paralyzed. It was too much water. Schiester was just pouring it in, wasn't doing it in little trickles so Gavin could get *some* air; he was just drowning him.

Schiester may as well have shoved his head into the bucket.

Schiester barked out a cruel laugh. "I don't give a *fuck* if you have pointers on my technique, Stormbeck," he said. "Besides, only once more. It'll be hard to kill you if I only do this once more, even if my technique is less than *adequate.* Ziegler…"

Gavin couldn't speak before the towel was pulled over his face, dragging his head back, and the water was all he knew.

He tried to scream, tried to *breathe*. The water was a knife in his chest, and his lungs spasmed around it. His nose burned as water poured in. His eyes rolled back, and he convulsed mindlessly.

"Enough."

Gavin rocked forward so hard his head collided with the pole. He slumped to the side, gasping raggedly, choking on the water as it trickled out of his throat. The room spun dizzily around him. He coughed and more water streamed from his mouth. The once-icy water was warmed from his lungs. He shuddered and sobbed. The rope tying him to the pole was the only thing holding him upright.

"Please," he rasped, and his voice broke as his throat spasmed. The cold crept under his skin, freezing his bones. His lungs were on fire.

"I didn't have much time today," Schiester said conversationally, standing over Gavin as he shuddered at his feet. "If you'll put him back now, please, Ziegler…"

Through the rushing in his ears and the heaving of his breaths, Gavin heard Schiester's ringing footsteps leave the tiny washroom.

Gavin shivered violently and moaned when he felt rough hands on his wrists, fumbling at the rope. The knots would be harder to undo, now that the rope was wet. Gavin wondered distantly if Schiester knew that. Or if he cared.

The rope came away, and Gavin slumped to the floor. More water came streaming out of his nose and he coughed weakly. His head spun. He couldn't tell if it was from the drowning, or from hitting his head. He didn't fight as he was dragged away from the pole and into the center of the washroom. Goosebumps rippled over him again. He lay there, unmoving, completely untied.

He cried out in weak terror as he felt something rub against his skin, the texture coarse and scratchy. He peeled his eyes open – he hadn't even realized they were closed – and his breath froze in his chest as he realized Ziegler had knelt over him, and was toweling him dry.

He tried to speak, but his throat spasmed again. He coughed out another mouthful of water and turned his head to look up at Ziegler.

"Y-you…" he rasped. "Wh-why—"

"I'm going to have to fucking carry you back," Ziegler growled. "I don't want to get wet. Don't fucking move."

Gavin slumped against the floor, his skin itching from the touch. Still, he wasn't quite as cold. He whimpered softly as Ziegler dragged him upright by his shoulders and wrestled his shirt back onto him. He did his best to hold himself up on shaking arms while Ziegler tugged his pants on over his feet and guided them as far up Gavin's legs as he could with Gavin still lying prone on the floor. Gavin couldn't bring himself to feel embarrassed as he lifted his hips, helping Ziegler pull the jeans all the way up. Ziegler kept his eyes averted, only looking when he buttoned Gavin's jeans and zipped them.

"Come on," Ziegler said gruffly, and hoisted Gavin to his feet.

Gavin doubled over with a wracking cough, clutching Ziegler's arms as he fought to stay on his feet. He leaned heavily on the guard as he wrapped his arms around Gavin's chest and half-helped, half-dragged Gavin back to his cell. The water in his hair ran in rivulets down his neck and under his shirt. He was desperate to crawl under his blankets and huddle there until… until the next time.

Maybe I'll get pneumonia from this, like Sam did.

Even as he thought it, though, he knew that he hadn't inhaled enough. Sam had inhaled so much more. But if Schiester had continued that way, even another two or three times…

Ziegler dragged Gavin into the cell and pushed him roughly to the cot – but didn't drop him.

He didn't drag him in by his collar, either.

Gavin lay still, trembling, as Ziegler tied the rope to his collar again. Pointless and humiliating. Just like every other fucking thing in this fucking basement.

As Ziegler turned to go, Gavin wet his lips. He was still thirsty, even after that. "W-wait," he croaked.

To his shock, Ziegler paused, his back to Gavin, standing in the door of the cell. A muscle stood out in his jaw and he said nothing.

Gavin cleared his throat and winced as it burned. "Wh-why... You d-didn't..." He coughed weakly. Tears brimmed in his eyes, as much from coughing as anything else. "You didn't... h-hurt me."

The others did, when they could. Both on Schiester's orders and without them, if there was an excuse to land a kick to his ribs, drag him by his collar, press down on healing cuts, they did it. And Schiester smiled, every time.

Ziegler's hand curled into a fist. "I don't feel like it," he grumbled.

Gavin blinked. "I-I... don't..."

Ziegler pushed out an irritated breath. "You've confessed to a lot of shit," he said, turning slightly.

Gavin hung his head and said nothing. He fumbled for the blankets and did his best to pull them over him with shaking hands.

"A *lot* of shit," Ziegler continued. "Even stuff that I know for a fucking *fact* you didn't do, because... because you've confessed to doing some shit that happened to *me*." Gavin weakly raised his head to look at Ziegler. The guard waved the look away. "Like I said, I one-hundred-percent know you didn't do some of the shit you've confessed to. But... even the stuff you've confessed to while you're drugged out of your fucking mind... half of which I don't know if I believe, by the way, if you really are seeing things that aren't really there..." His shoulders shrugged up painfully by his ears. He kept his gaze fixed on the floor outside Gavin's cell. "I don't question Schiester. He's seen the worst of what your fucking world has to offer, and he's doing what he thinks is right. But for me?" Ziegler huffed out a breath. "I haven't heard you confess to anything that I think deserves this."

Ziegler stepped out of the cell and pulled the door shut behind him with a loud *clang*. Gavin watched him through watering eyes as he walked to the desk and sat down, grumbling as he found a wet spot on his shirt. He pulled out a book and opened it to a page he had marked with a scrap of paper.

Gavin pulled the blankets tightly around him, muffling a sob.

Chapter 31

Years ago

Isaac looked out over the surface of the lake, the ripples moving with the gentle breeze that ruffled his hair. *A good day for sailing,* his dad said on days like this, and then would chuckle like he'd made a joke.

It *was* a nice day. The sun was high in the sky, but the day wasn't too hot. The trees on the shore shimmered as the wind shook their leaves, and Isaac watched a seagull slowly circle above him before it settled, floating on the top of the lake like a duck. It was close enough to the tiny rowboat for him to see the oil-like shimmer of its feathers.

Isaac had no idea how far away the sea was – he'd never even seen it – so he wondered how, exactly, the ocean bird had found his lake, so far away from its home. He took a final bite of his sandwich and flung the crust towards the bird. It squawked and flapped its wings a few times, bigger across than any bird Isaac had gotten close to on land. It snapped up the crust and swallowed it whole.

He turned and grinned at his father, checking to see if he was watching. His dad smiled right back and brushed the crumbs off his hands, looking out across the water.

"You ready to keep rowing, bud?" he said.

Isaac nodded enthusiastically, and his father's smile warmed as he grabbed the oars in both hands and leaned back, pulling them through the water with practiced ease. Isaac's heart pounded faster, both from how hard he was rowing and with the excitement of starting to move so *fast* – and it was because he was getting stronger. He thought he must be rowing faster than he could run on land. He'd have to ask his mom to try racing him down the pier, next time she came to the lake with them. Her on the walkway, him in the boat. He figured he might not be able to beat his *mother,* but… maybe another kid. Maybe if Lacey could convince their parents to let him bring them…

The muscles of his back and arms burned, and he welcomed it. There was something wonderful about this: leaning hard into the oars, sending the boat all but flying over the water, with his dad watching with a smile. He was a good rower. His dad said so. He might even be as good as his dad one day, once he grew more. 'Filling out,' his mom had called it once, and ever since then he'd been asking for more meat with dinner. If he was going to fill out, he needed to fill himself *with* something.

"Hey, look at that," his father said, excited, and pointed over Isaac's shoulder. Isaac stopped rowing, looking behind him for what his father was pointing at.

His eyes went wide. Flying low over the surface of the water was the biggest bird he'd ever seen, all neck and wings and seemingly little else. His mouth gaped open, and he shot a glance back at his dad.

"What *is* that?" he asked, his voice low with awe.

"I think it's a crane," his dad said, shading his eyes with his hand. "Or a heron." He chuckled. "Not sure what the difference is. Still, that's pretty cool, right? I didn't know they lived in this area."

Isaac abandoned the oars and turned fully around to get a closer look. "Whoa," he said, as the bird beat its wings a few times and landed in the shallows all the way at the edge of the water. It stood on two spindly legs, like it was standing on stilts. "A *crane.*"

"Or a heron," his father said with a snort. "We can look at pictures in my bird book when we get home."

Isaac rose up on his knees for a closer look. "Yeah," he said softly, squinting as the sun shone brightly off the surface of the water. He pushed himself into a crouch, feeling the tiny boat wobble under him.

"Whoa, buddy," his father said, his hand shooting out towards Isaac. "Hey, sit down. You're too big now to be standing up in the boat." His voice was still warm, soft.

Isaac glanced back at his father, whose lips pulled into a wide grin. "I can keep my balance." He stood up a little higher, feeling a thrill as the boat wobbled again – but he stayed on his feet.

His father huffed, and his smile fell slightly. "I know you can, buddy," he said, his voice showing a hint of tension. "You're just… making your dad nervous. Have a seat, we can see if we can row closer."

"But I can see it from here!" Isaac said, standing all the way up. The seagull in the water near the boat started and took off from the water in a flurry of wings. The sudden noise made Isaac jump. He felt the boat tip under him and he pitched to one side, his hands flying out to catch himself. He tripped on the lunch box in the bottom of the boat and fell hard, the side of the boat hitting him right in the stomach. His mouth gaped open with the burst of shock and pain.

"Isaac!" his father shouted, and stood. Isaac felt the boat lurch even further to the side.

Stunned, he flipped over the side and fell face-first into the cool water.

Water rushed into Isaac's open mouth. All around him he could feel cold water and see fractured light, a wash of blue-green. He couldn't tell which way was up; black spots danced in front of his vision from the crush of pain. He felt paralyzed, like the blow had frozen his muscles. Water poured into his throat. It burned in his nose and suddenly, he could move again.

His limbs shot out in frenzied panic. He could feel the water filling his shoes, dragging on his clothes like they weighed a hundred pounds. He could swim, but terror clutched his limbs and crushed his chest. He let out a scream in a stream of bubbles, and the sound seemed miles away. His vision clouded as he opened his eyes. He distantly saw a circle of yellow, floating above him in a green sky.

Not the sky.

He shuddered as the water crept inside his lungs, forcing out the air. His stomach felt squeezed tight. He kicked hard, one last desperate attempt to reach the surface.

A hand closed around his hair and dragged him upwards.

He threw his head back and sucked in a gasp of air as he broke the surface of the lake. The water burned in his chest and he coughed, his eyes wide, his fingers clawing for something – anything – to grab onto. His nails dug into his dad's arms, and his dad let out a hiss.

"*I-Isaac,*" his dad heaved, his voice twisting like he was crying. Isaac clawed at his father's shirt, pulling himself up, desperate to breathe. "Isaac, buddy, I got you, I—" The words were drowned out as his father's head slipped beneath the surface of the lake. Isaac sobbed and grabbed at anything he could to keep his own head above water. His lungs burned like fire.

His father broke the surface with a gasp. "Isaac, it's okay, just, just hang on—" His father's hand shot out to the side, and Isaac felt the water slide past him in his wake. He turned his head and saw the side of the small boat, overturned now. His father heaved him up onto it, and he struck the keel, forcing more air out of his lungs. He dug his nails into the wood and clawed to stay on. His father remained in the water, clutching the side of the boat.

"Hey!" his father roared, waving his arm at a nearby boat. "Help! Help!"

Isaac moaned and coughed out another mouthful of water. His eyes slid shut and he slumped, exhausted. He couldn't *breathe.* The water rattled in his chest. He slipped off the side of the boat, back into the water.

"No, *no no no no,*" his father gasped, and heaved him back onto the wet wood. Isaac wailed brokenly and dug his fingers in again.

He could hear something, a scream, maybe, or a siren. Or the wind. He could barely lift his head to look around. His vision blurred as water dripped into his eyes. His head thumped back down onto the boat, and he drifted, his heart hammering in his chest. Every cough took his breath away, wracked through his body until he felt like he was drowning again.

Distantly, he heard a motorboat, getting closer. Closer. Then voices.

"Is he— Is he...?" A woman's voice.

"I, I d-don't know," his father shouted, and his voice broke. "P-please, *help*..." Isaac felt his father's hands under his armpits, lifting him, and another, unfamiliar pair of hands dragging him over the side of another boat. He shivered as his clothes clung to him. The boat wobbled, and another body landed beside him – his father. The boat lurched and started to move.

"*Isaac,*" his father sobbed, and Isaac felt his own heart twist at the sound. "Isaac, please, *please*... talk to me, buddy..."

"Get him on his side." The order came from a shaking voice.

Isaac hung limp in his father's arms as he was rolled onto his side. Water came trickling out of his mouth. He convulsed weakly, sucking in lungfuls of air. It didn't help. His chest felt heavy.

His father's voice again. "Isaac? Oh, god. Isaac, Isaac! Breathe, buddy, come on…"

Isaac coughed and obeyed. His throat felt like it would spasm shut.

His father's voice faded. "Can someone call 911?"

"Y-yeah, I, I think somebody already did…"

Isaac shuddered and started to cry. "D-daddy," he whimpered, reaching for him. "Daddy…"

Tears mixed with the water on his face as his father dragged him up off the bottom of the boat and crushed him to his chest. "Isaac, buddy, I'm *sorry, oh my god, Isaac…"

Isaac coughed weakly, gasping at air that didn't seem to reach his lungs. "Daddy…"

"I got you," his father sobbed. "I got you." There was a bump, a shudder, and Isaac was being carried. He clutched to his dad's neck, trembling. "Th-thank you," his father said with a shaking voice. The world tilted around Isaac. The sun shone in his eyes. He raised his head again and blinked as he saw someone coming towards him, brown hair pulled back in a ponytail, dark eyes that looked at him steadily, wearing dark blue clothes and a badge that shone on her chest. He clutched harder at his father as he fell to his knees in front of the woman.

"What happened?" she said crisply, sounding very serious.

"H-he just f-fell out of the boat," his father sobbed, shaking. "I d-don't, it happened so fast, he f-fell and the boat tipped over and he… he h-hasn't been acting right, he—"

"Did he hit his head?" Still in his father's arms, Isaac felt hands move through his hair, pressing down on his skull, pressing on his neck.

"I d-don't think so? I… I didn't see… He isn't breathing right, please, *please*—"

"Hey," the woman said, and his father fell silent immediately. Her voice softened. "What's your name?"

"J-Jonathan," his father whimpered.

224

"Okay. My name's Charlotte. I need you to breathe for me, okay? I need you to stay calm for him." Isaac's father took a shuddering breath. "What kind of boat?"

"A r-rowboat," his father croaked. Isaac's mouth gaped open. His lips felt numb.

"Hm. Looks like you took a swim, too. Where he fell, was it deep enough that you could reach the bottom?"

His father was silent. He shook his head.

Charlotte shrugged. "I mean, that's good. That means he probably didn't hit his head. Hey, buddy." Isaac whined as Charlotte squeezed his arm. "What's your name?"

"Isaac," he whimpered, his chest heaving. He couldn't *breathe.*

"Did he lose consciousness at any point?" Isaac flinched as something cold pressed to his chest under his shirt, then moved to the other side of his chest. "Take deep breaths, buddy," Charlotte said. The cold circle moved to two spots lower on his chest. "Yeah, sounds like he inhaled a lot of water."

"Lose c-consciousness?" his father said, distantly. "No... no, I, I think h-he was... awake..." His arms tightened around Isaac. "Wh-what, what should I—"

"Well, he definitely needs to go to the ER," Charlotte said. "I'd recommend you let us take hi—"

"Yes," his father said hollowly. "Can I... c-can I come with him?"

"Yeah, of course. Our cot's right over here, can you carry him?"

"Y-yeah. Yeah."

"Did you get hurt, or anything?"

"No."

"Okay, good. This is my partner, Ethan. This is Jonathan and Isaac."

"H-hello," Isaac's father said.

Another man's voice, now. "We'll take good care of him. Hey, Isaac. Yeah, right here."

Isaac whimpered as his father put him down on a small bed with wheels, sitting just outside the ambulance that was parked by the pier. Its lights were still on.

Charlotte looked at Isaac's father. "Dad, can you get his shirt and pants off? He needs to get dry. I can grab a blanket for you in a sec."

"Sure," his dad said flatly, as if from a million miles away. He reached out and gently guided Isaac's soaking wet shirt off over his head.

"Daddy," Isaac whimpered, panic creeping back into his chest. He clawed at his neck, his throat spasming shut, opening again. "C-can't, can't—"

"I know," his father breathed, gently removing Isaac's pants. A blanket was immediately spread over him. "The, the, the EMTs are gonna take good care of you, okay?"

Isaac's fingers wound in his father's shirt. "Dad…"

Ethan, the other EMT, put his hand on his father's shoulder, and he stepped away. Isaac whimpered softly as Charlotte pressed a button on the end of the cot, and it lifted into the air. The cot shuddered as they pushed it towards the ambulance and loaded it in.

Isaac's tears eased when his father climbed into the back of the ambulance and took his hand again.

Behind him, Charlotte was talking. "Hey, dad. He needs oxygen." Ethan clipped something to his finger, and behind him, beeping started. It was fast. "Oh, yup. Eighty-eight percent. Ethan, let's get a line started, too. So, Jonathan, he might not like the mask at first, so I need you to help me. Just hold it to his face. Once he's used to it, we can use the strap to keep it on, but for now, just hold it up. Okay?"

His dad looked at Charlotte with tear-filled eyes and nodded. Charlotte passed an oxygen mask into his hand, and he held it to Isaac's face.

It was smothering. Isaac sobbed and turned his head away, tears rolling down his cheeks.

"Hey, buddy, no," his dad said gently. "It's oxygen. It'll help. It'll help you breathe, buddy, okay? Can I give you the oxygen?"

Isaac looked back at his father. His lower lip trembled, but he nodded. He did his best to hold still as his father held the plastic mask over his face again.

Panic spiked in his throat, and he squirmed under the blanket. He shivered, suddenly, realizing he was freezing. Cool air blew over his face, smelling plasticky and wrong. Slowly, he felt his breathing come easier. The beeping behind him slowed down. The ambulance started moving with a lurch.

"Ninety-five percent. Much better." Charlotte shuffled along the other side of the cot, smiling gently. "Hey, buddy. Feeling any better?"

He *could* breathe better. He dragged in a deep breath. He could feel the water rumbling in his chest. It felt like when he'd gotten sick a few years ago, and his parents had taken him to the clinic and left with a bottle of pills that made his stomach hurt. Still, they made him better.

"Do, do I need antibiotics?" he said weakly.

Charlotte laughed. It was a nice sound. "Maybe," she said. "But not until we get to the hospital, at least. Dad, we can probably just use the strap now. Isaac, if we put the strap on the mask, can your dad let go?"

Isaac nodded and shivered again under the blanket. The ambulance bounced as it rolled over a bump.

His father patted his pockets, then drew his cell phone out of the pocket on his pants. It was dripping wet. *"Shit,"* he hissed, then glanced at Isaac apologetically. "Um, M-Ms. Charlotte…"

Charlotte glanced up from where she was assembling something on the counter, something with tubes and what looked like a needle. "Mm-hm?"

"Can I, um… c-could I… borrow a phone? I n-need to call my wife. What… what hospital are you taking us to?"

"Boulder City General is the closest," Charlotte said, reaching in her own pocket for her phone. She passed it to Isaac's father. "We'll be there in about twenty, if you want to tell her to come in the main ER entrance and go to the check-in counter. They'll take her back from there."

Isaac's father took the phone and dialed the number with shaking hands. He held the phone to his ear. "C-Carol-Ann?" he said, his voice weak. "Um… You need to get to the general hospital. Isaac's okay, but… we had an accident at the lake, and… no, no, he's okay. He's alright. He fell out of the boat but he's okay now. The E-EMTs are giving him oxygen. Yeah, he's… he's awake. Carol-Ann, listen to me. He's okay. He's doing okay. Just… scared me." His father's fingers moved slowly through Isaac's wet hair. "Yeah, I'll tell him." He held the phone away from his mouth. "Mom loves you, buddy."

Isaac nodded, another cascade of tears rolling slowly down his cheeks. "L-love you, mom," he rasped.

Chapter 32

"Brought you something," Sam called from Zachariah's doorway.

Zachariah jumped off his bed like he'd been shot, and Sam instantly regretted not knocking or clearing their throat or shuffling their feet first. The stems of the small bouquet of wildflowers were crushed in their fist.

"S-sorry," they murmured. "Sorry, I should have—"

"Sam," Zachariah breathed, his lips pale. "Come in. Hey, I was just... thinking of something else. Are... are those for me?" The abject terror that had seized Zachariah's body moments before melted as his gaze fell on the flowers in Sam's hand.

Sam glanced at the flowers, embarrassed now. "I mean... yeah. They are. I didn't mean to give you a heart attack over them, though."

Zachariah's shoulders hung around his ears. "Easy to do these days, I guess," he said airily.

Sam stepped into the room and shyly passed the flowers to Zachariah. They had no idea what any of the blooms were called – Edrissa would know, but she still wasn't speaking to them, not since they told her they weren't going to abandon their family for her – but the colors were beautiful. Mostly yellows and golds, with some blues here and there.

"I wanted to bring you something from outside, since you can't exactly, you know..." Sam trailed off as Zachariah stared at the riot of color in his hands. He held the flowers to his nose and inhaled deeply.

"Smells good," Zachariah said.

"Like... flowers?" Sam said as they raised their eyebrow at him, trying for playfulness, for just a moment of levity.

"Just like plants, mostly," Zachariah said with a shrug. "But plants smell nice."

"Fair enough." Sam looked at the flowers. "I should have... brought those in a cup or a vase or something. I could... Let me go..." They took a step towards the door.

"St-stay?" Zachariah murmured. He seemed to realize what he had said, and he turned bright red. "I mean... yeah, cup. Good idea. But you could... hang out after? I mean..."

Sam's throat tightened. "Oh. Yeah, I'll... I can definitely stay. Let me just..." They slipped out the door and hurried to the kitchen, grabbing a cup off the shelf and filling it quickly. With Zachariah's simple request, it was as if the entire world had been plunged into frigid ice and the only warm place left in the world was Zachariah's room. They carried the cup back to his room and knocked to announce their arrival, this time.

"Great," Zachariah said gently, holding out the flowers.

Sam took them and let them drop unceremoniously into the cup with a *splish* of water. They set the cup lightly on the nightstand beside Zachariah's bed.

"Nice," Zachariah, mumbled, almost as if to himself. He turned the cup slightly, so a particularly large flower sat front and center of the bouquet. His gaze appeared glued to it as his hands folded in front of him, his forearms resting heavily on his knees.

Sam stood beside him for a long moment before they turned to close his door. He didn't raise his head to look at them as they returned to his side and sat down next to him on the bed.

The silence drew out between them for a breath, then two, then ten. A minute passed, then another. Zachariah looked away from the flowers and at the floor.

"My mom grew flowers that looked a lot like those," he whispered. "But bigger. And red. She grew them in the box outside the kitchen window."

Sam's eyes fell shut and they pressed their forehead against his shoulder. "I'm sorry," they said. "I didn't realize—"

"No," Zachariah said, his hand finding Sam's. "No. It's... not bad. The flowers. I appreciate them. Thank you."

Sam nodded slowly and opened their eyes. "Is your mom... still alive?" Their fingers laced through Zachariah's.

"Yeah," Zachariah croaked. "Or at least... I think so. She was last time I..." His voice broke, and he tipped his head down.

"When you left Fort Meyers?"

Zachariah cleared his throat. "Um… no. When I, um… When I went to go work for, um Colleen Stormbeck. My mom threw me out."

Sam sat up, eyebrows pulling together as they looked at Zachariah. His head was bowed towards the floor. "Oh," they breathed.

"Yeah," he said. "She said that… if I was willing to… t-to 'be a thug for the worst people on earth, I may as well hurt people just like they do.'" Zachariah's throat bobbed as he stared at the floor. "I thought – I hoped – she was just overreacting. My dad tried to get her to change her mind. But she kicked me out, told me she never wanted to see my face again. She told me…" Zachariah huffed out a broken laugh and tipped back his head, tears glimmering in his eyes. "She told me I was just as bad as them, and worse, because I'd be doing the same things, and I still have a soul to lose."

Sam's stomach clenched. "Zachariah—"

"She was right," Zachariah said with a thin, bitter smile, lips quivering. Tears trailed down his cheeks. "I did those things." His palm was damp in Sam's. "But at least my dad took the money I sent him. For my brothers and sisters. I know they needed it. My mom wouldn't have taken it, if she'd known where it was coming from."

Sam pulled their hand away from Zachariah's and squeezed their hands together. Their old wound twinged. The pain of the injury, the ache of Isaac's absence, the terror of Gavin being missing – *kidnapped, it was a kidnapping, it couldn't have been anything else* – all congealed inside Sam's chest and settled around their heart. It sapped them of warmth and sucked at their limbs until they could scarcely stay upright. Tears pricked at their eyes and heat thickened in their throat for not the first time today. The room itself felt dark and empty, and Sam couldn't help but feel swept away in the despair of it.

But Zachariah was here. Zachariah was warm, and alive. Zachariah liked Sam, and had wide, gentle hands, and a kind face, and a gentle voice.

And Zachariah was *here*.

Sam turned their head and caught Zachariah's mouth in a kiss. Zachariah made a faint sound of surprise but didn't pull away. His hands gently cupped Sam's jaw, and his lips were so warm and soft. They tasted salty from his tears, but Sam didn't care. They'd tasted their own tears often enough the past few weeks that it hardly registered at all.

231

Sam gently pushed Zachariah down onto the bed, their lips never leaving his. He laid back onto his pillows with them and guided them to straddle his hips. Their mouth moved against his, slow and hesitant at first, then insistent, even desperate.

When Sam rolled their hips against his, they felt him hard against their inner thigh.

"Please," they gasped. "Can we do this?" Their cheeks were wet, too – when did that happen?

"Only if you want to," Zachariah panted.

"I want to," Sam whispered. They gasped as Zachariah ran gentle fingers through their curls. "Please, just… help me forget how much things suck right now."

Zachariah managed a laugh through his own tears, which hadn't ever stopped entirely. "Things do seriously suck… *ahh*—"

Sam buried their face against Zachariah's neck and pressed a kiss to the skin there. Zachariah slid a hand between the two of them and began to stroke Sam to hardness through their jeans. The room was silent but for the sound of fabric shifting and heavy breathing. The bed creaked as Zachariah sat up to take off his shirt. His chest was broad and muscled, his golden-brown skin perfect, unscarred, and warm under Sam's hands. Not like anyone else's in the family.

Maybe that's what Sam needed right now. Someone who hadn't been touched by the same pain that festered in every other person in this house—

—and Gavin, too, but he's not here—

Sam whimpered in frustration. Zachariah froze.

"Sam? Are you—"

"I'm okay," Sam grumbled. "I'm fine. I just… want to forget about everything. Just for a *second*."

Zachariah drew in a slow breath. "Yeah," he said softly. "Yeah, sometimes I… want that, too."

"Then kiss me, please," Sam said with their lips already pressed against Zachariah's.

Zachariah had no reply. He just cradled Sam's face and kissed them back, hard.

Chapter 33

A leaf the size of Vera's hand tapped against the windshield, startling her out of her reverie. She blinked and looked up at the farmhouse. *How long have I been idling?* She turned off the car and climbed out. Her muscles were stiff. She rolled her neck, pulled her shoulders back. Her body felt as tightly wound as a bowstring, ready to snap – and she stood just beside herself, looking in.

The afternoon sun streamed down, the rays at a slant. At the end of summer, and at the end of the day, the sun cast deep shadows. Vera's stomach twisted as she remembered the short days of winter up north, where the sun came out from behind the horizon for only a few hours – six or seven hours at the longest during the bitter months of December and January.

It's going to be a long winter.

Vera shivered, even in the heat. *We don't know if we'll still be searching then. Let's just make it through this day, then the next, then the next. We might find him, we might...*

Vera wondered when she'd made the switch from missing Gavin to mourning him.

Maybe Isaac was looking for a corpse. Maybe she was wrong about Daniel Schiester. She'd told Isaac that Gavin was alive, over and over and over again – because if she didn't believe that, if she believed that he was really dead, she would break right alongside Isaac. Her mind echoed with the sound of Isaac's broken voice from the morning they'd discovered Gavin missing. Her eyes burned with tears.

"Wh-what if he's dead?"

"I c-could have saved him..."

"Please don't let him be dead..."

She swallowed hard against the lump that formed in her throat and walked to the front door, stumbling on the uneven ground. Her legs wouldn't quite cooperate. The phone in her pocket moved against her hip as she walked.

Her eyes were unfocused as she opened the door. A flicker of movement caught her eye – Nata, standing from where he lay curled on the couch. He arched up in a languid stretch before circling and settling again. Tori stood up from behind the counter and set down a large mixing bowl.

"Hey," Tori murmured, and a tight smile flickered across her face. "How's the boy?"

Vera drew a heavy hand through her hair and kicked off her boots. "As bad as last time. Or… worse. I don't think he's slept since he got back from Saoirse's crew." Her socks brushed the floor as she walked into the kitchen.

"Shit," Tori muttered. She leaned on the counter and stared at the granite. "He taking his meds?"

"He's out of the prazosin," Vera said as she went to the fridge and took down the shopping list from its magnet clip. She dug a pen out of the drawer next to it and wrote *call Toby about prazosin* under the underlined word *meds*. "I stopped by the pharmacy before I came home. They don't have the new stuff in yet. I'll pick it up in a day or so. Or I'll have Isaac pick it up, if we're out."

"If Isaac's home to do it," Tori said softly.

Vera clutched the pen tight in her fist as her eyes squeezed shut. She blew a slow breath out of her nose, her back to Tori, and leaned her hands on the counter. "H-he'll be home," she murmured. "Finn's petition will go through in a few days, hopefully. Then they can check the town hall. Isaac isn't going *anywhere* until that's done."

Vera jumped at the soft touch at her back. She opened her eyes and turned around to meet Tori's gaze. Tori ran her hands up and down Vera's arms.

Tori pressed her mouth into a line before she said, "If he's been in the town hall the whole time…"

"I know," Vera groaned, pressing her face into her hands. "I… I know. But… I mean, *fuck,* we haven't been able to search a single building in Crayton until *last week.* And you know Schiester would have gotten suspicious if we *started* with the town hall."

"How's Isaac going to...?" Tori's hands tightened on Vera's shoulders. "I mean..."

"I don't know," Vera said with a painful shrug. She lifted her head to look at Tori. Her limbs felt like they weighed a hundred pounds each. "If Gavin is—"

"Please don't say if," Tori rasped. Tears brimmed in her eyes, ready to spill. Her lips trembled. "Please. Please don't say if. He... he *has* to be... I mean..." Vera's eyes were drawn to the scars on Tori's throat as she swallowed. "We've never... lost one of us before. I mean... if Isaac had lost *Sam*..."

"Gray has," Vera said. "Gray's lost... quite a few friends, actually. But never..." Vera cleared her throat. "Never a son."

If he dies... if he's dead...

If he dies alone in a cell, tortured, broken, because we couldn't find him in time...

No. He's not dead. He can't... be dead. After everything he's been through, he can't die like this.

Vera shuddered. The phantom collar tightened around her throat.

"Hey," Tori said, shaking Vera gently. "Hey. Come back to me."

"H-he thinks he's alone," Vera whispered with trembling lips. "He... at th-this point I... at this point I th-thought I was going to... to die. I th-thought Joseph was going to... to kill me. Schiester has had... *so much time* to hurt him. There's... nothing he couldn't have done during this time. Tori, he... h-he... if w-we g-go in and, and, and he's—"

"We'll deal with what we find," Tori said, soothing, brushing the hair back from Vera's face. "Hey. We'll—"

Vera shivered at the cold cement floor against her skin, the feeling of strangers' hands cutting the collar away, the gag shoved into her mouth to keep her from biting them. Everything she'd held inside, held back for Isaac, rose up and threatened to tear her down. Acrid despair crushed her chest.

"He thinks he's alone," Vera whimpered, her eyes wide, her cheeks wet with tears. "If he's alive, he... th-thinks he's alone." She gasped and wobbled on her feet. "Sch-Schiester's probably telling him he's alone. That we don't care. And... with how long it's taken for us to find him..."

"Yeah," Tori said, her voice shaking. "He probably is telling Gavin that. But when we find him—"

"He's gonna be so fucked up," Vera croaked. "What if we get him back and I…"

She felt a nudge against her leg and went still. She wet her lips and bent down to pet the cat, who looked up at her with his fathomless yellow eyes. Vera drew a deep breath into her lungs, let it out. When she straightened again, her head swam. She leaned against Tori and wiped the tears from her cheeks.

"S-sorry," she rasped. "Sorry. It's—"

"A lot," Tori finished gently. She laced her fingers through Vera's and squeezed. "This past month has been…"

"Hell." Vera sagged with exhaustion. Between missions further north and getting calls at all hours of the night with updates – updates that always, without fail, bore no news at all – she could barely stay on her feet.

She pushed away thoughts of the nightmares that plagued her when she *could* sleep. Nightmares of a cold cell, a collar and chain, a man who hurt her and held his knife to the throat of the only person in the world who could save her—

She could smell Ryan's blood. Bile crept up her throat. She swallowed it down and shook herself, forcing the memory out of her mind.

She could fall apart if— when they got Gavin back. She could afford to crumble once Gavin was safe.

If he's—

No. He's alive. He has to be. Schiester would never kill him without letting us know.

She could almost believe her own logic. She dug her nails into her palm, dragging herself back into her body.

"Wh-where's everybody else?" she murmured, suddenly and acutely aware of how quiet the house was.

Tori shrugged. "Gray's at Finn and Ellis's place, trying to fix their sink." She smiled ruefully. "I truly have no idea where we're supposed to dig up a plumber. I think the nearest one is in Westwood, and that's an hour away. And they know Ellis doesn't like being by themself, with Finn in Crayton right now."

Vera nodded vaguely. "Okay. And the others?"

Tori's smile fell. "Edrissa's out of the house somewhere, I'm not sure where. She said she needed some air. And—"

As if summoned by Vera's thoughts, a door creaked open down the hall. Vera looked up and saw Sam and Zachariah wander into the kitchen. Zachariah had bruise-like circles under his eyes, just like Isaac's. He looked up and flinched when he saw her. He relaxed a moment later, his hands shaking at his sides. His tan skin was pale and sallow after a month inside the house, out of sight of Schiester and his men.

If Zachariah was discovered, he was too small a prize for Schiester to keep alive for long – not while he had the son of Joseph Stormbeck to torment.

Sam's hair was tousled and unkempt, their cheeks flushed. When they saw Vera, their eyes widened and they took a hasty step forward.

"W-was Isaac home?" they murmured, and Zachariah reached out to take their hand. They squeezed his fingers, their eyes never leaving Vera.

"Yeah," Vera said softly. "He's back. He's, um... sorry he missed breakfast."

Sam chewed their lip. "He could... come visit, just for—"

"I don't think so, Sam," Vera rasped. "He's..." She swallowed. "Maybe tomorrow, after Gray gets back from their shift." Vera's chest ached with the lie, at the hurt that tightened behind Sam's eyes.

"Is he..." Sam faltered and stepped away from Zachariah, their hands still linked. "Can I-I do anything to help him? Help... Gavin?" They shrugged their shoulders up to their ears and wound their right arm around themself.

Vera's shoulders slumped forward. She cleared her throat and met their eyes in turn. She felt the intensity of their stares – Sam's and Zachariah's. Zachariah's eyes were bloodshot, his knuckles showing white as they gripped Sam's hand.

"Just... hang on. For him. For both of them. Gray will talk to Finn tomorrow and get a plan in place. This is the most dangerous part – for us, and for Gavin. If we storm the building and can't get in... or have the wrong place..." Dread curdled in her stomach.

There's no right way to do this. We have everything to lose, and Schiester will kill Gavin without a moment's hesitation if he finds out.

237

They just had to depend on how badly Schiester needed Gavin to hurt. They had to depend on whatever history Schiester had with Joseph being enough to buy Gavin some time.

But if he's dead...

If he's dead...

She couldn't stand to think about Gavin lying dead, cold, tied down in a cell because his family didn't fucking *try* hard enough to save him. Her stomach roiled and she felt her hand dart out to grab Tori's shoulder, to stabilize herself. Tori's hand settled on Vera's arm. Her fingers were cold.

Vera shuddered and blew out a slow breath. "Sorry. Jesus. We... we need to be patient. That's what we can do for him now. Once we meet with Finn, if they have a plan and they're sure... we move. Until then..." She ran a hand over her face. She felt like she'd aged ten fucking years in the past month. "Gavin just needs to fucking hold on."

Chapter 34

It was still Ziegler's shift when Schiester returned. Helpless tears smarted Gavin's eyes as the mayor descended the stairs to the basement again, his boots echoing off the cold cement walls.

Twice in one day? Gavin forced back a sob as he curled into a ball on his cot and pulled the blanket tight over his head. *Don't you have anything better to do?* Still, as hateful as he felt, it didn't protect him from the rising panic in his chest as the footsteps grew nearer and nearer to his cell – and finally stopped just outside of it. Shaking, Gavin raised his head and peeked out.

Schiester was staring at him with a mixture of rage and distrust. Gavin's mouth went dry as his muscles all locked at once.

Schiester reached into his pocket and slowly drew out the key to the cell. Just as slowly, he opened the cell door and swung it open. He stepped inside, drawing himself up to his full height until his hair nearly brushed the bars crisscrossing over them both. He wet his lips and opened his mouth.

"Put your hands behind your back, Stormbeck," he said, each word deliberately and perfectly formed.

Gavin's throat tightened beneath the collar and he obeyed without hesitation. Schiester made quick work of binding him, then took a step back, looking Gavin up and down. His cold blue eyes glittered in the dim light above. Gavin could hardly breathe past the terror clogging his throat.

In one smooth motion, Schiester pulled a cell phone out of his pocket. He tapped the screen a few times and held it out for Gavin to see. Gavin felt his heart tear to pieces in his chest.

On the screen was a video of Gray sitting at a table in the atrium of the town hall, helping a refugee fill out paperwork. They clearly didn't know they were being filmed.

Gavin was begging before he even realized he had opened his mouth. "Please, *no,*" he sobbed, already struggling to rise from the cot. "No, no no *please*—"

With his other hand, Schiester drew a handgun from the pocket of his coat and aimed it at Gavin's heart.

Gavin froze on the cot, but couldn't stop begging. "Schiester, *no, please*, not Gray, I've done everything you told me to do, they haven't done anything wrong, please, not Gray, please, Schiester, I'm *begging* you, no, please, no *no no*…"

"Shut up, Stormbeck," Schiester barked.

"Not *them*," Gavin sobbed. "Please, no, anyone but them…"

Almost anyone.

Schiester jabbed the barrel of the gun against Gavin's forehead and screamed in his face, "I said, *shut up!*"

Gavin's pleas trailed off into a broken, wordless wail as he stared at the figure on the screen. Gray – he hadn't seen them in weeks, or had it been months? – was there, they were *right there,* right upstairs, right above Gavin's head. He'd known – or hoped – that they had been, but now he *knew*. And they were about to be dragged down to the basement with Gavin and be put to death on the gallows just like Lucy and Topher had been. Gavin was going to watch Gray die today, in a few minutes, perhaps, and it was all because of him.

"Kill me," he breathed, through numb lips.

Schiester pulled the gun away from Gavin's forehead. Gavin barely had time to gasp before Schiester's fist, made even heavier with the gun, crashed against the side of his head. Gavin crumpled to the cot in a heap and stared up at Schiester, dazed.

"Another word, Stormbeck, and my men take them this moment. Do you understand?" Schiester hissed through clenched teeth.

Gavin pressed his lips together and nodded, blinking to clear his head.

Schiester blew out an exasperated sigh. "Very well. Now. You understand their life is in mortal danger, I take it?" he said flatly.

Gavin nodded vigorously. His temple throbbed with the motion.

Schiester snorted. "You may speak now, boy, if you're done with your ridiculous sniveling."

"Wh-what do you want?" Gavin rasped, eyes still streaming. "I've done… You've taken… everything you wanted. What's left? Do you… do you want to fuck me?"

There was a choked sound from the corner where Ziegler sat. Schiester's eyes flicked to his guard, and back to Gavin.

"Fuck you?" Schiester sneered. "I'd rather fornicate with an animal than fuck you, Gavin *Stormbeck.*"

Still, the tight line of Schiester's mouth betrayed a tension that chilled Gavin to his core. He wondered if he would survive being fucked by Schiester.

He wondered if a plaything had ever died on his father's cock.

Gavin swallowed hard past the collar. "Th-then—"

"If you're finished polluting this discussion with your disgusting notions…" Schiester waggled the phone in front of Gavin's eyes. "If you care about Gray Uriah as much as you claim, one would think that you would want to be very, very honest with me about what they may be doing? Seeing how lying ended for that nice young couple who saw fit to sacrifice their lives to save your worthless hide." Schiester gestured at the gallows along the wall.

Gavin's eyes filled with tears as acerbic guilt and prickly rage washed through him in equal measure. He forced himself to nod, unable to look away from the phone. Gray was right there, slightly blurry but *right there.* It was them. Their soft smile as they looked at the refugees, their gentle way of moving, their height as they stood to point them towards something out of frame. He could call out for them, if only he could scream loud enough. If they only *knew.*

Gavin tore his gaze away from Gray and met Schiester's eyes. Hate burned red-hot inside him. His lips trembled as he whispered, "What do you want me to do?"

Schiester smirked. "Just tell me the truth," he said with a cold smile. "That's all."

The truth is what got Topher and Lucy killed.

Gavin swallowed past the collar and the lump in his throat. He drew a quavering breath. "I'll tell you as much as I know," he lied through his teeth.

"Might as well," Schiester said. He tucked the phone back into his pocket.

Gavin nearly cried out at the loss, nearly begged Schiester to pull out the phone again, just so he could see Gray's face one more time. His plea died in his throat as Schiester hauled Gavin onto his knees by the collar, held him fast as he trailed the cold barrel of the gun along the sensitive scar on Gavin's cheek.

"As you said," Schiester murmured, "I've taken everything else. I *will* have the truth."

Gavin glared up at Schiester and tried not to shiver as he wondered if the gun was even loaded. This might be just another one of Schiester's games, another trick to torture him. Gavin's eyes flicked to the gallows along the wall. Lucy and Topher's deaths hadn't been a trick.

Schiester probably didn't even care about killing them. But Gavin knew, beyond a shadow of a doubt, that Schiester barely needed an excuse to kill Gray.

"Wh-what do you want to know?" he breathed through trembling lips.

The corner of Schiester's mouth pulled up in the shadow of a smile. "Ziegler," he said, not letting his eyes leave Gavin's. "Go and prop the door open."

Gavin's heart missed a beat. He blinked and tried to catch his breath.

"S-sir?" came Ziegler's reply. "The... door to the upstairs?"

"Yes," Schiester said evenly. "Prop it open. I want to ask our Stormbeck prisoner these questions with... a choice being in his hands."

"What the fuck—" Gavin gasped. Schiester shoved Gavin back against the bars of the cage. The barrel of the gun pressed against his throat, just above the collar, and he yanked against the rope tying his hands behind him.

"Ziegler," Schiester snapped. *"Now."*

"Already moving, sir," the guard said as he hurried up the stairs.

Schiester's smirk crept over his face like frost. "Now," he murmured. The upstairs door creaked open, and Gavin felt the pressure in the room change. "The truth. Or you might as well just scream for them, right? They could probably hear you now, with that door open. The sound could carry."

"What is this?" Gavin whispered. Fear constricted his throat. "What—"

"This isn't too much of a deviation from the plan, is it?" Schiester said, his teeth now bared in a wicked grin. "They *are* planning a rescue for you, aren't they?"

"No," Gavin croaked, desperately shaking his head. "Don't... don't do this. Don't... make this shit up out of nowhere and pin it on... on *them*. I know you—" Rage flared in him; he couldn't stop it. He lifted his chin, his eyes flashing. "I know you love doing that shit with *me,* but you will *not* do that to them, I will *not* let you get them killed—"

A slap whipped Gavin's head to the side. His ear rang, but the barrel of the gun stayed pressed to his throat. "Once a lying syndicate shit, always a lying syndicate shit," Schiester snarled in Gavin's face. Spittle flecked his cheeks.

"They're not coming for me," Gavin half-sobbed. Tears burned in his eyes. "They're not. They wouldn't. That's over—"

"Then why are they methodically checking every building and structure in Crayton?" Schiester said in a voice as flat and cold as his eyes.

Gavin's heart stopped. He searched Schiester's face, desperate to catch the lie – and just as desperate for it to be true. "What?" he breathed.

"What part of that sentence did you find confusing, Stormbeck?" Schiester sneered. "I'd be happy to walk you through it again, but slower."

"They're... searching buildings?" Gavin rasped. His throat was dry.

"Rather methodically," Schiester said. He pressed the gun harder against Gavin's throat.

"For... how long?" The tears in Gavin's eyes ran down his cheeks. He didn't try to stop them.

Schiester seemed to hesitate before he finally answered, "They started a week after I took you off their hands."

Gavin had no idea how long he had been in this basement. It could have been two weeks, or two months. He blinked and raised his gaze to Schiester. "Why have you been... letting them search?"

Schiester snorted. "I don't control who goes in and out of the buildings up here, boy. I am not your father. I don't feel the need to control the comings and goings of my own people."

"But..." Gavin felt dizzy. Something dangerously similar to hope was growing in his chest. "If you suspected..."

"I *suspect* many things," Schiester said airily. His grip on the gun had not loosened.

Gavin swallowed hard. "But... they—"

"Enough," Schiester said through gritted teeth. He slammed Gavin back against the bars so hard he saw stars. "Answer the question, Stormbeck. Are they coming for you? You claim to know them well. And if you lie..." Schiester pressed the gun against Gavin's shoulder. "...I will make sure Gray Uriah can hear the gunshot. But you will not die from it for some weeks afterwards."

Gavin trembled and pressed himself back against the bars. He stared down at the gun pressed into his shoulder, just below the collarbone. He shuddered and blinked tears out of his eyes. Slowly, he opened his mouth and asked one more question. "Is... is Isaac with them? When they search?"

Schiester held the gun perfectly still against Gavin. The barrel was beginning to warm with his body heat. Then, very deliberately, Schiester said, "No. Isaac Moore has not come further south than Burmingham since you were taken." The gun pressed in a little harder, and Gavin winced. "In fact, he spends a lot of time further north. He has become very close with a new group that travels around quite a bit. More time with them than with... well. You would call them his *family*."

Gavin's eyes fell shut, and tears streamed down his cheeks. *I broke him so hard he didn't even stay with the family,* he thought, sagging under the weight of his despair. *Sam must be crushed. Vera must hate me.*

Schiester gave Gavin's collar a cruel jerk, but Gavin's head sank low. He didn't try to hold back the weak sob that tore from his chest. "No," he said softly, as tears dripped off the end of his nose. "They're not looking for me. I don't know why they're searching buildings, but... it's not to find me." His sorrow tightened like a fist around his heart. He squeezed his eyes shut and slumped against Schiester's grip, weeping quietly. He was lost in guilt and pain. He nearly forgot the gun pressed against his shoulder, and his torturer bracing him against the bars of his cell.

Schiester drew in a quick breath through his teeth and slammed Gavin onto his back on the cot. Gavin cried out in surprise. His mouth snapped shut as he remembered the open door above him, guarded by Ziegler, who looked studiously away.

"Scream for them," Schiester growled as he pressed the barrel of the gun against the side of Gavin's head.

"No," Gavin whimpered.

"Call out to them. Right now." Schiester's eyes flashed in the dim light. He gripped Gavin's hair and yanked his head back with a vicious grip. "That's what you want, isn't it? I know you, Stormbeck. I know you won't hesitate for a second. Come on, now. They're just down the hall."

"Fuck, *fuck off*," Gavin gasped as he writhed against Schiester's iron grip.

"It's an easy choice, isn't it?" Schiester said through his teeth. "Scream for them, Stormbeck, or I pull this trigger." The barrel of the gun ground into Gavin's head.

Tears streamed over Gavin's temples. Schiester's hand tightened further, and Gavin barely suppressed a scream. He desperately shook his head against Schiester's grip.

Schiester's lip curled. "I'm done playing this game. Choose. Them or you."

"You know what I'm going to say," Gavin panted. "Please—"

A grin spread over Schiester's face. "I know. Say it. Scream for them. The door is open. Scream for them now. They can hear you, if you only scream. Them or you, Gavin Stormbeck. Them. Or. You."

"Me," Gavin sobbed. "You know I mean it, just fucking kill *me*." He squeezed his eyes shut and waited.

Schiester released Gavin's hair and leaned back. Shaking, Gavin opened his eyes and looked up at him, wrecked, terrified. Schiester was staring at him with an unreadable expression.

"Very well, Stormbeck," he murmured, his lips barely moving. "They aren't looking for you. They live another day to save helpless refugees, and you live another day to suffer." He stepped out of the cell without another word.

Gavin dissolved into helpless, breathless sobs. He rolled onto his side and pressed his face against the rough canvas of the cot so the sound wouldn't carry too far. The echoes of Schiester's footsteps faded as he climbed the stairs.

"Cut him loose, Ziegler," Schiester ordered tightly. "I'll be back this evening, before your shift ends."

Ziegler cleared his throat. "Agai— Yes, sir," he muttered.

245

The door slammed shut behind Schiester. Gavin glanced up and saw Ziegler standing at the top of the stairs, staring at the gallows.

"I'll be back this evening, before your shift ends."

Three times in one day.

Gavin's hands tightened into fists behind him and screamed his terror, his rage, his frustration. When his voice gave out, all that was left was his grief.

Chapter 35

Vera jumped as the phone in her pocket buzzed. She snatched it up and didn't even check the number before she flipped it open and held it to her ear.

"H-hello?" she said in a quavering voice.

"It's Finn," came the clipped reply.

Ice clutched Vera's chest. "F-Finn—"

"Hey. Is everyone there?"

"Isaac's back in town in the shack, Gray's with Ellis," Vera said. She tried to breathe slowly against the choked feeling in her throat. "D-do you have news? I mean..."

"I just wanted to let you know that I, um... I got an inspection scheduled of the town hall. Tomorrow."

The room lurched around Vera, and she fell against Tori, who stood just beside her.

"Vera?" Finn said, their voice starting to waver.

"Holy fuck," Vera breathed. She looked up and met the eyes of her family in turn. "It's... it's happening. Tomorrow." Her fingers ached as she clutched the phone tight to her ear. "I, um... I n-need to call Isaac and Gray. Let me... give me ten minutes."

"Sure thing. Um... stay safe."

"Yeah, you too."

Vera flipped the phone shut with numb fingers. She stared blankly at the floor, not even aware she wasn't breathing until her chest started to ache. She dragged in a shaky breath.

Sam broke the silence. "They..." They swallowed, and Vera raised her eyes to look at them. "It's... happening? Tomorrow?"

"Tomorrow." Vera could barely feel her lips as she spoke. Her fingers trembled as she selected the number for Finn and Ellis's phone and dialed. She held the phone to her ear. It rang only once before someone picked up.

"Hey," came Ellis's harried voice. *"What's up?"*

"It's Vera," she croaked. She reached out and steadied herself on the counter. "Is Gray right there?"

The moment of silence was deafening.

"Um... yeah. Wh-what's up?"

"Put it on speaker," Vera said.

"Oh, no," Ellis whispered, and there was a rustling sound. Then, *"Is Finn— You're on speaker, Vera. Is Finn... They're okay...?"* Ellis's voice sounded tinny and far away.

"What happened?" Gray croaked. They sounded broken. Hollow.

"Um..." Vera's throat tightened. "Finn called. They um... they're going to search the town hall tomorrow."

There was a clatter over the phone, a half-sob.

"Oh," Gray whimpered. *"I..."*

"He might not be there," Vera said quickly, her heart pounding in her chest. "We have to remember that. We—"

"But this is the first time we've been able to know," Gray said. Vera's chest ached at the desperation in their voice. *"And we... w-we're running out of places he could be. This is the... f-first time we've been able to... Vera, if he's not there, th-then... Does Isaac know?"*

"Not yet," Vera said dully. "I'm calling him as soon as I hang up with you."

"We'll all be over there soon," said Gray. *"Give us a moment and... we'll be right there."*

Vera shivered. Her hand tightened on the counter. She couldn't allow herself to hope, couldn't dare to think that maybe, just maybe, tomorrow...

She shook herself and cleared her throat. "O-okay," she breathed. "Sounds good." Her body felt encased in ice, scorched by fire. She raised her head and looked at the others. "Let's get Edrissa in here. Once everyone's here, we're making a plan."

Chapter 36

Gavin was dreaming – but somehow, he was awake too. The room spun around him, a dull kaleidoscope of gray and blue and black, the fractured edges digging at his skin. He shivered under the blankets, even as his nerves blazed. Sweat beaded on his forehead. It was warm under the blankets – three of them, now, each one earned by his confessions. And still, ice crept down his throat, crystallized inside him. He moaned softly and rubbed at the sting in the crook of his elbow.

He'd been here before. He'd felt this sickness in his veins, seen the broken edges of this room swirl around him before, just like this. He'd tasted the distant, bitter terror on his tongue from the cold blue eyes watching him, the creature made of shadows that stood just outside the bars of his cage.

He'd felt this before. He'd been this before. He could smell Isaac's blood, hear Sam's screams, feel his family's pleas like glass under his skin. He'd been trapped here before.

Where was *here?*

He pulled helplessly at the thick nylon collar around his neck. A rope was knotted to the ring that hung from it, coarse and scratchy against his skin as Gavin rolled over, whimpering. The rope pulled tight, and he choked. He rolled back, and the rope mercifully loosened. Tears glazed his face.

Something was coming. He knew, somehow, that something was coming, something that was waiting just outside the safety of the bars. His eyelids fluttered as he tried to see, tried to focus. His gaze fell on the specter standing outside and staring at him silently. As he watched, blue eyes became gray, white skin darkened to black. The hard line of a mouth rounded to full lips, and the figure grew until they stood several inches taller than the man who always watched his nightmares.

Gavin's throat felt scraped raw as he swallowed. "G-Gray?" he whispered.

Gray's mouth pulled into a smirk. Gavin recoiled at the disdain, the *bitterness* of their expression. He'd never seen them look like that before, not even—

Not even after he'd found the family again after shooting Gray in the chest.

Gavin whimpered softly. "I'm... I'm sorry..."

"Sorry for *what?*" Gray spat the words like acid through their teeth.

"For..." Gavin swallowed again, harder. "F-for... hurting... you. And the family. I'm... I'm *sorry.*"

Gray rolled their eyes. "None of us thought you were alive," they said flatly. They lifted their head, cast their gaze around the room. "This is where you've been kept?"

"I'm in the basement," Gavin rasped, pressing his face into his hands. The lights hurt his skin. "I've been in the, the town hall. I'm in the *basement.*"

"Yes, I know," Gray sneered.

Gavin pulled his hands away from his face and tried to push himself up to sitting. As he shifted, he thought he could feel water still burning in his lungs. *When did he drown me?* He couldn't remember. He couldn't *think.*

"A-are you... here for me?" Gavin whispered, turning tear-filled eyes towards Gray.

Gray blinked. "Here for... you?"

Gavin nodded, doing his best to muffle a sob as tears slid down his cheeks. "P-please... it *hurts.*" His fingers went up to brush the scars marking his nose, cheek, and eye, healed again after Schiester reopened them, cutting across his face in still-red lines that Schiester had forced him to look at in the mirror.

"Yes, I suspect it does," Gray said, and their voice carried a sardonic edge that made Gavin's eyes burn with more tears.

"I'm sorry," he croaked, and tugged harder at the collar. He couldn't remember how it felt to breathe without it. "But please, just..." He reached out with one hand, as if he could reach Gray from behind the bars. *"Help me."*

Gray cocked their head. "And why," they said coolly, "Would I do that?"

250

"B-because I..." Gavin bit down on his lip, his chest shaking with sobs. "Gray, *please*... I... I w-want to say I'm sorry to the others. Please, just... let me... l-let me see Sam. Let me see *Isaac*. Gray... *please*..." He shuddered and pressed his fist to his mouth to muffle the whine that tore from his throat. "Gray... p-please..."

Gray snorted. "Why are you here, Gavin?"

Gavin huddled against the bars. They leached the heat from his skin. He shivered at the relief against his sweat-slick forehead, the ache as his skin froze against the cold steel. He twisted weakly in the blankets. He couldn't stop shaking.

"I-I'm here b-because..." He lifted his head, searching for the ghostly figure with cold blue eyes. The room shimmered darkly behind the bars. Even Gray seemed to waver under the sickly lights.

Gavin's throat felt raw. "B-because..." His voice dropped to a whisper. "Because Sch-Schiester likes to... hurt me." He sobbed weakly. "Please, Gray, I... I'm *sorry,* I know I hurt you, and Isaac and Sam and Vera and the rest, but... please, I... he's going to *kill* me."

Gray's eyes were as cold as Schiester's as they looked steadily at him. They were silent for a long time. Gavin could feel his heart pounding in his chest, his skin beading with sweat, his hands shaking as he clutched at the blankets. He felt like he might be sick as the room tilted around him. He groaned and lowered himself onto the cot. Tears streamed down his face. He pulled his knees to his chest and lay still, shivering. It was as if he could see the noose hanging from the ceiling, even as he stared at the floor of his cell. The rope hadn't taken another life since—

A strangled sob left his throat and he covered his head with his hands. He shook with every breath.

He jumped and let out a wail as he felt a hand in his hair. Not soft, the way Isaac's was every time he came to this cell...

Isaac's never been here. He wouldn't leave me. He wouldn't leave me to die.

Gray wouldn't leave me.

Gavin forced his eyes open and looked up at the person touching him. Gray looked down at him with an expression that twisted their lips, darkened

251

their eyes. Not pain, not anguish, not anything Gavin would have given his life to see – he only saw *contempt*. He whimpered softly and wet his lips.

"Gray…"

Gray's fingers tightened in Gavin's hair and dragged him upright. Even as Gavin whined at the touch, it felt… strange. As if coming from miles away, as if it was only a memory of a feeling. Gavin's eyes watered as Gray shoved him back against the bars of the cage, tearing some of his hair out by the roots. He reached up to grab at Gray's wrist. His fingers closed on cold steel.

"What's your name?" Gray snarled, their eyes finally sparking with fury.

Gavin whimpered and tried to pull away. "Gray… no, *please,* just—"

He cried out as a blow snapped his head to the side. His cheek burned dully, almost as if he was imagining the pain.

"What. Is. Your. Name?" Gray said through their teeth, trembling with intensity.

Tears mingled with the sweat shining on Gavin's face as he sobbed. He knew the answer. He'd been called by that name every day for… not just the past weeks in this cell, but for longer than he could remember. His whole life. He'd had four months – one spent torturing his own family at his mother's command, and three spent loving them, being loved in return – when he was allowed to be anything else. The name he'd chosen, not the name he was born with.

He never had a choice. He was deluded beyond measure to think he ever had.

He forced himself to meet Gray's eyes, cringing away from the viciousness and the rage there. He opened his mouth to speak. Only a strangled whimper made its way out.

Gray struck him again, this time a backhanded blow across the face. Something wet and warm streamed down his cheek and moistened Gavin's lips. He flinched, expecting the taste of blood. It tasted like tears.

"What is your name?" Gray hissed.

"P-please don't make me say it," Gavin begged, weeping. "Gray, *please*…"

"You took Isaac and Sam. You *hurt* all of us. You tortured every single one of us." Gray was barely recognizable. Their face was a mask of fury. "I watched the look in your eyes as you shot me. You *liked* it. You *liked* watching me fall and choke and bleed."

It was true. It was all true.

"Do you have any idea how it feels to hear *your name* screamed by my family when they wake from nightmares?" Gray snarled. "Do you have any *clue* how it feels to be *hunted down* by the boy who tore my family apart, to be forced to house you, feed you, clothe you, *protect you?*"

"G-Gray…"

"My family went south with you and came back *broken*," Gray said, viciously. "They should have left you to die. *That* would have been justice."

"I-I know," Gavin sobbed. "Gray… I'm s-sorry, what c-can I—"

"Tell me your name," Gray snarled, kneeling on the cot in front of Gavin, forcing him back against the bars of the cage. "I don't want to hear your pathetic sniveling. Tell me your damned *name*."

The words tasted like blood as Gavin forced himself to say them. *"G-Gavin Stormbeck,"* he whispered through numb lips.

Gray lifted their chin. Their fingers loosened in Gavin's hair, and he slumped to the side, sobbing.

"That's right," Gray murmured. "Gavin Stormbeck." They stepped away from the cot and drew themself up to their full height. "You don't deserve my name. You *took* it, the same way you took everything from us. You were never Gavin Uriah. That was a lie, and you knew it." Their hand darted out and they grasped Gavin's wrist, pulling his arm straight so the fresh scars caught the light.

The word carved into his arm began to burn like a brand.

Stormbeck.

"This is who you are and who you'll always be," Gray snarled.

"No," Gavin whimpered brokenly. "Gray… p-please…"

"Syndicate *shit*," Gray spat, shoving Gavin's arm away. "Taking whatever you like, hurting whoever comes close." Gray grabbed Gavin's chin and jerked it up so he was forced to look at them. Their fingers seemed to press through his skin, as if he wasn't real, as if Gray's hand could pass right through him. His vision blurred with tears.

"Why *us?*" Gray whispered, and their voice broke. Tears welled in their eyes. "Why did you have to choose *us?*"

Gavin's lips trembled as Gray craned his head back. His fingers twisted in the blanket. All over his body, his scars burned – streaks of agony across his face, his back, his arm. The air boiled around him. And inside, self-hatred seared him.

"Because…" His throat felt like it was on fire, smoke crawling into his lungs and choking him. His eyes streamed tears. "You… y-you're good. I wanted Sam because they were easy, but then I wanted you all because you were *good*." He swallowed, trying to soothe the burn in his throat. "I w-wanted… all of you… because you're good. I've never… h-had that. I w-wanted to see… something that I've never had."

"Well," Gray spat. "Are you satisfied? Have you seen now what makes us so *good?*"

Gavin dissolved into tears. "I just wanted what you had," he whimpered. "Please, Gray… y-you understood before…"

"I didn't have the choice before," Gray said coldly. "When you're around, no one has a choice. You break everything you touch, don't you? Stormbeck son, born to rule, in command of all he sees. That's you, isn't it?"

"No," Gavin sobbed. "No, it's not… I n-never *wanted* that, I—"

Gray scoffed. "As if you wouldn't have always used your power to find more people to hurt. There's no end to the darkness inside you, is there? If we hadn't come along and given you something else, would you have ever stopped? Poor Stormbeck boy, you had to be *broken* before you stopped destroying lives. And that still wasn't enough, was it? You tortured them when your mother told you to. You broke when she hurt you. You hurt my family because you're a *coward.*"

"No!" Gavin wailed. "No, you… you don't understand, she would have *killed him* if I didn't—"

"You're right," Gray sneered. "I *don't* understand." They were starting to shimmer around the edges, to fade into the ghostly swirl of the room around them. "And thank god for that. I'm grateful that I'll never understand the mind of Gavin Stormbeck. I escaped you once. I don't need to be pulled in again." They took a step back. The bars seemed to part for them.

"Gray, *NO!*" Gavin screamed, lurching forward with outstretched hands. The rope on his collar snapped tight and a strangled whine punched out of him. "D-don't, don't leave me here, *don't leave me here, PLEASE!*"

"This is where you belong," Gray said, their voice echoing, fading. "The road of your life ends here. It could never lead anywhere else. This is justice, Gavin Stormbeck. This is retribution."

"Gray," Gavin sobbed, his chest desperately heaving. *"No."*

Gray nodded towards the gallows. The rope hung, seemingly from nothing, silent and still. "When your life ends," Gray said gently, "Don't think of us. I don't want us anywhere near your final moments. You will suffer, alone, and then you'll die. Schiester will dispose of your body. The myth of Gavin Stormbeck will fade."

"Please," Gavin whispered, his body numb and blazing all at once. "Please don't leave me."

"Count yourself lucky," Gray said, their voice barely audible anymore, "That Schiester hasn't raped you. If this were true justice, I think, he would do it. For Isaac's sake, at the very least."

The breath rushed out of Gavin's chest, and he collapsed to the cot, sobbing. He clawed at the collar. His head spun, the air too thin to breathe. He tilted his head back and screamed his anguish, sobbing Gray's name, Isaac's, Vera's, Sam's. Repeating the names of his family, over and over – the family he terrorized and hurt, but the family who made him *good*, for a short time anyway. The family he'd taken everything from, and in return had given him a home. They didn't have a choice – he knew that. But still... he was grateful. Even for things he'd taken from them at the point of a knife, not even knowing the danger he put them in for all those months, he was grateful.

As he sobbed his apologies, sobbed the names of the people he'd destroyed, a ghost with blue eyes stood in the corner, watching silently.

Chapter 37

"Isaac!" Sam cried hoarsely before Isaac could even walk through the front door.

They came barreling into his arms, burying their head against his chest and squeezing him tight. Isaac's eyes pricked with tears as he wrapped his arms around them and pressed a kiss to the crown of their head. He released them a moment later. He could barely breathe. His blood pulsed beneath his skin; his heart pounded in his chest; his every nerve throbbed.

Tomorrow.

I'm going to get him back tomorrow.

Isaac looked up at the others, who were crowded into the kitchen. Ellis was huddled in the corner, face pale, with their hands tucked under the small belly Isaac could swear they hadn't had the last time he'd seen them. Vera stood beside Tori. Vera's mouth was set, her gaze steady on Isaac as he walked in, tucking Sam beneath his arm. Edrissa shifted her eyes away, standing on the opposite end of the kitchen from Zachariah. Zachariah's face was haggard. He looked like he'd aged ten years in the three months since he'd reached the family. Deep circles were carved under his eyes, and his hands shook at his sides. Gray stood in the middle of it all, eyes wide but focused on nothing. Isaac thought he saw a glimmer of tears as they blinked and looked up at him.

"Um… h-haven't made the call yet?" Isaac croaked.

"No," Gray said weakly. "Wanted to… w-wait on you."

Isaac's throat tightened as he glanced around at the others. Every second they waited, Gavin suffered. Every inch of Isaac's body ached with terror, with the unending pulse of self-hatred that burned through him with each heartbeat: *my fault. My fault. My fault.*

"L-let's get it done, then," he rasped. He felt like he would jump out of his skin if he had to wait another moment. His hand twitched for the gun tucked into his waistband. Vera's eyes caught the motion. Her mouth twisted.

Silently, Gray pulled the cell phone out of their pocket and flipped it open. They dialed Finn and put the phone on speaker. They held the phone out in the middle of the group. It trembled in their hand.

It rang once. Twice.

There was a muffled clatter on the other end, and Finn's harried voice sounding out of breath answered. *"Hey."*

Adrenaline punched through Isaac's gut. Tomorrow, Finn was going to walk into the town hall and find Gavin. Tomorrow, Finn was going to let Isaac into the town hall, and they were going to save Gavin's life.

Tomorrow.

The possibility of failure didn't even cross his mind. Gavin was at the town hall; Isaac knew it with every fiber of his being. He was going to save him. The only way he was not going to have Gavin in his arms tomorrow night was if he was no longer *breathing.*

"H-hey, Finn," Gray said with a shaking voice. "The whole gang is here. You're on speaker."

"Good, good," Finn said distractedly. A shuffling sound. *"Sorry, I'm trying to get somewhere where I can talk. I've been staying with Vanya the past couple days."*

"Take your time," Gray said breathlessly.

There was the whisper of movement, the distant sound of a door closing. Finn's voice was more muffled than before. *"Alright, I can talk. Let's go over things."*

"What's the plan?" Isaac said, unable to keep silent any longer. He bit his lip and clutched Sam tighter. They leaned against him and squeezed him back.

"Well first, I hope the short notice is okay—"

"Yes," Isaac choked. "Y-yes."

There was a deep breath over the line. *"Okay. Good. So, here's my plan, the way I have it, the same way I've done everything else: I'm going to go to the town hall tomorrow to do a simple fire inspection. We've done half the town by now, and the town hall is right in line with the pattern I've been taking from east to west. There's no reason for his royal fucking fuckery to suspect I'm doing anything out of the ordinary."*

Isaac nodded as Finn spoke. His skin buzzed.

Finn continued. *"I'm not going to do a complete fire inspection, because that would be a waste of time. That building is old as dirt. But it'll probably have an alarm system. There will be a room with an alarm panel that I can check. Sometimes there will even be a premise map that'll give a detailed map of every floor... but I doubt it."*

"If DFS has been keeping captives in the basement, I doubt he'd leave a map up," Vera said harshly.

Isaac huffed out a breath.

"Yeah, that's what I was thinking. There will be an alarm panel that will probably give me a good idea of how many floors there are. We have to consider the fact that there might be more than one underground floor."

Isaac's breath rushed out of him. He hadn't considered—

"Isaac, this is where you come in," Finn said.

Isaac's body went rigid. Ice crawled into his veins. "Y-yeah?"

"If there are any floors that show up on a premise map or on the alarm panel that the mayor won't let me access, I figure there's a pretty good chance that's where to at least start the search. I'm going to have Gray with me on the inside, helping me with the inspection. It's definitely not a one-person job and I've had people help me with other inspections, so that shouldn't seem out of the ordinary if DFS decides to be looking over my shoulder the whole damn time. Once I get a good sense of where Gavin is being kept, I'll give Gray as clear an idea as I can. One of us will get a message out to you. A call or text, probably, so we can send details. But I'll figure it out day-of. If there is a premise map, I can even give you turn by turn instructions."

"I'll find a way in," Isaac said darkly. "I will."

"I know. I'll do my best to zero in on where Gavin is, but what's more likely is I can only give you an idea if he might *be there."*

"He's there," Isaac ground out through his teeth. "He *has* to be there."

There was a long pause over the line. Then, *"Yeah. It would make sense."*

Gray cleared their throat. "I'll be running interference inside and assisting in any way I can. Then, once we have him..." They blew out a slow breath through pursed lips, their free hand in a fist against the counter. "…I'll help Isaac and Gavin to the car."

Isaac met Gray's gaze and chewed his lip. Gray's eyes shone with tears. Their face hardened into agonized determination. Isaac blinked as he realized there were dried tear tracks on their cheeks. He swallowed hard and looked again at the phone in Gray's hand.

"I'll be waiting in the car," Finn said. Their voice broke. *"With my, um… med kit."*

Everyone was silent for a long moment.

Finn cleared their voice over the line. *"I know Vanya is working on gathering supplies for making a functioning fire department with… maybe even a transporting ambulance soon. I've been able to stock up from them."*

Gray's throat bobbed as they swallowed. "What are you planning on bringing?"

"Basic trauma stuff," Finn said in a monotone. *"Suture kits, tourniquets, trauma dressings, ten-gages, SAM splints, then… Fentanyl, ketamine, fluids, dextrose, epi, IV and IO kit, benzos, blankets and heat packs, vital signs stuff, my, um, airway kit w-with the surgical cric kit…"* Finn cleared their voice again. The sound came out twisted. *"I'm thinking about packing some IV antibiotics just in case…"*

"And…" Vera wet her lips. She was trembling. "And you think Gavin might… need all that?"

"You know we can't take him to a hospital, Vera," Finn said weakly. *"I'll have to fix whatever t-turns out to be wrong."*

Isaac's stomach clenched with nausea.

"Well…" Finn said softly. *"That's the plan."*

"We can't bring too many people," Vera said, her eyes unfocused. "Otherwise I would… I would go." She nodded slowly and looked up at Isaac. "You know I—"

"I know," he said gruffly. He shivered. Sweat prickled under his shirt. "That means that… I… should probably be down there already when Gray arrives." He absentmindedly rubbed his wrist against his hip, barely feeling the scrape of his belt against the fresh cuts that itched there. "I'll head back into town after this call, get a ride south. I'll make sure no one sees or follows."

259

"Where will you stay?" Vera said softly.

"In a fucking tent," Isaac snapped. "In an alley. In a dumpster. I don't care. I'll figure it out." Before the words were fully out, Isaac ducked his head. He glanced up at Vera, already shrinking with shame.

A muscle ticked in Vera's jaw. She stood perfectly still beside Tori, looking at Isaac evenly.

"I'm sorry," Isaac whispered. "I... I'm..."

"It's okay," Vera said, and Isaac raised his head. "I'm just... trying to work out the details."

"I know Vanya would offer their place, but we really shouldn't risk you being seen with... well, anyone," Finn said, sounding apologetic.

"I could ask Mathias," Isaac said. "He might say yes. But... that would be risky. For him."

"We'll figure it out as soon as we hang up with you, Finn," Gray said. For the first time since Isaac had left the farmhouse to search for Gavin, Gray sounded... not quite hopeful, but like there was a little bit of life in their voice again. Their fingers were white where they clutched the phone. "And... thanks, Finn. For getting this set up."

"Y-yeah," Isaac croaked. "Thank you."

The others all murmured their thank yous. Even Edrissa. She still leaned away from Isaac, her arms crossed in front of her chest.

"Well... I'll get going. Also, the inspection is scheduled for ten AM, so..."

"I'll be there," Isaac said with iron in his voice. His hand itched to hold his gun.

"Okay. Well... good, um, good luck, everybody. Love you."

"Love you," Ellis rasped, speaking for the first time. They were pale as a sheet, their hands tucked under their arms.

"Love you, babe," Finn whispered.

The line disconnected.

Isaac let out the breath he hadn't realized he was holding. He rocked forward, squeezing his arm even tighter around Sam's shoulders as his eyes burned with tears. His heart felt like it would leap from his chest with every beat.

260

Tomorrow. Ten AM tomorrow.

His hands went numb. He swiped at the tears running down his cheeks and into his beard. He felt something shift inside him, something that was about to snap. Blood pounded in his ears.

"Something we have yet to discuss in detail," Gray said softly, "Is that... once we have Gavin, Schiester will most likely come after us."

"Let him fucking come," Isaac growled. "I'll rip that motherfucker's head from his fucking—"

"If we kill him," Gray said gently, "We risk facing the anger of the entire north."

"If we kill Schiester, then we tell the entire *fucking north* what he's been doing to kids and innocent people with shit fucking luck when they come through Crayton," Isaac spat back. Edrissa drew away from Isaac, closer to Tori's side. Tori's hand settled on her shoulder and she stroked her thumb back and forth, soothing her.

Gray was silent for a moment. Then, they murmured, "We could just do that anyway."

Isaac froze mid-breath, rage crawling under his skin, solidifying into something like vicious hope. "Y-yeah?" he croaked.

Gray shrugged jerkily as they slid the phone back into their pocket. "Even if he took those pictures down, they're probably still in his office somewhere. If I see an opportunity – Gavin is the priority, he's the *only* priority, but if I get the chance – I'll grab them. Find a way to disseminate them. Those..." Gray's voice twisted. "Those people... Their families deserve to know what happened to them."

"But Gavin first," Isaac said brokenly. "I... I *need* to get Gavin out first."

Ellis shook themself and wet their lips. "Guys... Hate to be the guy to point this out, but he might not be—"

"He *is!*" Isaac cried, turning on them. They flinched back, staring at the floor. "He *is*. He... he *has* to be there. H-he has to be... *alive*." His chest tightened with a sob. "He's there," he whispered through numb lips. "He *has* to be."

Sam wound their arm around his waist again. Their hand brushed the gun tucked in Isaac's waistband. They froze and looked up at him with wide eyes. There was a hint of fear in their gaze. Isaac pushed down his guilt and looked away.

"All the same," Gray said, holding a placating hand out towards Isaac, "We should pack tonight, and be prepared to move. Regardless of how the plan goes."

"It'll work," Isaac said fiercely.

Gray's head fell forward. "Regardless," they continued softly, "We should be ready to move. Ellis, if you'll—"

"We've been ready to go for weeks," Ellis said, and shifted their feet. "We never really unpacked. Let's be honest... we knew this was going to get ugly. But once we have the idiot back..." They shrugged and stared at their shoes. "We can settle in then. Wherever it is we end up."

Isaac's throat constricted. "And I should get going," he murmured. "I don't have anything at my place that I care to bring with us. My weapons are already in the car. But I need to get back home, find a discreet ride south. I, um... I need to figure that out."

Sam's arm tightened around his waist again, and he looked down at them. When they stared up at him, tears welled in their eyes. He pulled them close and crushed them to his chest.

"Isaac," Sam whimpered against his shirt.

"I'll see you tomorrow," Isaac murmured against their hair. "I'll see you tomorrow, with Gavin. I'll have him tomorrow."

Sam shuddered and clutched at him. "I... I know."

Tears burned in his throat. He squeezed his eyes shut and kissed their forehead, trying to ignore the tears that ran into their hair. "Love you," he whispered. Dread settled in his stomach at how much the words sounded like *goodbye.*

He swayed from side to side with them, realizing for the first time how much he'd missed this. He *missed* having his little sibling in his arms, clutched tight. He'd barely seen them at all for the past...

Twenty-eight days.

They sniffled and pulled away. Vera was at his side, and she pulled him into a hug as well. He wound his arms around her waist and lifted her up off the floor.

"We'll get our boy back," Vera mumbled, her face pressed against his shoulder. "We'll get him back."

Isaac said nothing, only nodded. He set her back down and loosened his hold. When she stepped back, Tori took her place.

They all embraced him, one by one – Gray, Ellis, Zachariah. Even Edrissa walked up to him and stiffly stuck her hand out for him to shake. He could feel her fingers trembling in his grip. He kept his gaze down and bowed his head apologetically, only too aware of the rage that boiled inside him, just beneath the surface. When she drew back, she wiped her hand on her skirt.

When he turned to leave, Gray held out the phone. "Take this," they said. "In case we need to contact you."

Isaac tucked it into his pocket. "Sure thing." His voice was hoarse. "I just need to grab something."

He turned and walked down the hall to the bedrooms. When he stopped in front of the room he'd shared with Gavin, his stomach dropped. He placed his hand on the doorknob. It was cool under his fingers. He drew in a deep breath and turned it, pushing the door open.

His breath caught in his chest. It was exactly the same as he'd left it, the morning he'd discovered Gavin had been taken while he slept. The bedspread was rumpled, the drawer of Gavin's nightstand still slightly open. The curtain was drawn, but the last rays of the afternoon sun backlit the purple fabric, casting the room in a strange, dim light. As he caught his breath again, he was nearly brought to his knees; he could just barely catch a hint of Gavin's scent still trapped in the room.

Isaac forced down his tears, forced down the way his hands shook, the way he wanted to collapse to the floor and sob his heart out. He crushed his grief to dust inside himself. There was more room for the shame that way.

He didn't even have to look as he reached for the knife he had tucked between the mattress and the bedframe all those months ago, so that when the time came to protect Gavin from the threat he'd known, somehow, was coming, he could. His fingers wrapped around it. It felt dull in his hands. Heavy. Useless.

Useless. Useless. Useless.

He shoved the thought away and straightened up. The knife fit perfectly into the empty sheath at his belt.

As he walked through to the front of the house again, he looked at his family, still all gathered in the kitchen, huddled together as if for warmth. Tears tracked silently down Gray's face. Isaac bit down on his tongue, holding back his own.

"I'll see you all… tomorrow," he said, feeling the weight of the gun against his lower back.

"See you," Vera murmured.

"I'll call you with any updates," Gray said, wiping their face on their shirt.

"L-love you, Isaac," Sam said softly.

"Love you, too," Isaac croaked. He turned to go. His hand lingered on the handle of his knife as he pushed open the door and walked out into the golden afternoon sun.

Chapter 38

Gavin whimpered softly as he stirred, clawing at the collar. His head swam sickeningly and the room melted behind the bars. He shuddered at the sound of Gray's echoing voice as it evaporated into the shadows.

"Count yourself lucky..."

"Count yourself lucky..."

"Count yourself lucky..."

His head ached. His stomach heaved. He moaned, rolling to his side. The rope pulled tight with the motion, and the collar pulled tight on his throat. He clawed at the collar again, hands shaking, desperate to take it off – desperate to take a free breath without the nylon scratching deep welts into his skin, without the compression against his throat that made his chest tighten with panic.

He could scarcely remember how it felt to take a breath without it.

He floated, sick and wobbly, terror eating down into his bones and hollowing him out. Something moved along the edge of his periphery, and he gasped, bolting upright. There was nothing there. Only a deeper shadow, the whisper of a voice that he swore he knew.

Gavin Stormbeck.

He trembled and turned his head, searching for the source of the voice. All around him the shadows moved, slowly at first, then faster, writhing around him, enough to drown him. His eyes went wide, his chest rising and falling too quickly to pull in air. His skin felt like it would melt off his bones. His knuckles went white as he clutched at the bars, peering out, searching for the thing that he knew was watching him.

The sound of dripping blood echoed inside the cell. He whirled around and saw nothing. Heard only a whisper that made the hair on the back of his neck stand up.

"Gavin Stormbeck."

"NO!" he screamed to the empty air. "No, *no*... th-that's *not me!*"

"It's your name," the voice said, outside the bars again. Gavin turned, his heart hammering in his chest, and caught a glimpse of green-blue eyes that flashed with amusement. He knew the voice now. An unbearable chill gripped him.

"It's the name on your birth certificate," the ghostly voice murmured. *"It's the name I wrote down when you were born at Greenwood Hospital at eight fifty-six AM, April thirtieth, two-thousand-five. Six pounds, four ounces. You were a little thing, weren't you – Gavin Joseph Stormbeck."*

"No," Gavin whimpered, pressing his face into his hands. "No, no…"

"Your mother was in labor with you for seventeen hours," his father whispered. *"I've never seen her so fierce. She loved you so much… she wanted nothing more than to bring you into the world. She sobbed as she held you in her arms for the first time. Our little boy. Our little Gavin."*

Tears streamed down Gavin's face as he dropped his hands and slumped back against the bars. Sweat made Isaac's shirt stick to his skin.

"And you watched her die," his father said. Gavin could feel breath on the back of his neck. Slowly, his stomach heaving, he turned – and whimpered softly as he saw his father standing in the middle of the cell. His smile was serene, his posture relaxed, open. His smile widened as Gavin finally met his eyes. Gavin's lips trembled; his hands locked in fists at his sides.

"You watched her die. You didn't even move to help her, did you?" his father said gently.

"Sh-she was going to kill me," Gavin croaked, tears making his voice weak. "Dad, she was g-going to kill me—"

"No, she wasn't," his father said with a laugh. "What makes you think that? She *loved* you, Gavin. And you let my little whore shoot her dead."

Gavin forced his eyes shut, shaking his head as if he could clear the memory – the bullet tearing through his mother's skull, the coppery smell of her blood as it soaked into the carpet. The fear in her eyes as she died.

The relief, the bitter relief, as he watched Vera kill the woman he had called *mom* as she tortured him.

"Don't you even *miss* her?" his father crooned.

Gavin opened his eyes, and tears spilled down his cheeks. "I…" He bit his lip and winced at the constant pulse of shame under every heartbeat, under the collar. He dragged in a breath. "I…" His voice dropped to a whisper. *"I do."*

His father chuckled. "My son," he sighed. "You were our everything. Our empire, our playthings, our *legacy*, it all would have fallen to you. We didn't do a thing that wasn't for you, do you understand?"

"You raped Vera for *me?*" Gavin snapped, leaning forward, rage burning in his chest. "You did that for *me?*"

His father took a step back, his face falling into an expression of gentle pity. "I would have taught you how," he murmured. "I would have given you everything."

"I didn't *want* that!" Gavin screamed, the collar tightening on his throat. "You, you think I… *wanted that?* I spent my entire fucking adult life trying to get *away* from you because…" He swallowed, trying desperately to catch his breath. "…because I… I must have *known* that if you… e-ever found out I didn't rape my playthings, then you'd—"

"What else are playthings for, son, if not for use? For fun?" his father said, genuine confusion crossing his face. "You enjoyed fucking Isaac Moore, didn't you?"

The air froze in Gavin's chest. "Don't," he breathed. "Don't… that was… that was *different,* don't—"

"But you did enjoy it, did you not?" his father said with a smile.

"Stop," Gavin heaved, shuddering.

"You *could* fuck him after all, couldn't you? You think that would have been possible if you didn't really want him that way? Perhaps I understand the gentle times. You could almost chalk that up to lovemaking. You were so *generous* with your touches."

"I said *stop,*" Gavin growled, tearing at his hair.

"But that last time at home…" His father tsked. "With your bodyguard holding him down… He screamed like he was being cut to pieces." His father breathed a sigh, his eyes going unfocused, his lips pulling into a placid smile. "He screamed like my Vera used to."

"NO!" Gavin roared, throwing himself against the rope. He gagged when it snapped tight again, dragging him back. *"STOP!* You… you *know* it was different!"

His father cocked an eyebrow. "Was it?"

"YES!" Gavin sobbed. Shame and hatred clawed at his stomach. "She would have killed him, and I would have done... *anything* to save his life."

"Hm." His father inspected his nails. "Good thing the idea of saving his life gave you a usable *hard-on,* hmm?"

Rage swelled inside Gavin, pushing against his skin, burning him from the inside out. He stared at his father in horror. His father's lips slid into a grin.

"My son, the hero," he said, smirking. "Well, I'm glad *something* brought you around to seeing things our way. You would have learned to enjoy it, in time. It's in your *blood,* Gavin Stormbeck."

"My name is Gavin *Uriah,*" Gavin hissed through his teeth. He spat on the floor at his father's feet, his hands fumbling at the buckle of his collar. Tears streamed down his face. "The Stormbeck legacy means fuck-all. You're dead. My mother is dead. And I'm going to die a fucking *Uriah.*"

"Ah, no," came a sinuous voice that twisted in his mind. He froze. Bile crawled up his throat; every nerve in his body lit on fire. He turned his eyes to the phantom in the corner, blazing blue eyes standing out against a ghostly face, above a body made of shadows.

His father chuckled. "If you insist that you are *different,* little boy, if you insist that you are not my son..." He shrugged. "The collar suits you. And..." His eyes flicked to the scar of his name carved into Gavin's arm. "You've even been marked for us. Here comes your new owner now, son."

The shadow slid to the door of the cell. It seemed to melt through the bars as it crept closer to Gavin. Terror curdled in his stomach, snuffing out the rage. He looked up as the specter stood over him, obscuring everything and everyone else.

"What did I tell you about unbuckling the collar?" the ghost asked with a cold gaze that seared Gavin to his core.

"P-please," he whimpered, as shards of ice sank into his heart. "Please, no..."

The creature laughed. "I said I would find more... creative ways to restrain you." It turned and threw a glance into the corner of the cell. "Who are you talking to?"

Gavin shot a glance at his father, seizing with panic. There was no one there. His father had disappeared into the room that curled around him like smoke from a candle. "N-nobody," he rasped. "Nobody, *please…*"

The ghost flashed a smile, and Gavin caught a glimpse of sharp, needle-like teeth. It reached out with a gloved hand and dragged Gavin onto his stomach, pinning him on the cot with a weight that felt more solid than the press of the walls against his skin.

"You just don't learn, Stormbeck," the creature hissed in his father's voice. Gavin turned tear-filled eyes towards the other side of the cell, searching for his father. His arms were pulled behind his back, and rope tightened around his wrists. His collar was untied from the bars of the cage. "This crime will be easy to punish, though. I do believe we're nearing the end of your retribution. A day more, perhaps two, if I can bring myself to wait that long…"

Gavin's eyes flicked to the gallows that stood against the wall. Always there, silently calling to him.

He cried out as he was pulled from the cot and onto the cold floor. He shivered as the icy cement pressed to his skin, chilling him through the sweat-soaked shirt. The ghost dragged him to the side of the cell and forced him to his knees.

The blue-eyed specter shoved Gavin back against the bars of the cage, and he whimpered as the steel bars leached his body heat through his shirt. The ghost yanked the collar back, forcing Gavin to stretch as tall as he could on his knees, before he tied the collar to the bars of the cell. Gavin whimpered as his knees began to ache already against the hard floor. If he shifted, tried to relieve the crushing ache, his collar choked him. As he struggled and gasped, the ghost faded, sliding backwards out of the cage to stand behind the bars and watch.

Gavin's eyes slid shut and he twisted against the rope around his wrists. He whined softly as his knees ground into the hard floor. He opened his eyes and cried out in horror.

Fresh tears spilled down his cheeks as he stared up at the thing towering over him, a seething mass of shadows with a cruel slash for a mouth. Cold blue eyes pierced him. Terrified, he looked for the ghost that stood outside the cell as the collar closed around his throat. The ghost stood there, silent and still, watching Gavin and the creature both. Gavin turned his wide eyes up towards the monster that loomed over him once more.

The creature's lips pulled back in a snarl. Gavin's stomach dropped as he saw the rows of razor-sharp teeth, the creature from his nightmares – the one who looked like Vera, always tearing his father's throat out. The creature stared down at him, eyes blank and empty. The sound that came from its throat wasn't human.

Gavin prayed he would wake up before the monster devoured him.

It descended on him and ripped its teeth through his throat.

Gavin screamed. The sound was twisted, wet, the gurgling scream of a dying animal. The scent of blood flooded Gavin's nostrils and his stomach heaved.

Again, the creature lunged forward, tearing razor-like teeth through his flesh. He could hear the air whistling through the gash torn into his neck, could hear the blood spilling onto the floor. He sobbed helplessly and tried to twist away from the monster. The collar held him in place.

Again, the monster ripped into his flesh, feeding on his blood. His head spun. His throat burned with bile. And still, he did not die. The creature stared at him with soulless eyes, Gavin's blood streaming down its lips and chin in rivulets. The smell clung to the inside of his throat. His head pounded with every panicked, dying beat of his heart.

Still, his lungs kept drawing in air. Still, his heart thudded in his chest. Still, his twisted screams tore through him, as the monster bent down and drew a barbed tongue along his neck, tasting his blood. Behind it, the ghost watched, its cold blue eyes unwavering. No mercy came from those eyes. Only pain. Only more blood. There was another ghost standing beside the specter. It spoke.

"Sir…" it murmured.

"Hush," the blue-eyed ghost hissed.

Gavin sobbed as he met the other ghost's eyes. He thought it looked familiar. Sometimes, those eyes didn't bring pain.

"H-help," he pleaded, choking on the collar, on his own tears. Agony tore through his throat as the creature sank in its teeth again. "Please, ple-ease, please, *no, PLEASE!*"

270

The monster eating his flesh purred softly, as if pleased with his begging. Gavin shuddered as sharp teeth pierced him again. His eyes rolled back and he waited, desperately, to die.

"This is how your father died," the creature hissed in a creaking voice, as if its throat was desiccated from years of thirst. *"I tasted his blood. You taste the same, the two of you – torturers, rapists, sadists, murderers."* It groaned and sucked at the ragged flesh of Gavin's neck. *"Hmmmn. You're your father's son. Gavin Stormbeck. Your father's son."*

"Ahh," Gavin moaned, his vision going white from pain. It echoed through his body and crushed his throat. "No, *no,* I… *please…*"

"When was the last time your mother held you in her arms? When was the last time you made her happy?"

"Please," Gavin whimpered, gasping for breath. "Please j-just… k-kill me, *please…*"

Gavin shuddered at the huff of warm breath against his neck. *"Mmm… no. We both know your life belongs to him."* It nodded towards the ghost standing outside the cage, watching. Always watching.

"Please."

Gavin sobbed helplessly as his blood ran down his throat, the feeling almost like a memory, like the punch of a bullet through his chest, like the scent of his blood as it ran out of him and into the carpet. Beneath him, cold cement opened up, sucking him down into nothingness like a tomb. The walls melted around him. Cold blue eyes burned into him from outside the cell as the monster purred contentedly. It opened its mouth and sank its teeth into Gavin once more.

Chapter 39

Finn's ears were ringing, despite the cotton they'd shoved into them. They'd been setting off alarms for almost fifteen minutes – or, rather, they'd been sending the guard running all over the building and back, pulling each fire alarm and waiting for Finn to turn the alarm off. Then he'd report back on where in the building he'd been. Finn had to admit, there was a part of them that liked making Daniel Schiester's yes-man sweat as he climbed the stairs over and over. A walkie-talkie would have been much more efficient, but the mayor hadn't wanted to spare two of his.

"We've got some encrypted channels, and for the sake of security…" Schiester had said in that smooth, uncanny voice.

"I understand," Finn had said, forcing an uneasy smile.

No walkie-talkies, so the guard would sweat. After the second stair climb, he had shed his jacket, revealing the under-arm holster that really hadn't been concealed at all. Finn would have laughed, if they hadn't been so damned terrified. The guard may as well have started without the jacket. It wasn't hiding *shit*.

The guard, even with his sidearm, wasn't the biggest threat today – not even close.

Their fingers fumbled as they adjusted the device they were using to test the panel. The building's fire system was in surprisingly good shape, all things considered. Most of the fire alarms were still operational, and the panel was still in good enough working condition that it could probably have even sent the fire department if the alarms went off for real – if there was still a dispatching center to receive the signal, and a fire department to send. Finn had no idea who the emergency alert was being sent to, or if there was anyone left to hear it.

Still, the sound of the alarms was already making their head ache, which was why Gray was checking in refugees outside on the steps to the town hall today. Finn blew out a slow breath, trying to steady themself as the room spun around them – something else that they tried to tell themself was because of the blaring alarms, and not because of the barely-suppressed panic that made it hard to take a full breath.

Another alarm went off, coming from one floor up, in the south wing of the building. Finn winced even with the cotton stuffed in their ears, keeping their eyes on the panel. No activation. The siren was going, but it wasn't actually reaching the alarm system. Finn counted slowly to ten, trying to calm the beating of their heart as well as wait for the guard to silence the thing. The guard was supposed to stop the alarm in ten seconds if Finn didn't. A moment later, the siren went quiet.

If they were here for a real fire inspection, they would have written that down.

The guard came jogging back into the panel room, pulling the cotton from his ears. "Second floor, south wing, west wall about halfway down the hall. It doesn't look like there's another one in that wing."

"No, I wouldn't think so," Finn said carefully as they removed one earplug. "That covers the second floor in that wing, right?"

"I didn't see any other alarm things in any of the rooms on that side," the guard said. Finn couldn't remember his name. Zeller? Zimmer? Their mind jangled with nerves.

Finn looked back at the panel. "Alright. Let's check on the north wing now." The guard nodded and jogged away, his boots echoing on the wood floor in the panel room. The green carpet that covered the floor outside the room muffled his footsteps as he moved towards the stairs.

It didn't matter what that guard's name was. Finn wondered, with a cold wash of rage, whether the guard had hurt Gavin where he lay shackled in the... well, they didn't *know* Gavin was in the basement. Not for sure.

They knew for a fact that this building had a basement, though.

Their gaze wandered across the room, sliding along the wall until it settled on the pipes that supplied the sprinkler system. They'd been painted red, once, but the paint had long since blackened, peeled, and flaked away, leaving a little pile of reddish-brown chips lying on the floor along the wall. A massive pipe came straight out of the floor, bent, and branched out into four smaller pipes. The big pipe, Finn knew, was connected to the town's water system that had been kept running by some miracle, and by the stubbornness of a very ancient water tower pump. Three of the smaller pipes went up and disappeared into the ceiling to supply the sprinkler systems for the first, second, and third floors. Those were the only floors Daniel Schiester had said existed.

The fourth pipe disappeared into the floor.

Finn jumped as another alarm went off, this one coming from the north wing of the building. They clapped their hand over their ear. They'd forgotten to put the cotton back in after the guard had left, the guard that perhaps – *almost certainly has, the motherfucker,* Finn thought – hurt Gavin.

This is how I lose my goddamn hearing. Finn glanced at the panel where one dim red light shone. *More than halfway done.* Finn turned off the alarm and pulled their hand away from their ear. The guard jogged in a moment later.

"That was in the conference room, second floor, north wing, east side," the guard rattled off. Zimmer. Finn thought his name was probably Zimmer.

"Thank you," Finn said, their gaze moving over the panel, counting the remaining lights. They turned their head to glance back at... Zimmer. "Next one?"

He huffed and turned to jog back up the stairs. Finn pushed the cotton back into their ears and waited for the next alarm.

They couldn't keep their gaze away from the fourth pipe disappearing into the floor. There could be a number of reasons that the mayor said there was no basement. Maybe it was caved in. Maybe there was radon down there, so it was boarded off. Maybe the mayor just had something private down there that he didn't want to be disturbed.

Finn knew the truth, though. They knew it in their gut, just like everyone else had: Gavin was in the basement right this moment. And he was probably suffering at Daniel Schiester's hands right now.

After the mayor had led Finn to the panel room, he'd crossed his arms over his chest, leaning casually on the doorframe.

"I'll have one of my men assist you," he'd said. *"With anything you need."*

Babysit me, you mean, Finn had thought. *Guard me. Watch me.* They had forced a smile through their teeth. *"Thank you. Sorry about the alarms… The test shouldn't take very long. But they'll be going off on each floor—"*

"I understand," Schiester had said. *"We've moved our check-in tables outside. It's a beautiful day today."* Schiester had straightened up then. *"I have some business I need to attend to, if you have no other questions. If something comes up, please let…"* Why couldn't Finn remember the guard's damn *name?* *"…know and he will pass on your needs. Otherwise, thank you for your services today. It feels like progress, to have such a necessary service renewed. I am eternally grateful for our first responders."*

Finn had gritted their teeth. *You would have killed me along with the others you've slaughtered if you thought you could get away with it, you mother*fucker, *you evil torturing hypocritical piece of shit.* Their jaw hurt even now from clenching it so hard.

Above them, an alarm echoed through the hall. The light on the panel flicked on. Finn silenced it.

They tried their best not to imagine what Gavin had experienced for the past month. Gavin, trapped in this sadistic asshole's basement, probably hurt within an inch of his life, forced to atone for everything he'd done, even after he'd done everything he could to make it right… Gavin had been prepared to *die* to make everything right.

He'd *tried* to die to make everything right.

The guard walked into the panel room. Finn looked at him expectantly. Zimmer's face was pale, but flat and emotionless, as he spoke. "Second floor, north wing… the m-mayor's office."

Finn turned around, their eyes moving over the panel, counting the lights. "Alright. I'm guessing there should only be… two more on that second floor, if it's the same as the third."

Whatever-his-fucking-name-was nodded, then turned slowly to go back upstairs.

The phone burned in Finn's pocket. Once they'd gone through all the alarms, once they were *sure* there was a basement in this building instead of just an assumption from a dumbass medic who had maybe forgotten how riser rooms worked, they would send a text to Isaac to let him know they were finished. There was no premise map in this room – they'd been right about that, and if they gave a shit they'd make a note of that, too – so there was no map to help Isaac into the basement. Still, they had a pretty good idea of which door on the outside led to the basement from their walk around the building at the start of the day. It was locked, of course. If Finn couldn't get to it and unlock it from the inside, they could always—

They flinched as another alarm blared, but they were grateful for the distraction. They were almost finished, and they needed to *focus*. They silenced it and waited for the muffled thumps of the guard's boots as he came down the stairs. They pulled the cotton out of their ear just as he walked back into the room.

Zimmer shrugged tightly and crossed his arms over his chest. His hands were clenched into fists. "Second floor, north wing, west wall, uh, the first room off the stairs. And I checked the other room up there – the alarm is damaged, I think. Doesn't have a thing I can pull."

Finn fumbled in their pockets for a pen. Really, they should have been writing *all* of this down. They scribbled a line on the notebook that lay open on a chair in front of the panel. They could barely read their own writing. Their pulse pounded faster and faster in their throat.

"Alright," Finn said, pushing out a shaky breath. "That just leaves the first floor. Would you mind—"

The guard was already out the door.

Finn slipped the cotton back into their ear, waited for the blare of the alarm. When it pierced the air, the panel stayed dark. *That one's broken, too.* After ten seconds, the alarm stopped.

Finn's head spun as the guard came back into the room and told them the location of the broken alarm. Then the next one, and then the next one, both of which worked. The tips of Finn's fingers were numb. Their mouth felt too dry to speak. They glanced up and saw the guard standing in the doorway, staring at them like he'd just said something.

Finn cleared their throat. "S-sorry, what?"

"I think there's one more, but before I forget…" Zimmer trailed off, and his eyes flicked to the floor and back. "The mayor wanted to debrief with you on your findings, when you were done. So, once we finish with these alarms, I'll go get him and you can fill him in on how today went."

All the blood left Finn's face. They steadied themself against the wall as a wave of nausea crashed over them. "Debrief?" they mumbled, and cleared their throat. *He can't fucking kill me before I even get a text off to Isaac, he does* not *fucking get to kill me when Ellis and our baby are still out there in the world, fuck, shit...* "Usually I go back and write up a report of—"

"Yeah, well, he just wanted to make sure there was nothing really wrong that he needs to focus on today," Zimmer said. There was a moment of hesitation, a flash of something across his face that Finn didn't quite catch. Their throat tightened as they swallowed.

"Oh," they said, trying to steady their voice. "Okay. That's... I can do that, no problem. There are just a few small problems, nothing too big." They had to force themself not to glance at the corner again, where that one ancient water pipe disappeared into the floor, headed for the basement where Finn was sure Gavin lay in chains, and if Finn couldn't save him, if Isaac walked into a trap, if someone died today because Finn ended up getting put against the wall and shot before they could warn the others—

"Okay." Zimmer shrugged again. "Well, I'll just... go pull this last alarm or two and then we'll be done... or was there something else that still has to happen?"

A lot more has to happen. I need to test the detectors and the horns and strobe lights and the battery packs for this panel and the actual water pipes and the—

"Um, no," Finn croaked. Their ears were ringing so loudly it sounded like another siren. They cleared their throat again, and coughed when that didn't relieve the feeling of a collar around their neck, tightening. "Let's just... sure, yeah, we'll test this last alarm, and then I'll talk to the mayor."

The guard nodded once, then turned and stalked down the hallway.

Finn snatched up the keys that hung on a hook right beside the panel. With shaking hands, they activated every single alarm, one by one, even the three that hadn't been activated at all because they were in the basement that didn't exist. They had to just *pray* that the electronic locks on the doors in this building were all working, and that the alarm would open that door to the outside and that Isaac could get into the building that way.

They slammed the panel shut, locked it, and thrust the keys into their pocket. They didn't bother picking up the bag of tools they'd brought, just turned on their heel and walked as quickly as they could towards the front of the building, their hands shaking at their sides. The phone lay unused in their pocket. They didn't dare risk pulling it out and sending a text to Isaac – not while they were still in the building. Not while DFS might be able to capture them, go through the phone, find evidence against the entire family, and have them all put to death.

They couldn't risk their family.

Not Ellis.

They shoved the front door open and blinked against the morning sun, already high in the sky. They found Gray and met their eyes as they nearly tripped down the stairs; Gray looked up from the paperwork they were filling out with a hollow-faced refugee, Gray's eyes wide with surprise and fear. Then their gaze darted to the town hall. The muffled alarms echoed across the square. Their face went pale, and they shot to their feet.

"E-excuse me," Gray gasped, and turned to the volunteer seated at the table next to them. "Marie, could you... I have something I have to..." They turned and rushed down the sidewalk, digging their hand in their pocket for their keys. Finn turned the other way and forced themself not to run.

Their heart beat so hard in their chest, they thought it might burst. They knew Gray was headed towards the car, pulling it around to the back parking lot that was almost always empty. The car had Finn's medic bag in it and the family's supplies for the run north, for once they rescued Gavin. But first, they had to get a text to Isaac. They whipped the phone out of their pocket and sent a text, their fingers flying over the screen.

There's a basement. Door on north side should be open.

Their hands shook as they turned back to the town hall and jogged towards the back of the building. As Gray pulled the family's dilapidated car into the lot, the muffled sound of the fire alarm buzzing through the air beeped once, then went dead.

Chapter 40

Cold, metallic terror shot through Gavin as the door slammed open. He shivered, curling in on himself and trying to ignore the heaving of his stomach as the last of the drugs in his system made his head spin. There was something on his periphery, like a word he couldn't quite find, a face he couldn't quite place, as if the memory would come flashing back if only he could *focus.*

And he could, sometimes. Schiester's friend must have been messing with the cocktail because sometimes, he *could* remember.

He swallowed hard, the collar a constant pressure against his throat. He tugged the blankets over his head as the sound of Schiester's boots echoed from across the basement. The scar on his arm seared with pain, and the scars on his back ached in anticipation and in paralyzing fear. His throat closed like he was being drowned again. His skin prickled as the *click, click, click* of Schiester's boots down the steps reached the floor and moved towards him. He pressed his hand over his mouth to muffle a sob.

"Good morning, Ziegler," Schiester said in a breezy voice. "He was good for you, I trust."

There was the scrape of a chair across the floor, the rustle of clothing. "Yes, sir. Just slept, mostly."

Mostly. Ziegler left out when Gavin had screamed himself awake, clawing at his collar, sobbing that something with Vera's face, his father's face, *Schiester's face* was eating his flesh and feasting on his blood. The memory felt so immediate, as if it was real, as if it had actually happened hours ago. Gavin swallowed as his skin ached from the cold.

"Good. Good. Now… your shift is over, but if you would be willing…"

There was a pause. "…sir?"

"Upstairs, someone is conducting an inspection of the building for *fire safety,* of all things. Important, I suppose, but… if you would be willing to keep an eye on them, I would be most appreciative."

The hair on the back of Gavin's neck stood up. He huddled under the blankets, desperately hoping against hope that if he made himself small, and disappeared into the blankets, he wouldn't be hurt today. Praying that if Schiester just forgot about him, if he just left Gavin alone...

"Absolutely, sir, I can do that." Gavin could hear just in his voice how tired Ziegler was.

"Thank you. And... when they are done, bring them to my office. I'll want to... discuss their findings."

Gavin's breath froze in his chest.

They?

There was a shuffling of boots on the floor. "Yes, sir. Can do."

"Thank you, Ziegler. Of course, you will be compensated for your overtime."

"I... thank you, sir. I wasn't... worried about that."

Gavin hesitantly pulled the blanket back and cast his gaze at Ziegler. He was standing in front of Schiester, his back straight, his head bent. He was clutching his lunch box. "I'll go check on the inspector, then, sir."

"Thank you. Report to me – immediately – if there are any problems."

There was something about the way Schiester said it that made Gavin's skin crawl. Ziegler turned to go, climbing up the stairs with heavy footfalls and disappearing through the door at the top. Gavin knew better than to scream when that door opened.

Schiester's cold blue eyes flicked to Gavin's, and Gavin let out a whimper. He shivered and pushed himself back against the bars, making himself as small as he could, as Schiester's mouth pulled into a grin.

"I have something new to try, Stormbeck," Schiester said evenly, digging into his pocket.

Gavin groaned. "N-no... you, you did it again to me yesterday... didn't you?" He pulled mindlessly at the collar. "Schiester... *please,* not again..."

"Relax, boy," Schiester said as he pulled out a tiny vial and a syringe. "Not the same thing. No, I feel like watching you *beg* for your food today, and *this*..." He nodded towards the syringe as he drew up a small about of the liquid in the vial. "...should make that just... *excellent.*"

Gavin shivered. "Schiester... what... what *is that*—"

"Nothing for you to worry about," Schiester said with a smile. He flicked the bubbles out of the syringe and slid the vial back into his pocket. He pulled out a set of keys and unlocked the door to the cell.

Tears stood in Gavin's eyes. "Schiester... please, *please* don't..."

Schiester tilted his head and surveyed Gavin, his eyes moving up and down his body, from the scars on his face, to the collar around his neck, to the tattered blanket that he had wrapped tightly around himself. "I suspect you don't remember what I said to you last night, do you?" he said with a sardonic twitch of his lips.

Gavin swallowed hard. "Last... n-no, you... you *drugged me* last night. *No,* I don't fucking *remember.*"

Impotent rage crushed his chest. His palms itched to hold a knife, to take it to Schiester, cut him to pieces and savor his screams as he bled out over Gavin's hands and onto the floor. Gavin had never wanted to tear someone apart so much as he did Schiester. Schiester, who had forced him to rip out Isaac's heart, who had forced the Stormbeck name back on him again. Gavin trembled with his longing to grab the syringe from Schiester's hands and plunge the needle into his throat, to find the carotid and *rip—*

Schiester chuckled at the rage that darkened Gavin's face. "No, I'd expect not. Well, I suppose I'll repeat myself." He took a step closer. Gavin shrank back against the bars. "What I *said,* while you were speaking to what I can only assume is the twisted creature who was your father—"

Blue-green eyes flashed across Gavin's vision, a mouth pulled into a charming smile.

"—is that I think I'll only require one more day with you."

Terror flooded Gavin, sharp and acerbic and strong – but something else followed just behind, washing over him: ragged, bitter relief. He slumped against the cot, his chest quivering, his eyes burning with tears.

Only one more day of this. Then it's over. Then, it'll be done. His eyes flicked to the gallows, looming over him like a shadow. Like a monster.

"Okay," he croaked, and a tear escaped to run down his cheek.

Schiester snorted. *"Okay,"* he huffed. He took another step forward and grabbed Gavin's arm. Panic burst through Gavin, his gaze moving between the needle marks on his veins, and the syringe in Schiester's hand. He forced himself to stay still.

At least it's just this and not...

"Count yourself lucky..."

He wasn't sure who the voice echoing through his head was.

"Count yourself lucky..."

He tried to turn his arm over, exposing the inside of his elbow. He was frozen in confusion and surprise as Schiester leaned forward and jabbed the needle into his arm, just below his shoulder, and injected the liquid into the muscle. Gavin winced as it burned. Schiester retreated with the syringe.

Gavin blinked and looked up at Schiester. He rubbed absently at the burning in his arm. "Wh-what—"

"I told you," Schiester said serenely as he stepped out of the cage. "Something new today. Are you hungry?"

Gavin felt frozen to the cot. "I... y-yes..." He swallowed hard. His mouth was so dry, and hunger was a dull, constant ache inside him. He could tell, in the weeks he'd been here, that he'd lost weight. Isaac's shirt hung loose on his shoulders in a way it hadn't before.

"Good," Schiester said with a curt nod. "We'll wait about fifteen minutes, and then you may beg for your food. Although..." Schiester laughed. It made Gavin want to punch his fucking teeth in. "...you may begin now if you wish, I suppose." He shrugged. "I like to hear you beg, either way."

Gavin groaned as he lowered himself to the cot. The needle marks on his arm itched, and he rubbed at them. "P-please," he breathed, covering himself with a blanket again. *"Please."* He wasn't sure what he was begging for. He eyed the gallows again, the rope hanging from the ceiling, a perpetual, silent promise.

Schiester laughed. "Speak up, Stormbeck, or be silent."

"Please!" Gavin sobbed, burying his face in his hands. "Please," he whimpered. "Please kill me."

A sigh. "Christ, you are so like your father. So *dramatic*. It's a pity I never realized it before he—"

"Before he made you kill your friend. Yeah, I got it," Gavin snarled. He trembled and pulled the blanket tighter around himself. He knew better, by now, than to think he could provoke Schiester into killing him. He knew better than to think he could escape even the final few hours of his pain.

The basement was silent as the grave. Gavin tore the silence apart with a desperate sob. "Kill me," he whispered beneath the blankets.

Schiester cleared his throat. "Beg, boy, or be silent."

Gavin pressed his hands over his mouth and stifled another sob. Tears streamed down his face and onto the cot.

He counted his heartbeats. He counted his breaths. He didn't try to count seconds; time in here didn't seem to work like time in the real world anyway. In here, he could blink and wake up feeling gutted, weak, missing the hours that had passed while Schiester smiled in the corner. In this place, seconds, minutes, hours – they were all irrelevant. Gavin measured time with the changing of his guards, the pain in his body, the scars that Schiester sometimes allowed to heal.

He rubbed at the stinging muscle in his shoulder, waited for something to happen – for the room to fade away, for the voices to creep into his mind, for the hallucinations that Gavin *knew* were coming. He waited for the sick lurch in his stomach. He waited for the things he saw in his nightmares, the horror that gripped him, the flashes of things he could only half-remember, the things that scurried away into the deep darkness of his mind if he tried too hard to bring them to the light. He shivered on the cot, wishing Schiester would give him a time, a measure, of how long he'd suffer this time.

He jumped and cried out as an alarm pierced the air.

A red light flashed above him, cutting through the cold blue press of the lights overhead. He slammed his hands over his ears and turned his gaze towards Schiester. Gavin went cold when he saw him.

Schiester was looking up at the ceiling, at the flashing strobe light, with terrifying fury. Below that, though, was a flicker of something that he had never once seen on Schiester's face – and it caught in Gavin's throat and burned him from the inside out.

It was *fear.*

Schiester dug his hand into his pocket and fished out the keys. "Change of plans, Stormbeck," he yelled above the piercing siren.

Gavin scrambled backwards on his hands and whined softly as the rope on his collar snapped tight with the motion. He trembled as Schiester unlocked the door and stormed in. When Schiester's fingers fumbled at the knot tying his collar to the bars, Gavin sobbed weakly and pushed against Schiester's hands.

A fierce backhand snapped Gavin's head to the side. Stunned, his mouth fell open. Schiester untied the knot and dragged Gavin onto the floor, one hand gripping the ring of his collar, the other hand fisted in his hair.

"Please!" Gavin sobbed, his head ringing with the siren. "Please, *no!"* He gasped with the freezing cold press of cement against his skin.

The siren went dead, and the strobe lights ceased flashing above him. He whimpered as Schiester's hand tightened in his hair.

"Come on, Stormbeck," Schiester growled. "Come on, *walk*." He dragged Gavin out of the cell and towards the gallows.

"No!" Gavin pleaded, his hands grabbing at Schiester's, trying desperately to break free. "Schiester, no, *please*…"

Schiester released the collar just long enough to whip his hand across Gavin's face again. Gavin cried out and slumped in Schiester's grip. Blood dripped from his mouth.

"Not exactly how I *wanted* to do this," Schiester hissed as he dragged Gavin up the wooden steps, "But I'll settle for it." He shoved Gavin onto his stomach and pulled his arms behind him.

"No." Gavin writhed under Schiester as his wrists were bound behind him. "No, *no, please*…"

"You beg for death nearly every day now, Stormbeck," Schiester spat. "I'm giving it to you."

Gavin froze. His body screamed at him to get up, to fight, to be like Isaac. He slumped with exhaustion. *It's over now. I don't have to do this anymore. I get to die a Uriah.* Tears streamed down his face and onto the wooden platform. Schiester finished tying the knot and dragged Gavin to his feet.

Gavin couldn't feel his legs as Schiester forced him to stand, yanking him up by the collar when he collapsed to his knees again. Gavin's heart hammered in his chest, a blur of sensation, throwing itself against his ribs. Gavin could barely breathe. He was empty inside, hollow. Schiester slipped the noose around his neck and pulled it tight. When he stepped away, Gavin managed to stay on his feet. He realized distantly that the sound of sobbing was coming from him.

Schiester descended the steps and walked to stand in front of Gavin, his face twisted with rage. He looked like the monster from his nightmares, his hallucinations. He raised his hate-filled eyes to Gavin's, his hands fisted at his sides. His chest heaved with each furious breath.

"You are being charged," Schiester hissed, "With the crimes of torture, kidnapping, murder, rape, and every other *fucking* crime anyone with your name has committed against the people in this world."

Gavin nodded jerkily; his vision blurred with tears.

"And for that – the penalty is death." Schiester could barely get the words out. His jaw was clamped shut, and Gavin could see him trembling. "You may g-give your last words now." His lip curled, and Gavin shivered at the hatred that twisted Schiester's face.

Gavin swallowed hard. His mouth felt too dry to speak. His heart ached in his chest. The rope burned against his wrists. He swallowed again, and his lips trembled as he opened his mouth to speak.

"M-my name is Gavin Uriah," he croaked. His knees nearly gave out under him.

Schiester's face contorted in a rictus of fury. "I hear your last words. I now put you to death."

All the breath rushed out of Gavin's lungs. Tears poured down his face. He could feel them collecting in the divot of the scar carved into his cheek.

Schiester walked around the gallows and stood by the lever. He reached out a hand to pull it. Gavin squeezed his eyes shut and forced down a sob.

I love you, Isaac. I love you, Gray. I love you, Vera. I love you, Sam. Please—

The upstairs door burst open and banged against the wall.

Gavin flinched, and his eyes flew open. His head snapped to the side to look up the stairs. His heart pounded in his throat. He let out a twisted sob.

Isaac stood at the top of the steps, his gun held tight in his hand, his eyes wild and blazing with fury. The gun was pointed right at Schiester's heart.

"Step away," Isaac snarled. "Step away, you mother*fucker,* or I'll put one in your fucking chest."

Chapter 41

Isaac's heart lurched as he locked eyes with Gavin. Every muscle in his body froze, his hand spasming around the gun, his breath turning to stone in his chest.

Gavin's alive. He's alive.

He furiously blinked back the tears that burned his eyes and shoved down the ache in his chest as his heart hammered wildly against his ribs. Gavin's green eyes burned into his, wide with terror and shock. Agony flashed through every nerve in Isaac's body as he realized where Gavin was *standing*.

Gavin was standing on… fucking *gallows,* the noose around his neck, and Schiester… that *motherfucker*… had his hand on the lever. Isaac's hand spasmed around the gun. His finger twitched on the trigger.

He couldn't shoot Schiester this far away. If he fell onto the lever…

Isaac's throat tightened as he slowly stepped down one stair, then another. His stomach burned at the terror in Schiester's eyes.

"Ah, I'd stop right there, Isaac Moore," Schiester said, his voice shaking. His hand tightened on the lever. Isaac froze. "Don't take another step."

"You pull that lever, I put a bullet in your head," Isaac growled. His chest ached with each breath as he came down another step. "If you move… I swear to god, if you move…"

Schiester's eyes flicked past Isaac, to the open door, then back to Isaac again. His lips twitched. His hand loosened on the lever. Isaac came down another step and he let his eyes find Gavin's again. In the cold, blueish light of the basement, the scars on his face stood out more than usual. Blood stained his mouth, looking almost black against his pale skin.

"Isaac," Gavin whispered, swaying where he stood. Isaac's throat tightened. "Isaac… *no*…"

Schiester's mouth pulled into a tight grin. "Ah, yes. Seeing things again, are we, Stormbeck?"

Isaac's blood ran cold. "*What* did you just call him?"

"N-no," Gavin whimpered. "This... th-this f-feels real, I... n-no..."

"Doesn't it always?" Schiester said through his teeth. Gavin fell silent with a broken sob.

Isaac's fingers ached around the gun. "I *said*," he hissed, "*What* did you just call him?"

Schiester smiled smugly, his lips pulling back over his teeth. "I'll let him answer for you, *Moore*," he spat. He glanced at Gavin. "What's your name, boy?"

"M-my name is..." He shook his head, his eyes still fixed on Isaac and streaming tears. "M-my... please, Schiester, *don't*—"

"What is your *name?*" Schiester roared. Gavin and Isaac both jumped. Isaac's finger tightened on the trigger as he went down another step, then another.

"G-Gavin Stormbeck," Gavin sobbed. His head fell forward. For the first time, Isaac realized Gavin didn't just have a rope around his neck. Isaac turned his gaze to Schiester's again, frozen with the rage coursing through his veins.

"You fucking *collared him?*" he breathed.

Dark delight burned in Schiester's clear blue eyes. "Retribution," he said simply.

Isaac felt like he might throw up. "Wh-what... what did you *do?*" Somehow, his legs carried him down another step.

Schiester's hand tightened on the lever. "What should have been done *years* ago," he ground out.

Just a few more steps. Isaac's legs shook under him. "Wh-what..." His gaze flicked towards Gavin. "Gavin, I..."

"*Isaac,*" Gavin sobbed again, twisting his arms against the rope tying him. "Please, g-get out of h-here, *no...*"

Isaac nearly collapsed on one knee as he reached the last step. The gun shook in his hands. The rope was around Gavin's neck; Schiester's hand was on the lever...

"I've made him feel the *gravity* of what he's done," Schiester said fiercely, a feverish light in his eyes. "He's been punished for his crimes. And today, he pays for them with his life. A little earlier than I was hoping, but…" He shrugged his shoulders in a tight, jerky motion. "Sometimes things don't turn out like—"

"*Shut up,*" Isaac snarled. "Shut… *shut up.* Let him go. Now. Or I swear to god, I'll shoot you right fucking now."

Schiester tilted his head back and laughed. "Isaac Moore. You don't seem to understand the situation. Shoot me, and I *will* pull this lever. And I've got a man in the building now, loyal to me. It's only a matter of *time* before he returns to this basement, at which point he will kill you, and I can execute my syndicate prisoner in peace."

Tears welled in Isaac's eyes and he blinked them away. Every nerve was screaming. "I…"

"I'm giving you an opportunity, Moore," Schiester said, almost gently. "Leave. Now. If my men pursue you, I will call them off. I will leave your family in peace. But this one…" He jerked his head towards Gavin. "…stays with me, so he can properly pay for his crimes. Crimes that *you* have so carefully, conveniently overlooked."

"I'm not leaving without him," Isaac spat through his teeth. "I'm… I'm *not leaving him.*"

Gavin sobbed weakly. "Isaac…" he whimpered.

"Leaving with him is not an option. You leave alone, alive, or you leave in a body bag. I'll even bury you together, if you wish," Schiester said coldly. "Those are your options. Those are your *only* options."

Isaac's chest felt so tight he could barely draw breath. The gun in his hand lowered an inch. He swiped the tears out of his eyes. His stomach roiled, and he tasted bile.

"Please," he croaked, shaking. "Take me."

Schiester snorted. Gavin sobbed.

"I don't *want* you," Schiester said, laughing. "What on… why on *earth* would you think I want *you?*"

"Isaac, *don't,*" Gavin sobbed. He blinked over and over, casting his gaze around the room, stumbling as he turned his head. "I… is this…?"

Isaac's heart sank, leaving him hollow, empty, numb. He could barely feel the cold air on his skin, chilling the sweat on his shirt. All he could see was Gavin, and the man who was going to kill him.

"Y-you want to hurt him?" Isaac murmured, looking at Gavin. "Then... t-take me. I... I'll hurt, for him."

Schiester blinked. "Excuse me?"

"Look at him," Isaac rasped. Schiester shot a glance at Gavin. "Look, he... h-he doesn't want me to hurt. It'll... hurt him, if you hurt me. And I... I-I'll take it. For him. *Please*." He was barely holding back a sob.

Schiester's gaze moved over Isaac in cold fascination. "Jesus *Christ*," he breathed. "He really does have you perfectly trained."

Cold, vicious rage flooded Isaac's veins. He swallowed hard, nodded. He forced himself to look at Gavin. "I..." He swallowed again. "Y-yes. I... I w-want to... be good for him. I want you to... to hurt me, Schiester." His legs shook under him and this time, he let them fold. He fell to one knee and tilted his head back, the gun held loosely in his hand now. "T-take me," he whispered, pushing the air past his lips. "I... I c-can be good for you. H-hurt me, please."

"Isaac, *no!*" Gavin shrieked, stumbling forward. Isaac stifled a cry as Gavin tripped and choked on the rope around his neck. Gavin staggered to his feet, gasping and coughing. "No," Gavin sobbed weakly. "Isaac, don't... don't *do this!*"

Isaac forced himself to look at Schiester again. "Th-this is what I was made for," he whispered. "Please. Take me."

Schiester let out a gusty breath. "Incredible," he murmured, eyes fixed on Isaac. "The great Isaac Moore... no one would ever know." He chuckled. His eyes flashed with satisfaction. "No one would ever know that you're just a *whore* who needs a collar and a master." He looked up at Gavin. "And to imagine Gavin *Stormbeck*... good lord. You're right. If he really does care for his plaything that much..." Schiester took a step forward, his lips parted with that cold, sadistic smile Isaac had only ever seen hints of before. "How does that sound, Stormbeck? Want to have your pet back?"

Another step forward, away from the lever.

"No, *please*," Gavin sobbed, yanking hard on the rope around his wrists. Tears streamed down his face. "Isaac, please, *run...*"

"I w-want to be with him," Isaac croaked, his eyes fixed on Schiester. "I w-want…" He swallowed thickly. The words burned his tongue, but he pushed them out. "I want to… Please, l-let me be his… his plaything again. Please… h-hurt me for him."

"No!" Gavin screamed.

Schiester's smile pulled wider. "Good boy," he said coldly, and took another step towards Isaac, away from the lever.

Isaac snapped the gun up and fired. It punched through Schiester's chest. The shot deafened Isaac and he watched Schiester stagger backwards as if in slow motion. Schiester's eyes went wide, shocked, and his hand flailed to the side. Reaching for the lever.

"NO!" Isaac roared, and launched himself forward from where he was kneeling. Schiester's fingers scrabbled against the lever. Isaac threw himself at Schiester with all his strength and tackled him. Isaac's gun dropped to the floor. Schiester hit the cold cement floor with a hollow thud, gasping, pressing against the wound on his chest. His crazed eyes were fixed on Gavin. He reached again for the lever.

Seams popped in Schiester's bloodstained shirt as Isaac dragged him away from the gallows.

"Nnnh… *no*," Schiester heaved, blood bubbling in his throat. He coughed, and red bloomed on his lips.

Isaac threw Schiester to the floor. A ragged cry tore out of him. Isaac snatched up the gun off the floor and pinned Schiester under his boot. Schiester gasped. A wet scream gurgled in his throat. Isaac aimed for Schiester's head and fired. The bullet tore through his face and his head slammed back against the floor. He lay still.

With shaking hands, Isaac shoved the gun into his waistband and whirled to face the gallows. He leapt up the steps three at a time. He thought his heart would burst as he loosened the rope and yanked it off around Gavin's head. Gavin fell to his knees in front of him, gasping.

Isaac fell with him, dragging him into a crushing embrace. Isaac's hands tingled as he clutched at Gavin, feeling his cold skin, his shaking breaths. Gavin shuddered against him, heaving weak sobs. Tears wet Isaac's shirt.

"Isaac," Gavin sobbed. "Isaac, you… you *came*…"

"Of course I did," Isaac growled. He pulled back just long enough to pull Gavin into a fierce kiss. Gavin's lips trembled against his. Every inch of Isaac's skin was on fire. "I'm… I'm so *sorry*…"

"Th-this…" Gavin pulled away, casting terrified eyes around the room. "Th-this… f-feels real…"

Isaac drew the knife from its sheath at his belt and began to saw through the ropes around Gavin's wrists. Sweat and tears stung his eyes.

"Is this… i-is this… real, Isaac?" Gavin breathed.

Gavin's words finally reached Isaac, and he froze. His throat worked to swallow his bile. He leaned back and looked Gavin in the eye. *"What?"*

"Is this…" Gavin wet his lips, and for the first time, Isaac realized Gavin's scars weren't just a trick of the light. They *were* darker than before, carved deeper, as if…

As if Schiester had taken a knife to them to open them again.

Isaac shuddered with rage. "Gavin… I… we need to get you out. We're getting you out, *now*. I just…" He began to cut through the ropes again, tears blurring his vision. When the rope snapped under Isaac's knife, Gavin pulled his arms in front of him, rubbing at his wrists. A scar on Gavin's arm caught Isaac's eye. Without thinking, he reached out and grabbed Gavin's wrist, tilting his arm up towards the light.

Stormbeck was carved into the skin in thin, haphazard lines.

Isaac's breath froze in his chest. Fire raced along his body, searing him down to his bones. He couldn't breathe. Couldn't move. Couldn't *think*.

Stormbeck.

Slowly, he raised his eyes to Gavin. Gavin's eyes were red, with dark circles carved under them, and he trembled under Isaac's gaze.

"He did this to you?" Isaac hissed.

Gavin blinked, searching Isaac's gaze in disbelief. His eyes welled with tears. He wet his lips. "I…"

Isaac lurched forward, his fingers fumbling at the black nylon collar around Gavin's neck. Gavin gasped and jerked back.

"N-no," he breathed. "I… I c-can't take off the collar or he'll… he'll *punish* me…" Gavin's voice dropped below a whisper. "He'll *hurt me,* Isaac." He clutched at Isaac's hands, pleading.

"He's fucking *dead,*" Isaac snarled. "We have to go, Gavin. Come on. We have to *go*."

He staggered to his feet and pulled Gavin up beside him. His heart ached as he realized Gavin was thinner than he had been a month ago, his cheekbones jutting out more sharply, the bones of his hands and wrists standing out. The shirt – Isaac now realized it was *his shirt* – hung on Gavin's shoulders, making him look smaller, not like when Gavin had worn his shirts before. His wrists were scarred, rubbed raw from the rope. And still, Isaac's eyes kept sliding to the collar around Gavin's neck, and the raw, red skin beneath it.

Isaac whimpered softly. He pulled Gavin's arm around his shoulders. His own arm went around Gavin's waist and he stumbled forward, half-carrying him down the stairs of the gallows. As they passed by Schiester, Isaac didn't spare him a second glance. He gritted his teeth against the sound of Gavin's whimpers. They slowly made their way up the stairs, Gavin sobbing the whole way.

"Isaac," Gavin whispered, over and over. "Isaac. Isaac. You came."

Chapter 42

Gavin could barely draw breath past the collar as Isaac half-dragged him up the stairs. He looked back dizzily, his eyes darting over the cold, dark basement that had been his prison, his death sentence, for what had felt like an eternity. He stared at the noose hanging from the ceiling, empty and silent. His gaze fixed on Schiester and what was left of his face, still bleeding out over the floor, the dark red stain creeping over the cement. Schiester lay unmoving. There was no rise and fall of his chest, no glint in his cold blue eyes. His eyes were blank and unblinking, staring upward at the ceiling, spattered with blood from his caved-in face. Gavin swallowed hard. It felt like knives going down his throat. The room swam dizzily around him and he stumbled.

Isaac jerked Gavin upright in an iron grip. Gavin's gaze flicked to him. His heart caught in his throat as he looked at Isaac – his hair was longer than before, his beard thick and roughly cut, with patches of dark red and brown along his jaw. He looked *bigger* than the last time Gavin had seen him, his muscles standing out starkly under his skin. Gavin felt fragile next to him, weak and *broken*. He bit his lip at the sight of tears streaming down Isaac's cheeks.

"Isaac," Gavin whispered. His head buzzed like a current ran through it. "Isaac."

Isaac said nothing, only set his jaw and pulled Gavin up another step, his arm wrapped around Gavin's waist.

The walls stayed put. They didn't melt or disappear into the shadows. The air felt like normal air, slightly warmer this far up the steps, and it touched Gavin's skin, filled his lungs. It didn't press him down against the cot or caress him like a physical touch. He cast his gaze across the basement as Isaac dragged him up another step. There was no ghost standing in the corner, watching. The monster was dead, lying empty at the bottom of the stairs.

Gavin clutched Isaac's shirt and tried to force his legs to move. They were heavy, useless things that wouldn't obey him. His heart pounded in his chest, so fast and loud he could hear it in his ears. A wave of nausea crashed through him and he groaned.

Isaac lurched to a stop, his gaze fixed on Gavin. "Hey," he murmured, and cupped Gavin's face with his free hand. "We're almost to the top. Finn's... w-waiting outside, with Gray. We'll—"

"Gray?" Gavin murmured. His voice cracked. "G-Gray is—"

"We all are," Isaac rasped. "Vera is protecting the others, and we're all ready to move. Only Gray and Finn could come south, though. But the others, they... they're waiting for us."

"And you," Gavin said. His skin broke out in a cold sweat. "You came."

Isaac's mouth twisted, and his eyes filled with tears again. "Yeah," he croaked. "I... yeah."

"F-for *me*," Gavin whispered. His fingers felt numb. "You came for *me*."

Isaac let out a strangled whimper and held Gavin tighter. He helped him up another stair. "I came for you," he said softly. The tears welling in his eyes fell, wetting the front of his shirt.

Gavin swallowed hard as shame struck him like a bullet. "I d-didn't mean it," he said desperately, his eyes wide. Isaac turned to look at him again. "I didn't mean it. The letter. I... Sch-Schiester made me write it, Isaac... He said he'd... Isaac, I didn't want—"

"I know," Isaac said. His gaze pinned Gavin in place. "I know... Gavin, I knew from the very first *morning* that—"

Gavin crumpled forward with a sob. He clutched at Isaac's waist as he teetered on the stair. *"Isaac,"* he sobbed. "I wrote it to hurt you, Isaac, I thought... I didn't *mean it,* you *know* I didn't mean it, I didn't mean— I *love* you, Isaac..."

"I know," Isaac said brokenly. A muscle stood out in his jaw as he reached the top of the stairs. "I know." His hand settled on the door handle and he pushed it open.

Gavin's breath caught in his throat. Isaac tightened his arm around Gavin's waist and took his full weight as he stumbled down the cool, dark hallway. It felt like a lifetime had passed since Schiester's men had first dragged him down this hallway, bound and terrified and numb. The dim yellow lights cast a sallow pall over Isaac's face, deepening the shadows under his eyes. Gavin's stomach roiled. Tears burned in his eyes and he cast a glance behind him to make sure Schiester – or his ruined, faceless ghost – wasn't following him.

"Almost out," Isaac murmured. "There's an, an emergency exit just—" He jutted his chin at the door halfway down the hallway. The door at the end of the hall led to the garage, Gavin remembered. "We just have to—"

Gavin's heart lurched as the door to the garage burst open. Ziegler rushed through, his gun held tight in his hands but pointed at the ground. His eyes widened as he saw Isaac, supporting Gavin as he sagged in his embrace. Isaac's hand jerked towards the gun in his waistband. Ziegler snapped his own gun up to point squarely at him.

"N-no," Gavin breathed.

Isaac shoved Gavin behind him, keeping one hand locked on Gavin's shirt, holding him up. Gavin stumbled and clutched Isaac's arm.

"Don't reach for your gun, Isaac Moore," Ziegler said softly.

Isaac's throat clicked as he swallowed. Gavin could feel him trembling. "Please," Isaac whispered. "Please let him go."

A muscle stood out in Ziegler's jaw, his face thrown into stark relief in the dim lights. He shuffled his feet forward a step.

"Ziegler, *please,*" Gavin begged. Isaac took a sharp breath. "Just... I'll g-go back downstairs, just... please let him leave." His hands shook. Sweat prickled on his skin and soaked into his clothes. He felt strangely hollow, eaten by the terror that was somehow still growing inside him.

Ziegler looked straight at Isaac. Ziegler's hands tightened on the gun as he ground his teeth together. Gavin could tell he was holding his breath.

Isaac pulled Gavin closer – putting his body between Gavin and the bullet. Always, always taking the pain for everyone else. Isaac looked at Ziegler. "You... you kn-know what he's doing to..." He wet his lips. "You *know* what he's been doing to people who come through here that—"

"I do now," Ziegler croaked. "I... I mean, I knew about some of them but..." He shuddered, and his gun lowered an inch. "I never knew there were so *many.*"

Isaac shivered. Goosebumps stood out on his skin. "Please," he murmured. "Please, he... he d-doesn't deserve this. I..." He whimpered softly, and tears spilled down his cheeks. "I love him, *please...*"

"The ones who came through a few weeks ago," Ziegler murmured. "They... Lucy and—"

"Lucy and Topher?" Isaac gasped. Shame crashed through Gavin, seeming to crack his ribs wide open. "They... did they..." Isaac froze when Gavin sobbed weakly. Isaac's eyes never left Ziegler, but his hand tightened in Gavin's shirt. "Did Schiester—"

"They seemed like good people," Ziegler said, his voice wavering. "They seemed like—"

"Did Schiester *kill* them?" Isaac snarled. Ziegler jerked the gun up to point at Isaac again. Gavin could feel how hard Isaac was shaking. "Did that *motherfucking*—"

"How did you know them?" Ziegler said, his voice hollow. His finger was on the trigger. "Were they—"

"They were part of the fucking *resistance,*" Isaac growled, and took a step forward. Gavin stumbled behind him. "They've been, been working with Tori to... They were *good people* and you fucking—"

"Their picture is up on his wall," Ziegler murmured. His shoulders slumped. "He... had all their pictures up on the wall like a goddamn *serial killer.* There are... *dozens* of them. And he..." Ziegler stared at Gavin over Isaac's shoulder. "Y-you..." He blinked and looked to Isaac again. "Where's Schiester?"

Gavin whimpered as Isaac went rigid, pulling him close against his side, angling himself so he was still shielding Gavin with his body. Isaac drew in a shuddering breath and forced it out. "If y-you... need someone to stay behind, to t-take the punishment, I can—"

"Isaac, *no,*" Gavin sobbed, trying to worm his way out of Isaac's embrace. He was so *weak.* His hands shook and his knees gave out under him. Only Isaac's arm around him kept him upright. "I..." He turned tear-filled eyes to Ziegler. "You c-can tell them... G-Gavin Stormbeck killed him, I—"

Ziegler sucked in a breath. "S-so he's dead, then." His voice sounded empty, haunted.

"I-I did it," Gavin whispered.

"*Shut up,*" Isaac hissed. "I am *not*—"

"Please don't hurt him," Gavin said, pleading, staring straight at Ziegler. "He... *fuck,* is this...?" He squeezed his eyes shut and shook his head. Helpless rage burned in his chest. "Ziegler, I swear to *Christ,* don't you hurt him—" His voice broke.

"He doesn't deserve this," Isaac rasped. His arm wound so tight around Gavin's waist that he couldn't pull away. "I w-won't... He's *not* going back down there. It was my fault. I killed Schiester. But please... *please* let him go. He d-doesn't deserve..." His hand inched towards his waistband. "If you need someone to stay, I'll stay. Just *please*..." His throat bobbed as he swallowed. His voice dropped to a whisper. "Please let him go."

"He..." Ziegler's hands shook so violently he almost dropped his gun. "He's killed *so many* of them," he whispered.

Gavin's heart lodged somewhere in his throat. The room spun around him. He felt like his limbs were filled with lead, dragging him down. His fingers tangled in Isaac's shirt.

"Some of them were just kids," Isaac breathed. "Lucy and Topher were resistance. They... they're the *reason* we survived. They're the ones who..." Isaac whimpered softly. "*Shit.* They... we wouldn't have m-made it out of the city if—"

"I'm going to go back out there," Ziegler said, angling his head back towards the door. His gun lowered until it was pointing to the floor at his feet. Then he holstered it. "I'm going to go back out there for a second. And wh-when I get back, I—"

Isaac lunged forward, dragging Gavin behind him. Ziegler stumbled backwards. His eyes widened and his hands fell open at his sides. Isaac staggered towards the other door and shoved it open. Sunlight streamed in. Ziegler let out a breath and fell back a step.

Gavin's skin was slick with sweat as Isaac half-carried him out into the sun. Gavin's vision was going gray. Fresh, warm air drifted over him. The collar around his neck was soaked, rubbing against raw and tender skin. The world was fuzzy at the edges, like he couldn't quite focus his eyes. And again, that hollow, gnawing hunger inside him. His heart thundered in his chest.

"Isaa—" His tongue felt heavy in his mouth. He blinked away the sweat dripping into his eyes – or was it blood? He couldn't smell any blood. The scars on his face ached.

"Almost there," Isaac grunted as he dragged Gavin down three steps and onto a sidewalk with grass on either side. Another building stood in front of them. A shop, Gavin thought maybe. The white bricks hurt his eyes after so long in the dark.

"Isaac," Gavin mumbled. He clutched at Isaac's arms. "Isaa—" His stomach heaved, bringing up only bile. A black spot appeared in his vision. "N-no…" He collapsed in Isaac's arms. He felt like he weighed a thousand pounds.

"Gavin," Isaac whimpered, lowering him to the damp grass. It felt so good and soft. The sweet smell of it was thick in his nostrils. "Wh-what…"

Gavin's stomach lurched. *The injection.* He tried to raise his hand to point to his arm. "Sch-Schiester… he…" His eyes fluttered shut, opened again.

Gavin stared up into Isaac's eyes. This wasn't like the other times, when the drug had slid into Gavin's veins and made the world twist and warp around him. Now, the darkness was *inside* him, eating him alive. He could feel his pulse in his ears. His shirt was soaked in sweat.

"Wh-what… what is this?" Isaac said, shaking, his gaze darting over Gavin's body. "What did he—"

"G-gave me… something." Gavin could barely understand his own words. "Isaac…"

"No," Isaac whispered. "No, *no*, he… what…"

"In… m-my arm," Gavin slurred. He reached again for his shoulder. Isaac pulled the short sleeve back, revealing a tiny smear of blood from where the needle had pierced his skin. Isaac's face went white.

"Did he—"

"Isaac," Gavin whimpered. Isaac's face floated above him, blurry and fading. Gavin could barely feel his fingers as they twisted in Isaac's shirt. "Isaac, I… I l-love—"

"No no no *no no no no*," Isaac sobbed, holding Gavin close. "No, *no, no, please…*"

"Isaac… hnng… n-not like the other t-times…" Tears rolled back into Gavin's hair.

Isaac's lips trembled. "Other… was he… *poisoning you?*"

Gavin shivered, despite the warmth of the sun on his face. He was freezing cold. "D-drug… hallucinations… Isaac—"

"No!" Isaac heaved a strangled sob and clutched Gavin to his chest. "Gavin, *no…*"

"Th-thank… Isaac, I l-love—"

"No, please, *Gavin*—"

"—l-love you—"

Isaac's tears fell on Gavin's shirt as he cradled him close. "No… I c-can't… Gavin, please, *don't…*"

The world shuddered around Gavin. His fingers lost their grip on Isaac's shirt. He was floating – no, he was being sucked into an abyss, being devoured, being dragged away from Isaac. Away from the sun.

Gavin's eyes rolled back. He heaved a broken sob, searching for Isaac's gaze, desperate to find him. To look at him, one last time. He needed to find Isaac.

The darkness rose up and ripped him out of Isaac's arms. He disappeared beneath its icy surface.

Chapter 43

Isaac's mind was blank with cold, empty panic as Gavin slumped back in his arms. Gavin's face was pale and shining with sweat, his dark hair wet and black where it stuck to his temples. Isaac held Gavin for an eternal, excruciating moment, shaking so hard he could barely breathe. He broke out of the ice encasing his limbs to fumble at Gavin's neck, searching for a pulse. His fingers burned as he brushed the collar.

Gavin convulsed weakly. A low, throaty groan punched out of him. It barely sounded human.

"G-Gavin?" Isaac breathed, every inch of his skin on fire.

Gavin's eyes rolled back, and he began to seize.

"No!" Isaac sobbed. His hands locked on Gavin's shirt. He couldn't make himself let go. He mindlessly dragged Gavin into his arms, holding him as Gavin's body jerked, the muscles rigid beneath his skin like he was being electrocuted. "No, *stop, NO!*" Isaac screamed. "Please, Gavin, *please…*"

He jumped as the phone buzzed in his pocket. He clutched Gavin to his chest with one shaking hand and fumbled for the phone with the other. He could barely see straight as he flipped it open and dialed a number. He held the phone to his ear, unable to hold down his terrified sobs.

The first ring cut off midway. *"Isaac?"*

"Finn!" Isaac cried. "Finn, he—"

"Oh, god. What happened? I… I'm in the car with Gray in the back parking lot—"

"H-he's seizing!" Isaac sobbed. "Finn, p-please, *please,* I need you—"

"Shit," Finn breathed. There was rustling on the other line. *"I'm coming with my bag. Where… where are you…"*

"Outside on the s-south side," Isaac sobbed. "Finn, fuck, *fuck,* Jesus Christ, Finn, *please…*" The veins stood out in Gavin's neck. His face was beet red, his features twisting with each jerk of his body. His eyes were blank, as if empty. *"NO!"*

"Fuck, shit, I'm coming. I'm coming." Finn was breathing hard. Isaac heard footsteps behind him and whirled to see Finn dashing around the corner of the building with a brown, heavy-looking backpack on their shoulders. "Shit," Finn spat as they fell to their knees beside Isaac.

"Wh-what's *wrong* with him?" Isaac sobbed. The world spun around him. There wasn't enough air. He couldn't breathe. "Finn, Finn, *do* something—"

Finn stripped the backpack off their shoulders and let it drop to the grass with a thud. Before they reached for it, they grabbed Gavin and gently eased him out of Isaac's arms. Every time Gavin jerked, Finn's hands tightened on him. They lowered him onto the grass, on his side.

"He's not *breathing*," Isaac sobbed. He reached for Gavin, clutching at his arm, grabbing at his side. *"Finn—"*

"People usually don't breathe through seizures," Finn murmured. Their hands swept over Gavin, starting at his head, down his neck – then Finn's hands stopped. They stared at the collar.

Isaac's hands jerked forward and fumbled at the buckle. It slipped out of his grasp with each convulsion. Finn shook themself and kept their hands moving down Gavin's back, pulling his shirt up. Finn paled as they both stared at Gavin's back. Isaac's heart broke as he saw the *dozens* of new cane marks, mostly healed now.

"What happened?" Finn said, clipped.

"I g-got him out," Isaac whispered. "I, I got him out, and he started to faint, and… and *this*—"

"Is he— Did he hit his head? Did you see if he—"

"No," Isaac sobbed. "Didn't… Schiester was going to, to *hang* him and, and he—"

Finn gasped. "Did he?" they breathed. "Did he actually—"

"I stopped him," Isaac whispered. "The rope never—"

"What else?" Finn snapped. Their hands moved over Gavin's chest and abdomen, then his hips, then his legs.

"He s-said… Schiester *gave* him something," Isaac breathed.

Finn's hands froze as they reached for Gavin's arm. "Schiester—"

"He said Schiester injected something… into his arm. Here." Isaac pointed to the muscle below Gavin's shoulder. "Said he—"

"He could have given him *anything*," Finn said weakly. They reached for their bag with shaking hands.

"Wh-what are you going to do?" Isaac sobbed. "Finn—"

Finn retreated with a tiny vial and a syringe. Their fingers trembled as they drew up the contents of the vial and flicked the syringe until the bubbles rose to the surface. "Hold him," they said darkly. "I don't want the needle to break off in his damn leg."

Isaac blinked. "Finn, what—"

"*Hold* him," Finn barked, and pinned Gavin's leg down on the grass. They leaned their knee just above Gavin's. His convulsions jolted through Finn. Isaac held Gavin's hips down with shaking hands.

Finn plunged the needle into Gavin's thigh, straight through his jeans. Finn's hands bucked with each convulsion. Still, they managed to hold the syringe steady as they injected the fluid. They pulled back the syringe once it was empty.

"Wh-what was that?" Isaac croaked.

"Midazolam," Finn said weakly.

Tears blurred Isaac's vision. "What—"

Finn leaned back, releasing Gavin's leg. They zipped the backpack up and swung it up over their shoulders again. "We have to *go,* Isaac," they said through their teeth.

Isaac whimpered. "B-but—"

"It's not going to work for a few minutes more," Finn said, taking in short, panting breaths. "And we need to *move.* Where's Schie—"

"He's dead," Isaac growled.

All Finn's breath left them at once. "Then we *definitely* have to move," they ground out. "Isaac, we… it's hard, but we need to carry—"

Isaac was already pulling Gavin's seizing body into his arms. Finn nodded and grabbed Gavin's legs. "Let's fucking *move,*" they snapped.

Isaac's arms ached as he held Gavin. His hands slipped against Gavin's sweat-slick skin with each convulsion. He held Gavin tight, even as Gavin's head thumped against his chest like a second heartbeat. Isaac stumbled on the edge of the sidewalk as Finn shuffled forward. Each time Gavin jerked, he went stiff as a board between them. Isaac dimly realized that the sobs breaking on his ears were his own.

"Gavin," he whispered. "Gavin, Gavin, please, *please* don't go..."

Finn muffled a sob and kept moving. They rounded the corner and hurried towards the back parking lot.

Isaac's heart leapt when he saw the beat-up car idling in the lot. The door on the driver's side opened and Gray staggered out, their gaze fixed on Gavin, who was still seizing in Isaac and Finn's grasp. They lunged forward a step. Isaac could read the horror on Gray's face even through the blur of his own tears.

"No," Gray mouthed, their hands outstretched.

"Get in the car," Finn barked. Their voice echoed across the empty parking lot. "Get in the car, Gray."

Gray stood frozen, staring at Gavin.

Finn sped up and Isaac stumbled to follow. Gavin's sweat was soaking through his shirt. Finn reached the car and yanked the back door open with one hand. They clambered into the back seat, doing their best to support Gavin's legs. When they were all the way in, they reached out and helped Isaac guide Gavin into the back.

"Gavin," Gray breathed.

"Get in the *fucking car*, Gray!" Finn screamed.

They leaned out the door to shove Isaac towards the front, then pulled the door closed behind them. Isaac staggered to the front passenger door and yanked it open. He collapsed into the seat and slammed the door shut. Gray scrambled back into the car and threw it into gear. The tires squealed as the car tore out of the parking lot.

Isaac whirled around and reached out for Gavin. The convulsions were coming slower now, and more sluggish. His hand closed around Gavin's cold and clammy fingers.

"I don't see any major injuries," Finn mumbled as if to themself. "But if Schiester... Jesus Christ, he could have given him tricyclics or Tylenol or cocaine or something household like fucking *diphenhydramine...* Jesus fucking… *fuck*…" Finn froze, staring down at Gavin's arm as it went limp. They reached out with a shaking hand and pulled Gavin's hand out of Isaac's grasp. They froze when their gaze fell on the scars on Gavin's arm – the scars that spelled out *Stormbeck*.

"What is *that?*" Finn breathed. Their face went pale, standing out starkly against their auburn hair.

"Wh-what is what?" Gray said nervously from the front seat.

Isaac swallowed his tears. "He… Sch-Schiester—"

"Carved *this* into him?" Finn hissed, horrified.

Gray drew in a tremulous breath. "Carved *what*—"

"He fucking carved the name *Stormbeck* into his arm," Finn snarled, visibly shaking.

The car swerved as Gray jerked the wheel. "He *what?*" they cried, their lips pulling back over their teeth in a snarl.

Isaac shivered and looked back towards Finn. "Finn," he croaked. *"Please…"*

Finn bit down hard on their lip. Their throat bobbed over and over, and their eyes filled with tears. They stared down at Gavin's arm and leaned in to take a closer look at the crook of Gavin's elbow. Their hands trembled.

"Are those fucking *track marks?*"

As Isaac looked, fresh horror crushed his chest. Finn tilted Gavin's arm up towards the light, and Isaac burned with rage as he saw the marks along Gavin's veins – some old, some probably as new as yesterday. He swallowed bile and raised his gaze to Finn.

"H-he said Schiester was… drugging him," he croaked. "Giving him things to make him hallucinate. But that this time was… was *different*. Because it went in his muscle." He wet his lips and leaned forward, reaching for Gavin's hand again. Gavin's face was slack – but not like when he slept.

"Wh-why is he unconscious?" Gray said, their voice shaking. "Finn—"

"I gave him something for the seizure," Finn said darkly. "It's normal. But I don't know what *caused* the fucking seizure."

"F-Finn," Isaac moaned. "Is he… F-Finn, is he *breathing…?*"

"Not enough," Finn snapped, already digging into their bag.

They pulled out a device that looked almost like a balloon with a mask attached. Finn's hands shook as they reached over the back of the seat and grabbed their oxygen concentrator. They flicked it on and plugged a bit of tubing into the device. The other end connected to the mask thing in Finn's hand.

Finn rolled Gavin onto his back. Gavin's eyes lazed under half-closed lids; his mouth hung open. Finn sat up against the door and shifted Gavin until his head was in their lap, his legs folded against the other door. Finn settled the mask over Gavin's face and gripped his chin to seal it over his nose and mouth. Slowly, they squeezed the balloon-shaped part. Isaac watched desperately as Gavin's chest rose.

"This is kinda normal," Finn said numbly. "It might be from the midazolam, might be from the seizure. Shouldn't last very long. A few minutes, maybe. Jesus, he's so goddamn *sweaty*…"

"Wh-what can I do?" Isaac said weakly.

Finn's eyes snapped up to Isaac's. They were wide, feverish, as if Finn was moments away from crumbling. Isaac's mouth went dry.

"Um…" Finn squeezed the bag again. "I need vitals. Look in my bag for the—"

Isaac lurched forward, pawing through the bag on the floor of the car. "I think I know… The pulse… oxi…"

"Pulse oximeter, yeah," Finn said breathlessly. They nodded as Isaac pulled out the little device and clipped it onto Gavin's finger. Gavin's hand was limp as Isaac pressed the button on top of the oximeter, turning it on.

Finn watched the device carefully, squeezing the bag with an absent-minded blankness on their face. Isaac held his breath as he waited for the numbers to appear on the tiny screen.

"O-one-twenty-eight," he breathed. "That's—"

"His heart rate," Finn said. "Eighty-nine on the SpO2. Not great, but not…" They trailed off. "N-not the… the *worst*…"

"Wh-what now?" Isaac breathed.

"Shit, Isaac, I don't *know!*" Finn sobbed. "I don't *know* what the fuck Schiester gave him! I mean, Jesus Christ, there are a thousand goddamned things that cause seizures and diaphoresis! It's—"

"What's—"

"It means fucking *sweating!*" Finn snapped. "I, I don't have a *goddamned motherfucking clue* what to do. He... I mean, I can check blood pressure and blood glucose, but that's about as much as I can do. Jesus Christ, Isaac, I was expecting him to be *injured,* not..." They fell silent and squeezed the bag again. Gavin's chest rose. It reminded Isaac of Gray, when Gray had been sedated, intubated, a machine breathing for them like their body was an empty shell.

Gavin's sweat soaked into the seat below him. He took a shallow breath on his own.

"Oh, thank *Christ,*" Finn breathed, and took the mask away from Gavin's face. He heaved another slow, shallow breath. "That's gonna have to do for now," Finn said weakly, and leaned forward to grab the blood pressure cuff and stethoscope out of the bag.

With Gavin's head still in their lap, they wrapped the cuff around his arm and puffed it up. Finn turned Gavin's arm over and placed the stethoscope against the inside of his elbow. Tears glittered in their eyes. They watched the dial carefully as they let out the air, the stethoscope pressed into Gavin's arm – right over the marks Schiester had left with a needle.

"One-forty over eighty-two," they mumbled, and took the stethoscope out of their ears. "I mean, pretty normal for after a seizure. Now..." They fumbled in the bag again and took out a small pouch. "I mean, just to cover all my fucking bases, since I have *no fucking clue*..." They pulled out another small device, a strip of what looked like plastic, an alcohol swab, and a tiny needle covered by a plastic protector. They slid the strip into the device, which beeped as it came on.

Isaac shivered as another wave of cold gripped him. He glanced at Gray. Their hands were locked on the wheel, their knuckles white, their eyes darting between the road and the rearview mirror. Shadows slid over the car as they drove under the row of trees that flanked the main road on either side.

Finn set the device on Gavin's chest and grabbed his hand. Isaac swallowed. "Is that—"

"For blood sugar. Might as well, but I don't see the fucking *point*..." Finn's movements were empty, as if they were on autopilot, watching

307

something they'd done a hundred times from a distance. They mechanically reached for Gavin's finger, wiped it clean with the alcohol swab, and pricked it with the needle. They squeezed a drop of blood onto the strip and set the device on Gavin's chest. Finn bandaged the tiny wound and set Gavin's limp hand down gently against the seat.

The device beeped, and Finn held it up to look at it.

The screen read *32*.

"Son of a *bitch*," Finn breathed.

Isaac's eyes went wide. "Wh-what… what does that… *mean*…"

"It means," Finn said, their body rigid, "That that motherfucker gave him *insulin*."

Chapter 44

Isaac clutched at the edge of his seat. His fingernails dug into the worn fabric. "Wh-what... C-can you... *fix it?*"

Finn lurched forward and pawed through their bag. "You bet your fucking *ass* I can," they breathed.

Isaac shoved his hand against his mouth to muffle a sob. Beside him, Gray heaved a sob of their own. Tears streamed down their face.

"D-do I need to stop somewhere?" Gray croaked. They swiped at their eyes. The car cleared the row of shops, the walls of trees, and sped into the open fields of north Crayton. Wheat rose up on either side of the car like golden waves. "Do you have everything you need here?"

"I do," Finn said. "I... give me just a sec. I can fix this. I can *fix* this." Finn's hands flew over the bag and they grabbed another pouch. They zipped it open, and IV supplies crackled in their plastic wrappers.

Finn eased Gavin's head out of their lap and let it fall back against the seat. They maneuvered themself around until they crouched on the floor behind Isaac's seat.

"Hey," they said, not looking at Isaac. "Scoot your seat forward, I need—"

Isaac pulled the lever on the side and slammed the seat forward as far as it would go. He spun around again and stared at Finn. Every heartbeat was a stab to his chest. Gavin's face was still lifeless, his eyes half-open, blank, sightless. His lips were parted as he drew in his shallow breaths. His hair was plastered to his forehead. Finn tied a rubber tourniquet around Gavin's arm and let the veins fill with blood.

Isaac swallowed hard. "W-will you... b-be able to start an IV with—"

"Yeah," Finn murmured. "These marks aren't bad. A few dozen of them, maybe. If he was a years-long heroin user or something it would be tough,

309

but…" They shrugged. "This definitely isn't the worst I've seen." They set up the IV tubing and cleaned the inside of Gavin's elbow.

"Now, Gray," Finn said softly. "Try not to go over any bumps? This IV has to be perfect."

Gray nodded wordlessly. They were clenching their teeth together so hard their jaw was twitching.

"Wh-why?" Isaac rasped. "Wh-what—"

"I'm giving him dextrose," Finn said as they prepped the needle. "I can't miss."

"Why?" Isaac whispered.

Finn drew in a deep breath. "Dextrose is necrotic. It kills tissue. Makes it rot. If I miss the vein, and the dextrose goes into his skin or muscle, he loses the arm."

Isaac whimpered. His nails dug harder into the seat. *"Shit,"* he breathed. "Be—"

"I won't fucking miss," Finn said through their teeth. "Sharps out, Gray. Careful. No bumps."

Isaac held his breath as Finn slid the needle into Gavin's skin. It went in smoothly. Finn pulled out the needle and attached the tubing to the IV still in place. They flushed the syringe of saline into Gavin's vein and taped down the IV.

"It's good," Finn murmured. "You're good, Gray."

Gray let out a gusty breath.

Finn reached into their bag and pulled out a bag of fluids. They attached more tubing and let the fluids run into it until it came dripping out the end. Finn clamped it shut and screwed the tubing into the IV. When they opened the tubing again, the fluids ran into the IV. Finn hung the bag from the hook above the window.

Isaac's mouth was dry. "H-how long…"

"Minutes," Finn said. "Really not that long." They reached for the pulse oximeter that had fallen off Gavin's finger and clipped it back on. "Hm. Pulse of one-ten, pulse ox of ninety-three… Not as bad as it could be. Jesus *Christ*, he's sweaty. He…" Finn's hand froze over Gavin's chest. "Isaac, is this… *your*—"

"My shirt," Isaac croaked. "He... he had my shirt the whole time." Tears brimmed in his eyes again. He couldn't look away from Gavin. He could almost believe that Gavin's skin was gaining its color again, just the faintest flush in the pallor of his cheeks. He lay still, unmoving, breathing shallowly.

"This is gonna make him feel like *shit,*" Finn murmured, tapping their finger against the bag of fluids. "I mean... well, not this specifically, but having your blood sugar tank and then skyrocket again is *terrible* for you. He'll feel hungover for at least a few hours, maybe days. But we've got enough food that we can keep his sugar up until the insulin wears—"

Isaac clutched Finn's arm as Gavin's eyes fluttered open.

"Gavin," Isaac sobbed, dragging himself over the center console to join Finn in the back seat. He stepped over the medical bag on the floor, carefully avoiding the IV tubing, and lifted Gavin's shoulders. Isaac settled himself against the door so he could cradle Gavin's head in his lap. Isaac stared down at Gavin, his hands slick with his sweat. Gavin's eyes rolled as if he was looking for someone. Something hot and bitter stabbed through Isaac as Gavin's eyes finally met his.

Gavin's eyes went wide. "I... Isaac..." He reached up with a shaking hand. Isaac clutched Gavin's hand in his, pressed Gavin's palm to his lips. Tears spilled down his cheeks.

Gray heaved a sob and pressed their hand to their mouth. Their left hand stayed on the wheel, white-knuckled and shaking, as Gray lurched forward with each sob, barely looking at the road anymore. They glanced in the rearview every few seconds.

Gavin blinked slowly and turned his head to take in his surroundings. "What..." He sounded like he was talking through a mouthful of cotton. "Wh-what... is th-this—"

"This is real," Isaac whimpered. He dragged Gavin up off the seat and crushed him to his chest. His lungs ached. "Gavin... Gavin, I love you..."

Gavin's fingers slowly wound in Isaac's shirt as he pulled him close. His grip was weak, his fingers trembling. "Isaac... what..."

"Schiester gave you insulin," Finn said dully. Exhausted, they sagged against the seat. "I'm giving you sugar to counteract it." Gavin glanced, bewildered, at the IV in his arm. He shuddered and reached for it.

"N-no," he gasped. "No, *no, Schiester, no,* this… this feels real, *no…*"

Finn seized Gavin's wrist and forced it away from the IV. "Don't pull that goddamn line, Gavin," they huffed. "Come on, this isn't—"

"I th-thought it was *real*," Gavin wailed. "Schiester… k-kill me, kill me, *please…*"

The words burned in Isaac's throat. "It is real, Gavin," he murmured, cupping Gavin's face as he cradled him in his arms. "It is. We got you out, and it's real."

"N-not you," Gavin whimpered. "Not… not *you,* Isaac, he always hurts *you…*"

Isaac blanched. He swallowed hard. "Look," he said roughly, pulling Gavin upright and turning his head towards the window. "Look. You're outside. We got you out of that… that *fucking* basement…"

Gavin whimpered, eyes wide, lips trembling. His gaze darted across the landscape flying by the car. His hand gripped the seat that shook beneath him as the car rattled down the road.

Isaac guided Gavin's face until he was looking at him again. "What were these hallucinations like?" he murmured. "What happened? I mean…"

Gavin shook his head. "I d-don't…" he croaked. "It's hard to… *remember*, I just… sometimes I remember, sometimes the time is just… gone…" He reached up and touched his own face. "Is this…" He crumpled, curling into himself. "I d-don't know if this is *real,* it… it always feels so *real…*" He slumped in Isaac's arms, sobbing weakly.

Isaac looked to Finn. "I… Finn, why is he—"

"He might be confused from the midazolam," Finn said heavily. "And like I said, the dextrose is probably making him feel like shit. It'll take him a while to feel normal again. But we'll…" Their throat bobbed as they struggled to swallow. "Isaac… I'm—"

Isaac reached over Gavin and dragged Finn into an embrace. "Thank you," he whimpered against their shoulder. "Thank… *thank you,* Finn." Tears rolled down his cheeks as he released them.

"It's just hypoglycemia," Finn mumbled, looking down. "It's the easiest—"

"Stop," Gray snapped from the front seat. Isaac looked up at them. They gritted their teeth and stared at Finn in the rearview mirror. *"Stop that.* You saved his life, Finn. I…"

Gavin stirred in Isaac's arms. He reached up with one shaking hand and felt for the collar that had been around his throat. When his fingers brushed bare skin, he trembled.

"Wh-where's the collar?" he breathed.

Isaac cradled Gavin to his chest again. Gavin's head rested on his shoulder. His damp hair tickled Isaac's neck.

"Gone," Isaac growled. "It's gone, Gavin. You're… n-never going to wear that piece of *shit* ever… e-ever again."

Gavin sobbed and buried his face in Isaac's neck. Isaac rocked him slowly, holding him close, and trembled with the smell of Gavin's sweat and fear. Gavin shivered violently and curled up against Isaac. Goosebumps stood out on his skin.

"Gavin," Isaac murmured. "Are you—"

"C-cold," Gavin whimpered. "I'm…" He shivered again.

Finn glanced at the bag of fluids. The last few drops were running into the tubing. They reached out and clamped off the line, then unscrewed it from the IV. They reached out to help Gavin sit up.

"Let's get this wet shirt off you," Finn said gently. They reached for the hem of the shirt.

"NO!" Gavin screamed, twisting away from Finn's hands. He clawed at the seat behind him, barely seeming to register as Isaac's arms came around him again. "Please, no, *no,* please no, please don't take it—"

Isaac crushed down the helpless, confused rage inside him as Gavin heaved a sob, clutching the shirt, trying desperately to push away from Finn. "Gavin," he said, his voice trembling under forced calm. He didn't want to ask. He *had* to ask.

He drew in a shaking breath. "Why can't we take the shirt off?"

Gavin froze, twisting so he could stare at Isaac with wide, frenzied eyes. He wet his lips and shivered. "B-because…" Isaac held his breath, terrified for what was coming next. Gavin whined softly. "Because it's *yours,* Isaac," he breathed.

313

The air froze in Isaac's chest. He couldn't breathe the sigh of relief that pressed against his lips. "I... and..."

"I w-want... just one thing of yours." Gavin reached out and brushed trembling fingers gently across Isaac's cheek, trailing through his unkempt beard. "Please, Isaac. Just... let me keep... this one thing. He's..." Gavin bit down hard on his lip. "He's going to take... e-everything else..."

Gray let out a strangled groan and dashed the tears from their eyes.

"You have me," Isaac croaked weakly. "You have me. You... y-you'll..." Isaac pulled Gavin close and pressed his forehead against his. "I'll never lose you again," he promised breathlessly.

Gavin whimpered. "B-but..."

Isaac pressed a kiss to Gavin's forehead. The sweat was already starting to dry there. "Here," he murmured. "Finn is, um..." He nodded at Finn. "Finn has a set of fresh clothes for you, and a towel. I'm going to just..." His hands ghosted against Gavin's waist and gently pulled the hem of his shirt up. Gavin whimpered softly. "I'm going to... take this off, and we'll towel you down..." Gavin met Isaac's eyes. "And you can hold onto the shirt, okay? You can keep it. Let us just... g-get you dry, and warm. Can I do that? P-please, Gavin, I..." He blinked away his tears. "Let us get you warm."

Gavin looked back at Isaac in terror. Beneath that, though, was a flicker of hope, and a question. Isaac gently brought his hand to Gavin's face. "You're safe now," he whispered. "I'll never lose you... n-not ever. Never again."

Gavin swallowed thickly. He nodded, and Isaac guided the soaked shirt up and over Gavin's shoulders. Isaac bit his lip at the sight of the fresh cane marks on his back. Finn handed him a towel, and Isaac gently toweled off Gavin's hair. Gavin held still while Isaac dried his chest and back, and shuddered when Finn handed him a clean shirt. He pulled it on and immediately reached for the soaked, stained shirt in Isaac's hand.

Finn dug around in the back and returned with a blanket, wrapping it around Gavin's shoulders. Gavin took it gratefully and clutched at the edge of the blanket with thin fingers.

"Now, we... we need you to eat something, Gavin," Finn said gently. "Let me make a PB&J. Perfect for this sort of thing. It's got simple and complex carbs that..." They trailed off, staring at the scars on Gavin's face. They bit their lip and glanced at Isaac. "Let me grab the stuff for that." They leaned over the back seat once more.

Gray leaned their elbow against the door and muffled a sob of relief. Isaac gathered Gavin into his arms and maneuvered him until he was sitting between Isaac's legs, leaning against Isaac's chest, his own legs stretched out on the seat beside him. Finn unscrewed the jar of crunchy peanut butter and smeared a thick layer onto a slice of bread.

Isaac pressed a fierce kiss into Gavin's hair. He leaned back and cupped Gavin's cheek, his gaze darting incredulously over his face. His eyes filled with tears again as Gavin's fingers locked onto the front of his shirt.

"I think this is real," Gavin whispered.

Isaac wet his lips. "C-can I… Gavin, can I… kiss you?"

Gavin leaned forward without hesitation and pressed his lips against Isaac's. They both drew in a tremulous breath. Tears streamed down Isaac's cheeks.

Chapter 45

Isaac's arms ached from holding Gavin so tightly. Gavin lay still in his arms, maybe asleep – his slow, easy breaths fanned out against Isaac's chest and neck, his head resting lightly on Isaac's shoulder. His legs were stretched out across the seat and the blanket was pulled tight around his shoulders, despite the warm autumn day.

Finn watched Gavin carefully, turned completely around in the front seat. They'd been feeding him for two hours, practically having to force Gavin to keep eating the rations they'd brought for their run further north, in case the rescue went very wrong. They'd checked and re-checked his blood sugar. Once they were satisfied that it wouldn't dip again, they had left him alone. Still, they'd barely taken their eyes off him. Gray, too, watched him carefully in the rearview mirror.

Gavin's head lolled as the car rolled over a bump. He stirred, drawing in a slow, deep breath, his eyes fluttering open. He lifted his head. His eyes went wide and he went rigid in Isaac's arms.

Gavin's lips trembled. "Wh-where—"

"We're almost to the house," Isaac said, pressing a kiss against Gavin's temple. The sweat had dried on Gavin's skin, leaving his hair stiff and stuck to his scalp.

Gavin pushed himself upright with shaking arms. One hand curled in Isaac's shirt as he glanced around, eyes darting over the one-lane road winding through the tall bushes, shadowed by trees. "I…" He looked down at his arm, where Finn's IV had been. There was only a square of gauze taped there now. He ripped the tape off and ran his fingers over the mark from the needle.

"No," he breathed.

"Hey, *no*," Isaac murmured, cupping Gavin's face and pulling it up. Gavin's eyes met his, green and bloodshot and brimming with tears. Isaac bit his lip and stroked Gavin's cheek with his thumb. "Finn had to give you some sugar through the IV. You remember? You remember that?"

Gavin trembled and clutched Isaac's shirt tighter in his hand. "I…" He blinked, shaking his head. His tears ran down his cheeks. "I… y-yes…"

Isaac wet his lips. "Gavin… please… I don't know what the hallucinations were like, but… you're not in one. You're safe. You're with… w-with *me*."

Gavin's throat clicked as he swallowed. "N-no one's getting hurt," he rasped.

"No one," Isaac whispered through numb lips. "No one's getting hurt. No one's… g-going to get hurt. Please." He whimpered softly. "Gavin, you're… This is *real*."

Gavin looked down at his arm again. His gaze slid over the scars there, the scars marking him – *branding* him – as a Stormbeck.

"This is real…?" he breathed.

Isaac wrapped his hand gently around Gavin's forearm, covering as much of the scars as he could. "I h-have you *back*," he whispered. "We… we got you *back*." His heart ached when Gavin looked up at him again and met his eyes. He pulled Gavin close and shivered as Gavin pressed his lips against his neck.

The car jolted as Gray pulled off the lane and into the driveway. The sun was at its highest point in the sky; it shone against the white paint of the house, hurting Isaac's eyes. Gavin looked up at it, as if he couldn't believe what he was seeing.

"A-are we…" His voice cracked. Isaac reached for a bottle of water and handed it to him. He took it gratefully and took a long drink. "Are we… staying here?"

"No," Gray said, their voice dragging with exhaustion. "No, we… we figured that once we got you, *however* that went…" They shrugged jerkily. "We'd need to run. Everyone else is here. They were waiting for us. I *wanted* to have them all leave when we got you, but…" Their voice dropped, fading, as tears welled in their eyes. "They wanted to see you first."

"I want to see them," Gavin murmured, leaning forward to look out the windshield as Gray pulled up to the house, beside the family's other car.

"They already know we have you," Gray said as they put the car in park. "Finn texted them after—"

They cut themself off as the door to the house burst open. Vera came dashing out, Tori right on her heels. Sam scrambled to catch up. Ellis followed behind, their gaze sweeping the car for Finn. Zachariah followed, and Edrissa came last.

Isaac sat up. "Zachariah—"

"Schiester is dead," Gray said evenly. "And Mathias will do his best to circulate the news of what happened to Schiester's victims. I think Zachariah is as safe as he can be, up here."

Isaac relaxed only slightly. He allowed his arms to loosen around Gavin, and he opened the door. He gently eased Gavin out of his lap and clambered out – he *had* to stay on his feet, but his legs were weak with exhaustion and relief in equal measure. He reached a hand back in for Gavin. Gavin took it with cold fingers and let Isaac help him out of the car. Isaac winced as Gavin shifted his bare feet on the gravel driveway.

Vera all but skidded to a stop when Gavin straightened. Isaac froze, his gaze darting over Vera, taking in her wide eyes, her shallow, panting breaths, her clenched fists.

"Gavin!" Sam cried and darted past Vera to crash into him. They wrapped their arms around him as he grunted and stumbled back. *"Gavin,"* they sobbed, and pressed their face into his chest.

"Sam," Gavin breathed. His arms shook with how hard he squeezed them. He whimpered against their hair, and tears streamed down his cheeks.

Isaac wrapped one arm around Gavin and Sam both, and with the other, reached for Vera where she still stood frozen.

He swallowed hard. "Vera…"

"H-he's been cutting his hair," Vera breathed.

Isaac's brow furrowed. "What—"

"DFS," Vera said, swallowing hard. "H-he's been… cutting Gavin's hair."

Isaac turned to look at Gavin and held him by his shoulders so he could see his face. Sam kept their arms tightly around Gavin's waist, looking from Vera to Gavin and back again. Gavin turned away from Vera, trying to bury his face in Isaac's neck. Tears glittered in his eyes. Isaac clenched his jaw. Gavin's hair *did* look different. Isaac looked up at Vera.

"I don't—"

Vera crossed her arms across her chest and hugged herself. "He's been cutting his hair so he looks like *Joseph fucking Stormbeck*."

Fire licked along Isaac's skin, burning through his veins. His hands shook as he pulled Gavin closer. He tried to speak, and his voice failed him. Sam stepped away and wrapped their arms tightly around their chest. Their mouth twisted as if they were doing their best not to cry.

"H-he…" Gavin croaked. Isaac held him tight to his chest again. "He… kn-knew my father. *Hated* him. He…" Gavin turned to glance at Finn. "He was… in the Defense Corps."

Finn sucked in a breath through their teeth. Ellis folded themself against their side.

Gavin swallowed and went on. "Schiester said… he helped my dad take down the DC from the inside…"

"That mother*fucker*," Finn breathed.

"…and that when my father told him to slaughter the JDC… he refused." Isaac's head buzzed as Gavin drew in a shuddering breath. "And my father… forced him to torture and kill his best friend. And then made sure everyone else in the DC knew it. So Schiester didn't have a place there anymore."

"That *motherfucker*," Finn snarled. "I… I *knew* he was DC. And he…" They whimpered softly. "He… he *helped*…" They covered their hand with their mouth and pulled Ellis close, pressing a kiss to their forehead.

Isaac turned his gaze back to Vera. She was still staring at Gavin; Tori pressed against her side, looking up worriedly at her. Gavin whimpered and tore a hand through his hair.

"I'm sorry," he sobbed. "I… I'm… s-sorry, Vera, I'm *sorry*…"

"D-don't…" Vera said flatly. "Don't. It's okay."

"I can cut it," Gavin croaked. "I can… right now. We can go inside and—"

"No," Vera snapped. She shuddered and blew out a slow breath. "No," she said, more gently. "No. We… we should really go."

Gavin blinked and turned to Isaac. "Go?"

"We weren't sure what would happen once we rescued you," Gray said softly. "We didn't know if Schiester would know it had happened, or if he would pursue you, or…" Gray took a step forward and placed their hand on Gavin's shoulder. "Schiester obviously already knew where you were, and we're… so isolated out here that his men were able to approach with no one ever seeing them. And we…" Gray huffed out a laugh. "I thought this family could use some privacy to recover. But having a community around us that we can depend on is something that would… help, I think." With that, their eyes flicked from Finn and Ellis to Edrissa.

"Besides," Tori said evenly, her hand moving back and forth against Vera's shoulder, as if warming her. "None of us really wanted to stay in this place after… well. Yeah." She chewed her lip and looked at Gavin. "We figured you might want to find a new place to live, too, after… what happened. In this house."

Isaac didn't think he could hold Gavin tighter. He forced his arms to loosen, forced himself not to crush Gavin to his chest hard enough to make his body believe he was really here again.

"So…" Gavin swallowed dryly. "Where do we go?"

"Laporte," Gray said with a smile.

Gavin blinked. "Where—"

"Laporte is where Mathias has been sending the refugees that Schiester would have killed," Gray said, iron finding its way into their voice. "I've been in contact with a woman named Kali there. She's been coordinating the refugees and finding homes for them. I called her last night and asked if she would take us. She said yes."

"S-so…" Gavin quivered and clutched at Isaac's shirt with one hand, the other tightly gripping the damp gray cotton that he hadn't let go of yet. "So… I w-won't be… he won't…" He shoved his forehead against Isaac's neck. "I w-won't be… taken… again?"

"Schiester's dead, Gavin," Isaac said, choking back his tears. "No one's going to take you. Not ever." His arms wound tighter around Gavin's waist. "I'm never going to let that happen again."

"And they'll…" Gavin's voice broke. "The people in Laporte. Th-they'll let me—"

320

"Kali has assured me that you won't be harmed," Gray said, just a hint of cold, shivering anger showing through. "And the people in that town... understand what it means to make mistakes. They understand what it means to change, too."

"I didn't mean to make you leave," Gavin whimpered, glancing at the house. "I'm sorry, I... I didn't mean... for anyone to get hurt..."

"Hey," Isaac soothed, cradling Gavin's face between his palms. "Hey. None of us got hurt. Hey. Look at me." He caught Gavin's gaze and held it, his thumb gently stroking the scar on Gavin's left cheek – carved deeper, now, the freshly-healed wound still dark pink, almost red. Gavin's lips trembled as he looked back at him. Isaac pitched his voice lower. "Remember? No one got hurt."

Just you, he didn't say. *Just... just you.*

Gavin swallowed hard. "I don't want anyone to—"

"You're important," Isaac whispered, and watched how his words struck Gavin. Gavin's mouth twisted, and tears spilled over his cheeks. "You're important. We risked this because... because you're important. Because you're *worth* it."

"Stop," Gavin rasped, holding back a sob. *"Please..."*

"Gavin," Tori said. She stepped forward and held out a hand to him. "Hey... Gavin, it's..." She squared her shoulders and lifted her head. "We're a *family,*" she said softly. "And you're part of that family. Now we've..." She nodded to the family's other car. "We've got your stuff packed already. Sch-Schiester's dead and Mathias is going to tell people the truth of what happened. We're probably not in too much danger here, but..." She looked back at the house and shivered. "None of us want to stay here. It's just about an hour drive to Laporte. Won't take too long."

"Gavin," Sam murmured, taking another step forward. "Um... Nata was, um, really helpful when I was—"

"Your arm," Gavin rasped, staring at Sam's right hand. They had it close to their body, curled slightly. "Is it—"

"Not better," Sam said, blowing out a slow breath. "It'll never be... better, probably." They shrugged jerkily. Finn pressed their lips together and looked away. "But I'm figuring stuff out. How to do a lot of things one-handed.

But I meant… Nata was really helpful when I was getting better. Would you… w-would you like to hold him? While we drive to Laporte?"

Gavin shivered against Isaac's side, but nodded. "I… Th-thank…"

Sam's cheeks flushed as they turned and headed into the house.

"Everything else should be ready," Tori said, her lips thin. She was looking at Vera. "Want to start heading towards the cars?"

Vera shook herself, tore her gaze away from Gavin and the ghost she saw in his place. She nodded. "Yeah. Let's… let's get this show on the road."

Isaac looked up as Sam emerged from the house, carrying Nata in their arms. His round yellow eyes peered around, and he squirmed in Sam's grip. Gavin huddled against Isaac's side.

"Um…" Sam chewed their lip and adjusted Nata in their arms. "I can… hand him to you, once you get in."

"Y-yeah," Gavin rasped. He wobbled and lowered himself onto the back seat, his hands still clutching Isaac's arms. "I… yeah."

Vera stepped forward and dropped some shoes and socks onto the floor of the back seat. Gavin looked up at her gratefully.

"I'll stay in this car with Gavin," Finn said, reaching for the other door. "Ellis, if you want—"

"Shotgun," Ellis said, keeping their eyes down and away from Gavin.

Isaac climbed into the back seat with Gavin as Finn came in on the other side. He immediately pulled Gavin back into his arms. Gavin relaxed against his chest and reached out for Nata as Sam handed him in.

"He's a little grumpy," Sam murmured. "I woke him from his nap."

Nata let out a plaintive meow as Gavin took him. He clambered into Gavin's lap and looked up at him, whiskers twitching. After a moment he dipped his head and pushed against Gavin's hand.

Isaac pulled the door closed and gently maneuvered Gavin, so he was sitting in his lap again, his back against the door, his legs stretched out over the seat. Finn stared at him and Ellis reached back to squeeze their shoulder. Vera climbed into the driver's seat of the other car. Tori took the front seat and Zachariah, Sam, and Edrissa squeezed into the back.

Gavin's hand hovered over Nata as the cat stumbled in a circle in his lap once, twice. Finally, he curled up, his head resting on Gavin's chest, and began to purr. Gavin's hand shook as he gently petted the cat.

Isaac's eyes swam with tears as his arms wrapped around Gavin again, holding him as the car bounced over the driveway in reverse. He couldn't keep his eyes off Gavin, taking in his hair, dried sweat sticking it to his temples; his eyes, bloodshot and sunken; his lips, chapped and trembling with breathless, whispered words; his scars, cut so deep now that they puckered the skin around them. Isaac leaned forward and gently laid a hand on Gavin's face, cupping his cheek.

Gavin looked up from the cat and into Isaac's eyes again. Isaac shuddered with the wave of raw emotion that crashed through him, desperate relief and guilt and joy and shock that Gavin was here, Gavin was *here*, Gavin was in his arms, safe. Gently, carefully, he leaned forward and pressed his lips to the scar across the bridge of Gavin's nose. He pulled back and kissed the scar on Gavin's cheek. Then, the scar at the corner of his eye. Back to his nose, cheek, eye. Nose, cheek, eye. He tasted Gavin's tears as they poured down his face.

"I-Isaac," Gavin whispered, his voice shaking. "Is... th-this..."

"This is real," Isaac murmured. He rested his forehead against Gavin's. "This is real. You're... y-you're safe. You're *here*."

"N-no one's getting hurt," Gavin breathed. "This feels real."

Ellis cleared their throat. "N-no one's getting...?"

"Later," Finn rasped. They reached up and squeezed Ellis's hand.

Isaac settled, leaning his shoulder against the car door as Gray pulled out onto the lane. The car shuddered as they drove over the bumps in the road. Vera's car was right behind with the others.

The sun shone brightly on the hood of the car, so bright Isaac had to close his eyes. The wind moved through the trees that swayed on either side of the lane. Isaac rolled his window down, and he could hear the birds calling to each other, and the wind rustling the long grasses that smelled so good. With each heartbeat, Gavin relaxed in his arms, his head falling against Isaac's shoulder, his breaths becoming deep and slow again. A tear rolled down Isaac's cheek, and he hid his smile against Gavin's hair.

www.ingramcontent.com/pod-product-compliance
Lightning Source LLC
Chambersburg PA
CBHW031118210626
46816CB00016B/1640